PRA

"Jenni L. Walsh brings the inspiring true-life tale of horse diver Sonora Carver to life with profound sensitivity and impeccable historical detail. A beautifully written novel about courage, perseverance, and the unbreakable bond between a girl and her horses. I read it in one go!"

—MIMI MATTHEWS, *USA TODAY* BESTSELLING AUTHOR OF THE BELLES OF LONDON SERIES

"A winner of a story from start to finish! I fell head over heels for Sonora, her spirited horses, and her spunk, and was cheering from the sidelines the whole way. Heart pounding, immersive, and utterly fascinating—you won't be able to put this one down."

—SARA ACKERMAN, *USA TODAY* BESTSELLING AUTHOR OF *THE SHARK HOUSE*

"If you grew up binge watching *Wild Hearts Can't Be Broken*, Jenni L. Walsh's *Sonora* is your new favorite book. While the characters all feel familiar, the true story of Sonora Webster Carver and her diving horses is grittier than the Disney version. But that grit and determination are what make this story so inspiring. Don't miss this wild ride of a novel!"

—SARA GOODMAN CONFINO, BESTSELLING AUTHOR OF *DON'T FORGET TO WRITE*

"This one's for the horse girls, the girls who fell in love with *Wild Hearts Can't Be Broken* and hoped someday they'd be like the fearless, determined, strong Sonora Carver, whose love and belief in her horses made her an icon. In the pages of *Sonora*, Walsh's impeccable research and immersive prose expertly plunge the reader into the complexities, triumphs, and disappointments of the real Sonora Carver—a woman whose life inspired a generation—and into the fascinating community behind a bygone high-diving horse act that enthralled the country. This novel is not to be missed, a sure classic, just like the movie that first introduced us to Sonora's life."

—JOY CALLAWAY, INTERNATIONAL BESTSELLING AUTHOR OF *THE STAR OF CAMP GREENE*

Ace, Marvel, Spy

"Jenni L. Walsh captures the thrill of being on the court in a vivid and detailed portrayal of Alice Marble's rise to sporting greatness, as well as her struggles to fulfill her dreams both on and off the court. *Ace, Marvel, Spy* is a smashing success."

—BILLIE JEAN KING, SPORTS ICON AND EQUALITY CHAMPION

"All's fair in love and war—and tennis!—in Jenni L. Walsh's latest page-turning historical novel. Champion, editor, widow, and spy Alice Marble is a remarkable woman full of grit, determination, and unfathomable fortitude who made her mark on the world in irrevocable ways. Readers can't help but be inspired by this unflinching portrayal of a true American icon."

—KRISTY WOODSON HARVEY, *NEW YORK TIMES* BESTSELLING AUTHOR OF *A HAPPIER LIFE*

"The strength of this novel is its deep exploration of Alice's motives and emotions. The intensity and determination to pull through injuries and heartaches, to finish and excel at every task, and to assert her independence in a man's world, are evident . . . Recommended for readers wanting to learn more about a multi-talented tennis legend."

—HISTORICAL NOVEL SOCIETY

"Best-selling author Walsh (*Unsinkable*, 2024) delivers a page-turning delight starring tennis ace Alice Marble, who came from a modest background to reach the top of her sport . . . Whether Alice is in a nail-biting tennis match or in a tight spot with her mission, this book will have readers on the edge of their seats. Be sure to read the author's note about the fascinating, real Alice Marble."

—*BOOKLIST*

Unsinkable

"Walsh's latest (after *The Call of the Wrens*, 2022) is a heartfelt tale of two women in two times. *Unsinkable* joins the ranks of other spy novels written in this vein, but Walsh's prose truly allows the reader to enter the mind and heart of each character, bringing their motivations, flaws, and desires to light . . . Walsh skillfully crafts two well-rounded characters who grapple with internal and external conflict, and yet who honestly earn their resolutions."

—*BOOKLIST*

"An intriguing and thoroughly original novel merging the maritime journeys of Violet Jessop—a very real person who survived three separate shipwrecks—and the fictional Daphne Chaundanson, a brilliant young woman invited to join Special Operations during the dark days of World War II. In author Jenni L. Walsh's expert hands, separate tales are seamlessly woven together to create a remarkable dual-timeline narrative. *Unsinkable* is about the bravery of women and the stunning lengths to which they will go to protect others. It is a heart-stirring story of women who risk everything in order to claim their proper place in this world. Walsh takes readers on an exhilarating voyage of danger, sacrifice, and ultimate triumph."

—LYNDA COHEN LOIGMAN, *USA TODAY* BESTSELLING AUTHOR OF *TWO-FAMILY HOUSE*, *THE WARTIME SISTERS*, AND *THE MATCHMAKER'S GIFT*

"With elegant prose and superb attention to detail, Walsh pulls you instantly on board this beautiful tale of two determined, whip-smart, and truly unsinkable women. I was intrigued from page one, both Violet's and Daphne's stories sweeping me along through every harrowing moment until that perfect twist and captivating ending. A must-read for fans of unstoppable, courageous women."

—NOELLE SALAZAR, *USA TODAY* BESTSELLING AUTHOR OF *THE FLIGHT GIRLS*

"Jenni L. Walsh spins an incredible tale of survival and heartbreak in this riveting novel. Inspired by true events, the rich historical detail and tense plotting make for an unforgettable read. Historical fiction lovers, add this one to your list!"

—SARA ACKERMAN, *USA TODAY* BESTSELLING AUTHOR OF *THE CODEBREAKER'S SECRET* AND *THE UNCHARTED FLIGHT OF OLIVIA WEST*

"A stunning dual narrative spanning some of the marquee events of the early twentieth century. Violet and Daphne are compelling heroines of the first order, and one cannot help but root for their triumph from the first page through to the seamless, satisfying conclusion. Walsh is a master storyteller, and *Unsinkable* shows her skill at its best. Not to be missed by anyone who loves historical fiction and resilient heroines."

—AIMIE K. RUNYAN, BESTSELLING AUTHOR OF *THE SCHOOL FOR GERMAN BRIDES* AND *A BAKERY IN PARIS*

"An extraordinary story of two extraordinary women. Jenni L. Walsh expertly weaves together Violet's and Daphne's histories—Violet is real, Daphne an amalgamation of several real-life women—to craft a historical novel that is vivid and enthralling. There is intrigue and bravery, duty and love in these pages, and readers will keep turning them to the very end, eager to learn the fates of these two inspiring women. A joy to read."

—KATE ALBUS, AWARD-WINNING AUTHOR OF *A PLACE TO HANG THE MOON* AND *NOTHING ELSE BUT MIRACLES*

"I fell headfirst into this historical fiction tale featuring two powerful and resilient women, Violet and Daphne. Walsh seamlessly weaves together fact and fiction in a dual-timeline narrative that keeps the reader guessing, culminating in a satisfying conclusion. The courage of both main characters lingered with me long after I turned the final page. I am so looking forward to whatever Walsh writes next!"

—AMITA PARIKH, BESTSELLING AUTHOR OF *THE CIRCUS TRAIN*

The Call of the Wrens

"In *The Call of the Wrens*, Jenni L. Walsh chronicles two volunteers in the Women's Royal Naval Service during the First and Second World Wars. Spanning decades in a story that is both epic and intimate, *The Call of the Wrens* is an original and compelling tale of sisterhood and strength."

—PAM JENOFF, *NEW YORK TIMES* BESTSELLING AUTHOR OF *THE WOMAN WITH THE BLUE STAR*

"What a lovely surprise. The heroines in Walsh's latest can be found racing around war-torn Europe on motorbikes, relaying secret messages, and undertaking daring missions as part of the real-life women's branch of the Royal Navy. There's also giddy romance, family secrets, and shocking twists, making it an absolute treat for historical fiction lovers."

—FIONA DAVIS, *NEW YORK TIMES* BESTSELLING AUTHOR OF *THE MAGNOLIA PALACE*

"The lives of two women in two different world wars collide in unexpected ways in this powerful exploration of the British Women's Royal Naval Service, commonly known as the Wrens, a daring group of real-life women who were instrumental in both World War I and World War II. Laced with triumph and tragedy, bravery and redemption, this tale of finding oneself in modern history's darkest hours will break your heart and put it back together again, all in one delightful read."

—KRISTIN HARMEL, *NEW YORK TIMES* BESTSELLING AUTHOR OF *THE FOREST OF VANISHING STARS*

"*The Call of the Wrens* by Jenni L. Walsh is a beautifully written gem of a historical novel, shedding light on a little-known group of women, the Wrens, during both world wars. Walsh skillfully entwines the stories of Evelyn and Marion as they journey to find their voices and, ultimately, their calling. I was completely captivated by this richly drawn portrait of strength, survival, and love."

—JILLIAN CANTOR, *USA TODAY* BESTSELLING AUTHOR OF *BEAUTIFUL LITTLE FOOLS*

"In *The Call of the Wrens*, Jenni L. Walsh has woven a wonderful tale inspired by the real-life women's branch of the United Kingdom's Royal Navy. This dual-timeline novel features two courageous heroines, Marion and Evelyn, roaring around Europe on motorbikes during both world wars. Thrilling missions, family secrets, romance—it's all here. We need more books like this that show the remarkable contributions made by adventurous women during the darkest of times."

—ELISE HOOPER, AUTHOR OF *ANGELS OF THE PACIFIC*

"In *The Call of the Wrens*, Jenni L. Walsh lends her remarkable voice to the little-known, intrepid women of the Women's Royal Naval Service, women who revved up their motorcycles and risked their necks to heed Britain's call to win the world wars. Packed full of action and with a heart-wrenching twist, Marion and Evelyn's story reads like a battle cry for anyone who's had to fight against other people's expectations and find her own place, and her chosen family, in this world."

—CAROLINE WOODS, AUTHOR OF *THE LUNAR HOUSEWIFE*

"With a winning blend of adventure and romance, Walsh highlights the bravery and intrepid spirits of women destined to forge a path beyond the restrictive expectations of their era and circumstance. A winning treatise on courage and sisterhood, *The Call of the Wrens* will have fans of Kate Quinn and Erika Robuck rejoicing with each compulsively readable page."

—RACHEL MCMILLAN, AUTHOR OF *THE MOZART CODE*

Sonora

Also by Jenni L. Walsh

ADULT FICTION

Ace, Marvel, Spy

Unsinkable

The Call of the Wrens

A Betting Woman

Side by Side

Becoming Bonnie

MIDDLE GRADE

The Bug Bandits

Operation: Happy

Over and Out

By the Light of Fireflies

I Am Defiance

Hettie and the London Blitz

She Dared: Malala Yousafzai

She Dared: Bethany Hamilton

Sonora

A NOVEL

Jenni L. Walsh

HARPER MUSE

Sonora

Published by Harper Muse, an imprint of HarperCollins Focus LLC, 501 Nelson Place, Nashville, TN 37214, USA.

HarperCollins Publishers, Macken House, 39/40 Mayor Street Upper, Dublin 1, D01 C9W8, Ireland (https://www.harpercollins.com)

Library of Congress Cataloging-in-Publication Data

Names: Walsh, Jenni L. author
Title: Sonora : a novel / Jenni L. Walsh.
Description: Nashville, TN : Harper Muse, 2025. | Includes biographical information. | Summary: "Inspired by a true story of one of the first female horse divers, Sonora explores a world of daring feats and extraordinary adventures set in the heyday of the American carnival scene. This book vividly captures the spirit of a brave woman who defied societal norms to follow her dreams, diving into the unknown with courage and resilience"-- Provided by publisher.
Identifiers: LCCN 2025018489 (print) | LCCN 2025018490 (ebook) | ISBN 9781400246779 trade paperback | ISBN 9781400246793 | ISBN 9781400246786 epub
Subjects: LCSH: Carver, Sonora—Fiction | Women stunt performers—United States—Fiction | Stunt performers—United States—Fiction | Horses—Fiction | LCGFT: Biographical fiction | Fiction | Novels Classification: LCC PS3623.A446218 S66 2025 (print) | LCC PS3623.A446218 (ebook)
LC record available at https://lccn.loc.gov/2025018489
LC ebook record available at https://lccn.loc.gov/2025018490

Art Direction: Halie Cotton
Cover Design: Lindy Kasler
Interior Design: Chloe Foster

Printed in the United States of America

25 26 27 28 29 LBC 5 4 3 2 1

AS IN MANY OF my novels, I tell the story from the perspective of the main character. Sonora was a talented performer of her times, and while her act is no longer done today, she cherished her horses, and I find her tenacious, determined spirit to be truly inspirational.

As seen in the October 9, 1923, edition of the *Savannah Morning News*:

Wanted: Attractive young woman who can
swim and dive. Likes horses, desires to travel.
See Dr. W. F. Carver, Savannah Hotel

Chapter 1

MA TAPS THE NEWSPAPER. Presses on the print, actually, the tip of her pointer finger whitening each time.

"You should do this, Sonora," she prods.

"Uh-huh," I say, not taking her or the ad seriously, and focus my attention again out the window on my little sister beyond. Arnette's doing acrobatic-level feats from the river rope swing. Her yellow swimming suit blurs, mixing with the color of the leaves that show the earliest signs of turning.

"Sonora."

"Ma," I mock, not sounding like the eldest child I am, but I can't help emotionally regressing while dealing with Ma's . . . obsession . . . with the adverts in the dailies.

I sigh as she neatly tears the paper. She's serious about this one. But I'm not about to look a second time and give it credence. Instead, I chuckle at Arnette, the spitting image of me, despite being six years younger, who completes a flawless backflip from the rope. I taught her that.

I spoon cornflakes into my mouth.

Ma slides the torn square in front of me, going so far as to replace my cereal bowl with the newspaper clipping.

"Sonora," she repeats.

I have no desire to engage. A slew of ads have elicited declarations of "Oh, Sonora, if this isn't picture perfect!" since Ula—I refuse to call him Daddy—left us high and dry six years ago, right after President Woodrow Wilson declared war on the German Empire. "You'll be sent over, Ula," Ma had said with a note of panic. Her hand was a vise on his. "You're not too old to go."

As it was, he volunteered. Ula left with a quick kiss on Ma's cheek and a pat for each of his six young children. He never came back. It would've been easier if the flu or the war had taken him. But the allure of another life? Of another family? That stung like a hornet.

Ever since, Ma's obsession of running her thumb down the black ink has been unwaning and she's been in a constant state of wanting and being wanted.

FOR SALE: goldfish bowls

Not that we'd ever owned a single fish, nor did Ma have a plan for what to do with the glass bowls, but, "They're basically giving 'em away, Sonora. How can I pass that up?" What she meant was, how could she fill the void that losing her husband—and his salary—had caused? All I know is seventeen glass bowls didn't do the trick. The containers sat empty, precariously stacked in a corner for months until

Arnette and one of my brothers, Humphrey, roughhoused too closely.

WANTED: cosmetic maker
FOR SALE: unicycle

Ma pursued them all—*and more.* She seeks, seeks, seeks, then disregards whatever notion she had and moves on. It's as if she wants to be done with something before it's done with her. Which is silly when it comes to inanimate objects. But it's the only way I can rationalize her behavior and the discarded pestles and mortars, random nuts and bolts, and a slew of other forgotten items she leaves in her wake. Tinker Bell would surely have a grand old time.

But the ad that took the cake . . .

FOR SALE: Two acres on Burnside River, fifteen miles from Savannah. Five-room stucco cottage, modern conveniences, two-car garage, boathouse, private pier, six rowboats

I'd been scratching an itch to move about, visiting my aunt in Florida, when I received a letter from my ma.

When you come back, don't go to Bainbridge. We live on Burnside River now.

That wasn't a relocation to the other side of town. It was clear across Georgia. But there we were, my family of seven, crammed into two rooms so Ma could offer rented beds to hunters. It'd been her greatest venture thus far. The thing is, Ma's ideas are about as surefire as a toy gun. She quickly realized she had no actual desire to house lodgers.

But now she seems to have a desire for *me* to do something.

"Sonora, I think you should do this." There's that insistent *tap, tap, tap* again. "For yourself. For your family. For the people."

For the people?

What is this woman getting on about? The better question: How best to placate her so that I can quickly put an end to this conversation?

I look.

I read.

I sigh.

"Let me get this straight. You want me to perform with . . . what? A circus?"

Ma scoffs. "I see no such mention of a circus."

"Then enlighten me, Ma. What is this?"

"You'd be part of an *attraction*. The show must go on!" She demonstratively raises an arm.

"Really, Ma?"

She laughs. But then her hand covers mine. "You've always had your head in the sky, my dear. When you're not helping me here, you're off gallivanting, feeding that soul of yours. Does this not seem exciting? Read it again."

"I've read it twice," I counter.

She smiles. "You know what they say: third time's the charm."

I humor her.

WANTED: Attractive young woman who can
swim and dive. Likes horses, desires to travel.

The kettle on the stove screams. "I'll get it," I offer, as I always do. But I'm also eager to stand, to get out of her crosshairs, to turn my back so I can't see Ma's gaze trained on me. I feel it on my back as I pour hot water into her favorite mug. I add chamomile. She could do with some calming down. How can she even suggest I be an *attraction*? Bless her heart, it's another of her spontaneous notions. I shake my head, catching Arnette out the window again.

Whip those arms, I try to mentally communicate to her. It'll help her rotate faster in her tuck position. Arnette surfaces and immediately makes for the bank to go again. I long to be out there with her, perfecting my own dives, but I'm due at work soon. We have bills to pay. Many mouths to feed.

I set Ma's mug in front of her, preferring to remain standing, prepared to make my exit.

"Listen to reason, Sonora." Ma sips her tea, steam rising from her mug. She stares at me as she swallows, as if waiting for me to supply the reason. A song and dance we do often. This time I do nothing but stare back.

She sighs. "Don't you see? It offers everything you've ever wanted. And you've got all the qualifications. You're young."

I shrug. Nineteen. Whether or not that's young depends on who you ask.

"You're mighty pretty too."

I scoff. "You reckon so? Remember what Mamie Lou did?"

Ma shakes her head. "My mama was a straight shooter, God rest her soul."

"Straight shooter or not, she said after seeing me for the first time, she rushed to the chapel to pray because I wasn't anything for the eyes."

"Well, it worked, and it's not a sin to acknowledge you're a looker. Those big green eyes and that red-brown hair of yours, not a strand out of place."

Sure, right now, but I was out on the sycamore, minnows darting beneath my feet, only an hour ago. Wild child one moment, prim and proper the next.

But I know I'm not horrible to look at, not that it's done me any good with the boys. Roger Meadows and I were inseparable for a time. I'd even begun to doodle *Sonora Meadows*. I'd been a fool. After a few months' time, he moved on. So did I.

Ma says, "You've got the courage of a lion too."

"Now, that's not in the ad," I point out.

"No, but it should be."

Yeah, it should be. Diving from great heights, which I assume is what's being asked of this young, attractive woman, can be dangerous work. I've dabbled; I know. The funny thing is, I've never considered the idea of being courageous before. Having courage is like coming from old money. If a millionaire walks down the street and sees an item in a storefront that he wants to buy, he goes in and buys it without a second thought. That's how I feel about courage. I've never questioned it because I've always had ample amounts of it. For me, having courage is as natural as having fingernails.

Ma taps the want ad again, then stands to turn up the pressure. "You could do it. You swim like a fish, and I've seen you climb and dive from the old sycamore when you don't think I'm watching. Flipping and twirling all the way down. It's enough to stop my heart. But you do it. You do it well. And don't even try to deny your love of horses. You traded Humphrey for a horse, for Pete's sake."

I try to hide a smile. It's true. All of it: the flipping, the twirling, and the part about trying to trade my baby brother. I was taken with Sam ever since I saw him grazing in our neighbor's pasture. He was a beautiful stallion. I was a fanciful five-year-old with a sibling to spare. Mrs. Jenkins noticed the hearts in my eyes for her Sam. One day she jokingly asked me if I wanted to swap Sam for Humphrey. I kicked up so much dust running inside to fetch my nine-week-old brother that Mrs. Jenkins coughed out dirt.

"I *almost* traded him," I correct Ma. "You caught me running out of the house with him. He was barely out of his crib for ten seconds."

Ma smiles. "Always a free spirit, my Sonora."

"But," I say and glance again at the ad, "what does liking horses have to do with diving?"

"Can't say, which is why we should meet the man. And think, answering this here ad could give you the opportunity to travel more." She pauses. Ma waits for my eyes to lock with hers. "You can satisfy that wanderlust of yours."

"You've already mentioned that."

"For good reason."

Maybe. I can't deny I get antsy staying in one place. That

feeling's always been there. When I was younger, I wandered off so frequently that Ma had to lock me in the backyard. She never guessed I'd scale the fence, withstanding one reprimand and punishment after another.

God help me, I read the advert in full again.

My chest tightens.

It's nerves. It's from the thought of this Dr. W. F. Carver taking one look at me and saying, "No, thank you."

Or maybe even worse: him taking me on, then changing his mind, leaving me to pick up the pieces of my life and figure out what I'm going to do next.

I meet Ma's gaze, kneading my hands together. "You really think I should meet him? That he'd like me?"

"I really do, honey. The timing couldn't be more perfect. You're not married."

"Nor do I want to be," I say quickly.

I'm ignored.

"You never finished high school."

"Well, that's a kettle calling the pot black."

"You've always moved to the beat of your own drum." As she says this, she touches my bobbed hair. "You work as a bookkeeper at a department store, making fifteen dollars a week. How will that ever help support a family of your own?"

"Like you pointed out, I'm not married and I've no desire for more of a family. I've already got plenty with all of you."

I won't say it and hurt Ma's feelings, but I practically raised half my siblings, doing everything but holding them to my own breasts. Families nowadays are larger than most can afford.

Financial quicksand, if you ask me, especially when one of the providers runs off.

Ma sighs. "I could use one less mouth to feed."

I frown, all the while knowing having five instead of six underfoot would make life easier for her. "Mama, are you trying to rid yourself of me?"

Her hand covers mine again. "Of course not. I was being facetious. But I am being earnest when I ask, what do you want for yourself, Sonora?"

The question stops me. I glance again at Arnette, simply swinging now, head tilted back to collect the sun.

No one's ever asked me what I want before. I've just helped to take care of my siblings and worked a steady job at Adler's department store. Neither lighting me up inside, but necessary work. Reliable pay.

I'm not sure how to answer the question of what I want for myself. Not yet, anyway.

"Sonora, honey, ever since your daddy left . . ."

I squeeze my eyes tight.

She's quiet.

I open them.

She goes on, "You've only been half living, sweetie. I appreciate all you do for us, but you've been taking the easy route, protecting yourself."

From failure.

From love.

From figuring out a future.

From being abandoned again.

The words flash through my mind.

Ma acknowledges, "Now, I know I have my own holdups. And I know I've done little to encourage you. I'll admit I've been caught between needing you exactly where you are, doing exactly what you're doing, while also wanting you to stretch your wings. It's beginning to feel like I'm doing nothing more than clipping your wings, though, and this here job feels like it could be the ticket to you figuring out what you want for yourself, that's all."

My mouth goes dry. I swipe her mug and take a sip. I let what she's saying sink in. This conversation is a bit of a novelty for us, Ma and me acting more like two ships passing in the night the majority of the time. But maybe she has a point. Maybe this could be a good opportunity to figure out who Sonora Webster actually is. She's certainly not a bookkeeper, that much I know. "You're sure about this? About me meeting him?"

"I am, darling. It'll be good for you. For all of us."

"Okay, then. I'll meet him," I say in a small voice. I hold up a finger to keep Ma from talking. "I'll make no promises, but I'll meet the man."

To consider being a diver as part of a carnival act . . .

The seed has been planted in my own head, and I daresay I've picked up the scent of a life with horses without even knowing how they fit in with diving yet.

"I'm glad you'll meet him," Ma says, snatching back her mug, "because I've already spoken to him. We've got an appointment tomorrow evening."

Chapter 2

BY THE TIME MA and I click-clack into the Savannah Hotel the next evening, my initial allure at being a diver for a traveling carnival has lost some of its shine. Or maybe I've simply lost confidence in myself, fearing that Dr. W. F. Carver will take one look at me and laugh in my face. Ma, on the other hand, is still beaming at full wattage.

She eagerly bumps me with her hip, not breaking stride.

Both of us are in our Sunday best. Dresses on, hair pinned back, stockings straight, slips the appropriate length. Everything is meticulously so.

Except maybe for my twisting hands. The more time that passes, the more I believe coming here may've been a mistake. Why put myself in a situation to fail? This isn't black-and-white like the numbers in the ledgers I keep, even if that work is as boring as all get-out.

I scan the lobby, trying to spot Dr. W. F. Carver before he sees us. Perhaps there's time to pull Ma back by the arm and tell her I've changed my mind. I figure this Dr. W. F. Carver to be the slick type. Maybe in a suit, considering he's got "Dr."

ahead of his name. Or maybe in a red-and-gold ringmaster getup, as if he's just stepped out of a big-top tent.

A man stands, a commanding presence. A head taller than everyone else in the lobby.

I know it's Dr. W. F. Carver right away by how he focuses on me, as if deciding whether I could be his next prized mare.

And I've pegged him all wrong.

Not a doctor. Not in a black top hat. But in a ten-gallon hat, his wavy gray hair reaching his shoulders. Immediately his hand is out—even though he's still a good twenty feet away—and he's charging toward us, barely dodging other lobby-goers, as if he doesn't have a single second to lose.

"Ma, no," I whisper. "You can't mean to send me off with that man."

He could be a caricature of the Wild West, oversized belt buckle and all.

"Hush now, Sonora, you're being rude."

Rude or not, my mind is spitting nouns at me. Dr. W. F. Carver is—how do I say this gently?—a burly fella, likely double me in weight. Someone who seems more suited to be a cowboy, a rancher, or a renegade, even. But not what I'd imagine a showman to be.

And now here he is, taking Ma's hand first, shaking it as if she were a man.

Cross my heart, Dr. W. F. Carver is as big as a redwood or sequoia. Maybe getting close in age to those trees too, though it's hard to tell how old he is exactly with such weathered skin.

He takes my hand next.

His is calloused.

He shakes me like I owe him money.

"You must be Sonora."

His voice is formidable, just as his stride was as he barreled toward us.

"Yes, sir," I say. I wouldn't dare leave off that *sir*. If someone told me he once wrestled a bear, I'd only reply, "Why yes, I do believe he has. And he won. Poor bear."

"This way," Dr. W. F. Carver says without further preamble. "My son and daughter are just over here. Carver's High-Diving Horse Act is a family business, you see. Call me Doc, will you?"

High-Diving Horse Act?

It's the first I'm hearing those four words put together in that way, the want ad being one-sided, focusing on what I can do, not what I'd be doing with the horses.

Likes horses, I remind myself.

I do. I really do. It's a large part of the reason I'm even here. But does that mean I'll be diving *with* them?

I glance at Ma as we follow Doc. She's smiling from ear to ear.

"Here we are," Doc says. "I'd like to introduce my children, Allen and Lorena."

Both are sitting at a round table, enough chairs for each of us. I turn toward Lorena first, feeling too intimidated to lock eyes with another Carver man just yet. I reckon she's closer to Ma's age than my own. She's pretty, her hair such a deep red shade that I'm not sure if it's natural or if she paid for it. Where her father's complexion is ruddy and leatherlike, Lorena's skin is pale, smooth, with only a hint of wrinkles emerging between and around her eyes.

We exchange our hellos, and I sense a tinge of something in her voice, but I can't quite put my finger on what it is.

"I go by Al," Doc's son says, pulling my attention to him. The shake of my hand is so quick, it feels like an obligation more than a nice-to-meet-you. The bones of his cheeks are defined to a point that a fairy could enjoy a seat there. A green hue deeper than my own makes his eyes that much more penetrating, intimidating even. "Only my old man calls me Allen."

His tone isn't exactly friendly. Nor harsh. Maybe no-nonsense is a good way to describe it.

Doc enthusiastically gestures to the free seats. I take one. Ma takes the other.

Both Carver men are distinguished-looking. Same shape to those eyes. Same prominent cheekbones. Same straight nose. Same general likeness in how they confidently hold themselves with their backs ramrod straight. But the rest is night and day.

Al is more the type I was expecting to meet. Ten or so years older than me. Dark hair in a shorter style, highly glossed and slicked back. Fedora not on his head but on the table. Snappy suit. The kind of clothing you'd wear to close a deal. The thing is, I don't get the sense this Al wants to close anything with me. He may be physically at the table, but mentally he's already moved on, his attention out the window on the passing cars. Rude, yet that suits me fine. Let him judge the cars rather than me.

My eyes jump to his daddy. Meeting Doc's gaze is no better, not with how he's sizing me up.

"Her name's good," Doc says. "Don't you think, Allen?" When his son is noncommittal, he turns to his daughter.

"The name's decent for a poster, I guess," Lorena says, not unkindly, but in a manner I now see as perhaps sullen.

Ma chimes in, "I named her after my great-grandmother, a performer in her own right."

I cock my head at Ma. I've never heard such a thing before, and I get the sense she's talking nonsense to impress him.

"So it's in the blood," Doc bellows. "That's grand, Mrs. Webster."

"Miss," Ma corrects. After Ula left, she went from missus to miss, but insisted on keeping the same last name as her children.

"Apologies," Doc says, ever so slightly tipping his hat. "And I must say, you weren't fibbing. Your daughter is mighty pretty."

I can't help a glance at Al, whose disinterest is beginning to narrow my eyes. I'm here to help *them* . . . *him* . . . with their act. How is Doc nonplussed with his children's lack of enthusiasm? He simply goes on, saying, "The crowd will like her. I already do."

Ma says, "She can swim. Dive. This one is fearless, I can tell you that, Mr. Carver. But can you tell me more about—what did you call it?—the Carver's High-Diving—"

"Horse Act," Doc finishes. "Carver's High-Diving Horse Act."

"Horse," I repeat. "In what manner are the horses involved?"

"Well, they dive, of course. Horse and girl dive together."

My mouth drops open.

Together?

I'd gotten it correct, as incredible as this sounds.

He adds, "That's what Lorena here has been doing for years."

Lorena's chin is raised. Proud as a peacock.

I hate to ask it—this girl is already not overly friendly toward me—but I have to. "Couldn't that be dangerous for the horse?"

Doc inhales sharply, and I instantly regret the question. If his next words send me packing, I won't be surprised.

Fortunately, Lorena answers, though her words are just as sharp as her father's inhale. "No. The horses would dive on their own. It's how this whole show came to be. Isn't that right, Daddy?"

Doc nods and motions for her to keep on talking.

Lorena beams, looking pleased to do just that. "My daddy here was riding across a bridge when it collapsed underfoot. One would expect the horse—Silver King was his name—to belly flop, but instead he angled himself down and dove into the river. Daddy hung on, emerged from the water on his back, and Silver King swam against the rough current, getting them both safely to shore. My daddy recognized the potential for an act, and Silver King was more than happy to oblige the fans. No one *ever* has to force one of our horses to dive when there's water beneath him."

Doc squeezes his daughter's hand. "It doesn't stop a certain man from the SPCA from sniffing around. All he ever finds, though, is his own—"

"Doc," Al says, suddenly taking notice of our conversation.

It's interesting Al doesn't call him Dad. We're similar in that way. Though I wonder if Al calling his father by name is because of their show.

"Apologies," Doc says, hand to his heart. "The devil got in my blood for a moment. But the question's a good one, Sonora. What else would you like to know?"

I can see how Doc charms an audience. I can see the showman now in how he talks, moves. Winks. "How about pay?" Doc offers. "Money makes the world go around, does it not? Especially in the twenties. It's like the world's gone mad. Good for business, though. I'll tell you that much. And I'll tell you I'm prepared to offer my new diving girl fifty a week."

Under the table, Ma kicks my foot. I barely feel it. "Fifty?" I parrot, astonished.

"That'll go up, too, as we book more shows."

I'm stunned speechless. That's more than three times what I make as a bookkeeper, and I'm in Savannah's largest department store.

"We do shows in the summer and into the fall. We winter in Florida. We keep the act small, close-knit. You'd travel with us, live with us."

"But what about diving?" I ask. "I've dived plenty over the years, but never on the back of a horse." I twist my lips. I want to point out that it sounds dangerous. But maybe I have a screw loose, because I'm more intrigued than scared. "How do you know I can do the job?"

"Miss Sonora," he begins, "I could teach a pig to fly, as long as that pig has a thirst to fly. The thing is, most pigs don't. Do you want to learn to fly on a horse, Sonora?"

Do I?

Would that help answer Ma's question about what I want for myself? I'm not sure. Beside me, Ma blessedly doesn't kick me this time. She doesn't chirp in either.

"Look," Doc says. "I'm not going to pressure you, sweetheart. I love them horses more than I love these two." He thumbs toward his children.

I begin to laugh but stop short when Al and Lorena don't so much as chuckle.

My hands go into my lap.

"We've got a show this weekend. You go. You watch. You see what diving for me is all about. And if you think you've got the thirst, we'll talk some more."

"All right, sir."

"But, Sonora, I can't promise you the next girl I meet with won't say yes right away."

Or that his two children won't like *her* better.

I understand he's giving me the hard sell. Ma bought it from the second she saw the want ad. But me, it's the horses I need to see to help make my decision. Those beautiful, powerful animals may make the risk of being rejected or failing and being thrown out with the bathwater worth it. All I say is, "I understand."

With that, Al plucks his hat from the table, Doc tips his, and Lorena stands.

The three Carvers leave Ma and me sitting there.

In a matter of days, I'll see a girl diving with a horse for the first time.

And for the first time, I have a feeling my courage will be tested.

Chapter 3

BEFORE I KNOW IT, the weekend is upon me. I have mixed emotions about seeing the Carvers again, any of them, but I am intrigued to see their horses.

To see a horse dive.

With a girl on its back.

Wouldn't that be the bee's knees?

Ma and Arnette join me. My other sister, Jacqueline, stays behind to watch our brothers. Nighttime is kissing Savannah by the time we arrive at the fairground. We missed one or two of the other acts. To think, only days ago this was open land. And now, per the flyer Ma brought home, the grass is speckled with apparatuses for aerialists, high-wire walkers, and trapeze artists. And next up under the lights, there will be a diving girl. The Girl in Red, she's called.

I purposefully keep my eyes on my feet as we walk past idle chatter, voices in varying octaves of excitement, and toward empty seats in the grandstand. I've built up this evening and the horses in my head, and I want to be sitting on the bleachers, the aroma of candied air wafting all around me, before I raise my head and see all there is to see about the Carver's High-Diving Horse Act.

I take my seat. I press my heels together. I fold my hands in my lap. And I look up. And up.

My eyes are drawn to a tower.

A spotlight is trained at the top.

I find myself holding my breath.

Ma told me the tower is forty feet tall, but at the time the measurements were merely words. Now those words have taken shape. A series of two-by-fours painted white rise from the ground—higher and higher—in a crisscross pattern, dwarfing everything around them. Then at the top, a platform, outlined by streamers and a string of lights.

At the base of the tower, a second spotlight flickers on. Within the beam of light, there's Doc Carver, a sly half smile stretched across his weathered face. His cowboy hat is even larger than before. His jacket is adorned with tassels. A microphone stands before him.

"Ladies and gentlemen," he begins.

I sit up straighter.

Arnette grips my hand.

Unable to stop myself, I smile over at Ma. I'm surprised her own smile hasn't fully formed, but I see the intrigue in how her mouth hangs slightly open.

Doc Carver bellows into the microphone, "It is my complete pleasure to welcome you all to Carver's High-Diving Horse Act and the Girl in Red!"

At that, a third spotlight illuminates a girl at the base of the tower. The Girl in Red. She wears only a swimming suit and a helmet. Both red. One of her hands grips a ladder.

I expected Lorena, but as I squint, I don't believe it's her. Though at this distance and with her head beneath the red football helmet, it's hard to tell. The Girl in Red waves to the crowd. We cheer, Arnette's high-pitched voice vying for the loudest.

Then the girl begins to climb.

The spotlight follows her. Her water shoes are so white they reflect the light. Up she goes, never pausing, never looking down.

Would I?

At the top, she waves, then proceeds to the platform's edge. She dramatically leans over, one hand holding a rail, and the audience collectively grows louder.

It's showmanship I would do, I think.

There's a large circle-shaped pool at the tower's bottom, dug into the ground. The final spotlight is trained there. The water is still, untouched. I can't see its depth, but I can't imagine Doc Carver would allow one of his horses to be hurt. At one side of the tank of water, a ramp rises to a platform raised above the ground. A man is there. I squint again, trying to determine if it's Al. But no, it's a younger boy. A groom, I guess, to see to the horse after the dive.

The girl straightens from leaning over the tower's edge. Her shoulders visibly rise and fall as she walks toward the back side of the tower. Is it nerves? Would they ever go away?

Doc booms into the microphone, "We are the first act of

its kind, the only women—the only *performers*—to complete such a daring feat! Because of the dangers involved, I ask you to hold your applause. Hold your voices."

A hush falls over the grandstand.

I pull my bottom lip between my teeth.

Doc Carver goes dark.

The girl raises her arm.

She holds it.

She drops her arm.

It's a signal, I realize, for the horse. I can't see the horse, but in an instant, a galloping sound engulfs us. The mighty beast runs up a ramp barely visible in the night. I can feel him, as if his footfalls rumble every inch of the fairground.

The horse's shadow looms higher and higher. The strings of lights on the tower shake.

Then his head, neck, and shoulders appear. Within a heartbeat, the Girl in Red launches herself onto the horse's back. He's gray, my mind registers, before both the horse and the girl launch from the platform.

They become a single silhouette against the dark night: the horse's slender neck, his long legs, her torso.

I find myself sitting taller, stretching my own torso.

It's marvelous, each and every glorious second they own the sky.

And in that moment, my breath held and my body tense, I realize this is what I want for myself. I want to be on the back of a horse, owning the sky. And I want that feeling day after day, night after night.

Then they splash, the horse meeting the water first, the Girl in Red following on his back. Water sloshes over the sides of the pool, a crescendo to the dive.

Instantly, the crowd is on their feet. I climb onto my seat, desperately needing to see the horse emerge from the water. When he does, the girl is still on his back. She thrusts an arm into the air. There's nothing to hear save for applause, but for a moment, panic seizes me. The horse's expression is fierce, with his teeth bared and his nostrils sucked in, and I worry he's been hurt. If he is, the Girl in Red doesn't let on. I rip my gaze from him to gauge the reaction of the others in the grandstand. Ma has a hand over her mouth. Arnette may burst out of her skin. Most are clapping wildly. Some have tears in their eyes, as if they've witnessed something momentous.

They have.

I focus again on the horse. Droplets drip from him as he climbs a ramp out of the man-made pool. I blow out a breath; if he was struggling, he's successfully made it, not looking any worse for wear. In fact, his head is high and his tail is swinging freely. The girl slips off him. She bows.

I begin shaking my head. A little from disbelief at what I just witnessed, a little from awe, and a lot from envy at what the Girl in Red gets to do. Soaring through the air with that magnificent animal is her job.

If I thought I was enamored with Roger Meadows, then I need lessons in love. Because I've truly fallen in love this time, simply and completely, with the idea of this being my future.

All I can hope is that Doc Carver hasn't already hired a girl to teach to fly through the sky. I want to be his new Girl in Red. I have an unquenchable thirst to be that girl.

Chapter 4

I'm on my feet—"Excuse me"—pushing through the crowd. "Excuse me."

My sights are set on the Girl in Red, still bowing, and the magnificent beast beside her. He's passed to the groom.

I must hurry. I don't know how long the act will remain before they all are whisked away.

Doc Carver?

I strain to find him as I weave in and out of bodies.

Ma calls my name.

He must be around here somewhere, basking in a successful act.

There he is, in front of the microphone again, giving his thanks for everyone turning out to witness the making of history.

A history I need to be a part of.

As I approach, I smooth my hand down my white blouse and ensure it's fully tucked into my blue serge skirt. It's my next best after my Sunday best.

"Sonora!" I hear again.

This time I slow; I wait for Ma and Arnette. Impatiently. I try to calm myself. It wouldn't serve me well to bum-rush Doc and come across as too excitable. No, I want to appear competent, levelheaded, composed. With Ma at my side to underline my enthusiasm for the position.

Only—I realize, my smile waning—Ma's enthusiasm has wilted, lines between her eyes. "What?" I say to her as she joins me. "What's wrong?"

My attention flicks to my sister, whose expression is the complete opposite. In fact, my little sister looks like she'd steal my spot if she could.

Ma presses her lips together.

And, *no*, my heart sinks. She always does this. Ma gets some harebrained plan to feel more fulfilled—in this case to make *me* feel more fulfilled—then she goes after it like a bat out of hell only to up and change her mind.

It's why there's a rusted unicycle leaning against the barn.

It's why Ma never housed a single hunter.

It's why she's shaking her head at me now. "I don't know, Sonora. Maybe this isn't such a grand idea."

The irritation is there in my voice for all to hear as I say, "This is so typical—"

"Sonora, honey—"

"I'm young. A woman. Who can swim. And dive. I like horses. I desire to travel. That's the ad you shoved in my face. You asked me what I want for myself. And this is it. This'll make me feel alive, Ma."

I throw a quick look over my shoulder at Doc. He's leaving the lower platform that doubles as a stage.

"It looks dangerous. That's all," Ma tries. "And truly, honey, I was being facetious about you being an extra mouth to feed. You make an adequate amount at Adler's. You don't need to jeopardize your welfare for us."

"I'd be doing it for *me*, Ma." Arnette's eyes are still lighting up like the Fourth of July, and I know she's about to chime in, so I hold up a palm to silence her and focus on my ma, asking, "You don't think I can do it, do you?"

She must register the hurt in my voice; her face softens. "It's only that it's so high, seeing it in person. And the splash pool doesn't leave a large margin of error. How easy it'd be to get hurt. I don't want that for you."

I resist a glance at the tower and instead cross my arms. "I'm going to see this through, Ma. You asked me what I want. I want this."

I leave her standing there and chase after Doc, throwing out "excuse me" like candy at a parade. Finally, I've reached him.

"Mr. Doc Carver," I say to his back.

That *mister* is overkill.

When he faces me, his amused expression tells me he agrees.

"I'm glad I caught you," I say.

Doc beams. "How can I help you, little lady?"

He's friendly enough. What's missing is his recognition of me. "I'm Sonora. Sonora Webster. We met earlier this week?"

"Yes. Yes, of course."

"I'm interested," I blurt out. So much for composure. "That was incredible, and I'd very much like to be a part of your act."

Al crosses behind his daddy, his head shaking in my direction as if he's already dismissed me as ever joining them.

"Duly noted, Miss Webster. I'll be in touch if the need arises. Still a few kinks we're ironing out."

Again, he's friendly enough. But where's the enthusiasm from before? He couldn't have seen Al behind him. But did they talk about me and decide on a big fat no about bringing me into the act?

Doc tips his hat and disappears into an outbuilding.

I'm left dumbfounded, steamrolled. Denied?

Just as I had feared.

THE BEST THING ABOUT working at Adler's department store is their café that sells delicious tuna fish sandwiches, coffee with whipped cream, and a superb lemon pie.

I don't like the tiny closet I work in.

I don't like being cooped up indoors all day.

Frankly, I don't like bookkeeping.

Numbers make me twitch, despite them being a sure thing. I'm more of a right-side-of-my-brain kind of girl.

But considering it's been three months since I practically threw myself at Doc Carver's feet and I've heard zilch from him, it appears I'd better swallow that pill and accept I'm going nowhere.

I hate the heaviness of that thought.

I hate that I put myself out on that limb, only for it to snap beneath me.

I hate that my mind keeps replaying the exchange I had with Arnette the day after witnessing the Girl in Red fly on a horse.

"What do you reckon I did wrong?" I muttered to myself as we were swimming back to the shoreline after a dive.

Arnette lifted a brow. "That looked fine to me."

I blew bubbles into the water, then said, "No, I mean with the Carvers."

Leave it to an almost-teen to answer bluntly. "Maybe they just don't want you anymore."

"If that's the case, I wish he would've said so."

Instead of leaving me in limbo.

"Men." Arnette shrugged.

I frowned.

I frown now, the columns on my spreadsheet not balancing. So much for numbers being a sure thing. My supervisor, Mr. Murphy, is patient with me. I'm lucky I even got the job. Lord knows there are many more qualified than me. But Mr. Murphy came back from the war when Ula did not. He took pity on us.

I also hate being pitied.

It's why I dust off the pie crumbs from my blouse and don't leave my shoebox of an office until the numbers add up. I yawn no less than fifteen times on the trolley ride home. Sitting all day has the unfortunate result of somehow causing more exhaustion than running around. When I reach our long drive, I check the mailbox. Someone already got its contents. Or else there was nothing to be got.

The chances of a letter coming from Doc Carver began at seventy-five percent in my mind. As time went on, that dropped incrementally to fifty, forty-five, forty. Then thirty-nine, thirty-eight. Really, I should stop this game I'm playing with myself and accept that Dr. W. F. Carver and his High-Diving Horse Act have no business with me. But I'm a glutton for punishment.

The screen door slams behind me. My gaze falls on a stack of mail on the kitchen table.

Humphrey whizzes by, chasing . . . a frog.

"Better not let Ma catch you with that inside," I call after him.

"She's the one who told him to get it out of the house," Arnette says, coming into the kitchen, hands behind her back.

A twinkle in her eye.

"What ya got back there?" I ask her.

"Back where?" She's all innocent-like as she twists, still concealing whatever she's got.

Even though my little sister has instantly put my stomach in knots, I crack a smile at her antics. "If that's a letter for me . . ."

"You'll do what?" she says. "Jump around? Shout for joy?" Her smile falters. "Leave us high and dry?"

I step closer. "If they do want me. If I go," I say, and we both know without a doubt the devil himself would have to stop me. "I'd write. I'd tell you all about my adventures. Would you like that?"

She narrows her eyes. "Only to me."

I laugh. "If that's what you want, though I reckon Ma would like to hear from me once in a while too."

"But mostly me."

I nod. "I don't swipe extra cookies from the jar for any of our brothers or Jac, do I?"

She smiles. "And that's why you're my favorite."

"Only for the cookies?" I ask, putting on a faux frown.

I think Arnette would hug me if not for hiding that letter behind her back. She says, "You give me both cookies and love. You promise you'll write, Nora?"

"Cross my heart."

"Fine." She reveals the letter.

Addressed to me: *Miss Sonora Webster.*

And the sender: *Dr. W. F. Carver.*

Arnette barrels into my stomach, her arms winding around me before I've a chance to open it. "I've already read it," she says, her voice muffled. "I'm going to miss you terribly."

I drop my chin to the top of her head, holding her close.

I'm going to miss her too.

I'm going to miss the whole lot of them.

But it tickles me pink even to think it: *I'm going to be a high-diving horse girl.*

A horse diver?

A diving girl on a horse?

Diving horse rider?

I'll sort that out later, because I soon find out that this here letter says I leave tomorrow.

Chapter 5

PACKING IS A BREEZE; I don't own much, my prized possession a gold-plated vanity set that used to be Mamie Lou's. Then there are my books, a whole shelf of them, though only a third will fit in my luggage. I'll have to buy more wherever I go. Waltzing into bookstores all over the country is another thing I'm looking forward to.

For now, I walk from room to room. My excitement for what's ahead eclipses the heaviness I feel at what I'm leaving behind. A home. Familiar faces. A little sister who never minces words. A mother who mostly lets me do as I please; as she herself has said, the two of us similar to two ships crossing in the night, both intent on the single goal of keeping our family afloat.

I'm glad I'll be able to send money home, to still help in this way. Though Ma assures me it was never about the money. "It's about no longer clipping your wings."

I'd rather she'd speak to me plainly, no more silly sayings about boats or birds. But it's not her way. Nor do I blame her. Ma's done her best to pick up the pieces after Ula's leaving, but she's always felt a fingertip away from accepting the truth of things.

Not me. Not anymore. I'm about to take the greatest leap I've ever taken, putting myself in the most vulnerable position I've ever been in.

All that's left is stepping from the platform to a train car.

Who knew one step could be so frightening?

But I do it, and as soon as I do, the waving begins. Ma, Jac, Junior, Arnette, Daniel, and Humphrey, all lined up. A sight to commit to memory. I'm not certain when I'll return. It could be weeks, months, or years. I'm now at the mercy of a man who I get the sense doesn't know the meaning of the word *no*. A man whose drumbeats are ten times louder than my own.

I fill my lungs with air as I scan for a vacant seat.

Demonstrative waving catches my eye.

"Doc Carver?" I say to myself, questioning if I've somehow just conjured the man.

Though he must hear. "In the flesh. Saved ya one."

"I didn't know you'd be on here," I say, taking the seat beside him. "Your letter only said to collect my ticket and come to Florida."

"Sonora, it wouldn't be appropriate to let you travel to Jacksonville alone, now, would it?"

"It would've helped if my ma knew that ahead of time, sir."

He chuckles. "Let's not backtrack and call me sir. Doc suits me just fine."

Very well, but I'm serious about wishing I'd known he'd be here on the train. In my seat, I scour out the small window for

Ma. Spotting her, I point to Doc, then give her a thumbs-up. Ma's hand finds her chest, relief evident on her narrow face that I won't be making the four-hour trip without a chaperone.

I settle in. Well, as best I can beside this behemoth of a near-stranger. Who can apparently read my thoughts. "Lots of time to get to know each other, you and I."

I smile.

"I do hope you won't take offense."

I cock my head ever so slightly. "Because of how long you kept me waiting for your letter?"

He bellows a laugh. "No, not that. I had some ironing out to do. Business concerns that do not concern you. What I mean is your hair, your dress. Neither are as expected after our meeting."

Today my bobbed hair is down instead of pinned back. And my skirt, it falls just past my knees, how all the young things are wearing them now.

Doc waves his hand, as if overwhelmed. "Those creeping hemlines." His head adds in, shaking. "Thank the good Lord Lorena is too old to get caught up in all that newfangled flapper stuff."

I self-consciously tug my skirt, which in a sitting position has inched higher. These kinds of dictations aren't surprising, nor do I take offense; Ma has plenty of her own. But I'm baffled at how to respond to a man I barely know.

Probably for the best, considering Doc has more to say. "A lady should never let her knees show."

Ain't that rich, considering the Girl in Red was in nothing but a swimming suit during his act.

He's still going on. ". . . Never smoke. Never drink. Now, that goes for both men and women where I'm concerned. Oh, and profanity . . ."

"Never?" I guess.

"Mild," he corrects. "Sometimes life calls for it. Then, all right, let it fly. But anyone who stands under my banner in one of my acts is expected to adhere to certain morals, you see."

I snort, barely audible. Who is this man? And honestly, I need examples of what he deems inappropriate as far as cussing. So I ask, "Is *damn* a suitable word?"

His head rattles. "*Darn*. No. *Dern* is the best alternative."

Is that even a word?

I ask, "How about *oh my gosh*?"

"Oh my *word*."

"Really, I can't say *gosh*?"

He pins me with his gaze. "*Gosh*, and *golly* for that matter, are blasphemy."

Well, gosh. "What can I say then?"

He runs his pointer finger and thumb along his long mustache. "If you must say anything, I'll accept *gee*."

He doesn't say anything along the lines of "my way or the highway," but his serious expression doesn't make me eager to test him. He won't hesitate to send me packing, I know.

"Seems fair enough," I say, if it means I'll get to ride his horses. I'dyay eakspay inyay Pig Latin ifyay at'sthay atwhay isthay anmay eferspray.

"Sonora, you and I are going to get along just fine. Now, what would you like to know? Ask away."

Truly?

He widens his eyes. "Go on. I won't bite."

I don't believe that for even a second, but where do I begin? Dr. W. F. Carver looks like the reincarnation of Billy the Kid, yet he doesn't smoke or drink and only curses when life calls for some dern vigor. All that's clear is that he's a man who craves showmanship. So let's start there. "How did this all begin? You being in shows, I mean."

"Would you believe I was a dentist?"

"Honestly"—I pause—"no."

He belly laughs.

And I can't help having a fondness for the man, while being intimidated by him and simultaneously wanting to earn his approval. If I had a daddy, I wonder if it'd feel a little something like this, and I lean in, eager to hear more of his story.

"My great-, great-, great-, great-"—he scrunches an eye—"great-, and a few more greats for good measure, grandfather was John Carver. Came over on the *Mayflower*. First governor of Massachusetts. That means I come from a long line of politicians, lawyers, professors, doctors. Those types of professions. My old man had been a doctor, and I took up the notion of being a dentist. I stuck with it long enough until I had 'Dr.' in front of my name too. But the tooth-pulling business wasn't for me. I realized it the day I went to a gun club and blasted all the targets."

"Your daddy was okay with you changing your mind?"

"I was clear across the country in California at the time. He didn't have much say in the matter. A newspaper did an article about me, talking about how good a shot I was. Next thing I know, some enterprising men put up the money to take me around the world sharpshooting. I earned myself the title of Champion Rifle Shot of the World."

My eyes go large. "That doesn't sound like any small thing."

"The world's not a small place, that's for sure."

"What happened next?"

"Lots of fanfare. I exhibited my marksmanship for the Prince of Wales, Emperor Wilhelm, Grand Duke Albert of Austria." He whistles. "Those were some good times. I only came home because I was homesick for custard pie."

"You're lying."

He winks. "From there, I ran into an old friend, Buffalo Bill. Between the two of us, we had enough sense to make a dollar, and we started a company putting on melodramas about the Old West." He sucks through his teeth. "Huge success it was, but it didn't last. Nope, the two of us were like oil and water. We went our separate ways, each of us doing our own shows, trying to outdo each other every step of the way. I ended up catching the eye of a playwright who hired hundreds of cast members to give the show the old razzle-dazzle. Yours truly was the lead. Remember how Lorena told you about that horse of mine who dove off the bridge? That was my Silver King." Doc shakes his head, a content, faraway expression overtaking him. "King loved that scene. My muse for all that I'm doing now."

"And to think," I say, utterly enamored with the progression of his story, "it all began on the *Mayflower*."

He guffaws. "The *Mayflower* indeed. Though don't go reminding Allen he hails from Puritans. That boy is as hardheaded as a mustang. But he'll spook like an unbroken mustang too."

I can't help myself. "Al's pretty wild then?"

"The stories I could tell . . . When he was a boy, he ran away. Had his poor mother bereft."

"Why'd he run off?"

"This or that. Allen always thinks he's right."

I hide a snort; the apple doesn't fall far from the tree.

"What's he do? For the act, I mean."

"Ironically enough, he helps to break and train our horses. For as unreliable as he can be, never fail, the horses always take to him."

Al's unreliable. Always thinks he's right. He'll spook like an unbroken mustang. Not the most flattering way to speak of an employee, much less his own flesh and blood. And I have to know. "Doc, what made you change your mind about giving me the job?"

"It wasn't me whose mind had to change. I'll be straight with you. You've got some work to do when we get there in a few hours, Sonora."

I bite my bottom lip; I have a feeling he doesn't mean with the horses.

Chapter 6

ISN'T THIS A FEAST for the eyes?

A big ol' farmhouse, along with a few outbuildings.

The barn and stables.

A round pen for horse training.

The tower and a man-made pool for diving.

A natural pond that is already calling to me for a midnight dip.

A dirt track with a stretch of wooden bleachers marred from the sun, elements, and termites, if I had to guess.

"Used to be an old racing track before we took it over for the winters," Doc says beside me, the dust still settling from when we drove up to the property in his tin lizzie.

I'm beaming, taking it all in. Very serene. Very quiet. Not much commotion at all, save for a breeze tossing the tall grasses back and forth. Where is everyone? But more importantly: "How many horses do you keep?"

"I certainly picked you right if that's your first question. We've five at the moment." Doc claps his hands against his dungarees. "Shall we shake a leg and get you started?"

Suddenly, I can't move, much less shake a leg. Ma said I've only been half living. Protecting myself from failure, love, my future, abandonment. An ample list, apparently. What if I can't hack it as part of the act? What if Doc sends me packing? I'll be forced home with my tail between my legs. Back to a small, airless closet, if I can even get rehired at my old job. Back to diving from a tree branch and swinging low over a river, when I want to live fully, forty feet in the air above an audience in awe.

Or worse, what if, like Doc with his tooth pulling, I realize horse diving isn't for me? Where will that leave me, back to only half living and figuring myself out?

But no, I was born for this. I set my gaze on the tower, some of those nerves dissipating into a fieriness to climb the ladder.

"Don't be getting cold feet now," Doc says. "Hard to anyway when it's a good ten degrees warmer than back in Savannah." He laughs at his own joke, clapping me on the shoulder. "How about we meet the horses?"

"Please," I say, and just like that, I take another step into my new world.

KLATAWAH IS WRITTEN ON the first door. There's a row of stalls with chest-high doors, each enclosure opening to a shared paddock area.

"Allen turned out the horses earlier," Doc says, noting why there aren't any horses to greet us. I'm instantly let down at having to wait to meet them. I've been around horses all my life. Neighbor horses, that is, where I've stolen moments whenever I could here and there. I've offered to ride them, feed them, brush them. But here I'll be living with them. I can pretend they're all mine.

Doc cups his hand and shouts, "Where are Daddy's horses?"

There's a rumble of hooves. Overlapping neighs and whinnies. Then five heads appear in the five openings: a sorrel-colored head, a dapple-gray muzzle, two with roan markings, and last but not least, a head as white as snow.

I suck in a breath, overcome by these magnificent, beautiful creatures. "They know to go to their own stall?"

His eyebrows dance. "These are no ordinary horses."

He places his palms on either side of Klatawah's head and pulls him toward his own, holding him there for a moment, stroking the horse's strong jaw.

A lump of emotion forms in my throat, witnessing such a simple, shared affection—and I can't wait to get my own hands on a horse.

Apparently the horse in the next stall over shares my conviction, tossing its head in my direction. A real beauty with dark and light gray shades creating circular patterns all over her body. I step closer, mouthing the name on her door: *The Duchess of Lightning*.

"I know you," I say, slowly extending my hand. "That was quite the dive you did at the fair. Though, apologies, I thought you were a boy."

I swear she either thanks me or is laughing at my mistake with a string of whinnies.

Doc chuckles. "Lightning is never short of things to say.

She's got different sounds for each of us. Before long, she'll have a nicker for you too."

If I can only be so lucky.

Lightning sniffs my hand before accepting me, leaning in.

"Attagirl," Doc says, and I'm not sure which of us he's talking to. "Lightning is our largest, our bravest, our most loving."

The next horse down, the first of the two horses with roan markings, makes his presence known. "And then we have Judas."

I snort. "Judas?"

"That's right. And better believe he's earned his name. When we first got him, he tossed Lorena over his head. She called out how he's a Judas, and, well, the name stuck to him like white on rice. Aligns with this one"—he nods to the next horse—"who we call John the Baptist, because he clamors for the water. Both are characters. Horses have as much of a personality as you and I do. And I'll tell ya, these two are trouble. But we love you anyway," Doc says, stretching his arms to pet them both at once.

The horses all clearly love him, including the final one, Snow, whose coat is as pure and white as a new dusting of snow.

"Careful of her too," Doc says, his voice not wavering from that of a proud papa. "She's a glutton. At first we welcomed it. Snow would do anything for a carrot. It made her our easiest to train. That is, until she became so acclimated to her snacks that she had a tantrum if we didn't reward her to her liking. One time she nearly kicked her way out of her stall. Allen had to reinforce the planking."

Al. Whom I haven't yet seen, though maybe that's not such

a bad thing. But the rest of the troupe? "So, five horses," I say, "but where's everyone else?"

Doc looks up and down the stable, as if just realizing our only company have four legs and swishing tails. "Georgie, our groom, is likely starting on supper. We've a schedule and trade off who handles the grub. Vivian, who you know as the Girl in Red, has the day off. She's off somewhere, maybe holed up in her room. We don't train like other troupes when it comes to the animals, though. The acts with bears or lions train daily to keep the animals fit in mind and body. But once our horses are trained to dive, they've got it. Our focus is keeping them happy, healthy, exercised, and properly stabled and fed."

A vehicle suddenly rumbles up the long drive.

Doc cocks his head toward it. "That must be Lorena and Allen now."

He strides outside the barn, and it takes some effort for me to keep up as I follow after him.

"How's my girl?" Doc calls in greeting.

Al unfolds from the car. He's taller than I remember. Tall, dark, and brooding. Lorena is slower to emerge. She shakes her head solemnly. "Doctor says I shouldn't perform."

Doc removes his hat, runs his hand through his hair, then shoves his hat back on.

"Are you hurt?" I ask Lorena, scouring for visible bandages or braces. Perhaps they're beneath her blouse, skirt, or stockings.

Doc sighs. "Lorena tore a leg muscle last year. Had surgery a few months back, right around the time I put the ad in the paper. I was looking for a new girl in case Lorena wouldn't be able to perform. Now here we are. Here you are."

But what would have happened if Lorena's doctor appointment went differently? Would I be right back on the train?

Judging by Al's sour expression, that's exactly what he'd been hoping for. Lorena's isn't much better. Though if I were in her single-strap shoes and not able to dive anymore, I'd have a similar somber mug.

"I'm sorry you can't dive," I offer to her.

She nods as her daddy clamps her shoulder. "I've got big plans for Lorena nevertheless. Lorena, Allen, and Vivian are spearheading a second troupe for us. Being able to run two helps with the bottom line." His eyes are lighting up like Christmas morning. "That leaves you with me, Sonora." He pins his son with a look. "And why my decision to bring you on is weighted the greatest. Training starts tomorrow. But you, little lady," he says, switching his gaze to Lorena, who's already taking steps toward an outbuilding, "I'd like to get you in the offices to map out a plan now that I know this is officially a go."

"I've got your bag, Lorena," Al says evenly, squeezing her arm. So he's not a tin man without a heart—not entirely, at least. Lorena kisses her brother on the cheek. It's not until she's walking that I notice a limp.

I rock on my heels, not having a clue what to do with myself next. My own bags are still in Doc's tin lizzie. I'll get them, considering no one's offering.

"You're scrawny," I hear in a deep voice, stopping me in my tracks.

"Excuse me?"

Al already has their day bags at his feet. "You're nothing but a reed. Twenty pounds underweight. John will shake you right off."

I narrow my gaze. "I may be lanky, or whatever you want to call it, but I'm not weak. And John'll like me just fine."

"You're a kid."

"Which is it, scrawny or a kid? Webster would define those two words differently."

He shrugs, his face shadowed beneath the brim of his hat. "Are you referring to yourself, Miss Webster, or to the dictionary?"

It's my turn to shrug. "Both. I'll have you know, I'll be twenty next month. And as far as being a kid, I haven't acted like one in a long time. I cook, clean, care for my siblings, keep the house."

Al gives me a wry smile. "Sounds like you're ready to be a housewife more than a horse diver."

I turn up my chin. "I'll never be a wife. And don't you worry one more second about what I'm meant to be."

He shakes his head. "Guess we'll see what you're capable of. Doc doesn't give second chances."

I ignore that last part. I could easily point out how it seems his daddy has given him plenty. "Guess we will."

If my chin tilts any higher, I'll be gazing at the heavens.

"Doc still has an ad in the papers, you know."

I snap my head back at this. But my attention catches on another automobile coming up the drive.

Al turns. He curses.

Doesn't have the same morals as his daddy.

"Who's that?" I ask.

“No one that concerns you.”

I shore myself up with a breath. “I’m part of this troupe, so I reckon it does.”

“Sonora.” His voice is hard.

I instinctively take a step backward, and if I’m not mistaken, Al’s face actually softens at my reaction before he squares up to the incoming car, his mean mug back in place.

I quickly grab my luggage.

“Mr. Grover,” I hear as I make toward the farmhouse. “How unexpected.”

“I’m here to see your father, son.”

“His business is my business, and last I checked you’ve got no reason to be dropping in on us.”

“Now, Al, don’t act surprised I’m here. You know the SPCA doesn’t make appointments.”

SPCA? I pull my bottom lip between my teeth. I want to slow, to listen in to why an officer from the Society for the Prevention of Cruelty to Animals is poking around. But I also don’t want to push Al’s buttons any more than I have. In fact, I’d like to go back to Al pretending I don’t exist until he leaves with the second troupe.

It’s the horses I’m here for.

Chapter 7

SITTING AT MY NEW vanity, I run my brush from root to tip, the morning light catching the auburn in my hair. Mamie Lou raised me to start and end my day by brushing a hundred times. I always do; it's soothing, grounding, and satisfying. Though I crack a smile, remembering how Mamie Lou would scowl about how it'd only ever be a matter of time until I was off running, doing one thing or another that'd ensure tangles and knots.

Today that's horse-diving training.

I tap my toes beneath the table, hardly able to contain myself.

Last night at supper, Doc informed me I should be outside this morning at seven. It's a few minutes till. And I have plans to sit here until the very moment I need to go join him. No need to run into anyone. Supper was awkward, to say the least, and I've made mental notes of what to include in my first letter home to Arnette:

Georgie, the groom, is friendly enough but the quiet type.

Lorena doesn't have much to say either. Not last night anyway, most likely licking her wounds about not being able to dive this season. Not that I blame her.

Doc was as excitable as ever, yammering on about having two troupes to go out with next season. Not sure Al loved that. In his mind there is only one guaranteed troupe, considering he seems to be pushing for me to get a one-way ticket back to Georgia.

There was tension galore—when it came to Al and me, Al and his daddy, even Al and Vivian. Math hasn't ever been my strong suit, but I believe there may be a common denominator: Al.

One thing I have to tell Arnette about is this Mr. Grover fellow. I asked about him and his unexpected visit. Doc blew it off as nothing more than the man sniffing around as he's known to do. "There's no smoke, that I can tell you. And where there's no smoke, there's no fire. Harry's been known to use his position unlawfully, spiteful man that he is. How he works for such a fine organization is beyond me. But truth of the matter is, he's taken a special interest in Lightning, even though he hems and haws about all my horses. One time he tried to give me grief about the horses lying down, saying they were overworked, traumatized, or some nonsense having to do with our act. Shows what he knows. I'll have you know, with proper bedding, all horses will put their hooves up. It's why our stalls are a foot deep with pine shavings. Fresh too."

At the dinner table, he had elbowed Georgie. "He knows to replace any soiled shavings to keep my babies comfortable. We're fine. The horses are fine. But Harry will be back. Comes around at least once a year to check up on us. If Harold Grover ever thinks our horses don't *want* to dive, then we'll have ourselves some problems and he'll have a foot in the door. Fortunately, that's never been the case."

The idea of Harold poking around leaves me uneasy, even still this morning. I remember someone from a humane animal society once seizing a handful of steers from an old neighbor, the neighbor insisting there was no funny business going on. But who can really know what happens behind closed doors?

Only two minutes to go until I'm set to be outside, I pin my hair, remembering Doc's not a fan of the flapper-like length.

"Let's start living," I say to my glowing self in the mirror.

Then I'm off, gliding in my slippers over the hardwoods as quiet as a mouse. I ease the screen door closed, a pep in my step as I round the house, the platform of the diving tower poking out above the roofline.

I'm in my bathing suit, ready to climb the ladder. I assume Doc will want me to do some jumps and dives into the tank on my own before on the back of one of his horses. I think I'll start with showing him my back tuck, Arnette's and my favorite.

Turning the corner of the house, the first thing I notice is that no one's at the tower. I keep scanning, my gaze falling on the training lot and twelve hundred pounds of pure beauty, chestnut in color, a mane trimmed to stand up stiff. Klatawah.

The next thing I notice is a man leading Klatawah by a long rope in a galloped circle, the man wearing a fedora instead of a ten-gallon hat. Al. The common denominator. And no Doc in sight.

I puff out my cheeks, holding my breath there. Doc said yesterday I'd begin training with him. He's the one in charge who runs the whole dang show. Not *this* Carver, who turns as if he can sense me.

"On time," he says, turning back to his training, shortening the rope and thus Klatawah's circle. "I'll give you that."

I stop, popping out a hip. I've met his type before. Dismissive. Hardheaded. Can't be wrong. My ma married that type and was constantly putting him in his place. Suppose it didn't help matters, him leaving and all, but it's all I know how to act, so I lean in, saying, "Could it be the very first nice thing you've said to me?" I look toward the house, the barn, the other buildings. "Doc said I'd be training with him."

He deadpans, "Doc says a lot of things. There're clothes for you on the railing."

There are. A stack of them on the top rung of the fence. "I'm already dressed."

"Not for what we're going to do."

Klatawah's circle is smaller still.

"Which is?"

"Nothing on the tower. You haven't earned it." Hand over hand, Al shortens the rope some more, Klatawah slowly coming to a stop. Al runs a hand down the horse's bare back and pats his side. "There are three things a good rider has to have," he says, as if talking to the horse. "Steady nerves. The ability to think quickly." He finally faces me. "And the *strength* to act quickly."

No, sir, I didn't miss the emphasis he put on the word *strength*. And to that I say, "I'm not a weakling."

He nods toward the clothing but says nothing more.

It's maddening. He's maddening. And it really chaps my hide

that I find him physically attractive. I imagine he's even more so when he smiles, which is not something I've genuinely seen. But Al is a gatekeeper to what I currently want: diving with this magnificent horse. So I do as he asks—or rather, implies—and reach for the clothing.

I scrunch my forehead. He's stacked khaki-colored riding pants—the kind that lace up on the inside of the legs—beneath an old pair of Keds.

"What do I need all this for?"

"You'll be riding bareback, and until your legs and thighs are strong enough to hold you in place, you're going to thank me for Lorena's hand-me-downs as you slide all over."

Bareback?

Though, as I search my memory, I remember that Vivian wasn't in any type of saddle when she dove at the fair. Nerves prick my stomach. "How does she stay on?"

The hard lines of Al's face soften at my question. He doesn't ask me who *she* is, as if guessing where my mind went. He simply says, "Practice. And strength."

I soldier myself with a breath.

No saddle, no bridle, no stirrups, no bit for Klatawah's teeth. In short, nothing with which to guide him or for me to hold on to.

Al removes the rope from around Klatawah's neck. "If you don't think you can do it, Doc has interviews—"

"No. I can do it." I pull on and tie the pants and swap my slippers for the sneakers, then bend between two of the fence rungs to join Al.

I glance at the tower, today's training clearly going in a

different direction than I anticipated. Not that I'm vexed to be riding this majestic creature. It's only that I thought I'd be up on the tower.

Al cups his hands. "All right then, up you go."

I run my sweaty palms down my pants legs. This feels like a trick, like Al is going to get me up onto that horse only for me to fail. Dismissive. Hardheaded. And also shrewd?

I can't let him win.

I place my foot in his hand. He hoists, one of his hands repositioning to the back of my thigh.

Lord help me, my cheeks flush. There's nothing indecent in how he handles me. Merely a helpful hand. But it also feels intimate, his fingers digging into my upper leg, especially for a man who's done nothing more than bristle at the sight of me.

But I'm up.

I sit straight, shoulders back, head up, the picture of riding perfection.

"Now, stick."

Excuse me?

Al frowns. "Don't fall off, Sonora. Hug your thighs and calves against Klatawah's sides." He licks his lips, looking like he has more to say.

I cock my head at him.

Al bobs his, then says, "If you dig in your heels, he'll take off."

I say, "We wouldn't want that to happen, now, would we?"

He's a big boy. The horse, that is. My legs are stretched wide. It takes some effort. "Okay," I say, squeezing, instantly feeling the strain on my muscles. But . . . "I don't know what to do with my hands," I admit.

There's that wry smile again. "When he's diving, he'll have on a diving harness." Al runs a hand along the base of Klatawah's neck. "Here." Then Al taps the horse's side. "And here. A martingale and straps connect the two. A diver can hold on to that."

It isn't lost on me he says *diver* and not *you*. That's a battle for another day. For now I ask, "So where's the diving harness?"

"You're not diving, are you? We're going to crawl before you walk."

Actually, all we do is walk.

For what feels like hours, Klatawah and I do a four-beat gait. The entire time I squeeze my legs for fear of falling off. What I don't do is show the strain on my face, though my leg muscles scream at me, my back hurts, and my rear end is on fire. Nor do I show my frustration that Al is never at a loss for a way to correct me.

My posture is wrong.

I'm incorrectly holding my breath.

I'm looking down, whereas my chin should stay raised.

I'm reacting to the horse, when it should be the other way around.

Lorena comes by at one point, actually pointing out something I'm doing well: staying calm.

That night I lie in bed with a book, body pulsing, doubt churning, rereading the same paragraph again and again.

I think of the pond.

I think of the cold water having its way with my muscles.

It's all the thinking I need to do. I slip outside in nothing but a robe, a ridiculous robe that used to belong to Doc. Gray.

A scratchy wool. The thing wraps around me twice, feeling like the hide of a bull elephant. All I need is ginormous ears and a trunk to complete the look.

I hitch the oversized garment as I walk to avoid stepping on it and giving away my clandestine outing to the pond. Sneaking out for a nighttime swim isn't something I would've thought twice about doing back at home. I need this place to feel more like home.

At the water's edge, I dip in a toe, goose bumps erupting on my skin. Georgia would only be a few notches above freezing this time of day. Rather, night. But Florida gives me a few more blessed degrees.

I circle my lips and go for it.

It's colder than anticipated.

But folks have been doing cold-water immersion to ease muscles for thousands of years and have lived to tell the story.

I splash in, my breath coming out as a whoop, then in rapid fire, as I hold my arms above the surface.

That's when I hear an "ahem."

I turn to see the very last person I'd like to see after a grueling day of training together, he with his tightly pressed lips and his shaking head when I'd slip to one side or the other on Klatawah's back. His nonstop criticism. His overall demeanor implying that I won't be able to hack it.

"Go away," I spit out before I can stop myself.

Then Al does something that completely surprises me. He bursts out laughing.

Chapter 8

I CUP MY HANDS OVER my breasts, unable to stop another whooping sound as my arms sink beneath the water. "What are you laughing at?"

"You, of course. Sound rises, you know, and my window is just there." Al nods toward one of the second-floor windows.

"Anything else you feel the need to educate me on?"

I expect him to say something obnoxious, like how this is his land and he can do what he wants on it. Instead, he says, "I can't see anything. Honest."

The pond mud is soft and squishy. I dig in my toes to help keep my balance. To put it simply, I feel ridiculous, my rejuvenating nighttime swim now a spectacle. "You're a businessman," I point out. "Not always the most honest type."

Al crosses his own arms. "You don't like me."

I counter, "You don't like me."

We stare at each other, Al's face mostly darkened. But one side of his mouth is curled into a smile, as if he's enjoying this.

I'm certainly not.

"You can go now," I say, trying to retain a semblance of poise.

His gaze drops to my robe on the bank. He reaches for it.

"Oh no you don't."

"I'm not taking it, woman. I was going to hand it to you."

I'm quick to say, "I don't need your help."

"But you do."

I don't think he's talking about my robe anymore.

"I'm going to prove myself, I'll have you know."

Al takes one slow step backward, then another. "Just so *you* know, there are snappers in the pond. Hungry ones."

He leaves after that, walking away, at least having enough decency not to turn around when I hightail it out of the water naked as the day I was born.

I'M GRATEFUL WHEN IT'S Georgie the groom, not Al the Peeping Tom, at training the next day.

Though I do find it odd that Al has pulled a Houdini and is nowhere to be seen. Lorena interrupts my training at one point, apologizing for not giving me the warmest of welcomes. Back when we met in Savannah, she'd been surly about the idea of potentially not being able to perform. And now that she knows she's sidelined, she's dealing with those emotions. "But I never meant to be rude," she insists.

"And what about Al? Is he bent out of shape over your injury too?" I say in a teasing voice. "So upset he can't even show up to train me a second day?"

"Oh, he does that," Lorena says with a shrug. "Comes and goes. Disappears from time to time to clear his head or shake something off. It's just who he is."

Just who he is? That doesn't sound like any way to be; no wonder Doc says he's unreliable. But I'm not going to spend energy on *that*, not when Georgie is sheepishly looking at me, silently pleading for me to get back to training before Doc comes out and yells at him for slacking off. He's young, maybe thirteen or so. A quiet kid, but he sure knows his stuff about horses. He continues to put me and Klatawah through our paces, every muscle aching one gallop at a time. For a horse equivalent in age to a seventy-year-old man, Klatawah sure can move, and I slip all over his back, going so far as to dangle for a horrifying three seconds before I use his mane to right myself.

Georgie, ever the young gentleman, asks if I'm okay.

"I'm fine," I say.

I'm also sweaty and dusty, a horrible combination that I can feel on every inch of myself as I squint against the sun.

Finally, Georgie slows Klatawah to a walk, then to a stop, and I eagerly slide off, my eye catching on Vivian as she's climbing up the tower to practice her dives. I sigh, focusing again on Georgie. "Thanks, that was . . ."

"Longer than the last girl Doc tried out."

I perk up as Georgie helps me to the ground and I stumble forward a few steps. "Is it now? And where is Doc? Hiding in the bushes appraising me?"

I wouldn't put it past the man.

"Actually, I'm right here," Doc says.

Heat zaps through my body as Georgie's eyes go wide. He begins to lead Klatawah from the lot.

"Sir, I—"

"You're right in that I miss nothing, Sonora. Georgie worked you pretty good."

At a loss for what else to do, I extend my arms, the same color as the dirt, into a T shape to fully display my filth. "I think I need to wash up."

"Not yet, you don't. You've got three more horses to exercise." I glance toward Georgie, who is indeed whistling for Lightning. Surely Doc is kidding. My legs are about to quit on me. But he's not putting me on, and this isn't a Carver I can disappoint.

I allow Georgie to help lift me onto Lightning.

Then John.

Then finally, Judas.

"What, Snow doesn't get a go today?" I could joke. But I don't dare. All I want to do is be done with Judas.

I drop my head, allowing myself a low, slow breath, just as he throws his head back.

Pain sears.

My hands fly to my nose.

"Seriously, Judas," I growl, blood dripping from both nostrils, my body already beginning to sway from the sudden trauma.

Georgie is beside me, helping me down.

I thank him. Or at least I think I do.

He has my arm.

"That was your fault," I hear.

I follow the voice all the way to Doc leaning against the top rung of the fence. I crease my brows, even that small wrinkle of my face hurting my nose. Surely I didn't hear him correctly.

"Uh-huh." Doc nods, knocking the underside of his brim, nudging his hat up and back. "You were careless. Keep your head up. I know Allen taught you that yesterday. Next time you're liable to get your teeth knocked out."

Tears burn in my eyes at his harsh tone. But I won't let them fall. I won't give him any reason to think I can't cut it as part of his troupe, broken nose or not.

NOT BROKEN, FORTUNATELY. LORENA gives me a once-over in the farmhouse bathroom. Likewise, I examine her. She has dark features like her brother. Same pronounced cheekbones. Lorena's height—though she's crouched at the moment, me on the toilet lid, her kneeling in front of me—is the only semblance of Doc I see in her.

"Funny how neither you nor Al got your daddy's bright hair." He may be gray, but traces of red still dominate his brows and mustache.

Lorena leans back onto her heels. "We take after our mama, in more ways than one. Here." She hands me a towel with ice. "Bleeding's stopped. Keep this on it."

"Thank you."

Her brown eyes give off sincerity, most likely because that's exactly what she's being when she says, "You know, I had my doubts about you too."

"Like Al did . . . does."

She nods. "He may seem unredeemable at the moment, but my brother's one of the good ones." Lorena licks her lips, as if deciding how much to say. I give the slightest tilt of my head, welcoming whatever is churning in her pretty brunette head. "He's faced a lot of disappointment, that's all."

I open my mouth—there's a story there—but Lorena is quicker to speak. "It's only your second day, you're already black and blue, yet I'd reckon you're more determined than ever to stay on."

"I am."

"For yourself. For your family. For the people," I think, recalling my ma's words. Though the last few words almost make me laugh. It's not about being in the spotlight, not exactly. It's about being me—and without ever diving before on horseback, I know that's exactly how I want to live my life.

"I can see that. And don't worry, Doc will have you on the tower diving as soon as y'all reach Charlotte to set up for the first show there."

I lower my ice pack. "When's that?"

"Few more weeks. He'll want to do more training here first to increase your strength and your familiarity with the horses. Every morning, a few hours each go of it, just like you did today, though hopefully with less blood next time." She smiles. "Daddy's got to be certain you won't hurt one of his horses. But if you pass his tests, you're off to Charlotte. He'll have you watch the tower going up. Daddy likes when his divers see the tower being built. He says it's transformational or some mumbo jumbo like that. But you'll get your chance to dive. When you do, it's your grip on the harness that'll make all the difference." She reaches for a robe hanging on a peg, then strips the tie from it. "Like this," she says, showing me.

I watch, eagle-eyed, nodding, committing her movements to memory. "Thank you for helping me." I motion to my nose and to the robe.

"We're a family here. We all pitch in. All help out. You'll see."

"I'd like that. I'm sorry you can't dive this season."

She stands, shaking out her legs. "My old bones can't squat like they used to." She touches her knee. "And now I'm benched to managerial work. Part of me is excited, though, for a new challenge. I've been diving solo and on horseback for as long as I can remember. Two to three shows nearly every day of the summer. Part of me is even excited to be passing the baton to you. Though I won't be traveling with you to Charlotte. I'll follow after in another month or so with the horses. Vivian, Al, and me."

"So he hasn't disappeared forever?"

"You mean Al? He always comes back."

"Where'd he go?"

Lorena shrugs.

He couldn't have left because of our run-in last night, could he? But if not because of me, then what? Or who? His daddy? I don't see how disappearing solves a thing.

Lorena smiles, ever the peacemaker. "Don't worry about Al. He'll get to Charlotte eventually, Sonora. And when he does, show him what you've got."

Dearest Arnette,

Miss me yet? I promised I'd write from each of my adventures. This is me making good, coming to you from Lakewood Park in Charlotte, North Carolina, complete with a roller-skating rink, shooting gallery, catch-a-fish and other carnival games, pool and bathhouses, bowling alley, dance pavilion, food vendors, casino, and a gigantic wooden roller coaster that you'd die to ride—and yes, a zoo, including the ostriches featured on the other side of this postcard. I wish you were here. My act opens in a few weeks, so I'm not performing yet. Right now I spend my days training and helping Georgie groom the horses. It's been fun watching the fairground come together. The grandstand has been built. All the equipment for the high wire and trapeze acts is in place. Most importantly, over the past couple of days, I oversaw the tower going up. And up. At first it looked like a dinosaur skeleton. Then flooring was put down on the ramp and a handrail was put up on either side. At the top, the ramp now connects to the main part of the tower with a long runway that I'll dive from. At the very end, there's something called a kickoff board that the horses use to make sure they don't slip as they push off. Can you picture it all from when we went together in Savannah? The tower and ramp are painted a bright white here too, and there are lights strung along the railing. It's glorious. I can hardly wait to get my hands on the ladder and climb to the top. Can you see me standing there? I sure can. I'm counting down the days until Doc finally lets me up there. I'm working hard to be perfect in everything he does allow me to do. You've never seen a girl brush a horse so good or stick so solidly. I can't and won't give him any reason to think I'm not the right gal for the job. Once I get my chance to dive and the act gets rolling, tell Ma I'll be able to start sending money home. I'm out of writing room. Until next time!

With love and cookies,

Sonora

Chapter 9

I ADD OUR GEORGIA ADDRESS to the postcard. I smile, thinking of my sister receiving it. She'll be both happy for me and envious of me. I miss her. I miss the whole lot of them, always some hijinks going on with so many brothers under one roof.

Now it's primarily just me and Doc, an enigma of a man who can be hollering one moment and cooing the next. A man who razzed—or at least I believe he was joking—about cherishing his horses more than his children.

A voice says, "Would you like me to mail that for you?"

I jerk my head up to find the bookstore clerk with a friendly smile on his face.

"Oh, yes, thank you," I say. I reach into my shoulder bag for the two cents for the stamp. Ma insisted on sending me off with a little WAM. Walking around money, as she calls it.

"Is there anything else I can help you with?" the clerk asks.

I turn my head, salivating at the rows and stacks and heaps of books all over the store.

"We've got the latest from Virginia Woolf in, if you're interested. Have you read her before?"

I nod. "*Mrs. Dalloway.*"

"'Moments like this are buds on the tree of life, flowers of darkness they are.'" He smiles. "I've always been drawn to that line, the notion that even in undesirable moments, there is a hidden beauty and the potential for growth."

Al springs to mind. I wish that wasn't the case, but there he is at the forefront of my brain, pushing my buttons. Perhaps forcing me to grow. I've never worked so hard, even if it is partly to prove him wrong. Last night when I sat in front of the mirror and ran Mamie Lou's brush through my hair, glorious muscles protruded on my upper arms that weren't there before. "I like that line too," I admit. I run a hand over a stack of *To the Lighthouse*. "Do you have a favorite passage from her new book?"

He puts his pointer finger to his mouth. "Shhh, don't tell, but I haven't had a chance to read it yet."

I mime locking my lips. "Your secret is safe with me."

"But," he says, "should you find a favorite line, please feel free to come back and tell me."

"Oh," I say, embarrassed to admit I don't quite have enough WAM for a new novel. "I, um—"

"Why don't you borrow a copy. And like I said, come share your favorite line once you're done."

"That's very kind of you."

He removes a copy from the stack and pushes it at me. I accept it, holding it to my chest, then leave the store, intent on getting back to my room at the boardinghouse to curl up with my new book.

I'm two steps out of the store when I hear my name called in a fiery voice that could be none other than Doc's.

"There you are," he snaps. "What did I tell you about wandering around on your own?"

I press my lips together. Not a thing. But I'm not about to correct him. "Sorry, sir."

"You're my responsibility, you hear? Besides, once the show gets going, I don't want you rubbing elbows with the common folk. You're to be my new Girl in Red, mysterious, untouchable, one of a kind. If anyone gets to know you, you'll lose that panache and become old hat. Speaking of which"—he smiles a toothy grin, his hide apparently no longer chapped—"the tank is dug. Know what that means?"

In all honesty, I do not. Nothing with Doc is ever black-and-white. It could mean he wants me to stare into the water, contemplating the meaning of life. Maybe he'll want me to ride a horse around in the tank. Perhaps he wants me to swim on my own.

"You want me to dive with Lightning?" I ask, shooting for the stars.

"No."

"Oh."

"But I do want you to dive." He motions for me to follow him down the town's main street. Halfway down, just past our boardinghouse, is the entrance to the fairground.

"I'll just grab my suit from my room—"

He makes a noise. A harrumph, if I have to put words to it. "You think I won't outfit you properly? Who do you think I am? Go have a peek in your dressing room."

I light up like a Christmas tree. And there, as promised, is a modest red wool bathing suit with a rounded neck and a long torso. I rip it off the hanger, squeezing it to my chest much like I did with my new book.

Once appropriately attired, I follow Doc through the fairground. It's not yet open to the public, but there's still a frenzy of movement as concessions and vendors and performers ready themselves for opening day.

Where there wasn't a tank yesterday, now there is one. I can only imagine how many men it took to dig something so large. The hole is lined with a taupe-colored canvas, stretched taut over the edges to the ground, where railroad-sized stakes have been hammered through grommets into the grass.

"She holds thirty-five thousand gallons of water. Eleven feet deep, forty feet by twenty. Think you can hit that, Sonora?"

I assume he means as a target while diving. "Yes, sir. Absolutely I can."

"Then let's see what you've got."

My head tilts back and back and back as I search for the top of the tower. I won't lie, my insides do a nervous dance.

With a hearty laugh, Doc repositions my head so that I'm focused on another platform built into the tower. I thought it'd been there for support. "Crawl before you can walk, Sonora." They're the same words Al said to me. Doc explains, "You're starting at twelve feet."

For once, my feathers aren't ruffled. Instead, I'm relieved

as I climb the shorter distance. Once there, I flap my hands against the sides of my legs. "What do you want me to do?"

"Lorena has a whole routine. We slip in solo dives throughout the day to keep the crowd engaged. Why don't you show me what ya got. Something to really dazzle me. You mentioned when we first met that you've been diving all your life."

Did I? The man has the memory of an elephant. Wish he also had a greater proclivity for giving directions. This feels like one of his tests—to see what I've got. And I'm not about to fail and give him a reason to send me home. I do an about-face, line my heels up with the platform's edge, and perform my Sonora Specialty, a back tuck, all the while imagining myself back on the river with Arnette.

I know I've done it well. Knees to my chest, my arms whipping, hitting the water with straight legs pressed together. But when I emerge from the water and swim to the edge, I find Doc sunken down in a folding chair with a look resembling constipation on his face.

"What?" I ask.

"I thought you'd do something"—he circles his hand—"more elaborate."

I fight back a growl. If he wanted something more impressive, he should've asked for it. But no, this was my mistake. I should've given him exactly what he wanted to see, something more dazzling. "What does Lorena do?"

"Three somersaults instead of one, for starters. But also a log roll, water wheel, dead man's float, swan dive. She does something called the waltzing."

I've got nothing, my mind blank as to what any of those

mean. I bite my bottom lip, thinking over my next words. Then I decide to spit them out. "I can do them, once you explain how."

He sighs, which is as aggravating as hell, even more irksome when he questions, "Didn't the ad say I need someone who can swim and dive?"

I'm treading water both literally and figuratively. And I continue to tread carefully. "I can do those dives once I know more about them than what they're called."

Doc sticks a toothpick in his mouth, moves it around, takes it out. "Fine, I'll explain."

He does.

I climb the ladder to the twelve-foot platform, running his words through my head, mentally contorting my body in the ways he's explained. I'll start with the swan dive. I push off, arch my back, making sure to keep my legs straight and together. All the while, I stretch my arms long and straight in front of me, bending at the last moment to enter the water headfirst.

Ten out of ten, if I say so myself.

And Doc . . . I swim toward him to gauge his reaction. He's smiling. I could dance. What I do is get out of the pool, then climb the ladder again, and again, putting my new muscles to the test. I do it the next day, then the next day. Over the following week or so, my dives become more complex and the bruises on my body from hitting the water incorrectly become more pronounced. But soon I'm connecting skills, I'm keeping my core tight, I'm doing the dives exactly as Doc demands.

"All right, Sonora," he says one morning, after I've already done several dives. "All the way to the top."

Forty feet.

It's the first time I've climbed the full ladder. I've been shimmying up the old sycamore for years. My body knows how to reach, how to push, how to pull. Still, this is the highest I've ever gone.

I won't tell Arnette, but I wobble when I first look down from the high platform. I retreat a step and glue my hands to the railing.

Then I slowly bend forward, peering over the edge to see if perhaps I overreacted to the height. I did not.

"Well?" Doc cups his mouth to call. "You going to do it or not?"

I circle my lips. I breathe in and out. In and out. At first my instinct is to jump, to simply jump feetfirst. But if I do, it'll give my brain too much time to realize how far I'm falling. Instead, I swallow roughly and decide to do something complicated, three back somersaults into a log roll. I'll finish with a water wheel.

That's the plan. Now to get my feet to move. I inch to the end of the platform. I raise my arms. I just about growl when I see I have an audience, various carnival workers having stopped what they were doing to see my first—and hopefully not my last—attempt from the tippy top.

Then . . . I dive.

Chapter 10

SOMEWHERE IN THE FORTY-FOOT plummet to the pool, I lose control. It's hard to pinpoint when exactly, each movement of my body so intricately linked, the smallest error snowballing.

But I do; I lose it.

Hitting the water feels like smacking into cement, or at least what I'd imagine colliding with a solid surface to feel like. Falling off my bike, actually. But worse, a lot worse.

My lungs are paralyzed, unable to take in any air. Alarmed, I open my eyes beneath the water. It's blurry, distorted, my brain feeling rattled. But I have the wherewithal to be grateful I didn't land on my head or back or stomach. My right side took the impact.

Still underwater, I think I hear a loud chorus of *ohh* coming from those lined up to witness my inaugural dive.

Kicking and clawing, I scurry for the water's surface. There I fight to suck air into my burning lungs. I think my cheeks are similarly on fire from embarrassment.

I expect to see Doc on his feet, hoisted onto the tank's edge to check on my welfare. But after I swim over, I find him in his damn folding chair in the shade of a tree, lips twisted, his ten-gallon hat cocked to the side.

"That's to be expected for your first time," he says. "Up you go again."

It's *all* he says.

"Gee." No. "Damn. Thanks for your concern," I want to say. Instead, I clench my teeth and swim gingerly toward the exit the horses will use. I make my way up the inclined ramp to a small stage area. It's where I watched the Girl in Red take her bow. Right now I only want to keel over from pain. My muscles are no longer sore, acclimated to clinging bareback to a horse and twisting my body in every way possible, so why not introduce a new kind of discomfort?

With a huff, I stand straight, tentatively touching my rib cage, my gaze landing on none other than Al. It appears the prodigal son has returned. Beside him is Lorena, both of them under the shade of a tree. The two of them likely saw every second of my failed first dive. And I remember what Lorena said about Al coming here to Charlotte.

"He'll get to Charlotte eventually, Sonora. And when he does, show him what you've got."

I square my shoulders and make my way back to the ladder. I climb the forty feet. I stand on the edge of the platform. And I go again. There's no other choice.

Never before have I held my muscles so taut, kept my legs so straight, my bum so tight, my arms so close to my ears. My palms hit the water, the rest of my body following. There's a sting to my skin, but it happens quickly and fades almost immediately, so I easily forget the burn. I hear the whoops and calls and applause before I surface.

This time I *want* to bow. Lorena is beaming. Could it be that even Al appears impressed, his hands deep in his pockets and his weight rocking back on his heels? I smugly set my sights on Doc. He's moving in a similar way to his son, tipping the chair forward and back with his weight. There's that toothpick in his mouth once more. "Again," he says.

Let's give the man what he wants.

I clamber up the ladder, nerves pricking, ignoring the growing soreness in my rib cage. I do this more times than I'd like to count, until I'm panting, until my legs are trembling and I'm a novel shade of red—from exertion and the tank water, not yet warmed by the sun.

On my current ascent, I hear, "If that's as fast as you're going to go, you might as well call it quits and get dressed."

"Don't hurry me," I snap at Doc, the margin of error entirely too small while doing these dives. "It makes me nervous." The words are out before I can think to stop them. I can all but feel his eyes burning into my back. It's the first time I've talked back to him. No one ever does. Not even Al and Lorena.

"It makes you nervous, does it?" Doc calls, his voice even. It's unsettling. So is his abrupt laugh. From halfway up the tower, I twist. He's looking up at me from beneath the brim of his ten-gallon hat, even more cocked than before. "Well, now, that's a pity. You go get your dress on and I'll buy you a lemonade. How about that?"

"I can dive," I insist.

"Last one for the day." He's not looking at me anymore. He's already standing and folding his chair.

"YOU'RE THE COLOR OF a chili pepper," I hear behind me.

I know it's Al. He has an annoyingly deep voice that I can't help liking the sound of.

I don't break stride toward my lodgings. "Very funny."

"That's a better response than last time I saw you." He means when I told him to go away. I keep walking. His pace increases behind me. "You should have your robe on."

"I'm not wearing that thing in public."

"Suit yourself." He catches up beside me. "What did Doc's hat look like today?"

I whirl on him, water flying from the ends of my hair. "His hat? Seriously?"

"I was on the other side of the tank. Couldn't see him. But his hat's like a barometer for his moods."

Fine. "It was the same ridiculously large cowboy hat he always wears."

"Yes." Al points at me. "However, how he wears it makes all the difference."

I cross my arms, cringing at the pain that radiates on my right side. "Go on."

"Just so it's clear, this time you'd like me to explain?"

I sigh and glance at the carnival workers walking by taking notice of me. Of us. "Never mind."

"Wait. Sorry. Was his hat on straight, angled to one side, or tilted up toward the back of his head?"

I roll my neck and think. "Angled."

Al nods. "Straight on means things are going well. Tilted up is a sign to watch out. He's fired up. But angled, he's in a cheeky mood. Or feeling cocky."

"So you're saying I'm not getting any lemonade."

Al chuckles. "Afraid not. But at least you're good in his book."

"I don't know if I want to be in his book. He's mean."

"You sound like a child."

I press my eyes closed. I do. "I'm tired."

"Yeah, well, I think that's to be expected." He squints against the springtime sun, not wearing a hat today. Maybe the lack of one allows for more blood flow to the right side of his brain where empathy lives.

And I have to know. "Why are you being nice to me?"

"I'm being nothing but professional. I see a performer who has done everything asked of her so far. Who looks like she's put on fifteen pounds of muscle. Who took a licking and got back up. Who I think could be ready to try diving on the back of a horse. Why don't we attempt the twelve-foot platform tomorrow with Klatawah?"

My eyes go large. Finally, I'll get to do what I came here for. But . . . "Do you have the authority to make the call that I'm ready for all of that?"

Al raises a brow, just one, something I've never been able to pull off. "You let me worry about Doc. Unless his hat's about to fall off the back of his head. Then I'll say it's all your idea."

I laugh. How odd in a conversation with Al.

He shoves his hands in his pockets. "So, tomorrow then?"

"Tomorrow."

And I couldn't be more excited, my insides doing a jig. Diving on horseback is why I'm here. What I've been working toward for weeks and months. It's why I left my home, my family. It's my *final* test to see if I can hack it as a diving girl. Tomorrow I either sink or swim.

Chapter 11

AL DIDN'T SHAVE THIS morning. I wonder why. I shouldn't be focusing on their family drama. I should be focusing on what he's saying. I'm finally here, in front of the tower, Georgie on standby with Klatawah.

And I *am* focusing on his instructions. "The top tower has a rail you'll sit on," Al is saying. "Klatawah is trained to run up a ramp and off the edge. As he goes by, you'll throw your leg over and mount him, all in one motion so Klatawah doesn't stop moving. He won't, in fact, stop. He'll go off either way. The goal is to have you dive with him, instead of hanging off like a monkey."

"How do I mount him while he's in motion?"

"We'll get to that later. We're starting with the lower tower, where there's no room for you to sit. The ramp is too narrow. In fact," he says, handing me thick socks, "put these on over your swimming shoes to protect your ankles in case they scrape against the railing. The low tower is narrow, only enough room for us to stand. We'll have Klatawah run to us, like he usually does, but I'll stop him so you can mount him. Then he'll dive.

You'll both dive. Make sense? When Klatawah dives, when he pushes off the kickboard, pull back with your weight. Not on the harness. That's really important. Body weight, not harness. We don't want you yanking Klatawah. Or you rolling over his head."

I nod. I swallow. I blow out a breath. I do all the things, those familiar nerves circulating through me like electricity, and I'm glad I don't have an audience today, all the carnival workers with their heads down on their own to-do lists.

"Now," Al goes on, "when Klatawah first drops his feet over the edge, Lorena says you'll have the sensation that he's going to turn a somersault." Al shakes his head, his gaze intent on me. "He won't. This feeling of flipping over will pass once your brain catches up. So whatever you do, don't panic. We had a girl one time who spooked, and she shot off Lightning's back like a cannon. Would have been catastrophic if Lightning had landed on her. As it was, she landed toward the front of the tank. The fact she landed flat is all that saved her from breaking her neck. I really don't want you to break your neck, Sonora."

"Yeah, I'd like to avoid that as well."

"Any questions?"

I raise a brow. "About the low tower? Because you said on the high tower we won't stop him when I mount. How do I—"

"Yes, let's focus on the low tower for today. Crawl before—"

"—you walk. I know, I know."

I scratch an itch along my hairline as Al retrieves a helmet off the tower and places it on my head. He dips so we're eye level and fastens the clasp. "I have faith you can do this. More than fifty-fifty. Probably close to eighty."

I frown, but there's a piece of me that wants to give in to his teasing with a smile.

Especially when *he* smiles, an honest-to-God genuine one. Then he stands to full height and bops the top of my helmet. "But seriously. Weight back. Don't panic. Make sure your eyes are closed when you hit the water. *Stay* on his back. The tank is intentionally eleven feet deep. We first experimented with a depth of sixteen feet, but horses are too buoyant and they couldn't reach the bottom to push back off. The horses were coming up sideways or rump first. No one wants to applaud the emergence of a tail."

"Right," I say. "Weight back—"

"On the kickoff, yes."

"Don't panic. Close my eyes." Which, frankly, will not be a problem. "Stay on for dear life."

He gives me a curt nod. "Georgie, get Klatawah into place, will ya? Sonora, you're with me."

We climb the ladder while Klatawah is taken to the beginning of a longer ramp.

It feels surreal. I'm finally doing this.

It feels horribly frightening too. It's less about what I'm about to do and more about being worried I'll fail. A girl can only face so much rejection in her life. Already I imagine Doc stealthily positioned behind a concession stand, watching to see if I can pull this off or not. And I must. I can't go home. Not when I'm *this* close to fully living. No, I realize. I'm not close. I'm already there. I'm living. I can't lose that now.

"Where do you want me?" I ask Al once I reach the lower platform.

He points to one side of the narrow ramp, only a few paces from the edge. "One last thing. Horses are like people, each with their own personalities. Klatawah happens to be impatient. He's not going to like it when I stop him. Get on quick; you know the rest."

I clear my throat and give a single nod. Al motions for Georgie to release Klatawah. Suddenly I have over twelve hundred pounds of sorrel-colored enthusiasm barreling toward me. For a second, I question if there's enough time for Al to stop him. But then Klatawah is slowing, standing. Al cups his hands. I step. I push off, barely having enough room to maneuver my body onto Klatawah's back, hands finding his harness. He's moving before my fingers fully wrap around the leather.

Then his front feet drop over the side.

I lean back.

I feel his back legs push off the kickboard.

We're going to flip.

I hold my breath.

Then we're not. It's just the two of us falling. Nothing more than a blink before I squeeze my eyes closed.

Water gurgles and bubbles around us.

I hold on tight.

I feel when his hooves touch bottom.

We're surging upward, up, up.

I clench my legs. My hands are in fists around the leather harness.

And we emerge.

My mouth falls open. I let out a huff. A "we did it" noise.

Al's whooping, running beside a cheering Georgie as they make their way to the incline we'll exit on. "Yes, Sonora!" Al exclaims, emphasizing his words with a single, cracking clap. "Yes!"

I loosen my grip to pat Klatawah's neck, only for panic to seize me. His nostrils are sucked in and his teeth are bared. Is my weight too much? Is he struggling to stay above water? I make a move to get off him when Al calls out, "Sonora, stay on!"

"But he can't breathe!"

"No." Al has his palms up. "Klatawah's a smart boy. It's his way of keeping the water out. He's fine. Trust me."

He's fine, I tell myself.

We're fine. We did it. We're better than fine.

Klatawah tramps up the incline, his weight going back and forth until we're on dry land. Water cascades off his ginormous body as he beelines it directly to Georgie.

"That a boy," Georgie says, palm flat, a sugar cube waiting.

Then there stands Al, his head shaking as if in disbelief. "That was remarkable. But, Sonora, I have some bad news for you."

He motions for me to slide off Klatawah.

My heart's pounding. My gaze jumps all over the place, trying to find what I could've done wrong. "What?"

What bad news could he possibly have at this amazing moment in time?

He motions again for me to hop down, his arms extended at the ready. I let him catch me, softening my landing, his hand pressing into my bruised rib. I'm too focused on what he's about to say to fully register the pain.

Al sighs. "Well, after a dive like that, like it or not, you're now stuck with me. Doc's not going to let you go anywhere."

MUSIC TO MY EARS.

Though I'd have to take Al at his word. Doc is nowhere in sight. Not for that first dive. Not for the dives that follow from the low platform over the next few weeks.

Like father, like son?

Both seem to disappear.

At least Al is here now. I lob a question at him as I put one arm, then the other through the sleeves of my ill-fitting, elephant-like robe. "Doesn't Doc want to make sure I'm doing it right? We open on the twentieth. That's in two days."

I think Al can sense my disappointment at Doc's absence. I think I can sense his too. "Don't worry," he says. "I've been doing this a long time. You're sticking better with your legs. Before you were ducking your head too soon, but now you're waiting until he's in midair. You're—"

"I'm dropping his harness when we emerge from the water."

"Uh-huh. It's easier for him to swim with you gripping his mane. You're keeping your head up so your nose doesn't get busted. Already learned that the hard way, didn't ya?"

He smiles. Al's been smiling more. Lighter. He's clean-shaven again too. It makes him seem younger, and I'm curious how much older he is than me. I can hear Ma's voice: *Too old for you*. Not that I'm thinking about Al for me. I'm curious, that's all. Much of my time is spent with Virginia Woolf when I'm not training or having meals with the troupe in our boardinghouse. But it's been nice to get to know Al, Georgie, Vivian, and Lorena better during our suppers, Doc skipping quite a few of them to do God-knows-what. The result is a more laid-back environment, where I learn Vivian is a beauty school dropout, Georgie can juggle, Lorena curses in Spanish, and Al can cook.

"What?" he questions when he dishes out tonight's meal, a three-tiered bread loaf with coleslaw, relish, cream cheese and cheddar cheese icing, and some other unidentifiable elements.

My face must show sheer confusion. "There's garnish," I point out, not knowing what to call the green and red stuff.

Al pauses, fork in one hand, knife in the other. "That's right. Parsley and radish roses."

Lorena laughs. "Al worked in a kitchen after he ran away. What were you, eleven?"

"Didn't get to the kitchen until I was twelve," he corrects.

But he says nothing further, eventually standing to leave the small room, and I wonder what more there is to Al's story. Here I thought he ran away for an afternoon, a night. However, it's not sounding that way. He returns to the table with something that shocks me.

A cake.

"I'm not sure when your birthday was, but you mentioned it was coming up. Twenty years old, is that right?"

I nod, gobsmacked that he remembered. I received letters from home but otherwise let the day pass like any other, my concentration on Klatawah and the low dive, on proving my worth.

"Well then," Al says as Vivian and Lorena look on, smiling, "looks like you're no longer a kid."

My throat tightens with emotion. The good kind, feeling like I am actually becoming part of the troupe. "What you mean is, I'm no longer scrawny."

He waggles his brows at me. "That too."

THE NEXT AFTERNOON, AL and I walk toward the dressing rooms after a very successful morning of diving. That makes twenty-one successful dives in total, and I'm eager to talk shop. I tilt my chin up, toward the high platform, having not yet dived from that height with Klatawah. With opening weekend in one day . . . well, time is running out. As if reading my mind, Al says, "I think you're ready for the top."

"For the forty-footer?"

"That's right. But here's the thing. And Doc told me to tell you this." Al scratches the back of his head. "You won't be going off the top tower until opening day."

"Excuse me?" I could vomit.

"I don't know, Sonora. I tried to get him to see reason," he says. "The old man only does things his way. He didn't do this with Lorena or Vivian. And he said . . ."

"What? What did he say?"

Al twists his lips. "I didn't want you, Sonora. I didn't think you could hack it. A waif of a girl who showed up on a fantastical whim. But I was wrong. And, well, Doc likes to point that out. Says I don't have a leg to stand on when it comes to any decisions regarding you. And he says having you dive for the first time in front of a crowd will feel more authentic."

My heart's pounding. "Feel more authentic? What does that even mean?"

He wipes his brow. "All he said is that it'll be for the benefit of the audience."

"Wow," I say, spinning in a slow circle. "What happened to you showing me how to mount a moving horse? '*We'll get to that later*,'" I mock, and Al looks like a kid summoned to the principal's office. I'm too riled up to let him answer. "My first real dive *ever* with Klatawah and . . ." I trail off, my heart skipping a beat, a horrifying possibility coming to me. "Please tell me I'm diving with Klatawah and he's not switching up horses on me too."

Al shakes his head, and I palm my chest in relief. Still: "I'm expected to do my debut from an untested height? What the hell happened to 'crawl before you walk, Sonora'? You've both spouted that nonsense at me. I'll tell ya, for someone who is so protective of his horses, this makes zero sense to me. Also"—I hold up a pointer finger so he doesn't get any ideas of interrupting me—"Doc couldn't tell me this himself? He sent his underling?"

Al frowns. "I'm going to pretend I didn't hear that last part, because you're understandably worked up. All I can say is Doc is cagey before opening day. Aloof and short-tempered. The Wild West comes out in him. He makes weird decisions. One time he . . ." He pauses, no doubt seeing the anger radiating from me. "*One time* doesn't matter right now. Listen, it's best to stay out of his way, which is why I'm glad I'm hitting the road tonight. You can do this, Sonora. I know you can."

My brain can only take so much. "Excuse me?" I say again, this time through my teeth. "Back up. You're leaving?"

"I'm sorry. I thought you knew. Lorena, Vivian, and I, we leave tonight with Lightning and John for the Texas shows. It's been in the works for months. But Doc decided today's the day we're heading out 'cause tornado season is over along the Gulf Coast. He wants us to get a move on to Texas."

I flap a hand because, yes, I know about the plans to send out a second troupe. But with opening day *so* close, I thought Al would be here. I scoff. "The only person who's been training me these last few weeks, who knows what I can do and what I struggle with, will be gone. Fabulous."

"You can do this, Sonora," he says again. "When Klatawah approaches, swing your leg in an arc, nice and high. Twist your body. Grab on."

"As simple as that, huh? Thanks, Mr. Carver."

What a kick to the teeth this all is.

It's not that I'm afraid of getting hurt on the dive, though that's a very real possibility. I've already bruised my nose and my ribs. I tweaked my ankle too, my foot getting caught against the low-tower railing.

But I will not allow myself to look like a fool. And how can I have *any* idea of whether I'll crash and burn when I've never mounted a moving horse before?

Then there's the fact that Al is leaving in a matter of hours. Why does this feel like abandonment? That's ridiculous. This isn't the same as when Al disappeared for a few days. Nor is this the same as my daddy going off to war and then deciding he'd rather start a new family when he came back. And even if Al never returns, it shouldn't matter. I want nothing more from him than his teaching me the business. Not a relationship. I don't want marriage or kids. I want to ride, dive, and feel free.

Guess I'm getting what I want in that regard.

I press my fingertips into my temples.

"It's fine," I say. "It's fine. The show must go on. Isn't that what we say?"

Chapter 12

It's nearly showtime.

Since Al left, I've passed the time reading my book, swinging on the trapeze bar, and swimming in the tank rather than training with Klatawah. Doc's orders.

Now the crowds have come for opening day.

And Doc is pacing.

Ironic, considering he's told me to calm down a number of times already. And he's not the one who'll be diving untested from forty feet in the air. Doc insists, "It'll be like riding a bicycle."

Okay, but one time back in Georgia I was pedaling too hard, trying to beat Henry McAllister, and I wound up with a bruised ego and a broken arm.

I tell myself Doc wouldn't let me do this feat if he didn't think I could. His love for his animals is unquestionable.

Still, dust kicks up around him as he wears a path in the patchy mix of grass and dirt. We're tucked away behind the building that serves as our office and dressing rooms. It's too hot inside, the thermometer showing a balmy day of just over eighty. Tendrils of sweat run from beneath my helmet down my cheeks. It's way too hot for Doc's awful hand-me-down robe I've yet to put on.

"I could wear a shawl," I suggest, continuing the thought from my head out loud.

"Say what?" Doc questions, his attention not on me but on the growing crowd.

"Over my suit," I begin. "I could wear a fringed shawl instead of a heavy robe. It's too hot with it on."

He shakes his head. "It's just your nerves."

"But—"

"Sonora, you're not wearing a shawl that reeks of flapper. That is not how I wish to portray you. This is family entertainment. Nothing more on the matter."

He keeps on pacing.

I fan myself.

It can't be much longer now.

I haven't wanted to question Doc, but with time running out, I have to know. "Even if I mess up, Klatawah will be safe, won't he?"

"Sonora, I've got a saying when it comes to horse diving. Ninety-five percent is the horse. The other five percent is you doing as you've been taught. I trust that Klatawah knows what he's doing. I wouldn't let this happen if he wasn't safe."

Good to know. Though it would've been nice if he included me in that sentiment. Even better, where is his reassurance that I can pull off my five percent in front of what looks to be thousands of spectators? They've crowded around the tank, a thick rope keeping everyone at a safe distance.

"So many people," I observe out loud.

Doc laughs, or maybe it's more of a scoff. Either way, he taps his temple beneath the rim of his hat. A hat, I note, that is crooked. "Seven thousand, according to how many have passed through the gate. And it appears they've all come to see us. That's what happens when you're a featured free act."

I scrunch a brow. "We're not charging?"

"Not this time. Got to get the tongues wagging first."

Running my hands down the torso of my red suit, I nod. I'm about to ask, "Is it time?" when Doc grumbles, "Let's go. Don't forget your robe."

I fight a growl. I fight my nerves. I fight the fear I'll mess up this dive for Doc. The spectators. Klatawah. Myself.

Even Al.

On the way from our troupe headquarters to the tower, Doc transforms. One second he's a bow strung too tight; the next he's showcasing a megawatt smile, with his ten-gallon positioned just right.

I follow after, my diving shoes slick against the grass, and offer Georgie a smile when we reach the ramp. Klatawah is calm, and I lean my forehead against his. "We can do this, boy."

He nickers, and I assume he's in agreement.

"I know you know what to do," I whisper to him, "but please don't jump without me."

Another nicker and what I hope to be another show of solidarity.

Robe off, a breeze blessedly hitting my skin again, I hang the garment on the railing.

The spotlight flicks on, encompassing me. It's exhilarating. It's the kick in the butt I need in order to climb. I don't think beyond the simple movements of advancing my arms and legs.

Doc hasn't said a word yet, a silence permeating the crowd as they watch me go up and up. The light tracks me all the way to the top, where a numbness comes over me, as if someone else is about to sit on a railing she's never sat on before, wait for a horse to run toward her, and throw herself onto his back—all for the *very* first time—before he plunges a distance greater than seven times her own height.

All my training with Al dances through my head, soured by the fact he didn't teach me how to mount a moving horse before he left. Also by the fact he's not here.

This'll be me, relying on myself. Like I've had to do so many times before.

I stand taller, shoulders back, and peer down at the thousands of expectant, excitable faces waiting to see a woman dive with a horse. It's hardly been done before. It'll be the first time for this crowd.

There's something extremely humbling in that realization.

Something energizing. Something soothing, and I think I can do this.

A second spotlight appears, trained on the stage. Doc steps onto it. "Ladies and gentlemen!" he begins. As he continues prepping the crowd, it's a different spiel than what I heard back in Georgia. "The most important quality of a diving horse cannot be taught," he's saying. "Willingness. You'll notice I don't hold a whip. I never have. I never will. If Klatawah doesn't wish to dive, he won't. But I can assure you, he will.

What you're about to witness will bring joy to both you and our majestic Klatawah, who was one of our very first diving horses, at first performing without a diver on his back. That has all changed. Horse and woman diving together. And tonight we'll have the pleasure of witnessing our lovely Sonora's very first dive on horseback."

The audience loves that, some with hands over their mouths, others outwardly giddy at the thought of watching something so novel.

Doc ends by asking the audience no short of three times if they're ready to witness history in the making. Then he gestures with a straight arm in my direction, and I have to assume this is my cue to get into place.

I step forward, raising my arm to acknowledge the boisterous, cheering crowd, before I boost myself up on the railing.

For a moment, I question if my tush is in the correct spot. If I should be closer to the edge. Or farther away. There's no time to debate the distance. Georgie doesn't wait for my cue. He releases Klatawah, his hooves beginning to crash up the ramp, causing my grip to tighten on the railing as the tower vibrates and shakes.

More than anything I want to be a good rider and diver.

In a matter of seconds, Klatawah will be going past. He'll dive with or without me. One outcome a successful dive. The other supreme embarrassment—and maybe all that Doc needs to cut me from the show.

I'll lose this piece of myself.

I'll lose the horses.

I'll lose the inkling of something I'm beginning to feel

whenever I'm around Al, a thought that's entirely too confusing to nail down. Especially in this moment, Klatawah only paces away.

A line from my book surges into my head, the line I've decided to share with the bookstore clerk when I return my borrowed book.

"Arrange whatever pieces come your way."

And right now, that's doing a series of moves I've never done before.

Swing my leg in an arc, nice and high. Twist my body. Grab on.

Klatawah is a breath away. My instincts take over. I'm swinging, I'm grabbing, I'm on Klatawah's back—in the nick of time.

Together we fall over the edge and Klatawah pushes off with his back legs. His muscles tense beneath my thighs and calves. I close my eyes, thinking we'll soon hit the water. But we're at a greater height than all of our other practice dives. It's freeing, a primitive thrill, having no contact with the earth while suspended in the air, flying. I look to gauge how much more we have to go, only to squeeze my eyes closed again, the water just a heartbeat away.

We plunge into the tank so smoothly that for a moment my mind doubts that we've even completed the act.

But we have.

I can hear that we have.

Klatawah's feet hit bottom and he noses himself toward the surface, the water feeling as if it parts for us.

I did it.

I did it.

"I did it," I muse as soon as we're above water.

I'm still astonished as Klatawah climbs to the stage for his reward. Still in awe that I've done this when Doc motions me to the ground. Still shaking my head when he reminds me to take my bow.

When he says, "That's my girl."

It's the first time I've ever heard him use the praise for a human rather than one of his beloved horses.

Diving . . . like that . . . with a horse . . . for everyone to see . . . for everyone to celebrate . . . felt like the most natural thing in the world to me. It's not merely a piece of me. It's all of me.

Sonora and her diving horse. That's who I am now.

Chapter 13

I DON'T EVEN CARE THAT I have to put on the hideous robe after my first performance. I'm on cloud nine. Why should it stop at nine? I'm at a ten.

Doc whisks me away to the dressing room, insisting he doesn't want me to be seen. "We'll continue to build intrigue when it comes to you."

Before he closes the door, leaving me to my post-dive bliss, he adds, "You did good."

I smile, my vanity mirror returning my grin. Instinctively, I pick up Mamie Lou's gifted brush. I run it through my hair.

"I did it."

I can't help saying it again. If only Arnette had seen it. Or Ma. Or even Al. I can picture him, hear him. "Yes, Sonora!" he would've yelled, following it with a single, earsplitting clap.

It's disappointing how I don't have a single friend in Charlotte to celebrate this moment with. I certainly won't count Doc. He's more dictator than friend. And while Georgie is dandy, he'd rather keep company with horses than humans.

That leaves a party of one.

I suppose it's better than no party at all.

Dear Arnette,

I'm in Tampa! Specifically at the Florida State Fair. We wrapped up a very successful season in Charlotte. Performing matinee and evening shows every day for the last few months has been grand. With Florida still being warm, Doc contracted us for a few weeks down here before we winter in Jacksonville. I take it you got my last letter? If so, you know I've been restless between shows. Lonely, too, and Doc still won't let me rub elbows with the spectators. Back in Charlotte he wouldn't even let me swim in the public pool. He's insistent that I maintain an air of mystery. But this fair is larger, one of the biggest in the country. I'm hoping Doc gives me more freedom to explore. If only you were here to explore with me. There's pen after pen of livestock. Endless exhibitions. Booths with bright-colored quilts, golden jars of honey and deep red preserves. Horse races. Ice cream and every confection known to man. Parades of elephants. Dancers. Games. Rides. There's one called the Dangler that you'd give up your firstborn child to ride. It basically whirls in a circle, people sitting in chairs that dangle (hence the name!) from long wires. It gets going so fast, the chairs become nearly horizontal. Yesterday I watched someone lose a shoe. Nearly hit a man. There's so much excitement and energy. Sometimes I almost pinch myself that I'm here. A poultry contest begins soon that I'd like to see, so forgive me for cutting this short. Let's see if I can sneak off to watch the judging without putting Doc in a fowl (get it?) mood.

With love and cookies,
Sonora

I'm two steps into our hotel's lobby when I hear, "There you are, Sonora!" Doc pauses, brow scrunching. "Where're you off to in a hurry?"

I evade, answering, "I'm not set to dive until the afternoon. Do you have me doing a solo dive this morning?"

"No, none of that. Not today. I need you here. The press is waiting. A man by the name of Addison Miles would like to interview you."

My jaw drops. We publicized our act in the newspapers in Charlotte and again here in Tampa, but in both cases, it was about the act. Not me specifically. I tuck my hair behind my ears. It's grown out, long enough where Doc is fine with me wearing it down.

"You don't mind?" I ask.

"Do I mind that they want to do a headliner on a pretty young woman as opposed to a wrinkly old man? Not for one second. It's nothing but good business sense."

"All right, then," I say, following him to meet the reporter.

Mr. Miles is set up with his camera, a pad of paper on his lap, a sofa opposite him for me to sit on, and a water glass on a small table between us.

Sitting down almost makes me edgier than plunging forty feet. I didn't become a performer for the glitz and glam. I came for independence, to live my life on my own terms.

Which apparently now includes interviews with fancy newspapermen.

"Miss Webster," Mr. Miles begins. He's very buttoned-up. Very slick, a pencil behind not one but both ears.

"How do you do?" I say, nearly laughing at myself, having never used that phrase before.

He smiles. "I'm well, thank you. Shall we begin? I am beyond curious to know how you found yourself as the star of Dr. Carver's High-Diving Horse Act."

I glance at Doc. "I think the horses are the true stars. I'm just along for the ride." Mr. Miles laughs at that, and I loosen my hands, which I'm gripping in my lap. "But to answer your question, I answered an advert to join the show."

"And why did you? Join it, that is?"

"I adore horses. I wanted adventure. I'm lucky to have both as one of Dr. Carver's divers."

"And what's that feel like, to dive?"

I smile like a goon. "It's sheer exhilaration. A feeling of being entirely free of the earth. It's deeply intoxicating."

"You almost make me want to give it a whirl. You certainly are garnering quite the attention. Do you find the fanfare distracting?"

When I first witnessed Vivian dive, the grandstand held its breath in complete silence. That is no longer the case, nor does Doc discourage the enthusiasm of the crowd. Wolf whistles follow me up the ladder. Spontaneous applause bursts out. A steady stream of cheers follows when I reach the top of the tower. Then there are the shrieks as I throw my body onto Klatawah's back. "I hear everyone, but it doesn't distract me. I focus on the dive."

"I have to imagine it'd be disastrous otherwise. Is it the commotion that made your horse falter in your last performance?"

I glance again at Doc, expecting him to step in and speak

to our show the evening before. But he remains standing off to the side, arms crossed, watching our exchange. I shake my head. "There was a reflection in the pool from one of the tower lights. Klatawah is a smart boy. He wasn't about to dive into a string of lights. But once the lighting was adjusted, he was pleased as punch to dive."

Mr. Miles nods his head. "A smart animal, indeed. And you yourself are quite impressive, Miss Webster. We'd like to take some photos to accompany the article. Any man who sees your picture in the paper will be a goner. With a pretty face like yours, they'll be lining up to see the show."

Doc's laughter is deep. "Ain't that the plan? Let's take them at the showgrounds with Klatawah, yes?"

The reporter agrees. With the fairground straight down the road from the hotel, it's a short walk, Mr. Miles and I side by side. On the way, he asks, "So what's next for you and Klatawah?"

Doc edges in to answer, hands framing his oversized belt buckle. "We have more shows entertaining the fine people of Tampa; then we'll be returning to our winter ranch. My son and daughter are already there planning a full season for us next spring."

Al's already in Jacksonville? I'd be lying if I said he doesn't cross my mind from time to time, a silly thought considering I've now spent more weeks without him than I have in his company. But somewhere along the way of him hollering at me to keep my head up, to him making me a birthday cake, to him saying he was wrong about me, Al has weaseled his way into being someone I don't mind being around. Plus, he knows his way around a kitchen. And considering Doc and I have been living on hotel food, which has left much to be desired, it's Al's cooking I'm after. Or at least that's what I tell myself I'm missing most about him. But, of course, I know the truth. Al's never seen me go off the top platform. And more than anything, I want to witness his reaction when I show him what I can do. Makes me wonder, have I crossed his mind the way he's crossed mine?

Chapter 14

OUR RETURN TO OUR winter quarters in Jacksonville begins on the train. Doc insists we only travel first class. The horses take up half a freight car. At the train station, we transfer them to a trailer for the final few miles.

I find myself wearing a smile, anticipation growing at the thought of trading the grumpy, tired Carver beside me for the younger Carver, the one who may actually be charming if I give him the chance to be. My brain flashes to when he caught me in the pond, to the sly smile on his face, to his witty words.

I'm back, dust kicking up all around the trailer as Doc brings us to a stop. I hop down from the trailer's cab, waving away the dirt, scanning the farmhouse, the barn, the training lot. Everything looks the same as I last left it. Except for an unfamiliar face.

A young woman has emerged from the barn.

None other than Al is close behind her, John on a lead rope.

I squint, thinking it must be Vivian, even though I don't

recognize her. But no. Doc says, "Ah, glad to see Al is already putting the new girl through her paces."

I scrunch my brows. "Who is she?"

"Vivian's replacement, if we're lucky. Unless we bring on another diver, we won't be able to run two troupes this year."

My lips circle, my brain catching up. "What do you mean? Where's Vivian?"

Doc makes a clucking sound. "She got spooked. John was being a toddler. He turned over in the pool to unseat her, and she whacked her head on the bottom of the tank. She's fine. But she's not coming back."

I touch my own head.

"So," Doc goes on, nodding to Georgie as he begins to unload the horses from our trailer, "as I said, I need a new diver if we're going to have two troupes again next spring. This young lady arrived earlier today. Shall we meander on up to the fence to watch her first go at things?"

"I reckon that'll make her more nervous than anything."

Doc waggles his brows, saying nothing more, and I follow after him, asking, "What do you know about her? Has she dived before?"

"I've been with you, Sonora. You know as much about her as I do."

"Oh." I scurry to stay in step with Doc. "So you didn't interview her?"

"Can't say I did."

That means Al must've placed the advert. Al met with her. Al invited her here. Whereas Al was originally against me from the jump. I rub at my bare arms, telling myself I'm not the jealous type.

But she sure is pretty, and tall. Lorena's hand-me-down pants don't bunch at her ankles like they did on me. And Al has no problem cracking a quick smile at whatever it is she's saying.

I quicken my pace to eavesdropping distance, propping my elbows against the top rung of the training lot fence.

Doc's got his ten-gallon on straight, and I've the urge to knock it to the side, to nudge him into a cheeky mood where he'll have no problem pointing out anything she does wrong.

Can't say I'm proud of thinking like this.

I won't *think this way*, I tell myself, forcing a friendly smile on my face.

"What's her name?" I ask Doc.

"Melanie."

"Pretty."

Doc's eyes are trained on the new girl. "Certainly wouldn't be a hindrance with advertising the show." He fishes a toothpick from his pocket. "Time will tell."

Al helps Melanie up on John, giving her the same instructions he gave me about sticking. He laughs at something I can't quite make out. Then he's leading John at a walk, just as he did for me.

Melanie is slipping and sliding, just like I did.

Al reaches out to brace her, something he never did for me.

From time to time, I glance at Doc, trying to gauge how he thinks things are going for Melanie. His hat goes untouched. He does nothing more than chew his toothpick and watch.

Al does more laughing than I care for.

But it's hard to clearly read either one of them.

Melanie returns to the ranch for more ground training the next morning. Then the next. Today I stay inside, intent on playing a few hands of solitaire instead of scrutinizing every grin, smirk, or laugh between Al and Melanie.

Excuse me, *Mel*—as Doc and Al now refer to her. Which thankfully hasn't been too often. At supper the past few nights, Doc and Al have only communicated with grunts and shrugs.

Lorena's been gone, Georgie escorting her out of town to see another doctor. That leaves me with the Carver men, and the long-standing tension that exists between them. The older Carver said to be unmovable. The younger said to be unreliable. They're quite the pair.

"Sonora," Doc calls from the screen door. "You in here?"

I flip an ace of clubs and move it to my top row. "Living room," I call back.

"Well, I want you outside."

I slowly turn over another card, wondering what he could want with me. I'm not set to exercise the horses until this afternoon, after *Mel* is done. For whatever reason, she only rides a single horse, whereas Doc usually has me work all of them.

Doc strides into the living room, intent on telling me why he needs me. Turns out, he wants me to show Melanie the ropes on the low tower.

"Why me?"

"Thought you might be the best one to show her how it's done."

"And she's diving already?" I ask him. I can't hide the peevishness in my voice, so I don't even bother. I rode for weeks before Doc let me up on the low platform to work on my solo dives.

"Sure is."

"A quick learner," I say, moving a ten beneath a jack, "seeing as she hasn't even been here a full week."

"Sonora," Doc warns in a low voice. It's a strange, unfamiliar sensation to be scolded in this fatherly way.

I sigh, dropping the playing cards. "She's at the tower?"

"Yup, with Al."

"Of course," I mumble.

"You all get started without me," Doc says. "I'll be out soon."

I haven't interacted with Melanie, except for those initial smiles. But I can rise to the occasion. I can be friendly. I can smile. I plaster one on my face, only for it to drop as soon as I'm outside and the tower comes into view.

"What's John doing here?" The question is cast at Al. "Why's she wearing a helmet?"

"Doc didn't tell you? Mel's diving from the low tower today."

"On a horse?"

Al looks at me like I've lost my marbles. "Why else would John have on a diving harness?"

"But . . ." She's only had three days of ground training. Melanie didn't ride the horse any better than I did. She hasn't done a single solo dive, that I know of. And now she gets to dive with John?

Emotion thickens in my throat, and I can do nothing more than stare at the dirt at the base of the tower's ladder.

"Sonora?" Al questions.

I have the instinct to run away, to distance myself from a situation that makes me feel inferior.

That's exactly what I begin to do.

"Sonora, stop," Al says.

I close my eyes. I do stop; I don't like who I am right now. He takes my arm, shifting us farther from Melanie, and whispers, "What's going on?"

"Nothing," I say, blowing out a breath. "Nothing. Melanie is waiting."

Melanie is actually as sweet as pie, all thank-yous and pleasantries as I explain where she'll stand, how I'll stop John, how I'll give her a quick boost up. Word for word, I instruct her in the same manner Al taught me. I can't help but like her.

"I'm not sure I can do this, Sonora," she confides.

Al is standing at the ready with John. I glance at him, then focus again on Melanie. "You *can* do this." Then I decide to reveal how it took me weeks to stand where she's standing.

"Truly?"

I nod.

With a final intake of air, she tells me she's ready. Even if she's not, twelve feet shouldn't do much damage. At least I don't think it will.

I motion to Al, and John starts toward us.

I do the things: stopping him, hoisting Melanie. Then John dives, whether Melanie likes it or not.

When they emerge from the water, she's still on John's back. As a relatively new rider myself, I assume she's done pretty well. It's hard to read her expression as we reset to our places. Al releases John again. I halt him, and I'm about to help Melanie mount when her voice stops me. "No, Sonora. I can't."

"What do you mean? You've already done it once."

"And that was enough." Her eyes are big, pleading. "I don't want to do it again."

My mouth falls open, as I'm not sure what to do. I close it. Open it. Look toward Al, whose head is drooped toward his chest. I'm turning back to Melanie when I hear the screen door slam.

Doc storms into view.

His hat is tilted back, way back. He's a man on a mission, walking toward us. No, toward Al. "Thanks for coming by, Mel," he says without breaking stride, without even a glance in her direction. She quickly descends the ladder, tears threatening to fall as her feet hit the ground. Then she's off, running toward her car.

I'm so confused.

John, likely equally so, takes his final steps before diving alone, not caring a lick that he doesn't have a diver on his back.

Al and Doc are having words.

At a loss for what to do, I climb down and run around the tank to meet John at the pool's platform. He immediately hunts for sugar. "Sorry, boy, that's Al's department, and he appears to be otherwise engaged."

The Carver men are now storming toward John—and by default, me. It's a conversation that feels private, Doc talking loudly, claiming, "I told you, Allen. I told you she couldn't hack it."

"Of course, the all-knowing Dr. W. F. Carver."

I'm not certain what I'm hearing.

"Find someone else," Doc demands. "Or you can kiss New Orleans goodbye." His voice softens. "Come on, John. You did good. Let's get you a carrot."

What a Jekyll and Hyde moment. One that leaves Al running a hand through his hair and blowing out a long breath. He's staring up at the heavens. I get the sense he's about to say something to me, but then he doesn't. He shakes his head—and leaves.

Chapter 15

THAT WON'T DO.

These Carver men and their bad attitudes.

I follow after Al, swinging my arms for momentum. He's fast.

He must know I'm behind him—I'm not treading quietly—but he doesn't let on. Through the screen door, down the hall, up the stairs, all the way toward his corner bedroom.

"Al," I finally say.

He doesn't turn, nor does he stop.

His bedroom is his private sanctuary, probably somewhere I shouldn't venture for more reasons than one. But I know when Arnette is in a huff about something, she needs to talk. Maybe Al is similar.

I'll take that bet.

He leaves the door ajar.

With the back of my hand, I give a soft knock before pushing it open.

Al's pacing, looking so much like his daddy in that way. But

I'll also bet that's one of the few similarities they have, or at least that's how Al sees it.

"That man is insufferable," he growls.

Yep, sure can be.

"He calls me Allen because he knows it gets under my skin."

I bite my bottom lip and listen, watching as he pulls a black suitcase from beneath his bed. He crosses to a dresser, opening a drawer and removing all its contents in a single armful. He throws it into his suitcase.

He does it again with the next drawer.

"No point in sticking around. Mel ended up being no good. Chances are the doctor won't clear Lorena to dive. That leaves us with one troupe. Doc's. That man won't ever pass the reins to me. You're a smart girl, Sonora. You know where that leaves me."

He begins to make his way to the bureau again when he pauses at the window, his back to me, his palms pressed on the windowsill, bent slightly forward as if he's under too much duress to stand to his full height.

"And he wonders why I ran away as a kid. I sure as hell don't. Should've never come back. Nor do I know why I stay. Bet he'll live forever too. I'm a fool for believing he'd let me run my own show." His head slumps toward his chest. "What a joke."

I take a tiny step closer. "You're not a joke."

Is that a laugh?

"I was talking about him. Not me."

"Oh, sorry." I bite my lip again, questioning myself and what I want to ask. It may not be the right time. But is there ever a right time to ask about someone's painful past? Or present? "Al," I begin, "why did you run away?"

He sighs, finally facing me. He looks younger than his thirty years or however old he is. He looks vulnerable.

I shake my head. "Never mind, you don't have to tell me."

"Maybe I want to." He perches on the windowsill, hands on either side for support. "Doc's always been a big personality. You can't go toe to toe with someone like Buffalo Bill and not be. He believes that sympathy bolsters weakness and strength is begotten by strength. He's strict. He's conservative. Controlling, though less so with Lorena. But me . . . he's always been hard on me. I've never been able to live up to his expectations. When I was eleven, I had enough. So I left."

"So young," I say, barely more than a whisper, glancing at his haphazardly half-packed suitcase.

"I felt bad leaving my ma and Lorena. It probably sounds selfish to put them through all of that. But in my mind, I was teaching Doc a lesson."

"Where did you go?"

"I snuck onto a freight train out of Colorado Springs. Took it to Denver. It was winter, so even though I had grand plans to join the circus, I had to find other lodgings. I ended up helping a family feed and water their horses in exchange for a spot sleeping in the loft of their barn. Got me through the colder months until the circus picked back up. Started by feeding and watering the elephants the same way I did with the horses." He huffs, the start of a smile on his face. "One time I got to drive a circus wagon. It was this big ol' thing with twelve horses in front that pulled a cage of tigers. My hands weren't big enough to hold the reins for that many horses, but I figured it out. Ended up knotting together half of them. I guided the horses with the other six."

"Resourceful."

"I stayed with the circus for five years, doing everything from riding bareback to selling tickets to working in the kitchens to announcing the acts. Of course, by then, with his own connections in the circus world, Doc had tracked me down. He tried to lure me with a place in his business, but I didn't want that. I went on a world tour on an ocean liner. Then another. I was nineteen when the ship I was on went head-to-head with a typhoon. We won, but I wanted to be back on land after that. Doc caught me in a weak moment, and I started training horses for his diving act. Last year was the first he brought up Lorena and me breaking out on our own."

I dare ask, "How's it been leading the second troupe?"

"I thought it was going as well as it could. Then this whole bit with Vivian, then Mel happened. Doc told me the first day she showed up that Mel didn't have what it took. If I'm being honest, I agreed, but I didn't want him to be right."

I scrunch my brows. "But . . . that doesn't make any sense. Why did you only do three days of training before having her dive with John?"

"I had no choice. Doc dictated every bit of that. He insisted we couldn't baby her. Either she had the bravado to do the job or she didn't, and he didn't see the point in taking weeks to figure that out. I tried taking it easy on her, which only made Doc's conviction stronger. Sympathy bolsters weakness, remember?"

"With me, though . . . you were so tough."

"There's the second half of Doc's saying. Strength is begotten by strength, Sonora."

"But you called me weak."

"I said you needed to put on muscle. You having the gall to dive was never in question. Neither was your mental toughness. Your body had to catch up, that's all. And it did."

His hand twitches forward, as if he wants to touch me. Maybe I want him to touch me too. I lick my lips. "I'm glad you were wrong about me." I say it in a light tone, eager to ease the tension in Al's shoulders.

And while he laughs, there's not much humor in it. "Turns out adding you to the troupe may be the only thing Doc and I have agreed on lately."

His suitcase sits on the bed like an elephant in the room.

"Anyone with eyes sees you and Doc butt heads, yet you've worked on his act for . . . what? The past ten years?"

"I did leave, a few times. God help me, I always come back, for Lorena, for the horses."

"What about now? Are you staying or going?"

I didn't take in his room until now, Al and his story such a demanding presence. But he has suits hanging from a peg on the wall. Another two drawers of clothes he hasn't hastily chucked into his suitcase. A desk littered with papers and newspaper clippings.

There, my eye catches on something familiar.

It looks an awful lot like me.

"What's that?" I say softly, crossing his room, my heart suddenly pounding in my chest at the discovery.

Al leaps from his perched position to his feet and tries to grab the clipping, partially covered with other papers. But sorry, sir, it's too late to hide the fact he has it. "You saved the article about me?"

"About the act," he corrects.

I haven't touched the newsprint yet, but now I do, and my breath hitches.

"Al . . ." I try to meet his gaze, but his is averted. "It's not the full article." It's only the photograph of me and Klatawah. But I don't say that. My chest is already too warm. "Well," I do say, "you did mention you love horses."

"I didn't save the photo because of Klatawah, Sonora. And I won't be staying on because of him either."

Chapter 16

I HAVE NO WORDS.

What a roller coaster I've been on with this man, beginning with a slow, steady descent of thinking he disliked me, that he begrudgingly trained me. Then progressing to him revealing he'd been wrong about me. Originally that felt like the turning point for me, where I began to soften toward him. But could this be the tipping point, sending me into a free fall of emotions, where I question if Al has feelings for me? Is that what he means? Is he willing to stay with the troupe—despite his daddy—for me?

And me? Could I have feelings for Al?

He stares at me. Is he waiting for me to answer this very question? But it doesn't matter if I do or don't.

Whether he's staying for me. Whether I want him to stay. None of that matters. It can't because of one simple thing:

Al leaves.

It's what he's known to do. He did it as a kid when he ran away. He did it more than once with the troupe after he'd had enough of his daddy. I witnessed his Houdini act with my own two eyes last year.

In general, men leave.

They have big families they can't provide for. They are responsible for fists through walls. Raised voices. The crash of china. Slammed screen doors. Then silence when they take off and never come back.

I know it all too well, and I don't want any part of men and marriage. I never have. I never will.

"Sonora, I—"

"It's okay, you don't have to say anything. It's a good thing you're sticking around."

He inches closer. Heat radiates from his body, enveloping me. Enticing me. His hand twitches toward me again. Al licks his lips, and I think he may try to kiss me.

But I can't let that happen. "Al, no. We work together." We do; it's not a lie, even if it's not the genuine reason for pushing him away. "Let's not complicate things."

He swallows roughly and retreats a step, looking like a puppy that's been kicked.

Tires on gravel pull our attention, saving us from a moment ticking on too long. I rush to the window. Lorena steps out of the car. Her smile's so big it's impossible to miss even from two stories high.

"Doctor must've finally cleared her to dive," Al says, barely more than a whisper. "Guess I'm going to New Orleans after all."

"Looks that way," I say, disappointed, but also deciding in that moment it doesn't matter if Al has feelings for me. It's as if the tracks are whipping Al in one direction and me in the other. And you know what—it'll make for a smoother ride this way.

Bird's-eye View, Fairyland Park, 75th and Prospect, Kansas City, Mo.

Dear Arnette,

Hello from Fairyland Park in Kansas City! It's only my second season, and I know already I'll never tire of the lights, the commotion, the sights, the sounds, the smells. But most of all, my horses. I got your letter about coming to a show. Last time I sent money home, I asked Ma about putting you on a train to see one here in Missouri. Or we're in Nebraska after that. I'll keep asking her, don't worry. For this season, we have Lightning and John. I ride Lightning whenever possible because John was improperly named. He should be the one called Judas. John's beautiful, with roan spots on his ears and body. And such a smooth diver. He's one of our biggest horses (after Lightning) too. But for whatever reason, he doesn't like bringing a rider out of the tank. It's not for lack of strength. It's because he's a total imp and wants to play games with us. After a dive, instead of swimming toward the incline, he'll stay in place and thrash about dramatically. To the untrained eye, it looks like he's having trouble keeping his head above water. It's all an act. During training, I stayed on and he promptly stopped. Horses can wear mischievous expressions, and John definitely did. He also wasn't done. The next thing he tried was flipping onto his side to shake me. Doc said many girls before me would let go and swim on their own but for me not to let him get away with it. So I tricked him. I let myself float off while keeping a grip on the harness with one hand. Once John felt my weight lift, he began swimming like the beast he is toward the incline. That's when I hopped back on, foiling his fun. He's a character. At least he keeps things interesting. You'll love him when you get to meet him—soon!

With love and cookies,

Sonora

Dear Arnette,

I'm in Nebraska at a fairground called Krug Park! I'm sorry I couldn't get you to Kansas City. Ma insists you're too young to travel alone. I'll keep trying. See all the trees in this postcard? They have something to do with a funny John story. There are similar trees next to where we built our tower. John spotted them right away and on our very first dive of the show he decided to have himself a snack midway up the ramp. The hooligan was still chewing when he got to me at the front of the platform. And he of course wanted to finish chewing before he made his dive. The audience found his antics hilarious. Doc less so. He had the limb cut off right after our performance. It's funny how each horse has a mind of its own. Lightning would never pull the stunts that John does. She's a true lady and makes everyone feel special by calling each of us by name. Or at least it feels that way. Her nicker for me sounds different from hers for Lorena or Al or Doc or Georgie. A real charmer, that one. She catches everyone's eye. (I'll include a photograph of her in my next letter home.) There's not a performance with Lightning that goes by without someone approaching Doc afterward wanting to buy her (no doubt to breed her). Doc always, always says no. Actually he doesn't *say* a thing. He glares at whoever's asking to purchase her until they scare and run off. Doc can be amusing as long as I'm not the one on his bad side!

With love and cookies,
Sonora

Before I know it, the final show at Krug Park—and of the season—is here. Doc and I are on our way to the tower, the crowds already hundreds deep, when I spot a face that tickles my brain and flips my stomach.

"I recognize that man," I whisper to Doc.

"Sonora, you've seen literally thousands and thousands of faces this season alone. Chances are you have seen him before."

Dark hair, ordinary face, average height. He really could be anyone, but . . . "No, that's not it."

"Very well. Go on, point him out."

Doc is *not* pleased when I do.

"Harold Grover," he growls.

I pop my lips, trying to place him. "The man who showed up at the ranch and talked to Al? The man from the SPCA?"

Doc scoffs. "Listen, Sonora, the SPCA has been known to do the Lord's work. But not that man. He's simply making good on his threat to poke his nose where it doesn't belong. Just do your job, Sonora, and he'll be forced to crawl back into whatever hole he came out of."

I can do that. This is the fourth fairground at which I've performed. I've gone off the high tower two to three times a day at each. That's one hundred and sixty-five times in front of an audience. But I'm shaky as I climb the ladder, and jitters plague me as I ready myself on the top platform. I wish I was diving with Lightning tonight, but I've got John. Hopefully he doesn't plan on using anything from his bag of tricks.

When Doc announces me, I step forward, waving my hand, then blowing a kiss to the audience. I've lost sight of Harold Grover. But he's out there.

"Where there's no smoke, there's no fire."

I remember Doc saying that, and I trust him to know it's true. He's been running this show for longer than I've been alive. Never before has a horse been taken from him, and I'm not about to let that change tonight.

I motion for Georgie, who releases John.

The ramp rumbles.

No nerves, only anticipation courses through me now. I could do this with my eyes closed.

Doc and Al have told me countless times that horses have personalities. I've told Arnette that John can have a mischievous look to him. Many would argue that horses don't have expressions. But this horse does. Right now, as he runs toward me, he appears smug, like he may try to unseat me once we hit the water.

And *that* has me double-checking that my helmet's on snugly.

"Easy now," I say as I throw my leg over him and land on his back. He trots toward the edge. We're nearly there when heat surges into my body. The harness: it's loose. John senses something is wrong. He comes up short. And I go over his head.

Instincts take over and I reach for a handful of his light brown mane. With my legs dangling over nothing but forty feet of air, I hold on. My breath comes quickly, fueled by a wave of panic. John stamps his feet, impatient to complete his dive.

But he can't. If he does, I'll go with him. He'll land on me. That'll be it, the end of the line for me.

"Drop!" someone yells.

A chorus begins, all saying the same thing.

"Let go!"

I could. I know how to hit the water safely. But John—he could dive as soon as I fall. I wouldn't have enough time to get out of his way.

"Let go and drop!"

His soft hair begins to slide through my grip.

It's as if John suddenly grasps how dangerous this situation could be for me. He stops prancing. I can feel the exact moment he solidifies his feet against the platform. He blinks down at me, as if saying, "Pull yourself up, you silly woman."

I swing my body and feet, trying to gain purchase on the kickboard. I can't reach. The crowd reacts to my every try.

John takes a step back, bringing me closer to the tower.

I swing.

He steps again.

And with his help, I'm able to get a foothold and climb onto the platform.

The grandstand goes wild.

This isn't the show they came for, but they got something unforgettable nevertheless.

I can see the headline now: *Sonora and Her Horse Survive a Death-Defying Dangle.*

I bury my head in John's neck, thanking him for being the smartest boy ever to know what to do.

But then, with the roar of the audience still carrying on, my mind catches on one person who likely isn't clapping.

I also remember something else Doc once said.

"If Harry ever thinks our horses don't want *to dive, then we'll have ourselves some problems."*

Chapter 17

On the forty-foot tower, I press my forehead against John's.

Will Harold Grover believe the harness loosened, causing John to spook? Would that matter? At the end of the day, John's safety was put at risk.

"You're okay, though, aren't you, boy?" I ask him.

John stomps his feet, ever the showman, and I chuckle, the thunking of my heart finally beginning to slow.

"Okay, then," I say, retightening the harness. "Let's do this right, shall we?"

The energy of the crowd pulses beneath us. I can sense Doc's gaze on me, but he's the last person I want to see at the present moment.

With the harness secure, I mount John. "Ready when you are," I tell him.

I don't have to tell him twice.

He launches forward, kicking off, and we dive toward the water. The familiar sensation of bubbles washes over me until we break the water's surface. I'm on John's back. I want to stay that way. Fortunately, John isn't up to his antics and doesn't try to unseat me. He swims toward the incline and onto dry land, where Doc is waiting.

"All's well that ends well!" Doc proclaims to the spectators. "Can I hear it for Sonora and the diving horse, who truly embrace that the show must go on!"

The crowd erupts once more. This time the applause is sobering, making me realize how differently these moments could've gone.

"Bow, Sonora," Doc sharply reminds me.

I'd forgotten.

I give Doc and the crowd what they want, then Doc whisks me offstage while Georgie does the same with John.

Doc pushes the bathrobe at me. "Put this on, please. And, Sonora," he says, "I'm proud of how you acted up there."

"You are?"

I could eat up those words with a spoon. I can't recall hearing the word *proud* ever coming out of Ula's mouth.

"But," Doc goes on, though I wish he wouldn't, "whether you get hurt or fall off or what have you, you bow to that audience. You wave. You smile. Just like I am now. You give them what they came here for, as if nothing has gone wrong. If you want to groan or cry or lick your wounds, you do so in the dressing room. Never in front of the audience. That's part of showmanship."

"But . . ." And I know I shouldn't say a thing. I still do. "But they already saw us fail spectacularly. There's no hiding that."

Doc lets out an exasperated breath. "That they did. Harold

Grover did too. I suspect I'll be seeing his weaselly face in three, two . . ."

Right on cue. "This is grounds for a full investigation, Mr. Carver."

"Doctor," Doc corrects.

"Doctor, professor, *governor* . . . ," Harold Grover says, and I wonder if that last one is in reference to Doc's ancestor John Carver. Harold's done his homework. He goes on, sneering, "I don't care what precedes your name. If you're mistreating your animals, I have the authority to take them. Lightning—and the rest of them."

Doc positions himself so close to Harold Grover that they're breathing the same air. "Your organization has the authority to open an investigation. If that's what you'd like to do, so be it. We have nothing to hide. What happened this evening was plain and simple: human error. Not animal mistreatment. Not by a long shot. John dove safely without any coercion of any kind. There's not a thing I've done in my past that I regret or that I'm not proud of."

At that, Doc takes me by the elbow and bullies us through the crowd. When I glance at him, he's still smiling ear to ear.

LONG AFTER OUR ENCOUNTER with Harold Grover, hours into our drive toward our winter ranch in Jacksonville, a thought comes to me.

"Doc," I begin, a question in my voice, "Harold—"

"Don't even utter that lowlife's name."

"It'll make what I want to say difficult."

It's not every day a seventy-something old man rolls his eyes. "Go on, then."

"What Harold said struck me as odd. He said he had the authority to take Lightning and the rest of them."

"He most certainly does not—"

I hold up my hand to stop him, while Doc's knuckles whiten on the steering wheel. "My point is, why is he singling out Lightning when it was John involved in what happened?"

"I've long suspected Harry's had his eye on Lightning, not for who he works for, but for himself."

"What're you saying?"

"I've got various theories. Many want to breed her because of her exquisite bloodline. Could be as simple as that, but I don't think so. I reckon it's personal. Lightning is the flagship of my show. My wife picked her out and was her primary trainer. It's with Lightning that the act began to really get some wind behind it. He steals Lightning, he takes something big from me, and in his mind he gets payback."

"But why does he have it out for you?"

Doc sucks on his tooth. "Oh, he'd give anything to see me get my comeuppance."

"What on earth for?"

"He claims I stole something from him a long time ago."

"A horse?"

"No, better. A woman. I made her my wife."

I rub my hands together. "Now we're getting to the good stuff. What was her name?"

"Josephine." Said in a whimsical manner I've never heard from the man before.

"And how'd you steal *Josephine*?" I ask, matching his lovey-dovey tone.

"I did no such thing, Sonora. I saw something I liked and I fought for her, like any man would do."

"Where'd this happen?"

"A rifleman competition. Her old man was competing in it. Truth be told, I wasn't in the market for a wife. Didn't think one would suit me. But there I was, unable to take my eyes off her. She was tall, beautiful, with raven's hair. Whereas my own mop was as bright as a hot pepper. I'll tell you who did sidle up to her, though."

"Harold Grover."

"That's right. I could tell Josephine wasn't interested in him. Horses have tells when they don't like a person. Won't let ya touch them. Avoidance. Could get mouthy with their bit, chomping and chewing on it. So there she was, this young pretty thing, responding in a similar way when he wouldn't take no for an answer."

"Chomping on her bit?"

Doc chortles, and I warm inside at seeing this softer side of him. "She was twisting her lips left and right, like she was using every lick of patience she had not to snap at him. My Josephine would never do such a thing. Can you believe in all the years we were married, she never once bit my head off?"

"I find that hard to believe."

He really lets loose a laugh now. "Easy, Sonora."

I smile. "So what'd you do? Save her from Harold?"

"Dern right I did. I tapped him on the shoulder, asking if I could cut in. His face turned beet red and he mouthed off how we were at an exhibition and not in a dance hall. Had himself a laugh at my expense. Between that and Josephine's clear dislike of him, I knew I couldn't leave well enough alone. I extended my hand to her. She took it. I spun her in a circle, never before having danced a day in my life, proving I got nothing but two left feet. Still, I managed to spin her right into my arms. I'm not sure what happened to Harry after that. Everything and everyone else disappeared except for Josephine."

"Doc, I never would've pegged you as a romantic."

"For the right person, I can be anything . . . and with her I was able to do everything. Josephine was the part of my life I never knew I needed."

I SIT WITH THOSE words. I see myself as a woman who's factored out a man from her life's plans. But I won't lie that it gets me toe tapping to think how a stubborn, independent renaissance man like Doc Carver rewrote his own playbook.

"You've been quiet," Doc remarks after we arrive at the Jacksonville Union Terminal and move the horses to the trailer for the final leg of our trip to the ranch.

"Just thinking, that's all."

"Life's marinade. Give whatever it is time to sort itself out. No need to put a stake in the ground until you're ready to build a homestead."

"Do you mean that literally or figuratively?"

"I mean it whatever way you want to take it."

"You're no help."

"And you'll figure it out."

There's that warm feeling again, and I'll happily sit in that.

Eventually Doc makes the final turn toward the ranch, only the long gravel drive to go. He calls out his open window to the horses trailered behind us, "Almost home!"

The horses are about to get a much-deserved break, relaxing in their extra-roomy stalls with foot-deep pine shavings, each pen with a water bucket checked multiple times a day. Doc believes horses should be able to drink whenever they're thirsty, not when someone decides they are.

"I try to replicate their natural habits as much as possible," Doc told me once. It's why Georgie always puts their hay on the ground instead of in a manger. Judas especially loves to stomp on it to squash any chaff. They graze in the pastures too, staying fit with only a small dose of training each day. As much as the horses enjoy performing, they also seem to relish a few months out of the spotlight.

The same could be said for me. But returning to the winter quarters feels different this year, maybe on account of Doc's storytelling. Prior to the season, Al and I went our separate ways, his admission that he was staying on because of me a confession that eclipsed any other elephant in the room. That is, until he almost kissed me.

I'm not sure what it'll be like to see him again.

But I'm going to find out—real quick.

Al's standing outside the farmhouse, his hands deep in his pockets. Doc emerges from the truck first, complaining of his sore back, sore legs, sore everything. He announces how he'll be taking a long soak in the tub, stopping only long enough for a quick handshake with his son. But there's the ever-present tension in their hello.

I'm determined not to let there be any weirdness in ours. Al's my trainer. My colleague. Al could even be my friend.

It's fine to be attracted to friends, especially when they have Al's confidence and charisma.

"Hello, friend," I'm almost tempted to say. Instead, I try for a more casual, "Hey there, how was New Orleans?"

He smirks. "I wager it was better than your last show in Kentucky. What'd I tell you about dangling like a monkey?"

"Suppose I wasn't listening during that lesson."

He closes the distance between us in a giant step, immediately shooting my blood pressure to the high heavens. "I'm glad you're okay. Doc said you refused to let go. Why?"

I ground myself; Al's acting normal. No reason for me to muck it up. I grin, saying, "A wise man once told me that a good diver has to have three things: Steady nerves. The ability to think quickly. And the strength to act quickly. The way I saw it, pulling myself up was better than cushioning John's fall."

"A wise man, huh?"

I pinch together my pointer finger and thumb, leaving a sliver of space between. "Maybe just a little bit."

The clouds move then, a shadow slipping away, the sun blinding me, stealing whatever expression crosses over Al's face.

A new cloud rolls in.

The moment passes.

It's better that way.

Chapter 18

PLANS ARE UNDERWAY FOR our next season—Lorena, Al, and Doc wheeling and dealing with various land and fairground owners. This year it appears we'll be combining into one troupe, all going to California.

It's not somewhere I've ever been.

Shorelines and mountain ranges. Deserts and valleys. Vineyards and volcanos. It's one of the states that has it all. Including Lick's Pier, where we'll be spending our entire season, first time I'll be staying in one spot from spring through fall.

"You're his new lackey."

I startle at Al's playful voice.

I'm at Doc's desk, and yes, by seeing to all his correspondences, this is what I've become. For various reasons. Partly because I *want* to help Doc. This business is important to him not only because it's his legacy but also because he built it with his Josephine. There's something so gratifying in seeing the show continue to grow. Beyond that, there are many hours to fill in the day. A girl can only exercise and brush a horse for so long. And thus, if I don't fill the remaining hours, I'll fixate on the fact Al has stayed for me. It's a thought that triggers a flight reflex but also a tingly sensation I've never experienced on account of a man before. I clear my throat. "This letter won't write itself."

Al laughs. "Who is Doc having you correspond with this time?"

I twist in my chair to see him. "A man at a museum in Omaha."

"Is that so? Must be tracking down a keepsake. Back in the eighties he ran a melodrama with Buffalo Bill called Cody and Carver's Rocky Mountain and Prairie Exhibition."

"That's a mouthful."

"It was a hit, but Buffalo Bill and Doc didn't get along. Bill's fault, I'm sure he'd say. Anyway, the show split into Cody's Show and Carver's Show, but it began in Omaha."

"Well, it looks like Doc has his mind set on going to Omaha. Me with him. He hasn't told me much, just asked me to schedule a date."

Al cocks his head. "Why's he taking you?"

"Are you jealous?" I tease, and then I instantly regret it. The power struggle between the Carver men is real. "He's only taking me because you and Lorena are needed elsewhere. Doc told me you, Lorena, Georgie, and the horses will be setting off for California while Doc and I do this quick errand."

Al bobs his head, his Adam's apple moving in his throat. "If you say so."

I turn to the desk, my back to Al. I can hear him moving toward the door. "You should stand up for yourself. Demand to be an equal partner in things. If you want to know what's going on in Omaha, why don't you ask him?"

Al's laugh lacks humor.

AL'S CERTAINLY NOT LAUGHING now, even in jest. He's been tasked with packing his daddy's trunks. Lorena whispered to me before escaping for a long trail ride, "Daddy always makes him pack for him. If I were you, I'd make yourself scarce. It's not pretty to see."

"It can't be all that bad."

"I've warned you."

In her defense, she did, and when I go into the room to deliver Doc's mail, I quickly see why she told me to stay away. Doc oversees the whole packing shebang, pointing, commenting, demanding, demeaning.

In response, Al's jawline is like a photograph: both are worth a thousand words. I've grown to recognize the shape of his face when he's holding in a laugh, when he's working up a smirk, how his jawline lifts when he's agitated, how it lowers when he's taken by surprise. Right now his jaws are tense, a divot forming in his cheeks as his teeth clench.

"That doesn't go there," Doc admonishes.

Al doesn't say a thing. He never does, a volcano building up inside.

"Allen—"

I put down Doc's mail. Now that I'm here, I decide to cut

in. "Why don't you step out?" I suggest to the younger Carver. "I can take it from here."

Doc snorts. "Can you, now?"

I raise both brows. "I don't see why not." I extend my hand, silently asking for the hat Al aggressively grips with both hands and that I worry he'll try to rip in half.

As if amused, Doc motions for me to get on with it then.

Al relinquishes the hat, and his daddy watches every step he takes to leave the room. In that time, I begin packing.

"Sonora."

I spin on him. "Yes?"

"I didn't like the hat going there when Allen tried, and I still don't like it."

In my mind, my hand is firmly on my hip instead of holding his stupid hat. "You could do this yourself, you know."

"I never have. My beautiful Josephine did it before God called her home. Lorena doesn't have a knack for it. But if Allen can't do this simple task, how can he expect me to hand the business over to him one day? I'll tell ya, if I did pack my own things, I wouldn't put my hat in a spot that'll crush and mangle it out of shape, that's for sure."

I allow a smug smile to stretch across my face. "Funny, neither would I. I'll have you know I've stuffed your hat full of socks to hold its shape."

Doc is known to do this thing where, when he's wrong, he blows by it. He shoves the situation on. "Don't forget my belt buckles."

"God forbid that should happen."

Behind me, I feel Doc tense. Any second now, he'll claim blasphemy and put me in my place. But then the silence stretches on and on. I smile, liking that the old man and I have found a sort of comfortableness.

OUR MUSEUM MAN IN Omaha is diminutive where Doc is imposing, soft-spoken where Doc is, well, not. I'd never peg Montgomery Evans and William Frank Carver as friends, but here they are greeting each other, Doc enthusiastically slapping Montgomery on the back.

"It's been a long time," Montgomery muses.

"Too long," Doc agrees.

The museum is more pawnshop than a low-voiced, hands-off establishment. What makes it gallery-esque are the plaques and signage that accompany the seemingly endless pieces hung on the walls, some overlapping in such a way that the emerald-green paint can't be seen.

While the men catch up, I peruse.

A bullet from the gun of Annie Oakley, said to be the very last one shot prior to her death last year.

A human cannon once used by Barnum & Bailey.

A deck of playing cards believed to have belonged to America's first woman croupier, Madame Moustache.

"It's just over here," I hear Montgomery saying, and I begin to pick my way back toward the two men, nearly impaling myself on a sword Sam Houston once wielded.

Doc intakes a breath, his gaze focusing on an item.

At first I'm not entirely sure what's put the satisfied look on his face. On the wall there's a hubcap, a rifle, a shield, and a set of horse reins. Actually, more than one lead. I quickly count. Six are tied together.

"Heh," I say, realizing what they are and who once held them. And here I thought we'd come here for a keepsake from Doc's old show.

"I could've shipped them to you," Montgomery says.

"It's always good to see an old friend. How much for me to take them off your hands?"

Montgomery shakes his head. "Nothing. They're yours."

"Not mine. Allen's."

IN THE HOTEL ROOM, I muse over what happened earlier at the museum. Rather, I try to figure out what it means that Doc hunted down the reins Al once used with the circus—the very pair he tied together so he could control the twelve horses pulling the cage of tigers. An act of kindness? Or future provocation?

There's a knock at the door.

It's late. Doc's snoring, the low rumble permeating the thin wall from his room. Well, from my room. But he insisted we trade because the bed over there was more comfortable.

Another knock.

"Coming," I call.

The face of the bellman shows confusion when I open the door. "I'm looking for Dr. Carver."

"We switched rooms. I hope that's okay."

The man ticks toward the next door.

"But," I'm quick to say, "he's sleeping. I wouldn't disturb him. Can I help you with something?"

"I've a telegram for him."

"Very well. I can take it. I'm his secretary," I joke, sort of.

With a nod, the man presents the small yellow sheet. He tips his hat, offers his services should I need anything, then leaves.

I skip to the bottom, reading the sender's name first as I retreat back into my room.

AL

Instinctively, I smile. But as soon as I begin reading from the top, my smile falls.

LIGHTNING INJURED -(STOP)-

SUGGEST YOU COME AS SOON
AS POSSIBLE -(STOP)-

LETTER TO FOLLOW -(STOP)-

AL

Chapter 19

It's impossible to sleep.

For one, my heart aches for Lightning, whatever has happened to her. Al used the word *injured*, so I'm hopeful she's already on the mend. But then, why cable us in the first place?

Al knows his daddy. I do too, and I'm horrified to tell Doc when he wakes. He's the type of man to kill the messenger. But I can also see him crumpling onto the worn hotel carpet, distraught over one of his babies.

I'm pacing outside his hotel door, telegram dangling between two fingers, wanting as little contact with Al's words as possible, when Doc emerges.

"Sonora?" he questions, and I can't even look at him. "Our train's not set to leave for California until this afternoon."

"We need to delay our departure."

"I've been awake for thirty seconds. Now's not the time for riddles."

"Al sent a telegram. He's also sent a letter we need to wait for."

"Why? Spit it out, Sonora," he demands, fear already lighting up his eyes. Al has cabled us in the past, but this is the first time I've paced, averted Doc's gaze, and now I shift my weight from side to side.

"Something happened to Lightning."

Doc rips away the telegram.

Twelve words that take seconds to read, yet Doc doesn't raise his head for well over a minute.

Without a word, he disappears back into his room.

AIRMAIL CAN TRAVEL FROM one side of the country to the other in a day. It takes upward of three days for Al's letter to traverse the rails from California to Omaha, then to be delivered to me at the hotel's address.

I haven't seen Doc in all that time. Meals are left outside his door. The radio, set to *Spirit of the West*, drowns out any noise coming from inside.

Al's letter is hot in my hands. I'm afraid to open it. It's addressed to Doc, the reason I give myself for not tearing into it.

Instead, I knock on Doc's door. Harder, until the radio quiets. I hear a string of coughs before the lock clicks open. Doc hasn't shaven. He's disheveled, in both hair and attire. He has the look of a man already in mourning.

"It could be nothing serious. An injury that's already healing," I insist, holding out the letter to him.

"We wouldn't have waited three days for this letter if it contained nothing. Read it."

"Me?"

"I cannot, Sonora."

I nod; it's the first semblance of weakness I've ever seen from the man.

He demands, "Out loud."

"Should we sit?"

"Rip off the Band-Aid."

Emotion clogs my throat, almost too thick for me to speak. "Okay," I croak. "Okay."

My hands tremble as I tear open the envelope; it feels as if I'm opening Pandora's box.

"'Dad,'" the letter begins, that single word unsettling, a nomenclature I've never heard Al use before. Doc's breath hitches, confirming it is novel to him as well.

I swallow and continue reading. "'The day after Lorena and I arrived here in California, I examined the setup. As you know, I've been opposed to the horses diving directly into the ocean. But with us having signed a contract to that effect, I wanted the horses to practice straightaway. I put John through his paces first. He went into the water like a trouper, immediately swimming for shore. The breakers were a challenge and turned him head over heels until he reached the shallow water where he gained his footing. I was concerned, but again, we have signed a contract.'"

I pause, glancing at Doc. I wasn't privy to the conversations surrounding this agreement or the fact the horses wouldn't be diving into a controlled environment. My heart pounds in my chest. It goes out to John as I imagine the whites of his eyes while he fought against the waves.

"Keep reading," Doc demands, a stoicism to his voice now.

I need to center myself first. I need a long breath. "'I hoped that he and the other horses would acclimate to the ocean. If they used the water currents instead of fighting against them, they could be carried to shore. The next day I tried Lightning.'"

Doc closes his eyes. He's been waiting for her name.

"'She made a beautiful dive with no hesitation. When she emerged, the breakers must have spooked her. I can only assume she wanted to find an easier way to shore. Instead of swimming toward land, she went away from it, going toward the end of the pier. I lost sight of her in the pilings, but she appeared again in the calmer water beyond the pier. She had decided to swim into the open ocean. Lifeguards pursued her in a boat. It scared her more and she swam harder away from them. Our girl has always been a strong swimmer. She outdistanced them for a while before she began to tire. She gave up, Dad. I watched her put her head down. Then she went under.'"

I pause, words lodged in my throat. I clench my jaw, trying to keep my emotions from overtaking me. Doc is a shell of himself, no reactions, no movements, his eyes trained on the back side of the letter I hold—which is still unfinished.

"'The lifeguards,'" I continue, but my words are unintelligible. "'The lifeguards,'" I repeat, needing to get through this, "'secured a rope around her and towed her to the beach. They had a pulmotor ready, but it was too late. I sent the wire because I had to let you know something was wrong, but I hated to tell you about her death in a telegram. I wanted to break the news to you as gently as possible. If that even is possible. I have called off the contract until you can get here. Lightning is together with Ma again, if that's any consolation. I won't risk losing another horse, and I know you will agree—'"

Doc's big hand knocks the letter from my hands, a hand that falls more from gravity than his own will. "We leave on the next train."

Dear Arnette,

I almost didn't send this postcard. I look at the photograph of the beach, the pier, the roller coaster and amusements in the background, and I can feel the energy, hear the enjoyment, see the expectations of a long, fun day under the sun. But that's not how it is for us. You got my other letter? I still can't believe Lightning is gone. It feels impossible. In my mind, the act and Lightning are synonymous. She was the first horse I ever saw dive. She was our largest, our strongest, our bravest. She was special, the horse that'll be remembered when anyone thinks about Dr. Carver's High-Diving Horses years from now. She was special to Doc too. His late wife's horse.

Doc canceled our contract. We were supposed to be here until we winter in Jacksonville. I'm not sure what's next for us or where we'll go. For now we're here, horrible reminders everywhere.

I'll write more soon. It's too hard today. The jovial setting of this postcard feels too much like a lie.

With love and cookies,

Sonora

Chapter 20

EVER SINCE THE DEVASTATING news of Lightning, there's an ever-present ridge between Doc's eyes. And paranoia on his brain.

Every knock on the hotel door is Harold Grover.

Every time Georgie shows his face, Doc believes there's something wrong with one of our other beloved horses.

Every look from Al or Lorena is a coup in the works.

Every time I ask to go for a walk on the sand or a swim in the surf, Doc pales and panics. He won't let me out of his sight, and I spend the majority of my time in a chair by the hotel window, reading a favorite of mine, a book called *Lolly Willowes*.

Doc is constantly mumbling to himself about how California was supposed to help the horses, not harm them. "One stop," he says. "We were supposed to spend the entire season here, to save the horses the stress of traveling from locale to locale."

He's constantly blaming himself. "I failed her. My pretty

horse. My precious baby. The river currents were fine, Sonora. I told you that story, when Silver King dove on his own. He started this all. I thought Lightning could handle the waves. I thought she'd ride atop them to shore. I was wrong. Allen thought it too. He didn't outright tell me no, but he was worried about the open water. How could I be so wrong?"

I cross the room and lay a hand on his arm, feeling a jolt of alarm. Doc has always been a sturdy fellow. But beneath the thick fabric of his coat, too warm for this weather, are the signs of a man becoming brittle from age. And loss.

Each day he seems to worsen.

One afternoon Al asks me what Doc wanted from the museum in Omaha. I tell him to ask his daddy, even though I know he won't.

Later I ask Doc what he plans to do with the reins. He tells me, "Not now, Sonora."

I'm not going to fight a man with no fight. I'm about to return to my corner to read when Doc says, "Never mind. There's no time better than the present. Fetch my son."

I find Al beneath the pier, skipping stones into the water, a pensive expression on his face. His jaw shows grinding teeth. I kick off my shoes and call to get his attention.

He turns, his shoulders rising and falling. "You're a sight for sore eyes."

"You torture yourself. You and your daddy, cut from the same cloth."

He removes his hat to run a hand through his hair. "Only when deserving."

"Yeah," I say, not unkindly, but I also get the sense Al has no desire to be absolved from what's happened on this very beach. "I'm here on official business."

I smile then, hoping it's contagious, or at the very least Al will lighten from my words.

"What's the old man want?"

I shift my weight, my bare feet disappearing into the sand. "I reckon to give you something."

"You know what it is?"

"I do."

"You won't tell me?"

"I won't."

His head droops, but not before I catch the amusement etched across his face.

"I have something for him too," he says. "Two things. The first is a new contract, the San Francisco State Fair in a few weeks. The second . . ." He wears a white polo shirt, tucked into black high-waisted trousers that've been rolled to mid-calf. His shoes are discarded farther up the beach by the boardwalk. From the back pocket of his pants he pulls a battered envelope. "Well, I've been wrestling with this."

"I can see that." The envelope is quite wrinkled.

I can also see he doesn't seem quite ready to hand it over. He begins walking toward the boardwalk, each foot sinking into the sand.

I ask him, "Did you win the battle with whatever that is?"

"Not yet. It's a subpoena of sorts, an order restraining us from presenting our act until it can be investigated."

I close my eyes, knowing full well who's behind it. "Harold Grover."

"He wants to shut us down."

"You mean he wants to take our horses as some ridiculous retribution for his bruised ego."

"Doc's told you, then, how he's wanted Lightning for years?"

The sand burns my bare feet. Doc has told me more than that, but I'm not certain if Al knows his ma is the reason this all began. "Yes. But a man like that, I have to imagine he'll want all of them now. So what do we do?"

"I have some thoughts on how to stop him, but it's up to Doc. You know he calls the shots. If he can get us out of it, we'll have a new show waiting for us in San Francisco."

"Diving into a tank?"

"Yes, never again the ocean."

For the first time in days, I feel something other than despair.

When we reach Doc's hotel room, Lorena is there. I'm about to leave, this feeling like a family affair, when Doc says, "No, Sonora, stay."

We all sit at a small breakfast table. From my vantage point next to Doc, I see the reins in his lap, concealed beneath the table.

Doc's voice is hoarse. "I've been at this a long time. Longer than I ever thought possible. Show business can be fleeting. Rather, audiences can be. Times are hard now, fewer people having two dimes to rub together, let alone some coins to get into our frivolous shows. But our horses and our diving act have shown no signs of fatigue. What happened with Light—" He cannot finish. Lorena squeezes his arm. "Thank you, sweetheart." He focuses on his son. "And thank you, Al."

Not Allen, but Al.

We all heard it.

Al's mouth parts, as if he wants to speak but isn't sure what to say. His mouth gapes farther as Doc reveals the reins, as they thud onto the table's center. Al swallows, hard. It does nothing to temper the emotion in his voice. "Where'd you get these?"

"Omaha," Doc says simply.

Al's gaze flicks to me, then back to the reins, a prized memory and now a prized possession.

"Lorena, Al, I know I don't say it enough. I may not have ever said it, in fact. But I'm proud of you both. The Carver name would be nothing without the two of you. Your mama and I started this gig, but it's been a family effort to make it what it is today. Lorena, you on the horses, on the books, in my ear."

Lorena releases something between a sniffle and a laugh.

"And, Al, my boy, my right-hand man. It's not that your ideas haven't been serviceable throughout the years. I told myself you were unreliable, but it's been me pushing you away. It's been me unwilling to share the reins. But I'm ready to do more than that now." He taps the straps, the ones Al used to control twelve horses at once. "I'm prepared to pass them on to you, son."

I cock my head.

Al's gaze flicks to me again, to his sister, before returning to his daddy. "What are you saying?"

"Carver's High-Diving Horse Act is yours."

"Mine?"

"That's right. I'm hanging up my hat."

Lorena laughs. "I'll believe that when I see it."

"Tickets have already been bought."

"Wait," Al says. "What are you talking about?"

"For Sonora and me."

It's my turn to say, "Wait, what?"

"I'm taking a trip, something that's long overdue. Now's the time."

"But—" Al retrieves the summons from his pocket again. "They're going to try to take the horses."

"As if you'd let Harry do that. We're Carvers," he says, tear-filled eyes falling on his children, children he once jested were less important to him than his horses. The old softie was just protecting his heart, if you ask me. Doc goes on, "The horses are our responsibility. They're counting on us." He sighs. "I'm old. I'm broken. I need you, Al, to do what I've failed to do to save the horses and the show."

Al slides the reins closer. "I've negotiated a show in a few weeks up north."

Doc nods. "Then you'd better make sure you've got horses to dive in it."

Chapter 21

THIS TRIP DOC INSISTS on going on feels ill-timed. Random maybe. Horrible for sure. And the whole thing selfish. Irresponsible too.

Doc agreed to the contract that resulted in Lightning's death and the investigation into the welfare of our horses, and now he's made it Al's problem to solve?

Granted, the man is in his seventies, maybe even eighties. He referred to himself as broken and unable to fix things. But to put the weight of saving the show on Al while we board a train set for Merced, our end destination Yosemite . . . well, it leaves a bitterness in my demeanor that I'm not doing well at hiding. There's something to the saying "If looks could kill."

"Cut it out, Sonora," Doc says over his shoulder as he makes his way down the train's aisle. "I can feel you glaring at me."

I grit my teeth; the man would be lost if I actually *cut it out* and let him fend for himself. I pack his trunks. I do his correspondence. I make his meals when it's my turn to cook. All that remains for me to do is lift a fork to his mouth. With how frail he appears, his hands gripping each train seat we pass for stability, helping him eat may not be long off.

I sigh, wondering what Al is doing in this very moment. When I found him on the beach, he said he had some thoughts on how to solve our problems. They'd better be great ones. I'm left on tenterhooks until he cables or writes.

In Merced we disembark. I notice a lopsidedness to Doc's gait. I go so far as to try to take his arm. He shakes me off. So be it.

That night we're to stay with an old friend of his, Charles. I've arranged for Charles to pick us up. He's a friendly man whom I immediately assess to always be on the verge of a smile.

Where he's sunshine, Doc is rain clouds.

As soon as we arrive at his humble home, tidy but little more than four walls, Charles suggests that Doc take a load off.

"I've been taking a load off all day," Doc grumbles as he stumbles toward a large chair. That, a radio, and a table are all that make up the homely living room.

"Let me show you what she can do," Charles suggests.

Doc glances at me. I palm my chest in confusion. "Excuse me?"

Charles grins. "I'm referring to the chair. She's new. Figured I deserved some relaxation after breaking my back all these years."

Doc backs himself up to the chair, all but falling into it.

"Now, watch here," Charles says.

With a push or a pull—I'm not sure what he does—the chair launches backward, Doc going with it until he's almost lying flat and releasing a "whoa," as if he's in control.

"She reclines," Charles boasts. "Called a La-Z-Boy."

"I feel ridiculous," Doc grumbles. Yet I note he makes no effort to move. In fact, he wiggles like a cat finding a comfier spot. "I'd feel better with my boots off."

Charles retreats a step. "I ain't touching your dogs."

I'm already rolling my eyes when I hear, "Sonora, will you be a doll?"

"So how do you two know each other?" I ask as I start to maneuver one of Doc's boots off.

"I used to be a cattleman. Doc here called upon my expertise on his show way back when."

"Best herder in the business," Doc says, lids tightly closed.

"And best showman I've ever laid my eyes on," Charles replies.

"I had a good run," Doc muses, his voice barely more than a whisper.

"What brought on Yosemite?" Charles wants to know.

"I've never been," I begin, wiggling Doc's boot. I tug, nearly flying backward as it gives. "As far as Doc—"

His foot's swollen, badly.

"Doc," I say, "why didn't you say anything about this?"

I'm quick to remove his other boot.

"Or this?"

He waves a hand. "It's nothing."

"It's not nothing. Both your feet are swollen double the size. I'm surprised they didn't mushroom out of the top of your boots."

"Here," Charles says and nudges over a matching ottoman. "Put his feet up on this."

I do exactly that. "I think we should call a doctor."

Doc's eyes shoot open. "You'll do no such thing, Sonora Webster. I don't want any doctors barging into Charles's home."

Charles clears his throat. "Now, Doc, if you need—"

"No, nope, no siree Bob. I'm right as rain."

The hell he is. Doc's always been as healthy as a horse. I don't think I've ever seen him sneeze. "Charles," I say, "could I borrow your phone?"

He nods. "Mrs. Henretta is on the party line for what feels like twenty-four seven. Let me just—"

Doc barks, "I thought I said no."

I raise my brows. "You'll have to get out of that chair to stop me."

As expected, he either can't or won't. Soon I've called on a doctor, who arrives within the hour.

"Right this way," I hear Charles say to Dr. Jenkins, the men entering the small living room.

"So sorry for wasting your time," Doc immediately jumps in, struggling to sit up from his reclined position.

Dr. Jenkins lays a hand on his shoulder, gently guiding him down again. I can't help giving Doc a look my ma's given me plenty of times over the years—the one that says to cut the nonsense.

"That's cold," Doc says, swatting a hand at the stethoscope over his heart.

Dr. Jenkins ignores him, carrying on. "Arrhythmia," he says under his breath, then asks, "How long have you suffered from edema on your extremities?"

"How the hell should I know?"

I hitch at Doc's profanity, even a profanity as mild as *hell*.

"Doctor," I say, "I first noticed it today. He's hardheaded, though. Could've been going on for days."

The examination continues—eyes, ears, mouth, blood pressure—until Dr. Jenkins stands straight. "You're visiting our town, Dr. Carver?"

"That's right."

"You really shouldn't be. Where's home? Have a physician you're friendly with there?"

Doc's face hardens. "I live wherever I am."

"Well, I suggest you stop in at the hospital for some tests," the doctor says. "I'll make the arrangements."

Doc manages to sit up then. "The devil you will. I'm not going to any damn hospital."

Dr. Jenkins's eyes widen. He sighs. "Miss Webster, your father—"

"He's not my—" I shake my head. He may as well be. "What's wrong with him? Why's he in need of a hospital?"

Dr. Jenkins motions for me to follow him, already making his way toward the door. "Dr. Carver needs rest and should avoid any type of strenuous activity, which includes his blood pumping on account of his temper. It's why I'm not giving it to him straight. I'm going to write him a prescription," he says to me. "There're five drugstores in town. Take your pick."

"Medication for what?"

There's the sympathetic face I expect of a physician. "He needs to stay in bed. Better yet, get him out of Charles's and somewhere more permanent."

I scrunch my brows.

"I know nobody can manage his kind," he goes on, "but do the best you can."

Doc's voice thunders from the living room. "We're leaving, Sonora. Get my boots."

I lick my lips, running a hand over my forehead. "What's wrong with him?"

Doc's voice comes again. "What's good to eat in these parts?"

"Dr. Jenkins," I prod.

"It's never easy to deliver this type of news. You seem like a sweet girl. His heart is going back on him, Miss Webster."

I'm rubbing my forehead still. "I don't know . . . I don't know what that means."

"His heart is failing, dear."

Chapter 22

DOC GOT HIS WAY, as far as his stomach was concerned. We're at Angola's, an Italian restaurant.

It's only down the street from Charles's place, yet Doc's breathing became labored on the way here. Of course he'd never admit it. And I haven't told him the doctor's diagnosis, beyond the need for him to take it easy and also to take a dose of foxglove. Daily, the doctor had said. "For how long?" I asked, avoiding the root of my question.

But Dr. Jenkins laid his hand on mine. "Days, weeks, months. It's hard to tell."

It's also hard to tell Doc that his heart is failing. So I take the coward's way out. I don't tell him. It's also the way that spares me his hysterics; the chances are high that he would've barked at me for being wrong. That he's hunky-dory. Though part of me suspects Doc already knows his body is giving out, that it's the reason for this spur-of-the-moment getaway to Yosemite. Makes me wonder why. Makes me sad to think whatever the reason, we won't be going now, not when he needs to get back to his children.

I drum my fingers against the linoleum tabletop. I haven't cabled Al or Lorena. I should. I will. In time, once I know how to put it into twelve words or less.

A waitress approaches us with a friendly yet tired smile.

"I'll have the carbonara," Doc tells her.

Even that sounds like a bark.

It doesn't faze the waitress, though I do my best to communicate with my eyes that he's always been a grouch. Only now he's a grouch who's dying.

Lord help me, my voice almost cracks when I say, "And I'll have the lasagna, please."

Alone again, Doc reorganizes his silverware, his water glass, the saltshaker, the pepper. Everything has to be positioned just so. Satisfied, he leans back in his chair, his gaze casting onto a group of women at a corner table. They're talking. They're laughing. But I know exactly what goads the grimace on his face. They're smoking.

"Silly bunch of idiots," he says, and not quietly.

"Shhh."

"No, it's true." But at least this time he speaks through his teeth. "Don't they know how unladylike they look? Promise me, Sonora, you won't ever take up such an unbecoming habit."

He leaves off "after I'm gone."

But the words pound in my head and thicken my throat. I can only nod.

Our food comes. I barely taste it. We don't talk until Doc breaks our silence to say, "We'll head out tomorrow."

I let out a sigh. "Thank you for not fighting me on that. Al and Lorena will be—"

"No, you misunderstand. I'm speaking about Yosemite."

"Doc, you can't be serious."

"Serious as a heart attack."

I frown; this man is incorrigible. But as flawed as he is, Doc has wiggled his way into my heart. The closest thing to a daddy I've ever had. A man who's given me a shot at a life I'll hold on to with everything I've got.

I owe him this much. So I nod. So I say, "Okay, Yosemite. Then back to the troupe so you can rest."

Doc grunts. "If you insist."

It feels too easy, but I'll accept his acquiescence as a win; I need one right about now.

NEXT TO ANGOLA'S RESTAURANT is Angola's Motel.

Charles insisted we could still stay with him, but I declined. I don't want to be "on." I want to toss and turn and agonize and worry and cry and pound the mattress in the comfort of my own space.

And it's what I do, until I tire myself out, the future of Doc's health and the horses and the show all concerns that'll keep for a few more hours.

In the morning, I do my best to push it all down and focus on getting Doc to Yosemite.

We board a train after breakfast. The ride to Yosemite Valley is picturesque, yet I don't retain any of its beauty. At the station, Doc immediately makes for a stagecoach marked with a sign for Glacier Point.

I ask, "Been there before?"

He doesn't answer, a man on a mission. And that's fine; this endeavor is for him, not me. The trail is winding, to the point I worry I'll see my breakfast again. But finally the stagecoach stops, myself and the others all eager to get our feet on the ground. Rather, on the massive rock. That's all there is to stand on. The view is worth every twist and turn, every long minute to get here. I turn my body, a necessity to take in the full scene—mountain peaks, the tops dusted with snow; other rock formations; and far off a waterfall, the spray hitting the rocks in such a way a rainbow is visible.

"Spectacular," I utter.

Another tourist points out a formation called the Half Dome, a gargantuan rock with three rounded sides and one side that appears to be chopped off.

Someone else says we're at eight thousand feet. I rub my arms, registering the elevation with the gooseflesh on my arms, and scour for Doc, who's wandered off.

I spot him on one knee, eyes trained on the seemingly endless peaks.

Has he grown too weak? Fallen?

"Doc!" I run toward him. "Are you all right?"

"I'm more than fine." His eyes remain trained on the valley. "I'm where I'm meant to be. Many believe my horses are the great loves of my life. But it's always been Josephine. I proposed to her in this very spot. Down on one knee, just like I am now. Josephine didn't hesitate to spend her life with me." He snorts. "I would've hesitated if I were in her shoes. I know who I am. Rather, I know how I can be. Bullheaded, cantankerous. A vulture going after what I want, how I want it, when I want it. You know what she told me once?"

"What's that?"

"My Josephine told me that vultures mate for life. That we'd be vultures together. She didn't see them as aggressive, opportunistic creatures. Josephine said they're patient, strategic, curious birds. Affectionate. Devoted. Josephine was all those things." He wipes the emotion from his eyes. I'm on the verge of doing the same. I'm on the verge of thinking it might not be so bad to have someone like that in my own life. "I told you before, Sonora, I was willing to change for my Josephine. She softened me. With her gone, there's been no one all these years to blunt my edges." He takes a shaky breath, on account of his memories or his condition, I'm not sure which. Maybe even the elevation. He extends his hand for me to help him stand. "Thank you, Sonora. I've grown to count on you."

"You don't say?"

I catch the start of a smirk. "Al needs that too, someone to soften him. He's a lot like his mama. But he caught some of me, poor kid."

I smile politely, unsure of his meaning.

"You're good for him, Sonora."

"Oh, we're not—"

"No, not yet. I can see that. But one day. You'll be a Carver. I can feel it in my bones."

What can I do but smile politely once more? I don't have the heart to tell the man I don't plan on ever marrying, be it Al or anyone else. But didn't I just think having someone may not be so bad? Didn't Doc rethink his plans all those years ago when he cut in and asked Josephine to dance?

Doc dusts off his pants, one of those universal signs that says, *I'm done here*. He straightens his ten-gallon hat just so, perfectly straight. He's the most at peace I've ever seen him.

AT THE WESTERN UNION offices, I stare at the blank paper. Our train back to the coast leaves in ten minutes. Doc is on the platform waiting for me. I'm nearly out of time.

Arriving at three, I scribble. *Eager to hear about the horses.*

I add my name.

For the life of me, I still don't have the words to tell Al that his daddy is dying. He'll see for himself as soon as we return. Overnight Doc has worsened, despite the foxglove medication that the pharmacist says will strengthen his heart muscles and regulate its rhythm. Doc is pale. The swelling in his feet hasn't improved. He's developed a cough that leaves him short of breath. Exhaustion shows in the droopiness of his eyes, the slump of his shoulders, his shorter strides. Gone is the man who bounded, bellowed, and bewitched audiences at every turn.

It's sad.

Has he let go now that he's had his moment at Glacier Point? Is he content to leave the show entirely to Al, to simply trust that his horses will be okay?

On the train ride back, he sleeps. Every so often I put my hand beneath his nose to feel for his breath. His chest moves too shallowly to register the rise and fall.

It feels crucial to pray that we'll make it back to his children in time. Somehow we do. Al's on the platform, a silly grin on his face, an expression that both excites me, making me think he must have something positive to say about the horses, but also kills me because I'm about to drop a load of bricks on him. We disembark, almost all of Doc's weight on me as he shuffles his feet, and I watch as the lines of Al's smile are exchanged for deep creases between his brows.

"Sonora?" He takes a giant step toward his daddy. "Doc? Dad, what's happened?"

I blow out a shaky breath. "Let's get him to the hotel."

Once Doc is settled in bed, Lorena at her daddy's side holding his hand as he sleeps, I whisper to them what Dr. Jenkins told me.

I expect theatrics from Lorena, a cold shoulder from Al. I've kept this from them. But Lorena's arms wrap around me first, Al's encompassing us both.

Lorena cries. Al is stoic. I let myself be held between the two of them, fighting back my own tears. Once we break, exhaustion has its way with me. I slump into my corner chair. I could sleep for days. I've only just closed my eyes when my shoulder is tapped. Al motions for me to follow him.

I close the hotel door behind me, turn toward him, and I'm pulled against his chest into a second embrace I'm not expecting. An embrace that's soft yet firm and that has the ability to release every fear, worry, and doubt I've been carrying with me the past few days. It's also a comfort that catapults Doc's words into my head.

"You'll be a Carver."

I pull away, unable to meet his eyes as I do.

"Thank you," he whispers.

I tick my gaze toward him. "For what?"

"For everything. For going with him. You don't baby him like Lorena. Or ruffle his feathers like I do. You're what he needed; it's why he took you with him to say goodbye."

"Goodbye?"

"At Glacier Point."

"Al, it felt like a 'see you soon' to your mama."

He lowers his head. "Yeah, maybe it was that."

"What happened with the horses?"

I need good news. I need to focus on something that isn't a Carver man.

Al's demeanor transforms as he stands taller, his jaw looser. "I think I did it, Sonora. I've saved them."

"Really?"

"Yes."

"How . . . how did you do it? What did you do?"

Al opens his mouth, but I hold up a palm. "Tell us together. Your daddy should hear it too, straightaway."

I return to the hotel room before waiting for Al to respond.

"Go on," I say when he follows me back inside. Doc is awake, if barely. Lorena is leaning over him, talking quietly.

I'm beaming without even fully knowing what I'm beaming about. "Doc," I say, "Al has news for us."

"Lorena was"—he coughs—"just saying how Allen"—he shakes his head—"how *Al* saved the day. Go on, then, son. No beating around the bush."

Al steps forward, chin raised, shoulders wide. I can already see how he'll make an excellent showman. "I began with an invitation," he says in a booming voice. "The investigation wasn't into Lightning's unfortunate death but the overall health of our horses. So I invited any veterinarian who'd like to examine our horses to do so. As you said, Dad, no need to beat around the bush. But while they did that, I took matters into my own hands."

One of Doc's eyes scrunches, as if he's trying to guess where the story is going.

"If Harold Grover has his way," Al says, "he'll have our horses in cages, their fates unknown. So I loaded up John in a trailer with a sign that said, 'They want to put me in jail for jumping in a tank of water.' I drove all around town, stopping outside the courthouse. I had the thought to bring John inside, straight up the steps and through the main doors. But with the steps being made of marble and our horses never shod, I quickly rejected that idea. Instead, I asked the judge who'd be presiding over our case to come outside to have a look at one of our horses for himself."

"And?" I say.

"And the judge saw without a doubt that John is one of the most cared for horses that's ever lived. The reports from the vets supported that. The judge threw the whole case out of court."

My mouth falls open, and I let out a huff, equal parts sheer joy and utter relief.

Doc motions for his son to come to him, clamping a hand on Al's shoulder until a fit of coughing overtakes him.

When he stops, Lorena kisses his forehead, whispering how he needs to get some rest.

We leave him then.

That night he slips into a coma.

In the morning we take him to a hospital.

I see it clearly now. He passed the reins to his son. He told his Josephine he was coming. He made sure his horses were taken care of. Then he let go.

Chapter 23

We bury Doc in the Carver plot in Winslow, Illinois, where he was born.

The day is warm and sunny, and while the man I've come to admire was neither of those things, the weather seems to honor a man who was a trailblazer in his own right.

One of the first men, only a teenage kid, to file papers for a homestead in Frontier County, Nebraska.

An accomplished marksman who gained worldwide attention after achieving a record of ten thousand hits a day, the guns becoming so hot from such rapid shooting that an attendant dunked the guns into barrels of water to cool them off.

An actor in a stage show like nothing anyone had ever seen before, requiring a cast of hundreds of cowboys, pioneers, Indigenous people, and even a herd of horses for the action scenes.

It, of course, led to his greatest accomplishment, which was birthed on the day Silver King inspired Carver's High-Diving Horse Act: becoming a showman.

And now, for us, the show must go on. It's what Doc would want.

Diving is what I want. It's become what I need. That moment, the sensation of complete separation from the earth. Freedom. Adventure. Doc gave that to me, and for that I'll forever be grateful.

AS SUMMER CONCLUDES, WE leave for Sacramento and the California State Fair.

The tank is dug.

The tower is built.

A new horse is added to our family. We've lost Lightning. But this new horse is actually a trade Al made for Judas, who Al says had become too unpredictable to safely ride.

I ask Al about the new horse. "How do you know he can dive?"

Said horse—Apollo is his name—snatches a carrot from Al's palm.

"I don't. First things first, I have to see if he *wants* to dive. Some horses won't budge, and I won't force him."

I run a hand down the white blaze mark on Apollo's face. The rest of him is a light tan, almost golden in color. The thing most noticeable about him, though, is that he's painfully thin, his hip bones jutting out. It worries me. "And if he's one of the horses that doesn't budge?"

Al clucks, Apollo crunching away on the carrot. "We find him a new home. It's happened before. Getting him well enough to dive from the top will take weeks, so . . ."

"A lot is riding on him being willing to dive."

"That's right. He won't be ready to be part of the act this season, no matter what, but I have big plans for him—for us—next summer. What do you say, Apollo? Want to see what you can do?"

The horse noses at Al's pockets. I smile. "At least we know food motivates him."

My words trigger a memory.

"Snow would do anything for a carrot. It made her our easiest to train."

Remembering Doc's words squeezes at my heart, reminding me of how much he has shaped the show—and me, even if that forming of who I am now came by way of some rather tough love from Doc. I drop my gaze, needing a moment.

"You okay?" I hear Al say.

I meet his eyes. They are warm. Caring. Al's been an onion I've had to peel back, much like his daddy in that way.

"I'm fine," I say. "Just hoping Apollo will be good for the show. He's got big shoes to fill. You do too, Al."

"I know," he says. "I know."

Then we stand there, neither of us saying a word, both of us lost in our thoughts, until Apollo nudges Al with his head, hard enough for Al to stumble. "He's in the mood for some carrots, I'd say. No time better than the present to get him to the low tower to try him out."

He may mean him and Apollo, but I take his use of *we* as an invitation to tag along.

Once the weeklong fair is set to open, the fair director estimates one hundred and fifty thousand people will grace the grounds. But right now, before the crowds descend, it's quiet, the sun not long for the sky, most exhibitors done with their prep work for the day.

Al walks Apollo with a lead rope attached to the diving harness. The excess is wrapped around his arm and elbow. He begins to unravel it, holding the rope out to me. "Will you take Apollo up to the low tower, then toss the rope to me?"

I smile, glad to be useful and included. Georgie could easily take my place. Lorena too. Though I know Lorena just finished practicing her solo dives and is likely soaking in a bath.

"Come on, boy."

Apollo follows me up the ramp to the low tower with little coaxing. A good sign. Once on the tower, Al instructs me to gather the remaining length of the rope and toss it to him. "It'll untangle," he says, "and should make it here." *Here* being the dry land on the opposite side of the tank.

Even before the rope leaves my hand, I know my throw is futile. The rope is heavy and long. I didn't coil it enough. It lands mid-pool, the thick rope quickly absorbing the water and sinking.

I stifle a laugh, though it's nearly impossible to keep it in at the frown that blooms on Al's face. "Now what?" I motion to my dress. "I'm not in the proper clothing."

"Sonora." It's all Al says, and I catch his meaning: neither is he. The man is wearing nice pants and a jacket, an attempt to look professional now that he's the face of our company. No tie, but still. He sighs. "Guess I can't ask anyone to do something I'm not willing to do."

I'm going to enjoy this.

Al balances on one foot, removing a shoe and his sock, not

breaking eye contact with me. I swallow another laugh. He sighs again. He lets out a prolonged breath, really selling it. He groans. He moans. He makes every sound possible before finally swinging one bare foot, then the other over the waist-high edge into the pool.

"Cold?" I tease. My first contact with the pool that morning had me wishing I was still in my warm bed.

"Water's fine," Al says, a smirk appearing. "Why don't you join me? As I recall, you don't need a suit."

My cheeks heat, Al looking mighty proud of his comment. He swims toward the rope. I have to point out, "Looks like it sank all the way to the bottom."

He narrows his eyes. "You're enjoying this."

"Not even a little." If I wasn't smirking, Al might have believed me.

One last sigh from him that I wager is more for show than true exasperation, and then he dives beneath the water.

I press my lips together, again having a hard time stifling how amusing I find this whole situation to be. I completely lose control when he emerges, his usually slicked-back hair now long around his face. "Look, Apollo, you and Al have matching manes."

Al extends his arm and his pointer finger at me in a playful manner before restyling his wet hair. Then tugging the rope behind him, he returns to the far side of the tank and climbs out.

He doesn't bother with his shoes. For some reason, this continues to amuse me. I giggle. He points at me again. "Training is serious, Miss Webster."

"Yet you look the opposite of serious, Mr. Carver."

This time he snaps his teeth at me. It's so unexpected, so sexually charged, so uncharacteristic of how he's ever reacted to me. My cheeks are entirely too hot, and it does something funny to my stomach that I'm not sure how to define. All I can think to do is clear my throat and say, "What do we do first?"

"It's up to Apollo now." He winds the length of the rope around his arm until it doesn't droop. "I've got the lead."

"A successful mission."

He eyes me, a mixture of humor and . . . heat? "I've got the lead," he repeats. "Now I'll give Apollo a gentle tug. Either he'll come to the edge and go off, or he won't."

"Simple as that?"

"Yeah, well, we'll see how simple it actually is." His gaze moves from me to Apollo. "Okay, boy, just a gentle pull. It's up to you to take a step."

He does. There're still three feet to the edge.

"Little more," Al says, and Apollo doesn't have any issues moving forward until his head is hovering over the edge. In order for him to take another step, he's got to be willing for his head and neck to stretch over nothing but air.

"You don't have a carrot, do you, Sonora?"

"I can get one," I offer. So far I've done nothing besides reassuring Apollo with "that a boy" and "good, good."

"Nah, I don't want him left up there alone. I think he'll do it. His eyes are steady, not looking all over. Apollo." Al's voice is soothing, soft. "Apollo, let's get those feet a little closer to the edge. You can do it, boy. I'm going to give you another small tug, all right?"

Al does, and Apollo shuffles closer.

"Little more."

That brings Apollo to the edge.

I hold my breath.

"Now it's up to you, boy. Nowhere else to go but down. One more tug. Your choice. But I'd really appreciate it if you'd make the leap."

Al nods at Apollo, pulls ever so slightly. Apollo doesn't budge. "It's all right. It's okay. I'm going to try one more time. If you don't go, we'll call it a day. We'll try again tomorrow. But I think you can do it, boy. You can do it. You're perfectly safe. Perfectly fine."

Al's voice is so earnest, so sincere. Hypnotic, even. I'm convinced. I'd jump.

"Okay, here we go, Apollo."

Al's wet jacket clings to him. I watch as his arm muscles flex, the rope losing more slack. Not enough to pull Apollo over, but enough to encourage him to take the final step.

It's all it takes. Apollo jumps.

I slap my hands over my smiling mouth. How remarkable to witness the bravery of this horse for the very first time. So trusting. So strong.

The splash is large. Al instantly runs from his position at the far end of the pool to the landing. It takes only a few seconds, but in that time, Apollo doesn't seem to know what to do. He flails.

Al calls out, "It's okay, Apollo. To me. Swim to me. This way. Yes. Head up." Al shortens the rope hand over hand as he coaxes, pulling Apollo in. Al stands on his toes, arm elevated, angling the rope as high as possible to teach the horse to keep his head up. Soon Apollo's feet hit the ramp that'll take him out of the pool.

He's done it.

Apollo too.

I clasp my hands together, rocking onto my toes.

Al's eyes lock with mine, and he looks like a kid in a candy shop. Apollo noses into Al's pocket. Al pulls out a carrot. "That was ugly as hell," he says to me. "His feet were spread as if he was trying to fly instead of dive. It's why he belly flopped. But we can work with this, Sonora. He's got potential."

I smile. A tiny part of me thinks Apollo may not be the only one with potential.

Chapter 24

By now, I've sat at my dressing room table many times prior to a dive, Mamie Lou's brush in hand. Funny for me to spend so long brushing my hair when it'll go under a helmet anyway. But here I am, this simple act feeling like a pre-dive ritual. And tonight, the very first show without Doc, I crave normalcy.

I'm sure Al will be great. He's a natural-born showman, with the charisma and—I'll admit it—good looks to captivate a crowd.

There's a knock at the door.

Speak of the devil. Al pops his head in. "I have something for you for tonight's opening."

I have on my red suit, my robe. My helmet's on the table. My diving shoes are already on. "Am I missing something?"

"No, not exactly," he says, coming closer, hands behind his back. "It's a gift, something you've wanted for a while."

"Arnette," I say in a playful voice. "Is that you back there?"

Al doesn't know I've been jockeying for my sister to come to a show. His furrowed brows emphasize his confusion.

"Arnette's your sister? Sadly, no, she is not the gift. Lorena picked it out." He reveals the rectangular box. "But it was my idea."

"Your idea, huh? Let's see what it is before you go and take credit."

He snorts and hands over the box.

There's a simple red ribbon tied around it. I pause before opening, a quick glance at Al. Considering I don't want a man in my life, him staying for me could've toppled us. That almost kiss could've done us in. But neither did. Our working relationship has been playful. There's been banter, laughter. Flirting, even.

This I like.

Presents I like even more.

I finally lift the lid—and gasp.

"Al."

His eyes flick from me to the box and back to me. "You're impossible to read. Do you like it? This is what you've wanted, right?"

"It's beautiful." I pull the shawl from the box, letting the lace and beaded material cascade to its full length. It'll be just long enough to cover my backside and hit mid-thigh, the fringed bottom giving another inch or two of coverage. An improvement from Doc's robe that goes well past my knees and is thick enough to warm an Eskimo.

"You like it?" Al asks, rare vulnerability lacing his question.

"Very much so. Here," I say, turning my back to him. "Help me get this horrible thing off. No disrespect to Doc, of course."

It takes a few thuds of my heart before his hands clumsily

settle on my shoulders to remove the robe. I hold out the shawl for Al to take. Like a gentleman, he helps me into the flowy garment one arm at a time.

He comments, "Fits like a glove."

I chuckle; such an odd thing to say.

His hands don't linger.

I face him, thinking it may've been nice to feel his touch a few beats longer. "Thank you. This was very thoughtful."

"Yeah, well . . ." He massages the back of his neck. "I heard you complain to Doc about having to wear his robe a time or two."

Seconds pass without us saying anything more. It's something I've noticed has happened a few times between us. And heaven help me, being in Al's presence is like a drug. I want more of it. But I'm not sure it's good for me long term. I don't mean to beat a dead horse—a horrible expression—but I've long known that I don't want a husband. I certainly am not pining for a man who has a habit of disappearing.

"Big night," I say finally. "Shall we get out there?"

A hand on each lapel, he snaps his jacket straight. And smiles. "It's showtime."

LORENA'S SOLO-DIVING ACT GOES first, one beautiful dive after another. She warms up the crowd spectacularly. A crowd I was convinced would include Harold Grover with a stick up his backside after not winning the case against us. But he's not here, or at least I don't see him. Has his grudge died with Doc? Or is it one that'll pass from father to son? My gut tells me the latter, and the thought squeezes my insides.

Lorena's spotlight goes off, darkening the tower. Standing at the base of the ladder, I blow out a long, slow breath just as Al takes the platform, microphone inches from his mouth. He does the closing for his sister's performance, the crowd loving her, then the spotlight once again trains on the top of the tower. It's my cue to begin climbing in that direction.

I hear a little girl exclaim, "Mommy, look!"

"Wasn't Lorena sensational?" Al bellows into the microphone, the applause that follows buying me more time to clamber the forty feet. "Next, we present for your entertainment the most exciting act in show business today . . ."

A second spotlight turns on, hitting me, illuminating me as I climb. I move at a breakneck speed, something Al says will add to the allure of danger. There are gasps. There are cheers. There are the catcalls that wrinkle my nose.

"Please," Al goes on, "turn your eyes to atop this lofty tower."

His words are timed with me arriving, the spotlights becoming one, me standing tall, raising my hand to wave. Al speaks *lofty* in such a way that it makes it seem as high as any human could possibly go without the benefit of oxygen. He gets his desired reaction: hands cover mouths, children point. I imagine some hold their breath.

Al finishes his spiel, all gusto and enthusiasm, while I visualize Klatawah running toward me.

Then he is. To the utter delight of the crowd, Klatawah and I make the dive. And Al's first show is an absolute success.

Dear Arnette,

I hope all is well at home. So much has been changing on my end. With Lightning. With Doc passing. With Al running the shows now. And even with Judas gone and us trying to make something of a new horse called Apollo. It's like getting to know a person. Is he shy? Stubborn? Loyal? Brave? I think he may be brave. Malnourished too. Georgie has been trying to fatten him up. I see how stressed Al is about making Apollo work for us. I know he feels a lot of guilt after the loss of Lightning. Right now John and Klatawah are our main divers. But Klatawah is thirty and Al doesn't want him diving next season. Lorena has been looking for a new home for him. It'll break my heart not to brush and ride him every day. But I understand. Horses are expensive to care for. The future of the show can only work if we can afford to keep it going.

The good news is that Klatawah is a Thoroughbred, so Lorena doesn't think it'll take long to rehome him.

I've learned so much about horses since joining the act. I've heard of Thoroughbreds, which Al claims can be temperamental. He says we got lucky with our Klatawah. But did you know there are warmbloods and coldbloods? Apparently horses that are warmbloods (Lorena says they can be called standard-bred as well) are best for leisure riding and racing. They are agile and quick. Coldbloods are slower, but they're stronger, meant to pull heavy carriages and carry a lot of weight. Apollo is a six-year-old coldblood, with hopefully many dependable diving years ahead of him. Training has been going slow. He'll make the dive from the lowest platform, which is a crucial step. However, he looks a mess while he does it. Al refuses to bring him any higher than twelve feet until he's not smacking against the water with his belly. We leave soon for the winter ranch. I'll write you next from there! Sorry I spent all of this postcard writing about random horse details. But part of me knows you eat it up as much as I do.

With love and cookies,

Sonora

Chapter 25

USUALLY OUR HORSES TRAVEL via train, Doc sparing no expense. And it may be what people are calling the Roaring Twenties, with excess galore, but that's not Al's style. He's not into big hats, big belt buckles, big personalities—or big spending.

So . . . "We drive," he says. "All of us, including the horses."

Apparently over the past few weeks, Al ordered a trailer to be made with very specific specifications to transport our horses. Georgie—barely sixteen and able to drive—and Al will take turns behind the wheel.

For his sister and me, Al has purchased an automobile. In my mind, *these* purchases equate to big spending. However, Al insists it'll be more economical over time. Plus, he says, roads are different now. More are paved; fewer are gravel.

I'm waiting with Georgie outside our hotel. Lorena hasn't emerged yet, notorious for her slow packing. The horses are trailered. All that's left is my ride.

An automobile approaches, massive in size.

It honks.

I shake my head, immediately knowing it has to be Al. "Seriously, that thing is gigantic."

Georgie whistles, which sets me into a fit of giggles. Georgie is wonderful, with the horses and as a human being. But mostly Georgie disappears into the background. Dependable when you need him. Inconspicuous when you don't. To see him admiring this ridiculous car gives me endless amusement.

When Al stops the car, Georgie immediately circles it, mumbling about all the finer attributes of this Studebaker Commander, as he calls it.

Also a Victoria, whatever that means. With jump seats set behind the front seat and a back seat. A store compartment covered with black velvet. A heavy-duty bumper on the front.

"That bumper had to be specially built," Georgie muses.

Al shrugs, exiting the driver's seat. "Who knows. I got her for a steal."

"Couldn't find anything larger?" I tease.

"You'll want big. There's a reason Doc always got Lorena her own train cabin. You'll see."

As if the mention of her name manifests her, Lorena emerges from the hotel lobby, arms full. "Little help here!"

I scrunch my eyes; for the second time this morning, the characters who've become my family are causing me amusement. "What do you have there, Lorena?"

"Candy and crackers," she says innocently.

"Sure." She does indeed have a bag overflowing with treats. "What you got in your other arm?"

I'm referring to the furry, if not adorable, bundle she's also holding.

Lorena smiles widely. "Her name's Claribel. She's a Pekingese."

Al shakes his head, as if he expects this from his sister, and strides toward the lobby for her trunks and suitcases.

"No way," Georgie calls out from the back of the car.

I put a pin in the dog and investigate Georgie's new discovery. "Okay." I admire the tire cover. "This I like."

"How can you not like Claribel?" Lorena grumbles.

The tire cover has a picture of a diving horse painted on it with the words: *The Great Carver Show and High-Diving Horses.*

"I like Claribel just fine," I assure Lorena. "As long as she doesn't wet herself on the drive."

Once packed—turns out I *am* grateful for the gargantuan size of the Studebaker—we begin to drive caravan-style, Georgie and Al in the truck-trailer combo behind us.

I'm first to drive, a bit shaky, to be honest, controlling such a sizable vehicle. It takes some effort to wrestle the wheel the way I want it to go. When I tire, both body and mind, Lorena and I switch places. Claribel on my lap, I quickly realize her appeal—and softness. Another appeal of our driving arrangement is not having to abide by train schedules. We cut across the country at our own pace, allowing the horses a break whenever Al or Georgie sticks out a hand through their window to wave us down.

"What do you think next season is going to look like?" I ask Lorena on day three or four. Around us is a whole lot of orange dirt and brittle-looking shrubs. "Will we have just the one troupe?"

"I'm not sure yet," she says, eyes on the road, hands firmly on the wheel. "Ideally, I'll lead one troupe."

"You'd do the diving and the announcing?"

"It'd be a lot," she acknowledges. "Maybe I'll have Claribel dive in my place."

I laugh, poking a finger into Claribel's fur. "She'd soak up all the water with her hair."

Lorena blindly reaches over to pet her pooch, afterward sinking her hand into the open bag of jelly beans between us. "We wouldn't want that, would we, sweet pea?" Then thankfully in her normal voice, she adds, "But we'll see. We have a few weeks to figure it out. All we know for certain is that there'll be a troupe led by you and Al."

She says *you and Al* in a way girls used to tease on the playground.

I narrow my eyes at her, not that she can see me, the diligent driver she is, but she must sense my reaction. Lorena hides a smirk as she chews her candy. "What?" she says. "Something is clearly going on between you two."

"Nope," I say matter-of-factly.

"What about the shawl?"

"You have excellent taste, Lorena."

"Fine." She pops another jelly bean into her mouth. "What about how he stayed with the troupe because of you?"

"After his disappearing trick the year before, you mean?"

"He came back, but—again—fine." She glances at me. "How about the birthday cake or all the nice things he said about you or—"

"Listen, Al is swell. And I'm pleased as punch to work together, but—"

Lorena lets out an unintelligible sound as she struggles with the wheel. Within a breath, we're bumping off the highway and into the dirt.

I cocoon Claribel against me, watching as Lorena lifts her foot from the accelerator and tries for the brake, slams down on it. But the heavy behemoth we're in has too much momentum. We careen up and up toward a ridge, holding our breath the entire time. Between the slope, friction, and Lorena's insistency with the brake, we begin to slow. A huge boulder ultimately does the trick to halt our forward motion, but not before our front wheels plow overtop it. Jelly beans flying, hair whipping, both of us screaming, luggage thunking against the back of our seats, we're thrown forward against the dash and steering wheel. I manage to twist my body in such a way to protect Claribel from the impact.

Then all's quiet, save for our quickened breaths.

The Studebaker, much like a seesaw on top of the boulder, teeters back and forth. In front of us, there is nothing but the drop-off of the ridge.

"Are you okay?" Lorena whispers, as if talking any louder will send us over the edge.

I rub my head, pulling my hand away to find my fingertips red. Despite the fact I'm clearly bleeding, my body feels like I've been drained of all my blood, leaving behind a wooziness. I lie, "Just a bump. You?"

"I think I banged just about everything." She gingerly reaches up to adjust the rearview mirror. "Al's going to kill me."

I don't dare shift my body weight to look behind us, but I have to imagine Georgie and Al witnessed the entire escapade of us flying off the road and now dangling from a ridge. "He won't get the chance if we don't get out of this thing."

We continue to seesaw, the heavy front bumper fighting against gravity. My stomach fights to keep down the jelly beans I've eaten.

"We need to go toward the back of the car," I determine. "You first, then I'll hand you Claribel."

Lorena groans as she moves. The car matches her moan, shifting farther. Crawling at a snail's pace, she transfers her weight to a safer portion of the car. Handing Claribel to her brings us ten pounds closer to survival.

It's my turn . . . when one of the back doors is thrown open. Al—face stricken, hair out of place—appears. His eyes take stock of his sister, then quickly fall on me. I see the moment relief floods his senses.

"Out, out. Come on, both of you get out of there."

He yanks Lorena, ignoring her protests as she cries out in pain. She took the brunt of our collision against the steering wheel.

I begin to crawl over jelly beans, crackers, and displaced suitcases, thankful all that hurts is a pounding in my head and an ache in my knee.

A tire or some mechanical part grinds. The car dislodges, now tipping more down than up.

"Hurry, Sonora," Al pleads, reaching a hand toward me. As soon as our fingertips touch, he pulls me free, momentum having its way with us: Al on his back in the dirt. Me on top of him.

I'm not sure whose heart pounds more frantically, but I can feel his as if it's my own. We're nearly nose to nose, his gaze dancing over my face. "You're bleeding. Sonora . . ."

Now would be the time to roll off of him, but he repeats my name, pinning me there with his voice. "That was scary," he goes on. "You scared me, the thought that I could lose you." He licks his lips. He stares into my eyes. "Sonora, marry me."

In one of Doc's radio shows, this is where the show would end. Doc would grumble, "Come on, not another cliffhanger."

But in real life, the moment goes on.

And on.

And on.

Al expects me to say something.

But I'm stunned speechless.

Chapter 26

WHAT'S A GIRL TO do when someone proposes out of the blue?

I decide on a joke. "I think you may be the one who bumped your head."

The casualness in my voice is the complete opposite of my mind, which is screaming, *What the hell was that? Surely he's lost his mind.*

"No," he insists. "This all just put a lot of things into perspective. Life is short."

And perspective is often fleeting.

"Well," I say, the surprise of his proposal successfully overtaking the shock I felt on account of the crash, "I'll let you off the hook. Drama's over." I punctuate my words by extracting my body from on top of his.

"Sonora . . ."

There's so much earnestness in his voice, it almost physically hurts my insides. But adrenaline can make a person do and say crazy things. All I can think to do is remove myself from this moment while still maintaining the good working relationship I'd been talking about with his sister before the crash.

"Wow," I say. "We really made a mess of things, didn't we?"

I hold my breath, hoping to tiptoe away from his proposal and praying for Al to focus his attention on the Studebaker. Like I am. Really intently. Some very long seconds pass where he says nothing.

I turn to Lorena, Georgie supporting her, Claribel cradled in her arms. "What hurts?"

"*Mierda*. Everything." Her use of profanity, even in another language, likely has her poor daddy rolling over in the grave. "I can't believe I did that. I don't even know *how* I did that. The wheel got the better of me, I guess."

Al throws down his hat, a complete contradiction to his calmer words, as he says, "It'll be okay. There was a gas station a few miles back. We'll drive there in the trailer. We'll get a tow. We'll get the car fixed up. Minor setback. Good thing for that specially made bumper, huh, Georgie?"

Now Al won't even look at me. It's better this way.

I lag behind the men as we walk toward the trailer. After Lorena is helped up to the bench seat, I offer to stay behind.

"And stand on the side of the road? That's not safe."

It comes from Al, but he's focused on his sister as he says it.

I close the trailer's passenger door, giving it a smack for good measure. Another punctuation mark, perhaps.

AFTER THE MISADVENTURE—BOTH the car accident and the offer of matrimony—things slowly return to normal.

The Studebaker is fixed.

I treat the proposal like it never happened, all smiles and friendliness and professionalism where Al is concerned. And I sigh in relief when Al follows my lead. The situation could've soured very easily. I very easily could have been kicked out of the troupe on account of a bruised ego.

Turns out, there are larger things to focus on. The first is a one-thousand-pound, six-year-old gelding who seems to have forgotten everything he's ever been taught. Somehow, though, Apollo is the lesser of our current two problems. The second is Lorena, whose injuries in the crash have her saying, "I can't dive. Either we find another girl or we go out as a single troupe this season."

I close my eyes, mentally exhausted from the past few months of Lightning, Doc, Al, Lorena, Apollo.

Basically, everyone and everything in my universe has been on my heart and mind.

It's why I'm walking to the mailbox at the end of the drive for something to distract me from it all. It's sunny. The birds are chirping. A slight breeze tousles my hair. All glorious things.

I hesitate as I reach for the mailbox door, certain this'll be the time, while Al and Lorena are in the office trying to figure out next season's shows, that a letter from Harold Grover will arrive, dangling a threat over us. He'll send some official-sounding hogwash that'll put the wind up all of us.

I puff out my cheeks and bite the bullet.

I just about do a jig when I recognize the handwriting.

Arnette's.

She's become my rock, sending postcards but also letters about all that's been going on. She has such a carefree outlook on the world.

When I told her Al proposed and I awkwardly shot him down, she responded in one of her letters back, *He'll just have to get over it if he wants to keep you as his star, won't he?*

When I told her Apollo had regressed, she wrote, *Well, whatever you taught him worked once. It can work again.*

I tear open the envelope, eager for whatever ray of sunshine is awaiting me.

I scan.

I read.

I squeal.

Mama has finally agreed to let me come visit you.

I hug the letter to my chest.

She wants one of us to see you with our own eyes after the accident.

I've assured them I'm fine. But I'm happy my ma doesn't fully believe me.

I'm running.

Suddenly I can't wait to tell Al and Lorena the news, not that they'll have the same level of excitement that I'm experiencing, but I want to tell someone.

I quickly read the rest as I go. News about my brothers. About my sister Jacqueline. New jobs. New sweethearts. Poor grades. Ma answering more ads. Nothing unexpected, but it all still fills my bucket.

Steps from the office, I force myself to slow so I don't burst in like a bat out of hell and scare the living bejesus out of Al and Lorena.

"I don't know," Al is saying. "There's no way we can do two troupes. With Apollo. With you being hurt . . ."

Lorena frowns. "I'm sorry. I wish I could perform."

Interesting, I think to myself, glancing at my sister's letter. This moment suddenly feels serendipitous. Arnette is coming to visit. Arnette loves horses. Arnette's been diving as long as she's been able to walk.

One plus one plus one equals three.

I've yet to be noticed. I put on a confident expression, eyebrows high, mouth quirked into the hint of a smile. "I've got the solution."

Al's amusement is instant. It's there in his relaxed cheekbones and in how his mouth parts into the start of a smile. "Whatever it is, yes."

IF ONLY I COULD snap my fingers and Apollo would stop his frog jumping and dive correctly.

I run a brush down his neck, dust trailing off, the sunlight catching on the particles as they mix with the dirt outside the barn. I say, making conversation with Apollo, "My sister should be arriving any day now. Maybe any second. I believe my exact words in the cable were for her to get her patootie here as quickly as possible."

He nickers.

In my mind, it's a laugh.

"I haven't actually told her about diving yet. So don't you go telling her. It'll be a surprise. No way Ma would've let her come if I spilled those beans. But once she's here, I need you to get your act together, sir."

He nickers again.

I raise a brow, assuming he's being fresh with me. "None of that. You ride splendidly, I want you to know. But Al's going to have to let you go if you can't dive"—I emphasize—"*from the low platform*. We haven't even gone to the high tower yet. It's not safe for you. For me. Won't be for my sister either, and I certainly can't have that. But I don't want you to go. I'd miss you."

I stop brushing him long enough to wipe hair from my face. Apparently too long. Apollo nudges me to keep going.

"I'll have you know, this relationship feels very one-sided."

"Hmm," I hear behind me. "I may know a thing or two about that."

The moment could be extremely awkward—if I didn't sense the humor in Al's voice.

I face him. "At least we all know where we stand."

"Sometimes my memory ain't the best."

I smirk. "Sounds like something you should work on."

He ups my smirk with his own sly smile. "Oh, there's something I'm working on."

I'm beginning to lose the thread here. But two seconds later that doesn't matter; Georgie is pulling up the drive. And with him is our most precious cargo yet: my sister.

Chapter 27

TO UNDERSTAND ARNETTE IS to understand a lightning storm. It can be unpredictable. It can be beautiful. Calming. Destructive. Unresting. Magnificent. I once heard that when lightning strikes wet sand, it can produce one-of-a-kind glass.

Let's hope Arnette interacting with water will transform our next season. Whether or not she can dive successfully will mean the difference between us going out with one troupe or two.

But first, before we get into all of that, a proper greeting.

I run to my sister, enveloping her in a hug. When I left, she was pushing twelve, her head aligned with my breastbone. That's certainly not the case anymore. Pulling back to see her better, the two of us eye to eye, I ask, "What on earth have you done with my little sister?" I cup her cheeks that have clearly lost all their baby fat.

She frowns, but I know that frown. She's putting me on. Inside, she finds me hysterical. Her smile cracks. "I'm all grown up, Sonora."

It's my turn to frown. She's not a kid anymore, I'll give her that. But I won't go any further than her being a young lady. A junior in high school, to be specific. Whom I'll have to keep my eye on, judging by the way Georgie is still lingering nearby with a goofy grin on his face. I move us out of his earshot. "You're something," I say to her, "that's for sure." I playfully narrow my eyes. "How is it that your bubs are bigger than mine?"

This reddens her cheeks, and I'm pleased to see her confidence has its limits. I grab her hand. "Come on, let me introduce you to the gang. You already know Georgie." Hopefully not too well. Al and Lorena have made their way outside. "This is Lorena. She's great. And this is Al."

He clears his throat. "And what about me? Aren't I great too?"

The question catches me off guard. It's always been Al's way to adopt a flirtatious tone when it's the two of us, something I'm relieved still exists. But with all eyes on me, I'm uncertain how to answer an otherwise innocent-enough question. Everyone here knows about Al's adrenaline-induced proposal. I huff out a laugh, buying myself time. Then I say, "Sure."

Sure?

Not my finest moment. Arnette saves me. "I suppose I'll be the judge of that, depending on if you let me ride one of your horses. I want to do what Sonora does."

I'm touched.

Al arches a brow, amused. "How about I teach you to ride? Then we'll see about diving."

My sister's jaw drops. My stomach clenches with nerves. I want this for her—it was my idea, after all, to bring her here—while simultaneously being concerned for her safety. Arnette's head turns to me. I'm nonchalant, the cool big sister. "I mean, if you wanted to try to learn."

"I sure as hell do."

"Okay then," I say, adding a clap. An honest-to-God clap, like I'm a male football coach. I immediately feel a fool but push on. "Let's get to work."

I'M ALL KNOTS, WHITE knuckles, and locked kneecaps as I lean against the fence to watch Arnette train with Al.

She's riding on Apollo, not from the tower, but in the training lot. Al wants to determine how comfortable horse and rider are together. I'm grateful for that. A horse that ditches its rider on dry land is dangerous. From forty feet high and in the water, even more so.

Al still hasn't given up on Apollo. And on day four of Arnette's visit, I'm relieved she's still in the mix too. Melanie only lasted three days. But my little sister clearly has the moxie—and muscle—that Melanie did not have. She's fearless, at one point dangling from Apollo with an earnest smile on her face. I get a furrowed-brow glance from Al, as if he's saying, "Maybe a little too fearless?"

I shake my head, assuring him all's fine, while unease pricks at my stomach. It's a weird sensation, having endless amounts of pride in Arnette and wanting to believe she's able to accomplish anything and everything. While the older, protective sister in me was emotionally at my limit after watching only the first hour of ground training.

It'll only get worse once she moves to the tower in a few days. Which ends up happening the next day, Arnette running to me at the fence to say, "Nora, guess what? Al says I can start diving in the morning."

"Oh?" I say, multiple questions in that single word.

So quickly?

Is she being pushed along like Melanie?

Or does she show true potential?

Or maybe it's because she's only with us for a week before she's back to Georgia, back to school. The plan is, if Arnette has what it takes, we'll begin working on my ma to convince her to let Arnette join us for the summer season while school is out.

"Arnette assures me you've taught her to dive," Al says. "I'd like to see what she can do."

Turns out, she also has ample amounts of moxie while in the air from the lower platform, but not as much control as I'd like with how she rushes through the movements, her excitement getting the best of her.

"I'm ready for the high tower," Arnette announces, already climbing.

Al shrugs in my direction. "I'm okay with it if you are."

I throw up my hands, all the answer Arnette needs. She scurries up the ladder like a possessed squirrel. She's remarkably fast. Ma will kill me if this goes south. I should have her perfect the low dive first.

She's nearly at the top. Forcing my decision.

I hold a clenched fist to my mouth. Would she stop now if I asked her to? Likely not. "Careful, Arnette," I call out. "Put some thought into the dive you're doing."

In other words, stop rushing.

I watch in anticipation and hopefully not dismay.

She dives—an impressive swan dive—hitting the water with little splash. Arnette emerges, the largest of smiles on her face. She did it. She did it well. Not only that, but if Arnette's expression is any indicator, she's hooked. And mentally, I'm already preparing what I'll say to our ma to let her return in May.

IT TAKES SOME CONVINCING.

Ma has to be reminded that the horse's skill accounts for ninety-five percent of the dive. Arnette only has to hold on for the last five percent, for which she'll be properly trained.

She also has to promise to write letters home—more frequently than I've been doing.

But the biggest factor of them all: Ma has to agree to let another of her daughters stretch her wings in a way she's never imagined. Jacqueline's job at Adler's is far less death-defying.

In the end, Ma relents, just as she did with me. By mid-May, Arnette has taken her junior-year finals early, then promptly arrives at the ranch—with one month to train before she heads out with Lorena.

I'll be honest, being separated from my sister is a point of contention for both my ma and me. Something that leaves Al confused. "But," he says, "the plan all along was to have two troupes. That's why we needed another diver."

I know this. His confusion makes complete sense. However, there are times when reason and emotions do not align. This is one of those times. I also know I have to get over it.

Seeing Arnette train over the next month—and knowing she can do all the tricks—will help. Along with the fact Al decides to say goodbye to Apollo. It's bittersweet. He's a beautiful, pleasant-natured horse, who has thrived in other ways. Such as eating, the boy solid as a rock now. He simply has no talent for diving, a crucial element of our show. A crucial element for having two shows going at once, in fact.

I find Al pacing in his office. Apollo left only hours ago with Georgie.

"You'll miss him. I will too. But you did what was right," I tell him.

"Yeah, well, right or not, I need to cancel some of our contracts as a result of rehoming Apollo. We have John and Snow, but both are getting too long in the tooth to do two or three shows a day, seven days a week. I'll need both of them on a single troupe so they can take turns. That means we're back where we started with not being able to have two troupes this year. Hence the contracts I need to cancel."

"So that's it?" I slump into a chair opposite his desk.

"My back's to the wall, Sonora."

Literally. He has himself propped up now, his chest rising and falling in defeat.

"Can't we find another horse?"

"You saw what happened with Apollo. Either I back out now or I risk having to back out days before opening day. That'd be detrimental to the Carver name." He runs a hand through his wavy dark hair. "I need to write the fairground managers to let them know we can't come after all."

"And go back to a single troupe? What will that mean for Arnette?" My heart's breaking for her. I caught her trying on my red diving suit only this morning. I shake my head, answering for him. "We'll share the dives. And I'll write the managers for you."

"You don't need to do—"

"Consider it done." Within a few hours, I've written and mailed three letters. Lorena immediately begins strategizing. "Two beautiful sisters. It's not the worst thing. I can use that in our promotions."

If Arnette is ready, a detail I sometimes overlook in my excitement. Then reality sets in, and as Mamie Lou would say, I'm about as nervous as a long-tailed cat in a room full of rocking chairs to see my sister go off the low dive on a horse for the first time.

Al's chosen John for her inaugural dive. In my mind, a questionable decision, considering he's the reason Vivian quit after whacking her head on the bottom of the tank. The last thing I need is my sister's brains scrambled. But John is the more experienced horse.

Together, Arnette and I climb to the low tower, and I'm biting my lip the entire time. Arnette's reached that stage in her adolescence where anything I say is countered with an agitated, "I know."

But does she? Does she really?

I double-check John's harness. Then Arnette's helmet. Despite her knowledge of all things, I remind her where to stand, how I'll stop John, how I'll give her a quick boost up. Word for word, she gets the same instructions I gave Melanie that Al gave me.

"You ready?" I ask her.

She grins. "We were born for this, Nora."

I nod. "I think so too."

At that, I motion for Georgie to release John. He barrels up the ramp toward us. I stop him. Arnette launches herself on, little help from me. And they dive.

She stays on his back!

They emerge.

She's still on.

Not only that, but Arnette's proclaiming she's ready for the top tower. I'm doing all the things: pointing a finger at her, shaking my head, laughing. Al's reaction is pretty similar, only he also calls out, "Fat chance of that happening today."

Good.

"But soon," he adds. "Well before your first show."

I'm good with that too. I'd have some words with him if he tried to pull a Doc and make my sister do her first forty-foot dive on opening night.

Arnette shrugs. "Had to try!"

Lorena's tense voice cuts through the excitement. "Guys."

I hadn't noticed her coming up to the pool. But there she is, holding a letter. "Guys, we have a problem."

"No," Al says. "Today's a good day. Today is not a day for problems."

"This can't wait."

From the tower, I strain to hear and call out, "What is it?"

"Those contracts you canceled the other day . . ."

"Yeah?"

"They're not canceled."

Al's brows knit in confusion. "What on earth does that mean?"

"I wrote them," I insist.

"That you did," Lorena says. "But they're not letting us back out. All three of them. Apparently they got together and decided it's too late to fill our spots. So they all say no."

I ask, "Can they do that?"

Al throws down his hat, stopping short of stomping on it. "They just did."

Arnette's head has been on a swivel, following whoever's been talking. Now she's the one to call out, "What's this mean?"

Al sighs. "It means the show must go on."

Somehow.

Chapter 28

AL PROCLAIMS, "WE NEED another horse."

Which, yes, seems to be stating the obvious. The question is how to find one *and* train one in a matter of weeks, when the process generally takes months.

To answer that, Al means to take to the streets.

For the past few days, I have driven out and around the countryside with him in the afternoons. Eyes peeled into every pasture and field we pass, on the hunt for—as Al puts it—a pretty horse, an intelligent horse, a horse that will prove to have courage and pride. It's not clear to me how Al can ascertain those attributes from the driver's seat, but I've called his attention to quite a few horses now, and he hasn't pulled over for any of my suggestions.

"Some of it's a gut feeling," he says, easing off the gas and leaning over me, shortening my breath as he gets a better vantage point out the passenger-side window.

"Like you're some horse whisperer?" I tease, ignoring the fact he's basically in my lap.

"If the shoe fits." He returns to his side with a grin, and I can't help the magnetic pull I still feel toward him, even with him the appropriate distance away. I fight the pull, though, the need to push him away stronger, and listen intently as he goes on. "To keep running with the shoe analogy, you could look at a loafer and know if it's too large or too small, right?"

"I suppose."

"Well, I look out into that there pasture, and I can tell the brown one is too small, the sorrel one too young. The black one is past his prime." He straightens and accelerates again. "It's the personality that's the largest factor."

"We'll find the perfect diving horse," I insist, even if it is reassurance without any certainty.

"We have no choice but to do just that." He sighs. "Can't believe I've agreed—again—to the contracts. I never should have promised them in the first place, knowing Apollo was struggling. If my father could see me—"

"Don't you dare do that," I chastise. "Your daddy would be proud of you for trying to make this right."

He shoots me a rueful look.

"Cross my heart."

He laughs lightly. "In that case, thank you."

"My pleasure."

Al taps against the steering wheel. "Seriously, though, thank you, Sonora. You're always there. Life has thrown us quite a few curveballs of late. Throughout it all, you've been a constant at my side. A listening ear. A voice of reason. A partner . . ." I can feel his eyes shift from the road to me, but his words have pinned me in place and, for the life of me, I can't pull my gaze from the window.

Part of me fears what he'll say next.

Another part of me is dying to hear whatever it is.

"Sonora." He pauses. "Look at me."

I do.

"I hope you'll never stop being those things for me, and I hope I can be those for you too. I've, um, grown to love you and—"

"Al—"

"No, let me get this out. Even if you say no."

I hitch my breath, fully grasping where he's going with this and already slowly shaking my head, while my heart—and Doc, if he were here—might very well be calling my head a fool.

"You said," he goes on, pulling the car off the road, stopping us, and twisting his body toward me, "that last time I asked you to marry me was in the heat of the moment, the excitement of you dangling over a cliff." He chuckles softly. "But look around—there's nothing exciting going on out here. It's just you and me on what could be a futile hunt for a horse to save our business. But that's okay, because you're beside me. I'd like it to always be you and me. As husband and wife. So, Sonora—"

"Al." My next breath may be the largest one I've ever taken. Exasperation doesn't fuel it. It's the simple truth of knowing Al could be everything I want, *if* I wanted to be somebody's wife. That's never been part of the plan. But could I be willing to alter it? I don't think I'm ready to make that decision on the side of some road. "That was beautiful, and you . . . well, you truly are great." I smile softly, hoping he'll remember our banter from Arnette's arrival and he'll match my grin. But he only twists his lips, hanging on my every word. "I feel for you too. I really do. It's only that I don't see myself getting married and being reliant on someone else. My daddy's gone. He didn't die; he chose to leave us. Then he chose to start an entirely new family. That broke my ma. It broke all of us."

Al reaches for my hand. I let him. "I'd never do that. Not to you."

I nod; this is him acknowledging that he's left before. And it means something for him to assure me. It does. But it's not enough to eradicate the fears and a mindset that's been built, rock by rock, since I was a child. "Families nowadays get too big. They can't afford them all. They fight. Nobody is happy in the end."

"You don't think we could be happy?"

"You already make me happy. Very happy." Funny, intelligent, caring, thoughtful. Easy on the eyes. Al is all those things and more. But do I need him to be my husband? Do I want to take that risk and have everything change? For him to lose what he feels for me? For me to ultimately harbor the same grudge I hold against Ula? We've never kissed. I haven't allowed myself to get attached. We've never crossed any boundaries. Nor do I think we should, and I shake my head. "Can't we remain as we are? Could that be enough?"

"Okay," he says, licking his lips and turning back to the steering wheel. He's nearly impossible to read with his reaction and that single word, a word he only repeats: "Okay."

The road ahead of us is a long, steep incline. I think again of a roller coaster with a big drop-off on the other side.

Our wheels turn over. Al clucks his tongue. I'm still uncertain what's currently churning in his head. But then he says, "Maybe the third time will be the charm." And he says it in a lighthearted way, a smirk bookending his hopeful comment.

I roll my eyes, matching a playfulness I'm grateful for. "Al, you've never been short on charm. Well, except for when we first met."

He chuckles softly. I'm grateful for that too. I squeeze his arm, knowing he's a kind man who won't hold any resentment against me where most others would. We reach the crest of the hill. There's a pasture on the other side.

Al squints.

He slows, then pulls off the road, parking us at such a precarious angle I fear the car may start rolling. "There," he says. "You see him?"

"Which one?" There are three.

"The paint."

"I don't have a lick of clue what that word means."

"A paint horse is often a quarter horse."

"A coldblood?" I ask, throwing out the only term I know.

He shakes his head. "No, and I know we usually go for those. But a paint could work. They're versatile. Not to mention powerful, athletic, and with unequaled beauty."

"Which one is he?"

"The brown one that looks a bit like a cow."

"Well, let's go get him."

Al grins. "Give me a moment."

He gets out of the car and walks to the fence. While the other two horses spook, the paint is curious, locking his icy blue eyes on Al. It's as if the two of them are sizing each other up. Then the paint kicks up his heels and runs off, following the other two.

Back in the car, Al says, "I want him."

"What makes you want him after that?"

"A feeling."

I motion with my hand in a "by all means" way.

Al's all but vibrating as he descends the hill, then turns down a dirt drive. A farmhouse awaits us half a mile in. By the time we're out of the car, a man has emerged and waits for us on the porch.

"My name's Al Carver," Al calls as we approach. "I want to buy that paint of yours."

"Glad to know you, Mr. Carver. But you're not the first one."

"What will it take to have him?"

The man snorts. "Wouldn't sell him to my worst enemy."

"Sir?" I ask.

"The horse is a menace, should be wearing horns. I joke about changing his name to Lucifer, I do. You can't tame him, can't ride him, can't put him to the plow. He's nothing but a pretty face to hide the fact he's as mean as the dickens."

"I still want him," Al insists. "How much will he cost?"

I give Al a look that I hope expresses he's lost his marbles. But his attention is solely on the farmer.

"Son, I've sold him three times already. Folks always bring him back."

Al's adamant. "I won't."

It's taking every ounce of me not to stop biting my lip and question what on God's green earth Al is doing. The farmer is being honest with us, and Al knows better than anyone we don't have time for a horse that can't be tamed.

"Come on now," Al persists. "How much?"

"I don't think you're catching my drift here. I've been using him as nothing more than a decoy. Put him out there in the pasture. Folks stop to look at him, and I end up selling one of the others."

Al stands his ground. "I can't use any of the others. I've got to have that one."

"Well, okay, but what if I don't want to lose my decoy?"

"I'll pay you double his worth."

"Only if I can keep it when you bring him back."

"Done."

The farmer extends a hand. "Then I reckon we have ourselves a deal."

Al shakes, and my eyes must be twice their size, wondering what has possessed him to purchase a horse that very well could be possessed himself.

Chapter 29

ARNETTE MAY BE TALL, hippy, and on her way to becoming an adult, but her current facial expression screams teenager. "You can close your jaw now," I say to her, picking at the long grass that flanks the porch steps we sit on.

My sister snaps her mouth closed, only to open it again to lament, "I can't believe he was going to propose *again* and you said no. Al's a dish."

"Technically I didn't say no. I said I didn't want things to change because, yes, he is important to me."

"It's still a no, Sonora. How'd he take it?"

I flap my lips, much like one of our horses when disgruntled. "Fine? I don't know. He's Al. I don't think he knows how to do unfriendly. But it's better this way. We have a contract. Multiple contracts, in fact, in a matter of weeks." I point toward the gravel drive. "He'll be pulling in any minute with that new horse. Our job is to greet them with nothing but smiles. And *no* reservations, even though I have a whole slew of them."

"About the horse or about saying no to Al?"

"Enough out of you." I refuse to spend brain power on this right now—not when I hear the crunch of tires.

Arnette salutes me like I'm a general.

I stand and smooth a hand down my dress.

"You know," my sister observes, "you look awfully pretty. Is that lipstick?"

"I always wear lipstick."

"And I always think before I speak." She raises her brows at me, as if challenging me to deny the fact I put some extra effort into my appearance. And, okay, maybe I have.

"You know," Arnette goes on, and I really wish she wouldn't. "It would've been better for us all if you said yes. When Lorena gets back from the doctor and hears all of this, she'll be as disappointed as I am."

I frown. "Whose side are you on?"

She stacks her hands over her heart and says in a funny voice, "Love."

I laugh. "You're too much." The trailer with Al, Georgie, and our new horse comes into view, and I perk up. "Do me a favor and leave whatever's going on between Al and me to me, you hear?"

"Because you seem to have that *all* figured out."

I hop off the stairs, leaving this conversation behind. The thing is, Arnette's not wrong. But what I said to Al isn't wrong either. No matter how I feel about him, I don't want things to change, because change isn't always positive. Change can go south. "You're back!" I call out as Al jumps down from the trailer.

And Lord help me, my stomach tingles. The way his face lights up. He's so hopeful. So eager. So attractive.

Arnette outpaces me, getting to the boys first. "Got my horse in there?"

"Your horse?" Al smiles. "We'll see who Red Lips wants to ride with."

Arnette snorts. "That's his name?"

I join them. "Well, go on, bring him out. I can't wait to see him again."

Honestly, I'm less than enthused, considering how the farmer talked about him. But horses are smart; they can sense emotion. And right now I want Red Lips to feel nothing but welcome.

I tell myself it's him I've dressed up for . . .

Georgie rounds the trailer to get our new friend, bringing him out and around. I'd forgotten how handsome Red Lips is. The majority of him is white, but he has perfectly placed brown markings, much like a cow. "He's beautiful."

Al says nothing but "Yeah."

An odd response from him. "What do you mean, 'yeah'?"

He leans closer, his next comments meant only for me. "I'm a little skittish about him, if I'm being honest."

"Excuse me?"

He retreats a step and drops his head toward his chest, like he can't believe what he's just gone and done by buying this horse.

Arnette is approaching Red Lips, Georgie talking to him in a soothing voice.

I say to Al, "What was all that bravado yesterday, then? You *had* to have this horse."

He removes his hat, only to settle it back on his head. "I

know, I know. I just thought that sometimes it's worth giving someone the chance to prove all the naysayers wrong."

He's talking about the horse, right?

I'd think so if Arnette didn't turn at that exact moment and widen her eyes at me. Al didn't purchase this horse the farmer compared to Lucifer, immediately after I rejected him, to try to prove some point, did he?

I shake it off, intending to do nothing more in this moment than meet our new horse. "Hello, Red Lips," I say, approaching his shoulder, his ears ticking toward me. "I'm Sonora. Such pretty eyes you have."

He paws at the ground, something I've learned horses do for various reasons: impatience, anxiety, boredom.

"Aching to run, boy?" I ask, lifting a hand to the side of his neck and petting him there. He offers me no visible signs he's not a fan. In fact, he does the exact opposite, nudging me, telling me he wants my attention.

I drop my mouth in surprise and look at the others. "Would you look at that? He—"

Suddenly Red Lips uses his teeth to take hold of the ruffle at the neck of my dress.

One second I'm wearing the garment.

The next I'm standing in nothing but my slip.

Arnette's hand muffles her laugh.

The boys stand there catching flies.

The damned horse nickers.

And never before have I been more mortified.

I DID WHAT ANYONE would do. I fled, cheeks blazing.

Now I've taken up residence at the window in my room, sulking and embarrassed, watching Al and Lucifer—I mean, Red Lips—in the training ring.

After his impish start, I don't have high hopes for how he'll react to the halter and lead rope. But as Al puts on both, I'm shocked. Red Lips initially acts disgruntled, but the fire in him dims, ultimately dwindling to a manageable smolder. Either Al truly is a horse whisperer or I've witnessed a miracle.

Al works him for some time before glancing toward the tower, and I know exactly what idea is rolling around in his head. He wants to see if Red Lips will dive. If he won't do that, the rest doesn't matter.

Al whistles, loud and piercing. Georgie emerges from the porch area, a jump in his step, like he's ready to help the boss, but also like he's been caught. I lean out the window, spotting Arnette on the steps, a Georgie-sized space now vacant beside her.

In no time, Georgie has Red Lips on the lower tower. Al is opposite him at the tank. The same setup Al and I used when testing out Apollo. The only difference: Georgie manages to toss the rope to Al without either of them taking a dip.

I'm on tenterhooks as Al coaxes, soothes, and gently tugs Red Lips toward the edge of the twelve-foot tower.

Red Lips steps confidently right up to the kickboard.

It almost seems too easy.

The next tug Al gives is minimal, barely there. And Red Lips jumps.

Al's back is to me as he skirts around the pool and to the incline where Red Lips will walk out. If only I could see his face. I imagine he's astonished. I also imagine he's thinking this is too good to be true. I hear a whooping sound, and I lean out the window again to find Arnette cheering like a maniac.

Al reacts to her. Then his gaze flicks up to me as if he knew I'd be watching.

"None of that now," he calls to my sister. "You'll go and jinx it."

I smile, liking that I guessed what he was thinking. He says something else to Georgie, likely wanting them to go again, to make sure the first time wasn't a fluke.

They set up.

And Red Lips does it again, as smooth as a veteran diving horse.

I run in place, flailing my arms, excitement taking over my body. We've done it. We've found our new horse. Most likely. As long as Red Lips can dive with a rider. But I'm so excited I'm already two steps ahead. In fact, I'll go so far as to say we'll be going out with two troupes. Now, to get our handsome hero fully ready for his first show.

Chapter 30

AL SAYS THAT IN an ideal situation, it takes about two years to properly train a horse. We're talking fully trained as a consistent perfect-ten performer. But that's not to say a horse can't be diving from the forty-foot tower in a shorter amount of time.

Say . . . a few weeks. Because that's all we've got.

Some horses are never successful, even with nerves of steel. Others are unable to control their legs in the air, like we saw with Apollo. Still others are poor swimmers, stroking harder with their forefeet, making themselves uneven and often causing themselves to roll over onto their sides. Some try to shake off a rider for sport, as John does.

So far, Red Lips has the nerve and the leg control, and he's a fantastic swimmer. Three for three, with only number four in question: Will he carry a rider?

It's what we've all been most nervous about, considering the farmer's warning that he can't be ridden.

"I'll try," Arnette says, all of us circled around our new star horse.

"Not a chance," I say. The girl conquered the top tower with John, and now she thinks she's an expert?

"Why don't I try him on the ground first?" Al suggests.

Georgie shrugs, while Lorena pops a hand on her hip and says, "What if he's got a thing against men, and that's all who've tried him so far? I think you and Georgie should sit this one out."

I chuckle, mostly because Al doesn't look even mildly convinced of that theory. "If you want to try him, Lorena, then go straight ahead."

"I wasn't talking about me," she says. "I mean for Sonora to give it a go. She'll be the one diving with him, no?"

I snort. "Well, thanks for volunteering me."

But truth be told, I've been dying to ride him. He may've torn off my dress—and laughed about it afterward—but I tell myself he was picking on me because he likes me. He's an eight-year-old boy, after all. I remember Frankie Phillips in the third grade. Picked on me until the cows came home.

I pet his neck. "No beating around the bush, I suppose. Shall we give this a go, Red?" Like with all the horses, I've spent ample time brushing him, and during one of those times, we had a chat about shortening his name. He seemed amicable, his tail swishing like a happy dog. "We'll do just fine. Won't we, boy? You're smart and strong and oh so handsome."

Arnette laughs. "Enough of that or else Al will get jealous."

That's worth a glare, which only makes her laugh harder.

Al pulls her into a headlock, such a big brother thing to do. Very un-boss-like. Arnette squirms, laughing, until Al releases her and smooths out his button-down shirt, transforming himself back into the head honcho. Al's playfulness may forever be my favorite thing about him. "Now," he says, straining to keep a straight face, "if we're ready to get back to work, every second ticks us closer to opening day." Then he does indeed grow more serious, turning his attention to me. "Sonora, if you'd like to mount him, go ahead. If he'll let you on his back, we'll try the tower. Georgie, if Red shows any signs of misbehaving, step in. And, Sonora, I'll be here to catch you if you fall."

"Aw, what a gentle—"

I pin Arnette with a look, successfully putting an end to her antics. Then Red gets my full attention. I talk in a soothing voice. I encourage him. I praise him. There's no need for a saddle. We only have on the diving harness. Al gives me a leg up; then I'm on Red's back.

He whips his head around, as if frosty that I have the nerve to ride him. But over the next hour or so, he doesn't throw me off. He may only be tolerating me, but I'll take it.

I'll take it all the way to the low tower. There, I stand along the railing, waiting for Georgie to release Red to run up the tower's ramp. Once Red is on his way, I shake out my arms. He can do this. We can do this. But when he gets to me, he puts on the brakes before I try to stop him, like he's not so sure. Still, I climb on. I bring him to the edge of the twelve-foot tower, talking to him again in a quiet, reassuring voice, reminding him that he's already done this. The only difference is I'm tagging along this time. If he'll let me; it's got to be up to him. I can tell the instant he acquiesces, a vibration going through his entire body and his muscles engaging. He kicks off, and twelve feet goes by in a blink.

FROM THEN ON, I go out every morning to ride him and do training dives from the low tower until the day we set out for the fairs.

"Behave yourself," I say to Arnette when it's time for her to leave with Lorena, a new groom named Freddie, John, and Snow, and for me to head out with Al, Georgie, and Red.

"Don't behave yourself," Arnette counters with a cheeky grin.

"You seriously are incorrigible."

"Mama tells me the same thing."

"Don't forget to write her."

She raises a brow. "You're the one who—"

"I know, I know. I'll write more often. Please be safe. You've got so much talent in your body. Sometimes I think too much and it could burst free at any moment."

She nods, then bites her bottom lip, a seriousness coming over her that I rarely see. "Thank you, Sonora. When you left to come here and do this, I was so envious. You were living the life I wanted to live. Now here I am. Mama never would have let me have this without you going first."

"You mean without the ad Ma pushed on me." I laugh. "She has herself to thank for two of her daughters running away to join a circus act."

"She's doing better, you know. Hasn't been answering the ads like she used to."

"That's something," I say. Something good. She's healing. I personally wouldn't have grown enamored with want ads. But maybe my way of dealing with Ula by swearing off men isn't much better of an approach. A pin goes in that, not the time to psychoanalyze myself. But Virginia Woolf would insist I do it soon. After all, she's the one who said, "Growing up is losing some illusions, in order to acquire others."

Arnette stops my thoughts, reciting our farewell. "Love and cookies."

"Always. Now"—I pat my sister's backside—"don't keep Lorena waiting."

Tears fill my eyes as I watch her run to the trailer and climb in. Freddie, our second groom, honks the horn as they depart.

I don't realize Al's come up beside me until he says, "She'll be fine." He puts an arm around my shoulder, a nice feeling, and I lean into him.

AL, GEORGIE, RED, AND I get to the New York fair two weeks before opening day. Red and I practice every morning, noon, and night from the low tower. But we've yet to go off the higher one. Today's the day—mostly because there are no more days left.

Admittedly, I'm apprehensive.

Red is big, but John is larger, making him handle a rider more comfortably. Something that makes me happy since John's with Arnette.

Red is strong but not always consistent. We want him doing

a plunge dive, where his forelegs break the water first, the rest of his body—and me—following with as little drag as possible.

But he does this thing—we call it a nosedive—where he enters the water almost vertical, shifting his body so he enters nose first.

It doesn't hurt him, from what I can tell. But I worry about getting hurt myself. A lot can happen in forty feet; a lot more than the twelve feet we've been doing.

I take a steadying breath. Georgie is at the bottom of the ramp with the horse. Easy-peasy. Georgie and I have done this setup hundreds of times.

Just not with Red at this height.

But here he comes, trotting up the ramp, as if *he's* done this a thousand times. I smile, relieved at his confidence. He allows me to mount him just fine, another victory.

But then he's slow on the takeoff, like he's moving through molasses. He kicks off, though, leaving the tower behind and beginning to soar into the air.

A breath into it all, he begins turning over, more and more, on the verge of becoming vertical. And all I can do for the next forty feet is hold on and pray he—we—won't flip.

Chapter 31

THE WATER RUSHES TOWARD me. Rather, it's Red and I who are plunging toward the water.

There's no time to think, only to hold on. I squeeze my legs and hands with all I have, feeling my body shift more vertically with Red's movement.

Any more and we'll turn over. Any more and he'll land in the pool on his back—pancaking me between him and the cement-like water. The fall ends before that can happen. We hit the water's surface in the most up and down position I've ever been in. The water tears down the back of my helmet and suit. It tugs at my feet.

My hands, then my fingertips, almost lose the diving harness. I grip as hard as I can while my body floats off Red into a handstand position beneath the water.

A rarity for me, I panic, our entry bubbles creating a wall around me that feels impenetrable.

I continue to hold on, my stomach muscles straining to bring down my legs, to feel for Red beneath me. I know the instant he kicks off the pool's bottom, thrusting me up, the water's movements shifting, clearing away the bubbles. It takes three strong kicks, but I exert myself onto his back at the same moment he breaks the surface.

It's a point of pride for me to always ride a horse out of the tank.

Today is no different.

I don't dare let go, but I toss my head to free water from my eyes. The first thing I see is Al, white as a ghost, standing on the exit ramp's platform.

"That's it," Al says. "We'll find a new horse."

"No," I say. "There's no time."

"He almost flipped."

"John has nose-dived on me before. We ended up fine. Just like Red, and I survived." Even as I say the words, I don't fully believe them. Al and I know John's size makes it less likely he'll turn over. John's also an accomplished diver who knows how to throw up his long neck and head to better balance himself. But there's one other significant factor to take into consideration: opening day is tomorrow.

I stare down Al, both of us knowing this very thing.

Al rolls his neck, letting out a low growl. "I can't, Sonora. I don't ever say it because I know it makes you push me away, but I love you. And I can't put the woman I love at risk for some stupid show."

"It's not stupid, Al."

He does more than run his hands through his hair. He grabs fistfuls. "It's not. But you're more important."

"I'm not. Your daddy built this show decades ago."

He releases the hold of his hair to throw up his arms. "One show won't bring us down."

"It'd end up being more than a single show, Al. And I'm not willing to risk your daddy's legacy by giving up. How about a compromise?" I say this without knowing what that is actually. Horses are my life now, but I don't know them the way Al does.

He droops his head before eyeing me with such intensity it almost hurts. "He'll dive alone," Al begins. "As many times as he's willing to do it today. He needs a better feel for it. If, and I mean if, he improves, we'll try you on his back again from that height."

TO CONVINCE MY MA that Arnette should join the act, we told her that whole business of how a horse is responsible for ninety-five percent of a dive and how a rider takes care of the last five.

Maybe that was the case with Lightning, Klatawah, and John, but that math doesn't work with Red. He's too untrained.

I watch him go off the high tower again and again. Sometimes he does a body plunge like we want him to do. Sometimes it's the more dangerous nosedive. I wouldn't say it's quite fifty-fifty, but it's not eighty-twenty either.

I don't think the exact number matters, except when it comes to Red not flipping onto his back. That needs to be zero. So far he hasn't, and on opening day, I tell Al that I feel confident he won't turn over.

"You insist on this?"

"I do."

Al makes an unintelligible noise. "Fine. Then trust your instincts. Protect yourself. If he nose-dives, you're exposed. You know to duck your head. But you'll need to duck even lower, and you'll need to do it more quickly."

Either that or my face will make contact with the water. That'd be less than desirable.

When opening night is upon us, when the time's come for our act, when Al has the crowd eating out of the palm of his hand, Red and I go off the top tower as if we'd perfected it ages ago, hitting the water in an optimal plunge.

After that, our season—in New York, then St. John, New Brunswick—is a blur, one dive blending into the next. There's only a handful of performances where I have had cause to remember Al's advice on how to avoid face-planting in the pool.

If only this were my greatest of worries. But no, a letter comes in for us at the post office the day we're set to return to our winter ranch. Al climbs into the driver's seat, Georgie in the second row, me in the passenger seat, and he starts reading to himself.

"What?" I study his tense jaw. "What's happened?"

He keeps on reading.

"What's happened?" I ask again, tight as a drum, my heart beating out a quicker rhythm. "Is it from Lorena?"

"No one's hurt," he says, eyes still moving left to right over the paper. Finally, he groans. As the boss man, the stress of running both troupes, one from afar, lands on his shoulders. It can't be easy, especially with us having to build a tower, break it down after our two weeks or six weeks or however long we're at a particular fairground, then transport it to a new location, only for the whole process to begin again. For a girl who craves adventure and travel, it says a lot that I find it extremely taxing.

I impatiently wiggle my fingers for the letter.

Al finishes, passes it to me, then immediately puts the trailer into gear. I need a breath before I dive in.

It's about Arnette.

She's fine.

She's come through the end of the season unscathed.

I'm relieved, but only momentarily. The next line sinks my stomach.

We can't keep her on.

Lorena writes how it's only a matter of time before Arnette gets hurt.

I look up from the letter. "I wonder if she's still getting charley horses. Is that what Lorena means? I know Arnette's gotten them so badly she could hardly walk. Makes me wonder if she's still not squeezing her knees in the right spot."

Horses have an inner tube behind their forequarters that acts much like a shock absorber and gives riders something to brace their knees against before hitting the water. She may be overexerting herself, resulting in her muscles seizing.

Al motions for me to keep reading.

"'Too unorthodox'?" I question, pulling Lorena's words from the letter. "Lorena's never sure if Arnette is going to be 'skilled or dangerously awkward.' I don't even know what that means."

"I'm not sure either," Al says when I finger-tap that portion of the letter, him glancing over from the wheel. "But Lorena says she's tried to correct your sister's errors to no avail. You read the same words I did; your sister is bound to hurt herself. No one wants that."

"Is she simply not holding her body tight enough? Or maybe it's her grip? You know, the grip I do on the harness helps. Maybe if—"

"And who taught you that grip?"

I twist my lips. "Lorena."

His point is made; if Lorena taught me, she would've shown Arnette the same thing.

I sigh. Georgie's hand squeezes my shoulder. I'd forgotten he was in the trailer with us. I wonder how he's feeling about the news that Arnette can't stay on. I've suspected he's been carrying a torch for her.

"Listen," Al says, "I know this means a lot to Arnette. And to you as well. But Lorena is right. We're going to have to cut her loose if her safety is in jeopardy. There's also the welfare of the show. Harold Grover—"

"We haven't spotted him all season."

"Doesn't mean he's not biding his time. He easily could've been at any of those shows that Arnette slipped up at. It's all the opening he'd need to start another investigation into us."

I open my mouth to argue but stop. Arnette means the world to me, and no part of me wants to crush her. But this show is my world. "How are we going to tell her?"

Al presses his lips together. I shift to see Georgie, who avoids all eye contact with me. "You want me to tell her, Al, don't you?" I huff a breath. "Coward."

He chuckles. "Damn straight. Arnette's as unpredictable as a lightning storm."

"You did not just say that."

He looks abashed. But it's not that. It's ironic how in tune Al and I are, me having likened my sister to the very same thing. But I'm also in tune with my sister, and I know exactly how she's going to react.

IT'S NOT PRETTY. ARNETTE'S stomping and subsequent cold shoulder are reminders that she's still a teenager, one who is bound to begin her senior year in a matter of days. She was going back to school no matter what, but now it's the returning to perform next season that's not seeming likely.

The day after I arrive at the ranch, I take a rather surly Arnette to the train station. "Go home, give Ma a kiss, and graduate cum laude. Forget about all this riding nonsense."

"It's not nonsense."

No, it's not. "We've each got our thing. I'll be front row and center once you find yours."

She's mollified—enough, at least, to give me a hug when the train's horn sounds for departure.

I watch her embark, then stand there. It's not until the train pulls out of sight that I heave in a long sigh of relief, simultaneously devastated to know my sister isn't coming back but relieved to know she'll be safe and sound back home.

There's a touch on my lower back. "You okay?"

"I will be," I say to Al.

A hand on either shoulder, he turns me to face him before his arms trail down my arms to find my hands. Immediately I want him to do it again and again, the feel of him on my skin like a drug.

His Adam's apple bobs.

"Are *you* okay?" I ask him. In the past, I've successfully restrained myself from crossing any boundaries and touching him. But my emotions are already too strained to hold back. I run a finger along his jawline. Today it tells me he's nervous but expectant.

"Yes, I'm more than okay. I feel more confident this time."

I cock my head. "What's that mean?"

He takes my hands again, holding both between us. "I've got a present for you."

"I'm listening."

"But there are parameters for said present."

"What kind of parameters?"

"The kind that require you to say yes first."

"To . . ."

"To marry me. It's a wedding gift."

"Oh."

Chapter 32

AL DIPS HIS KNEES to my level, us eye to eye. "I'm having a hard time reading that 'oh,' Sonora."

For good reason. I'm not sure what the tone of it means either. But I do know . . . "We've been down this road before, Al."

"But things can change."

"That's exactly it. I'm afraid, okay? Change scares me. Let's say we get married. After the bloom of the honeymoon wears off, you could become indifferent—"

"I could never—"

I press a finger over his lips. "Indifference is an emotion so pale that hatred may actually be preferable. And maybe that's where it ends up. But in either case, we'll no longer flirt and laugh. We won't be us. Then you'll grow tired of it all and you'll leave. You'll take the act with you, leaving me with nothing."

"Sonora, that's not going to happen."

"But how do you know that?"

"For one," he says with a sly smile, "you keep me on my

toes, like you're doing right now. Second, I am not your father. I'm not going anywhere. Third, because I'll keep coming up with reasons until you believe me, though this one might be the most important of them all: It's a leap of faith. A gut feeling. Think about Red. That farmer told us he's the devil. No one could ride him. Couldn't use him with a plow." He waves a hand. "You know the story. But I had that gut feeling about him. What if Red was a case of the right horse being in the right hands? What if that is what made all the difference?"

It reminds me of something his daddy said up at Glacier Point. "*Josephine was the part of my life I never knew I needed.*"

That has more credence than Red. I remind Al, "What about Red pulling those nosedives on me?"

"Hey, I never said there weren't going to be obstacles."

There's that sly smile again. A smirk I'd like to see until the end of my days. I've done this silly push and pull with Al for ages now. But maybe, just maybe he has a point. I run a hand down his chest, feeling him quiver beneath my touch. "So you're saying that you think I may not fit into marriage with anyone but you, is that it?"

"That's exactly it."

"Okay," I say.

"'Okay' as in you'll marry me?"

"You'll never leave me?"

"Never."

"Or grow tired of me?"

He laughs softly. "Not possible."

My heartbeat may as well be vibrating my entire body. An

electric current I've never felt before. And I know if I am truly going to marry, it's to Al. It's got to be Al who makes me his wife. But of course, I can't make it too easy on him, so I tease, "I mean, if you're going to twist my arm. However, that gift you first spoke of could certainly help in my decision-making." I follow my question with a cheeky smile, both of us knowing the gift doesn't mean a dang thing. I still want it, don't get me wrong. But it has no factor in me wanting to continue my life with Al in it. I'm ready to grow with him, to lose some illusions in order to acquire others.

"You've got to say yes first; then I'll tell you what the gift is."

"Yes, Allen Robert Carver, I'll marry you."

I'm off my feet so quickly I hardly know Al's got me in his arms, swinging me in a circle, a squeal leaving my lips—until his mouth finds mine. Our first successful kiss, and it's better than I've imagined. Slow yet hungry. Tender yet passionate. My feet touch the ground, the kiss continuing, and I lean into him, into my future husband. Goodness gracious, I didn't think those would be thoughts I'd ever be having. But he broke me in the best way, the way a good trainer earns the trust of a horse. Here I am, a woman in the right hands.

I'M ALL BUT BURSTING at the seams to get back to the ranch to tell Lorena. It's a bit of a kick in the pants that my sister left literally minutes ago. But I'll write to her and, of course, to Ma about the news.

I'm getting married.

Ma may keel over from shock.

Al doesn't let go of my hand from the station to the truck, the truck to the ranch, the ranch to the farmhouse, Al and me tumbling into the house, smiles for days.

"Everyone," Al calls out. He pulls me along, poking his head into the parlor. Georgie and Freddie are having at it with a game of cards. "She said yes!"

The boys talk over each other, but the gist is excitement from them both. Lorena comes running into the room, flour covering her from head to toe. "She said yes?"

"Yes, she did!" I say.

"Finally! Thank the good Lord," Lorena says, a hand over her chest, leaving behind a white print. Then she bum-rushes me, pulling me in for a hug, no doubt covering me with just as much flour.

I scrunch my brow. "You're baking?"

"Can't have a wedding celebration tomorrow without a cake, now, can we?"

Once free from her hug, I give Al the side-eye, good-naturedly of course, and softly elbow him in that knowing gut of his. "Someone truly was confident this time, wasn't he? Tomorrow?"

"I was optimistic."

Lorena sighs, a happy one. "My daddy was right, you know. He told me that he knew Sonora was going to be a Carver the minute he laid eyes on her."

I admit, "He told me something similar."

Al shakes his head. "Even from the grave that man is still getting his way?" But then he does something unexpected: he wipes his eyes. "He gave me Ma's ring. He did it before he died. I like knowing it was meant for Sonora all along."

I like that too.

MY WEDDING DAY IS no fuss. It's what I ask for. I wear my brown chiffon dress, brown suede shoes, and brown felt hat.

It's the nicest I've looked in ages, yet I may have to pinch myself to remind myself this is actually happening. I'm to be Mrs. Allen Carver.

We all pile into the truck, ending up at a justice of the peace. In what feels like a hazy whirlwind of a dream, the lay judge says all he needs to say, Al and I say all the right things back, my ring goes on, and then we kiss. My chosen family cheers.

And that's that.

Married.

I can hardly believe it, feeling more disoriented than I do in a diving pool full of bubbles.

There's cake. Merriment. We take a photo to send to Georgia. Ma will be sad she missed it but will be tickled pink I made it down the aisle.

I admire the ring on my finger. It's simple. A gold band and a tiny gemstone. Cushion cut, Lorena tells me. The sight of it warms my heart, knowing Al's mama wore it to show her commitment to another Carver man.

I steal a moment alone with mine. "I can't say I've ever imagined this day, but if I had, this is what it'd be."

The farm. The phonograph playing "I Wanna Be Loved

by You." Cake. There should always be cake. Maybe even a midnight dip for two in the pond.

"Though," I say, "I still think you promised me a little something for marrying you."

Al waggles his brows. "That I did, Mrs. Carver. Right this way. I'll show you."

Chapter 33

ONE WOULD THINK THAT on my wedding day, Al would pull me toward his bedroom, both of us giddy at what awaits us there.

It turns out his office is our destination.

I perch myself on his desk, one leg crossed over the other, a pose I saw in *Modern Woman* magazine. "Am I in trouble?"

"Would you like to be?"

I give him a suggestive look that ends in a passionate kiss. My bottom lip is the last for Al to let go of before he pulls back. "Or would you rather see your wedding gift?"

I'm all business now. "Gift, please."

Amused, Al chuckles. From his desk drawer he retrieves a small stack of papers. I've seen this type of document plenty of times before. "A contract?"

"Not just any contract. It's for the Steel Pier in Atlantic City."

"Ooh la la," I say. "I've never been."

"Not only that. We'll be there the *whole* of the season, Sonora. No tearing down and building back up. We can rent a little place right off the boardwalk and soak up an entire summer at the shore. It'll be a different kind of adventure, but an adventure nevertheless."

It's what Doc had hoped to do at Lick's Pier in California, to spare the horses—and us—the stress of moving from one fairground to another.

"Lorena too?" I ask.

He nods. "The money we'll save on staying in one place means we won't need to send out two troupes. She'll help run things. You'll dive on Red and John. Snow will be with us, as needed. Georgie will be with us. Freddie if he wants to stay on."

I smile. It sounds grand. "Thank you, Al."

He runs a finger down my forehead, smoothing the worry lines that've taken up residence there so readily over the past few months. "Anything to make you smile like that. And now that you've gotten your wedding gift, next stop . . ."

"Atlantic City," I answer.

"I was thinking more along the lines of upstairs, Mrs. Carver."

"Ooh la la."

TRANSFORMED.

That's what people are saying has happened to the Atlantic City boardwalk.

"The ballroom still stands, but this is where there used to be nothing but a large deck running around it," Al says.

"Here on the pier?" I ask.

"That's right."

Now in the place of the deck is a grandstand large enough to seat eight thousand spectators. It's no Michigan Stadium, which made headlines the other year boasting how it's the largest in the United States, sitting over seventy thousand rear ends. But eight thousand is a lot, especially with all that attention on me three times a day on a weekday and four performances on the weekends. That's over three hundred sixty thousand eyeballs gawking at me. I'd say that's a lot more than those football players are getting once a week. Doc would be proud of what Al's building.

"What do you think, Sonora?"

"I think the grandstand has certainly earned the *grand* of its name. What's next?"

I'm a kid in a candy shop. There's one of those down the street too, along with souvenir shops, tattoo parlors, pizza restaurants and carnival food stands, and stores with clothing and accessories. I already have my eye on a bedazzled clip for my hair.

Al goes on, "The stage is still being built, as you can see. When it's finished, it'll extend twenty-five feet overtop the water, and we'll get to it via a little bridge. The ramp for the tower will begin at the back of the stage. That way spectators will have a broadside view of it. They'll like that."

"And the tank?" I ask, pointing to a huge circle cut into a portion of the stage that's already been built.

"Yep, exactly there. Completely separate from the ocean."

What goes unspoken—because of bad memories—is that

there's no way in hell our horses will dive into the open water. The manager of the pier, Mr. Endicott, suggested it. Al put his foot down, his fist down, everything down. Sure, it's costing the Steel Pier more money to build it our way into the pier, but Al was willing to take a smaller cut in order to keep our horses safe.

"A hundred or so pilings will support the tank," he says. "It's all quite the undertaking. Which leads to something I want to talk to you about. In order to make this all work, we have to raise the height of the diving platform from forty to forty-five feet."

I shrug. "Shouldn't be a problem."

"Ideally not. But it's five extra feet for Red to start to turn."

"We'll be just fine." I kiss Al on the cheek, then twirl in a full circle, the warm sun and humid air hitting my face, to fully take in my home for the foreseeable future.

It'll be different from anything I've ever experienced. This isn't our typical fairground but a full-blown amusement park on a beach.

Opening day is drawing closer. Beyond the crashing waves, acrobats practice on water skis. There's a man—at this very moment—shoving himself into a cannon to be shot off into the water. Clowns are wandering about, two aerialists swing from a rigging that has to be over a hundred feet in the air, bands are practicing their sets, various rides are being built and tested, and carnival games are getting their final touches.

It's a feast for the eyes with so much commotion. For the nose too. Vendors are beginning to bag up popcorn and cotton candy. And I swear the scent of funnel cake is pumped into the air. Snow is so food-driven, I wouldn't be surprised if she starts chomping at nothing.

"Last but not least," Al says, "I'd like to show you your new dressing room."

"Yes, please."

On the way, my sights catch on a souvenir shop, and my jaw falls open. "Al."

"What?" He's distracted, his focus on the signage going up on our tower.

Steel Pier High Diving Horses, it says.

And while, yes, the signage is neat to see, I say Al's name again, because what I'm looking at leaves me with all the feelings.

"Yeah," he says, his gaze still not where I want it.

I paw at him, my hand falling short, unwilling to take my eye off a stack of postcards. "It's me. Red. It's our show."

I've been in newspapers and flyers, but never before on a postcard that advertises not only our show but the entire pier. That advertises *me*—in midair on Red's back. Who'd have thought I'd end up here?

Dear Arnette,

I've put off sending you this postcard for almost the entire summer because it feels cruel of me when you're back in Georgia. I've actually had it in my possession since before opening day. Is it horrible of me that I'm too proud of being featured in this way not to send it to you? I hope you'll be excited for me too. I do wish you were here and that things would have worked out differently with John. Did you get the hair clips I sent home for you and Jac? I've a matching one. Ma wrote me to say you've begun beauty school. Considering everyone has always called you the beauty in the family, I see that as exceptionally fitting. I hope you are loving every moment of it. I thought maybe the clip could come in handy for that. Write me soon. You've been stingy, and I fear it's because you're still upset you're missing this season. Al told me we're going to winter in a new location this year, a farm only a short drive away in Bucks County, Pennsylvania, but we'll be returning to Atlantic City for a second season. Maybe you'd like to come see a show then?

With love and cookies,

Sonora

Dear Sonora,

I'll admit I have been stingy and withheld letters since the summer. But that is behind me. So is beauty school. Mama wanted that for me. I did not want that for myself. I need to be where you are. I Know, I Know, Al and Lorena won't let me back on a horse. But there has to be something else for me to do on the Steel Pier. I intend to join you for your next season to figure out what exactly that is.

In fact, by the time you are receiving this letter, I shall be on my way to your place in Atlantic City. Maybe I'll even beat the mailman.

Your sister,
Arnette

Chapter 34

I BLINK LONG AND HARD. *Arnette.* What am I going to do with her?

The wall of my dressing room is inches away, which makes sense with the room itself being only six by six. I knock on it.

"Yeah?" Al calls back from his side. His office is larger, and because of the slightly increased size, his space has become more of a catch-all. It's where I keep my wardrobe trunks and where I hang my wet bathing suits. There's also a couch and a rocking chair in there.

I stand from my dressing table and, grabbing my keys from the key basket that Ma got me as a wedding gift, walk the few feet to his desk.

Al's posture isn't great. He's hunched. His shoulders are tense. He's poring over documents I can't quite make out. "What ya got there?"

"Presales for season passes. Projections. A bunch of numbers that no matter how I look at them aren't as good as we want them to be." He shakes his head. "That damned stock market crash. It's been over seven months since it happened. I was naive to think the country would be on the upswing by now."

I slink into the rocking chair. "Things have got to recover at some point, right?"

People are calling the day the stock market crashed Black Tuesday. It happened only a few weeks after we wrapped on our first season at the Steel Pier. We weren't sure there'd even be a second season. But here we are, enough people willing to scrape together their pennies to have a good time, most likely a distraction from all the other stuff going on.

"I don't know, Sonora. All I know is we can't have anything else go wrong this season or we'll be sunk."

I cringe. "Maybe it's not a good time to mention this . . ."

Al looks up from his projections. "Might as well spit it out."

"I have to run over to our place really quick."

"Why's that? I wanted to show you the improved stalls we've got in place for the horses."

We've fallen into a routine of marital bliss: Stopping into the office before heading out to the pier. Al will check on things. I'll swim in the tank or practice my dives. Then we'll lunch with a side of banter. The afternoon is for the horses—exercising them, brushing them. Then an early supper, a walk on the beach, a book for me while Al listens to the radio or reads the newspaper to survey the goings-on of the world.

As I say, bliss.

"The thing is . . ." I give myself a good rock in the chair. "I have to dash home because Arnette may be there."

"Arnette?"

"I got a letter from her today. She says she's coming."

"Here?"

"That's right."

"Please tell me it's only to watch a few shows."

"Something like that." I stand with the forward motion of the rocking chair and give Al a peck on the lips. "It's nothing to concern yourself with."

"I'm not sure I believe you, but I trust you've got whatever this is handled."

I smile winningly at him; then off I go.

THERE SHE IS, AS warned. Arnette's sitting on the porch of our small rental, head back, eyes closed, the sun illuminating her face and curled hair. Already, in a year's time, she appears older. I wouldn't go so far as to say wiser, but older, yes.

"Mama better know you're here."

She doesn't startle, doesn't open her eyes. She only says, "She does."

"And she didn't put up a stink about you coming?"

She opens only her left eye. "Oh, she did." Both eyes now. "But I'm over eighteen as of last month, so . . ."

"Have I ever told you that you're too much?" I close the distance to her, pulling her to a stand so I can give her a proper hug. "I've missed you."

"So you're glad I'm here?"

"I'm glad to see you. How about we start there?"

"I'd like to start with a tour so I can scour the opportunities. Unless, of course, you've had a change of heart and—"

"Nope."

"Had to try."

"I was thinking," I say, trying another tactic, one I already know will fall on deaf ears, but I owe it to Ma, and my own blood pressure, to try. "There are food stalls, and they're always in need of—"

"Sonora." Arnette pops her hands onto her hips. "You weren't much older than I am now when you joined the act. Why should you go after something that gives you life but not me?"

"I've already let you dive. *Much* younger than I was, I'd like to point out. I'd also like to remind you that it wasn't me who made the call that you were 'unorthodox,' or whatever Lorena called you."

Arnette frowns. But she's only deterred momentarily. "Aren't you the one who suggested I find my thing?"

I sigh.

She says, "Exactly. You know the ins and outs, the who's who. Won't you help me?"

"Fine, but only if you put that lip away," I say of her puppy-dog face. "Everything is down this way. Wait, where are your bags?"

"Already inside."

"But how . . . ?" I don't bother finishing my question of how she got inside. Arnette always seems to find a way.

Our rental is right off the boardwalk, the sand on one side, rows of shops with awnings on the other, with soaring hotels and larger buildings behind and above the storefronts.

"The feel of this place," Arnette says, pointing farther down to Steeplechase Pier where the Ferris wheel is the most spectacular of backdrops, "it's magnificent."

"Hardly anyone is here yet. Just wait until we're fully in season."

"I plan to do that very thing."

I laugh. Arnette's always been quick with that tongue of hers. But now it's coming out in a deeper tone. Still feminine. But the pitchy, youthful sound of her voice is long gone.

As we approach the Steel Pier section, it's livelier. At the ticket booth, which currently serves as a security booth, I wave to Butch and say, "She's with me."

He tips his hat.

"This is it," I say, proud as a peacock. "Last year the pier had a handful of acts. This year there are even more. It's a relief, honestly, with all that's going on in the country."

We're two weeks to opening day. Much like last year, the amount of commotion could make a head spin. In Arnette's case, it could make eyes light up. I don't want to crush her, but finding a gig in two weeks' time . . . and training for it . . .

Those prospects may be even lousier than the projections Al's grumbling about.

"Might as well start with the Globe of Death so we can get it out of the way that you will *not* be doing that." I point to a sixteen-foot caged globe.

Arnette raises a brow. "What goes on in there?"

"Oscar Babcock goes around and around on his motorcycle."

Now my sister presses her lips together. "You won't get any trouble from me. Passing on that one."

"Excellent decision. Anyway, his wife rides too, and three's a crowd. *But* there are a few clown acts."

"Pass."

"Sparky and Kelsey are quite popular. They do this waltz where—"

"Pass."

I laugh. "There are also animal acts."

"I'm listening."

"Mr. and Mrs. Pallenberg have bears. They're very nice."

"The bears?"

"I meant the Pallenbergs, but the bears haven't mauled anybody yet. They juggle, dance. Their grand finale is to row boats around in our tank. Who else do we have?" I scan the pier and the ocean. "We have the water sports gang who ride water skis, aquaplanes, and such. There's also the Hawaiians, five of them, who dive from a hundred-five-foot tower." I point, craning my neck back to see the top of the thin structure, little more than a ladder and platform. "Look, that's one now, all the way up top. Bet he has the best view of the whole island."

"Hmm, I wonder if those Hawaiians would like an even number."

I take her arm, turning her away, but my mistake: I aim her toward the rigging, where the aerialists are mid-act.

Roxie, with her auburn hair tossed back, has her teeth clamped tightly on a rubber bit. She flings her arms behind her body. Her leotard is platinum in color, making her look like a silver bird caught in flight. Her partner, Irene, is farther up the rigging on the same rope, frozen in an arabesque, her body tilted forward and her leg extended behind her in a graceful arc.

"*That*," Arnette says, nearly breathless. "That is what I want to do."

I'm the one to say it this time: "Pass."

Arnette's hands go together as if in prayer. "Come on."

"Come on, yourself. Roxie and Irene have been doing this for *years*."

Arnette chuckles. "Fine. Maybe an aerialist isn't for me. What about diving?"

Maybe, but a hundred five feet is awfully high. However, the water sports gang may be the ticket. They perform all sorts of tricks on and while being pulled behind aquabikes. "How about I talk to Mr. Amstead for you?"

"Truly?" Arnette's eyes are round, as if she expected me to give her the go-around before trying to send her home.

"This is important to you."

She throws her arms around me. "Thanks, Nora."

I hug her back, praying I'm not making a mistake and that Arnette's no longer *dangerously awkward*. One mishap or misstep as a performer is one too many.

Chapter 35

I SEND ARNETTE IN THE direction of the stalls to reunite with the horses, then go talk to Mr. Amstead.

He's agreeable, perhaps even more than I'd like him to be. It appears I'm once again caught between wanting to keep my little sister safe and wanting to see her happy.

But first, he says, he needs to see what she's got. We arrange a time for tomorrow to watch her swim and dive.

"Arnette!" I call, hurrying toward her at the horse stalls. The horse lodgings are new and improved this year. They're located on the way to the grandstand, and last season people would pass by and feed them, tease them. Drove Georgie crazy and Al mad. So we've fashioned a glass wall, allowing people to gawk all they want at our beautiful horses without any harm coming to them.

Arnette's petting John while chatting with Georgie. He's got that googly-eyed look going on again for her. Though, poor Georgie, it's not him she's bouncing on her toes for. It's me. "What did Mr. Amstead say?"

"I had to all but promise the man my firstborn child, but—"

"You and Al want children?"

The question is so far outside the realm of anything I've considered that it almost doesn't make sense in my brain.

Arnette laughs. "It looks like your head is about to explode."

"Yeah. Children, no. Diving for two isn't exactly in my plans." I shake away the thought. "But anyway, Mr. Amstead says he'll see what you can do at nine o'clock sharp tomorrow."

And at exactly nine o'clock sharp the next day, Arnette dazzles. Mr. Amstead is already nodding before she finishes doing the list of dives I'd seen when I peeped at his clipboard.

When she finishes, I tell her, "Guess you best write Mama to let her know you're staying."

That gets a squeal.

The next day we're both full steam ahead to ready for opening day. In a blink, it feels like it's here. The crowds certainly show up for the occasion. And continue to show up, day after day and night after night. Al's thrilled, after worrying about presales for so long. From a window in his office that I can only see out of on my tippy-toes, I notice quite a few sleepy-eyed children, sticky with cotton candy, who are determined not to miss tonight's show.

It never ceases to amaze me, even though I've been doing this for years now, how anticipation courses through me. I calm myself by sitting at my dressing table, running Mamie Lou's brush through my hair. It's got a helluva lot more volume from the sea salt air, a wave I've never had before. Al says it suits me.

I put on my bathing suit and drape my shawl over my shoulders. In the mirror, I meticulously apply makeup that'll be washed away once Red and I hit the water. Then I wait, listening to the faint sound of the boardwalk's music. Roxie and Irene are on now, "Springtime in the Rockies" playing. And if I know the timing of the song and their routine correctly, which I do, they're about to hit the climax of their performance. The crowd loves this part, when they use something called perch poles.

My act's the finale of the pier's first show of the night. We'll do two.

I leave my dressing room, following a long hall that pops me out near our stage and a tall wall that screens off-duty performers from the eyes of the audience. The other performers and I joke that it's our equivalent of Broadway's greenrooms, and where we take sunbaths, read, practice skills, gossip, gamble, and play poker and craps. Basically, all the things to keep us busy and entertained in between acts. It's been nice getting to know the other performers, something that wasn't possible in the past when we'd be in one location for only a week or so.

Along the way to the tower, I pass Jacob, who drives the boat that pulls the water-skiers. He wishes me luck. "Knock 'em dead," says Sparky, who is still dressed in the rear end of a horse costume. There's a bark, which I know to be from Claribel. Lorena's little fluff ball has taken a liking to Red. Which means Georgie is leading Red from the stalls up to the ramp. Claribel always gets herself all riled up when Red is on the move.

"The Stars and Stripes Forever" begins playing.

"Ah, Roxie and Irene must be swinging down," Arnette says, suddenly beside me.

A burst of applause follows.

"That's my cue," I say to my sister, not that she can hear me over the roar of the spectators. I step from behind the wall and toward the tower's ladder. As always, I time my ascent, arriving exactly as Al says, "Ladies and gentlemen, cast your eyes atop this lofty tower. We present for your entertainment the most exciting act in show business today—Miss Sonora and Red Lips, the famous diving horse."

From the lights of the buildings, the tower, the stringed lights here and there, and the glare of the Ferris wheel off the water, I can barely see. But it's muscle memory at this point. I step forward, raising my hand, the crowd welcoming me with the loudest of cheers.

I wave.

I get to do this, I think. *I get to do this every day and night.*

With the audience still thundering in anticipation, I seat myself on the railing and signal to Georgie to send up Red.

Off he goes.

The heavy drumming of his hooves is lost to the noise of the grandstand, but every bone in my body rattles as Red nears. Then here he is. In a single motion, I grab the harness and slide across his back until I'm in place.

Red's begun doing this thing where he stops at the tower's end and prances. It's the best word I have for it, like he wants a few moments of his own to show off what he can do. First he lifts one foot, then the other. Back and forth he goes, until the crowd's anticipation is at its height. Then he slides both feet over the edge of the platform.

Together we dive.

I feel it immediately. Not the weightlessness I've come to enjoy, but the panic-inducing rush of heat up my neck, knowing he's turning toward a nosedive—but more straight down than he's ever done before. I've split seconds to react; split seconds to decide what to do with my body. Usually when Red nose-dives, I duck my head to avoid the impact of the water.

This time . . .

This time he's too perpendicular, and I'm afraid any shift of my body forward will throw his weight too far. He'll turn onto his back and land on me. I could hurt him, hurt myself, hurt the act.

I decide. I stiffen my arms and hold my weight back in an attempt to stabilize our balance, exposing my upper half to the water. Instead of hitting the water at the crown of my head, where my helmet absorbs the impact, the wall of water breaks against my exposed face and eyes, which I didn't close in time.

The sting is instant. A dull aching sensation follows.

I struggle to stay on Red, but I refuse to lose contact with him or to let on to the crowd that anything went amiss.

Only seconds later, we emerge from the water. If someone told me I was underwater for minutes, my boggled brain would believe them.

Still, the act isn't done. I ride Red out of the tank, hopping down as I usually do to retrieve his sugar cube. I'm off-balance, woozy, as the crowd continues to go crazy.

I wave. I smile. I bow. I blink, the sights of the boardwalk now similar to a kaleidoscope. Al speaks into my ear, asking if I'm okay.

I nod. I will be, I assure him. I have to be.

Chapter 36

I HAVE A SECOND SHOW later this evening.

Before Al can ask me any more questions, I make for the dressing room. I grab a dry suit off the hook in Al's office, enter mine, and close the door.

Two hands on my dressing table, I lean forward, staring at myself in the mirror, water dripping onto the wood flooring.

It feels as if I'm peering through and around clouds, patchy bits of white fog floating before my eyes. Honestly, with the smack to the face I took, this doesn't come as a surprise. In time, it'll fade.

I change into my dry bathing suit, telling myself that my vision is clearing.

Al's coming into my dressing room as I'm leaving. "Are you sure you're all right?"

I smile. "Yes, of course. I hit the water weird, that's all. Things are just a little blurry, but it'll pass. It's already passing."

"Sonora—"

"I'm fine."

"I'd rather a doctor tell us that."

"A doctor will only tell me to rest. It's what the lot of them always say. We have another show tonight. Four shows tomorrow. I'm not about to do nothing, Al." I cup his face and run my thumb along his jawline. "I'm all right, and it can't be serious. It doesn't hurt at all." I realize it's the truth. I'd said it to convince him. But it's true, zero pain. "Fit as a fiddle. Now," I say, listening to the music outside, "I want to go see Red and let him know there're no hard feelings before we're set to go again."

Al kisses my forehead, my cheek, my lips. "If you're sure."

"I am."

And I dive again that night. I dive the next day too. What I don't do is tell Al that the cloudiness is still hanging around. That is, until I blink or rub, and it suddenly vanishes. Poof. I'm relieved, until something else peculiar happens. On occasion, it's as if a yellow lens slips over my eyes. When I flick my gaze up, however, it goes away. I can't find any rhyme or reason to it. All I know is it doesn't get in the way of my diving. That's what's important, especially when I look out Al's office window and spot someone in the growing crowd I wouldn't wish upon my worst enemy.

"What's he doing here?" I growl. I had hoped his feud had died with Doc. But no, there he is, vendetta written all over his face.

"Who?" Al says from his desk.

"The thorn in our side."

Al looks up. "Please tell me you're joking."

"I wish. He looks all smug, like he's hunting for trouble."

Al slaps down his pen. "Well, he's not going to find any. But I can see him wanting our horses more than ever with the state of the world. Speaking of the state of things, how are you feeling today?"

I turn from the window, taking a seat that's quickly become my favorite: Al's lap. "You ask me that every day."

"And?"

"And my eyes are *still* fine."

That's my answer any way you cut it with Harold Grover, as he continues to sniff around, coming to one performance after another over the next few days. And it stays my answer even after John, too, does a rare dive onto his nose. What are the chances? I duck into his neck to block the blow of the water, but my head still takes the impact.

I come out of the water smiling, ignoring the panic-inducing spots that dance before my eyes, as John carries me up the incline to the stage. Al puts extra gusto into his closing, praising John for bravely diving on nothing but his own volition.

All for you, Harold, I think.

I slip off the stage, wobbling off-balance both mentally and physically, and head toward my dressing room before Al can catch up with me. There I change into a dry bathing suit, and I'm whirling my shawl around my shoulders like a cape when, suddenly, it's more than a few spots getting in the way of what I'm seeing. It feels like I've been transported from day to dusk.

I rub my eyes.

The ruddiness remains.

I flick my gaze up. I blink. I rub again. All have been proven methods to reset my eyes over the past few days.

But not today.

I grip the back of my dressing table chair. Fear seizes me; the darkness is not lifting. Before, my injury had been a nuisance. A pain-free one, at that. And while I still don't feel any stinging or anything similar, my waning eyesight has advanced from being an annoyance to a potential hindrance.

I need air.

I push out of the dressing room, down the hall, into the "greenroom" backstage, and all but run into someone.

"Are you okay, Miss Sonora?" Georgie asks.

"Georgie. Yes, of course, I'm fine."

"Can I help you with something? John is all dried and ready to go."

"Wonderful, wonderful." I pause, wanting Georgie to be anywhere but in front of me with worry in his voice. "Actually, could I trouble you for some water? Just leave it by the ladder before I go on."

He dutifully scurries away, and I slump into a chair among the other performers. I scan, not seeing the familiarness of Arnette nor hearing the sound of her. It's disappointing; I could use a little of her frankness right now. She'd likely tell me to get back on the horse, literally, then take it from there.

I fill my lungs with air, an attempt to calm myself. *I'm okay. I'll be fine. It'll go away.*

"Sonora!"

I curse in Spanish, a little something I've picked up from Lorena.

Georgie did not in fact fetch me water. He delivered my husband, who kneels in front of me. "What's wrong?"

"Shhh." I stand, nearly knocking him onto his rear end, and disappear back inside. Al is on my heels. "You'll pull the wrong type of attention."

"Why? Sonora? What's happened? Have your eyes gotten

worse? I saw your dive with John, but you seemed to duck just fine."

I've the instinct to rub my eyes. Instead, I redirect to my neck, massaging there. "I asked for water, Al. Last I heard, that's not a reason to sound the alarms."

He shakes his head. "I don't think it's that."

"Well, you know what I know? I know we have a dive in a matter of minutes. And I also know that Harold Grover is still in the crowd out there, waiting for any excuse to take our horses from us."

I actually do not know for a fact that Harold's out there, but when Al closes his eyes, he verifies my assumption that the weasel of a man hasn't let us be. I wonder if Al knows about his daddy's quarrel with him, accusing Harold of abusing his position with the SPCA all because of a dispute over his mother decades ago, or if Al thinks it's all about the horses. "You don't need to perform again tonight. Lorena can do it. Or Arnette."

Al's already said before that he's not willing to put the woman he loves at risk for some stupid show. His words, not mine. The thing is, I'm not willing to put the show at risk. So I say, "No. Lorena's knee wouldn't hold up, and if my sister was too unsafe to dive for us before, then nothing has changed. There's no one to ride but me, and I happen to be more than capable of doing my job."

"Listen, Sonora, I'm not talking to you as a show runner. I'm talking to you as your husband and—"

"Funny, because I'm talking to you as nothing more than one of your performers, and I'm telling you I am fit to ride."

"The Stars and Stripes Forever" begins playing.

I cross my arms. "We've got to get out there, boss."

The *boss* bit may've been too much. Al's nostrils flare. But he steps aside, turning his body, allowing me to pass.

JOHN HAS ROAN MARKINGS, a gray coloring that makes it hard to distinguish him from the other shaded colors I now see as he barrels toward me on the tower. But we do it; we dive. It may be one of the best performances we've pulled off together.

Arm raised, waving to the appraising crowd, I recognize a certain man elbowing his way from the grandstand. Good riddance. He's gone.

But at what cost?

My vision remains cloudy.

When Al tries to talk to me after the show, I refuse to have any discussion. I want to sleep, that's all. I'll go to bed. My eyes will get a breather along with the rest of me. I'll wake tomorrow a new woman.

It was a soothing scenario, if only it would've played out that way.

While sunshine does stream into my bedroom in the morning, penetrating the muted curtain over my eyes and making it seem less damning, the grayness sticks around.

I sit in my nightgown for some time. I'm not certain how long. I don't necessarily think. I exist. Frankly, I'm surprised Al hasn't come poking. When I pad out to the kitchen, I see why. He's left a note to say he wanted to let me sleep and that he's gone to talk with the pier's manager, Mr. Endicott.

Good.

But also disappointing. Normally I would've gone into the office with him, then to the pier. The disturbance in my routine, the utter disruption that my eyes are causing, is maddening.

Through the blurriness, I pick up a second note, this one from Arnette. She's gone to have breakfast with Jacob from the Flying Hawaiians.

Someone else who is carrying on with her life.

I hadn't known Jacob was in the picture.

Curious, I make a mental note to have a talk with her about him later. More and more, little by little, she's been morphing from sibling to an earnest friend, the only person I've been honest with about my fears.

"My eyes aren't clearing up," I whispered to her last night.

"Can you see at all?"

"Enough, I guess."

"We'll take *enough* for now. And we'll figure out the rest as it comes."

I remember her words, shuddering a breath. I'm not set to ride until later this morning after Lorena warms up the crowd with her solo dives, but there's a fat chance I'm going to sit here by my lonesome and let thoughts plunder my resolve.

I throw on a dress and begin the four-block walk to the Steel Pier. My stomach instantly drops, the sunlight now disarming, making it even harder to see. I palm the brick wall of a building, trying to gain my bearings. I squint, enough to help me make my way backstage, where I promptly run into Al.

"I was just coming to see you," he says. His voice, flat in tone, is abnormally hard to read. "I have news for you."

"Good news, I hope."

"Depends on who you ask."

I cock my head, almost too distracted by the fact his facial features are largely lost to me to fully register his words. "Okay," I say, a suitable answer for most anything.

"Mel is on her way."

It takes me a moment. "Melanie? From a few years back?"

"The very one."

"I'm confused."

Al takes my arm and leads me to a quieter portion of the pier. He lowers his voice. "I know you'd want me to be honest with you. The thing is, Mr. Endicott caught wind of your eye troubles."

"How on earth—?"

"It doesn't matter."

"Was it you?"

Al's mouth falls open—that much I can make out from the movement of his face. "No, Sonora. But he knows. He threatened to cancel the act, so I telephoned Vivian. Pleaded with her, actually. But she wouldn't come back. Figured there was one other person I could try."

"Who?"

"Mel."

"Why her?"

"Besides your sister, she's the last one who's tried to ride for us, and I guess Mel's hurting for a payday, because she jumped at the chance."

"And what? Now she's suddenly brave enough to ride? I can't believe I'm saying this, but wouldn't Arnette be better? Melanie trained for all of three days *years* ago."

"Mr. Endicott says Mr. Amstead can't spare Arnette. The crowd's taken to her in their show."

Of course they have. I blow out a breath. "So today's shows?"

"They're off. Mel won't arrive until tomorrow."

"No." I pace three steps to the right, to the left, then back to Al. "That won't do. I'll do it, Al. I *can* do it. I don't know why you men possess the need to make me feel deficient just because of a little eye trouble. It's Sunday, as you very well know. It's one of our busiest days of the week. And those people *expect* to see a rider on a diving horse. They've paid their hard-earned money, in fact, to see *me* perform. I'm not going to disappoint them. I'm riding today, Al, and there's nothing you or anyone can say to convince me otherwise. John during the day. Red at night." Their unique colorings would make them easier for me to see during those times of the day. "Got it?"

"Do I even have a voice in this?"

"No," I say. "Now, I'll see you at the tower."

"What about a compromise?"

I huff. "I'm not a monster—what is it?"

"You dive today, but tomorrow you'll let a doctor give you a once-over?"

"If it'll make you feel better."

"It will."

I begin to leave, then stop. I come back to him. I press my lips to his. Then I ready myself to perform.

Chapter 37

AL COMES WITH ME to the doctor appointment. He really shouldn't. He should be supervising Melanie on her first day of shows. Lorena is doing the announcing and show running in his place.

But it's probably best I'm here and not there. I can't stand to watch Melanie doing my job. Not that I'd be able to see her all that well.

I knead my hands together. I've never had a poor experience personally with a doctor, but the profession in general makes me uneasy.

Al too. His knee is jiggling a mile a minute beside me as we wait in the aptly named waiting room. "He's the best eye specialist in the state. This clinic is used solely for eye cases. You'll be in good hands," he comments.

"Are you saying that for my assurance or your own?"

He squeezes my hand. "Can't it be both?"

This man. I nod just as a nurse enters the room. She calls my name, and we follow her deeper into the office. "First time in Philadelphia?" she asks, making small talk.

"Yes, ma'am," Al says. "Unfortunately, a quick trip."

"Well, the doctor is right this way."

The room is white on white, much as I expected. The doctor, too, wears white. Though, to me, it all appears an ugly shade of blurred gray.

"Mrs. Carver, I've a seat for you here." He taps it demonstratively. "Then I'll have a look"—he takes a piece of equipment from a table—"at your eyes."

I let the doctor do his thing, even though I'd rather not. Not knowing the prognosis means I can continue on, telling myself the blurriness, the grayness, the cloudiness will right itself and go away. But I've come all this way—at Al's insistence and our compromise—so I follow the doctor's commands and look up, down, left, right. He shines a light directly at my pupils. He asks me questions about how the injury occurred. Al chimes in from his point of view. Hearing the tremble in my husband's voice is hard, how he says watching the dive, not sure if Red and I would flip or land on our faces, almost brought him to his knees.

The doctor takes a step back, having completed his examination. "Mr. Carver, why don't you have a seat as well."

Al hesitates, and I know him. He's putting off the inevitable as I've been doing.

"It appears to me," the doctor begins in a solemn voice, "that the impact of the water has broken tiny blood vessels in Mrs. Carver's eyes. Both of them. Furthermore, it is my belief that the continued physical exertion of each ride thereafter has increased this internal hemorrhage to the point where more blood than the body can comfortably absorb has accumulated. This unabsorbed blood has clotted, and Mrs. Carver's retinas have begun to detach."

His words are numbing. And confusing. "What does that mean? My retinas have detached?"

"You see, there are three layers in the eye—the sclera, the choroid, and the retina. Each lies atop the next. Each with a different function. The sclera, the white of our eyes, is largely for shape. The choroid is a thin layer of tissue that serves various functions, such as absorbing excess light or allowing for adjustment in the position of the retina. The retina itself is what converts light into visual images that we then send to the brain. In your case, Mrs. Carver, the blood clot has slipped between the choroid and the retina, which has worked the retina loose. Think of wallpaper. If moisture gets between the paper and the wall, the glue will fail and the wallpaper will detach, yes?"

I nod. "I believe I've followed. So what can we do? Add more so-called glue?"

His voice is kind as he says, "In a way. Please know I will do everything within my power to restore the sight in your right eye. I'm afraid your left eye is utterly hopeless. Your right eye is only partially detached, but your left eye has been completely smashed."

Al's been silent. He now asks, "Spell it out for us, Doc. What's the worst-case scenario here?"

"I'll perform surgery. The worst-case scenario afterward is that your wife will eventually become fully blind."

No.

I think it, Al verbalizes it. Then he swallows roughly, audibly. "And the best case?"

The doctor clears his throat. "That Mrs. Carver will be only partially blind."

Chapter 38

I'VE BEEN IN SHOCK before.

Two such examples: when Ma told me Ula was never coming back and after the auto crash with Lorena. I'm having the same symptoms in this very moment: a cold sensation, clammy skin, labored breathing, and lightheadedness. And all because of the doctor's prognosis. Al hasn't said a word since Dr. Morganson left the examination room. All he does is palm my leg and rub his thumb soothingly over my knee.

Either partially blind or fully blind?

I'm at a loss as to how those two are the only possible outcomes.

I'm off-kilter. Usually Al would be telling me that everything is going to be okay. But he's not, and it's not okay that the pit in my stomach is so heavy I could sink straight through the floor.

Tears are about to replace the disbelief I feel when a nurse comes in. "Have you decided?"

That's right, a decision. After the prognosis, Al said something about getting a second opinion. The doctor said something about how time was of the essence if I wanted a chance of retaining any of my eyesight.

I do. I do very badly.

I stand, telling the nurse, "I'll do the surgery."

Al's head whips toward me. "Sonora, we can talk about—"

"Talking won't fix my retina."

He sucks on his cheeks, fighting back emotion. Then he concedes, "Okay, when would we get started?"

Right away. I'm led to a patient room. There's not much to it. A bed, really. I'm given a gown to change into that remains open at the back.

I tap one set of fingers against the bed, nervous for the doctor to return, for this process to begin, while my other hand holds my gown closed.

The nurse, Mrs. Davis, removes the pillows from the bed, placing them on a visitor chair. "Mrs. Carver, please make yourself comfortable. Dr. Morganson will check your progress daily. He's hopeful to operate in three to five days' time."

"What?" I say. "He's not going to operate immediately?"

The man himself enters at that moment. "That is correct, Mrs. Carver. I'd like to better appraise the extent of damage before attempting to operate, and in order for me to do my best calculations, I'd like to allow for the fluids and blood clot in your eyes to be absorbed as much as possible. For this, you're to remain perfectly still on bed rest."

Bed rest, two words that strike literal fear into me, the child who had to be locked in her backyard lest she run off, the girl with wanderlust and adventure in her blood, the adult who plunges forty-five feet into a tank of water on the back of a horse. This is who I am. Not someone who remains static, unmoving.

Emotion wells in my throat because I also understand that if I want to continue to be this adult, I need to do as the doctor orders.

A sniffle accompanies my nod. I lift one leg, then the other onto the bed. I shimmy backward until I can lie flat.

I cannot look at Al. It'll break my heart to see his heart breaking for me. Mrs. Davis hands me a mask to cover my eyes. I accept it; what choice do I have otherwise?

I LIE ON MY back in the blackness. The doctor is gone. The nurse leaves. It's only Al and me, his presence heavy in the room.

He asks, "Will you be okay if I go get some of your things to liven up the room?"

I press my palms into the bed, as if to get up. But I'm no longer allowed to do such a thing. I force my muscles to relax, but the question still comes out. "You're leaving?"

Even that simple question strikes fear in me.

His shoes scruff abruptly against the linoleum flooring. More gingerly, he takes my hand. "Never, Sonora. I promised you that I'd never leave you." He laces our fingers together. "And I never will. I only thought we could make the room feel . . . better."

"It's not as if I can see any of it."

The words come out more bitterly than intended. None of

this is Al's fault. It's not mine. Nor Red's or John's. It's simply a horrific thing that happened.

That happened to me.

That, no, I stubbornly made worse by insisting I continue diving. And now it's led me to this moment in time when I've been instructed to exist as immobile as possible. If I need to move my arms for any reason, I'm to do so cautiously. The rest of me should remain like a stone. Under no circumstance should I move my head, to any degree.

Already, after only minutes in this imprisonment, my muscles shriek to move. It feels as if my nerves have relocated to the skin's surface. The points of my body that press into the mattress—my shoulders, hips, and lower back—already ache dully, as if atrophying, something I logically know is not possible yet. Still, I cannot move them, cannot adjust.

I can only lie here.

"Go," I say to Al. "I'm not going anywhere."

"Let me at least get you the pillows."

I hear him move toward the chair where Mrs. Davis put them, but I say, "No, she took them away for a reason. The doctor wants me completely flat. I can do this. I have to do this."

Al's swallow is audible. "I know you can."

I SLEEP. IT'S A blessing to be unconscious, to pass some of the time I'm to exist in this unfamiliar, excruciating way.

When I wake I call out, "Al?"

Silence.

My breathing comes quicker. I'm alone. Or at least I think I am. Someone else could be in the room. I'd have no clue.

"Is anyone there?" I wait a few seconds, then say, more child-like, "Hello?"

Footsteps.

"Mrs. Carver, is there something I can help you with?"

My nurse, Mrs. Davis.

"My husband hasn't returned?"

"Not yet." There's a pause. She could be doing anything right now. Checking her watch. Frowning at the desperation in my voice. Looking out the window at a bird. Staring at me, her eyes full of pity. "Is there anything I can do for you?"

No, not really. Though, yes, I realize I have to use the restroom. I tell her as much.

"Okay," she says. "Stay right where you are. You're not allowed to get up."

She moves about the room. There's a clang. I picture her wedding band brushing against something metal. Her voice comes again. "I'm going to help you raise your hips the tiniest bit, just enough for me to slide the bedpan under you."

Her words are enough to trigger my desire to shoot to a sitting position, to rip off the eye mask, to exclaim, "Excuse me?"

I force myself to more calmly say, "Surely I can use the facilities?"

"The less you move, the better the chance the doctor will have of saving your eyesight. Three to five days, Mrs. Carver. No brushing your teeth, no brushing your hair, no changing your clothing. Another nurse or I will be here to help you with any needs you may have, such as eating—and relieving yourself."

When I say nothing, she grips my hips, and I bite back tears.

AL'S VOICE SHOULD BE a comfort. But I'm a mess of feelings. Embarrassment for him to see me in this weakened state. Anger at myself that I've worsened my eyes all on my own. Fear that my husband won't want me anymore. Anxiety that my life will never be the same. That *I* will never be the same.

"Sonora," he repeats. "Are you awake?"

"Yes."

"Are you thirsty?"

"No."

"Very well." I imagine him running a hand through his hair, his jawline tight, likely experiencing his own melting pot of emotions. I won't guess at them. "I brought a few things back with me."

What sounds like a photo frame clunks against the small table near my head. Glass is next. Flowers? He continues on. I stop guessing at what he puts down next.

All I want is to be unconscious again.

"Ah, Mr. Carver," a deep voice says. Dr. Morganson. "How is our patient?"

"Your patient can speak for herself," I say.

"Actually, I'd rather you don't talk and risk any unnecessary movement."

How to respond, when I'm not allowed to move an inch of my body . . .

"A model patient," Dr. Morganson says. "It's only been a few hours, but I'm going to slip off your eye mask and do a quick examination."

Fabric rustles as he moves closer. His hands pull at the mask. My eyes are closed.

"Go ahead and open your eyes for me," he instructs.

Light blinds me. As I adjust to the brightness, it's not lost on me how seeing in color has not returned, how life is still blurry. It's disorienting but not muddling enough to miss the utter worry etched across Al's face.

Dr. Morganson's examination is quick, and I'm relieved to once again plunge into darkness. Anything is better than seeing Al's drooped posture, the shape of him all wrong.

"I'll do an exam daily," I'm told, a hand suddenly on my shoulder. I startle at his touch, another emotion mixing into my melting pot: complete unease at not knowing what's to come.

DAY ONE TURNS TO day two, then three, then four.

Al visits me every one of them. I both want him to come and want him not to come. He sits with me. He tells me about the shows. I feel like a foolish corpse, unable to answer him, to gesture, to do anything greater than quirk my lips into a faint smile. Even that is difficult, despite how hard he tries to be the carefree, charismatic man I fell in love with.

It kills me to know how hard he tries.

It kills me to think I'm no longer the woman he fell in love with.

I've only broken my silence a single time, to make him promise me that Arnette won't come. Her whole life she's looked up to me. She can't see me like this.

"Dr. Morganson generally comes around this time," Al informs me. "Today could be the day."

Or there could be a day five, another twenty-four hours of yearning to scratch some itch or willing myself not to adjust my body, especially my head and lower back. Those two places in particular, where my body meets the mattress, are sources of endless, aching pain.

At the sound of footsteps, I'm about to find out if this torture will end or continue.

"Right on cue," Al says, a note of levity in his voice.

"I am a man of habit," the doctor says, matching Al's tone. "Let's see how Sonora is faring today."

By now, he's lost the formalness of calling me Mrs. Carver. And by now, I've learned to open my eyes a little at a time to keep the room's brightness from singeing my brain.

Dr. Morganson leans over me to complete today's examination. I search for and latch onto any details I can see. I notice a large, dark stain on his shirt. Ketchup, perhaps. Finally, he says, "I do believe we're ready."

"Really?" Al asks, stepping closer.

Dr. Morganson stands to his full height. "Yes. As I said, time is of the essence. I'd give Sonora's eyes another day or two if I could, but I fear it'd do more harm than good."

"But enough has absorbed?" Al questions.

"I can assure you I'll do my very best."

"Will it hurt?" I ask, the most I've spoken in days.

"No. First I'll administer drops, which will numb the surrounding tissue. Then I'll put an anesthetic into your lids. You'll experience nothing more than a prick. Once it has taken effect, you will feel nothing at all."

Perfect.

"And then what?" I ask. "What will you do?"

"I'll perform the operation."

"Tell me, please. What will you do exactly?"

The doctor glances at Al, then returns his focus to me. "Essentially, I will cauterize the choroid. I'll twist your eye to expose the back of it. Then, with a diathermy needle, I will pierce to the depth of your retina. When the needle reaches a point precisely between the choroid and retina, I will burn minuscule spots in the shape of a half-moon. If all goes as planned, scar tissue will form that will reattach the retina to the choroid. It's that glue we spoke of before. It'd act much like that."

"All right," I say. "Thank you." I think.

"I'll just give the two of you a moment," Dr. Morganson says before he steps out.

"You'll do great, Sonora," Al is quick to say.

I bite my bottom lip. This isn't an act or a dive where I have control of my body. This is the complete opposite of control, and I have to admit: "I'm scared."

Al's beside me in a heartbeat, lifting me from my prone position and taking me into his arms. I'm certain this is not allowed. Frankly, I don't care. He shudders, and I realize he doesn't want me to see him cry. I try to sink as deeply into his chest as possible, safe there. His arms tighten around me. "You're going to be fine," he whispers and kisses the top of my stringy hair. "No matter the outcome. You'll be fine. I'll be here. We'll figure it out together."

"Promise?"

"Always, Sonora."

Gently, he lowers me back to the bed. His expression seems as if he's memorizing me. But I'm the one who needs to do that. "Smile for me?"

What he gives me is forced.

"A genuine one."

It may be the very last time I ever see an inkling of happiness on my husband's face.

Chapter 39

As soon as I am out of surgery, my eyes are bandaged. I don't know if my vision has been fixed. "Dr. Morganson, can't I try to see after the medicine wears off?" I ask into the darkness.

"Not yet, Sonora. You're to remain immobile, even more so than before."

"For how long?"

He inhales deeply. "Three weeks. Maybe four."

I take my own deep breath before panic consumes me. "That long . . . But you'll check me before then?"

"Daily."

"So tomorrow, maybe things will be clearer?"

"That is the hope."

But do I dare let myself do such a thing as hope?

Sometime later I recognize the staccato footsteps of Mrs. Davis. "Have you come to feed me or change me?"

Her chuckle mixes with the sound of her setting something down on the bedside table. "I'm glad to see your humor is back."

"My humor has survived. We'll see for how long."

My shin itches. I instinctively reach for the spot, only for a hand to grab mine. "Sonora, you know better than that. Dr. Morganson has given me permission to sandbag you if I must."

"What on earth is that?"

"As it sounds. I'll line your body with sandbags so you are physically unable to move."

"That sounds like medieval torture."

"Torture would be not allowing you to speak for weeks. He only imposed that restriction for the days preceding your operation."

"How kind."

She pats my arm. "You'll get through it. It's nearly five. Are you hungry? I believe your husband said he'll be here shortly thereafter."

I can't help a frown. "He'll miss the night shows."

"I think it's you he misses."

It's a beautiful sentiment. It's also depressing. What if, after all of this, I'm no longer daring, courageous Sonora, one of the first in the country to dive on the back of a horse? No, it's too early in the process to fully play out that thought. "What's for dinner?"

"Your favorite."

I groan.

Mrs. Davis must've carried the dinner tray in with her. She now says, "Open."

We've done this song and dance before, her feeding me. It isn't one I fancy. But I do as she says, no doubt looking pathetic as I lie here with my jaw agape, like some wide-mouth fish.

The old Sonora would narrow her eyes at the discovery of what I'm eating; Mrs. Davis was, in fact, being facetious. As suspected, she's put meat loaf in my mouth, a food far from my favorite but one that's become a staple in these trying financial times.

I chew, barely. I've come to realize that I used to be a thorough chewer of my food. But now, with my head flat against the mattress, the back of my skull painfully rubs every time my teeth meet. I'll be lucky if I get out of this without a bald spot like a newborn or without bedsores. There are not only those vexations, but after days of being fed, I'm intimately conscious of the slow rhythmic motion of my jaw. I've become so in tune with how I chew that my focus seizes on the slow up-and-down motion of my mouth. And once my attention has become riveted on it, it feels as if my chin bones grow in size, too large for my face. A foolish notion, I realize. But I'm nothing more than a prisoner to my thoughts, both good and bad. Mostly bad, and in the end, I simultaneously feel and look ridiculous as Mrs. Davis continues to fork food at me.

I swallow, barely chewing and nearly choking. Ma undoubtedly would have chastised me about proper etiquette in my youth. But thinking of Ma isn't something I wish to do. She still knows nothing of my situation. Al and Arnette have been forbidden to write her about it. She'd worry. And I'd rather she not know what's going on until I know myself . . . in three to four weeks' time.

"Open."

THE FOOTSTEPS THAT ENTER the room are thumping, hurried. Unrecognizable. I'm immediately on edge. But then he speaks.

"Sonora."

And I feel silly for my heart jumping into my throat. "I'll have you know it's well past five."

"I know, I'm sorry. The drive here took longer than expected."

Hearing the exhaustion in Al's voice incites a feeling of guilt. The drive from Atlantic City to Philadelphia is a straight shot, but a shot that goes on and on for over an hour. "I'm letting you off the hook, then. Please don't come daily. I'm going to be here for quite some time."

"You're talking," he says.

"You're observant."

"Should you be doing that?"

"It's allowed."

He's silent. I picture him searching for someone to verify what I've said, but it's only the two of us in the room. I ache to reach for him, especially knowing no one will see me move. But I ache even more to be myself again at the conclusion of this ordeal. I remain still and instead ask, "Where are you?"

"I'm right here."

"You're a disconnected voice. Touch me."

Al moves quickly. His hand covers mine. His lips touch my forehead. "How are you feeling?"

Like I don't look like myself anymore, half my face covered in a bandage, the rest of me mummified beneath a thin blanket.

Like the muscles I painstakingly built, that convinced Al I was an able rider, are atrophying to gelatin.

Like I'm being held captive to a mind that is turning on me.

"I don't want to talk about me. Tell me about the shows."

Al chuckles. "It'll be a doozy."

"Doozy is my new normal. Go on, what's happening?"

"I'm not sure how much longer Mel is going to stick around. She began on . . . what? Monday? It's Friday, and she's thrown in the towel as far as riding Red."

"How does she get along with John?"

"She says she'll still ride him. But I think she wants to be done with all of it. She's not like you, Sonora."

That is swell to hear.

"So you need a new rider, for Red at the very least?"

He clucks. "Appears so. I've been thinking about Marty."

"From the water sports gang?"

There's silence. "Al?"

"Shoot, I'm sorry. I was nodding."

"It's okay." But honestly, the fact our conversations are different is something else that elicits feelings of ridiculousness. Al's jawline once portrayed a thousand words. Now a simple nod is lost on me. I focus my mind elsewhere, saying, "Marty . . . Has he expressed an interest in diving?"

"Well, I asked him if he'd try, and he was agreeable to that much. He's ridden horses all his life, which is why I thought of him. But as we know, diving on a horse is a different skill set than riding one, and a whole new ball game from doing tricks on an aquaplane. Still, I reckon he's got the nerve that Melanie's missing. We're going out early in the morning to give him a couple of trial dives from the low tower."

I picture the postcard of our act, the one with me on it. "Will the spectators expect a woman?"

"I don't know. Probably. I don't know what else to do here."

I bite my lip, wishing I could take back my question that clearly does not help matters. "Hey, Marty is a great idea. Worth a try, definitely."

Tension fills Al's voice. "Here's hoping it works."

A hope he must entertain because I didn't duck in time, because I insisted on riding after the initial dive that went wrong. "Al, I'm sorr—"

"Nope." His hand runs along my chin. "I don't want to hear any of that. All I want to hear is that you're improving. Listen, I should get back before the sun's down. But there's something I promised to ask you."

"Yeah?"

"Your sister. She'd really like to see you."

"No."

"It'd mean a lot to her. And frankly, she's driving me bananas with how much she's asking."

"She'll do that. And you . . . you should get on the road."

"Think about her coming at least?"

"What else is there for me to do but think?"

"HOW'D IT GO WITH Marty?"

The night and this morning have passed. Lunch with Mrs. Davis is behind me. Al's visit is both my favorite and worst part of each day.

"Red hasn't taken to him."

"It's only been a few hours."

"He took to you straightaway."

"What did Lorena say? Maybe it's because Red doesn't like men. Put him in one of my dresses. I recall he liked mine."

I expect a laugh, a chuckle, something that resembles our shared lightheartedness. Instead, I get: "Maybe. Red lets him mount him on the low tower, at least. Then as soon as they hit the water, Red tries to shake him. Marty wasn't able to ride him out of the tank a single time."

"What can you do but keep trying?"

Al snorts, just as another voice says, "Ah, Al, you're here too." The volume of Dr. Morganson's voice is low, as if he's just entering the room, and grows louder as he goes on. "Swell timing. I'm about to check Sonora's eyes. Mrs. Davis, will you do the honors?"

Her hands are gentle as she unwraps the bandage around my head.

I keep my eyes closed, my heart pounding. I've been waiting for this moment, praying that my eyesight has improved, even if it is only my right eye.

"Go ahead and open them, Sonora," Dr. Morganson instructs.

Mentally, I need a countdown. Breath held, I start with a slit, not enough to know much of anything. Then, slowly, I part my lids.

And my heart drops.

"The same," I say softly.

"That's fine," Dr. Morganson says. "We can't expect a miracle overnight."

It's not lost on me he uses the word *miracle*. Or that there's the shape of a frown on Al's face. The other day truly may've been the last time I'd see him smile.

Dr. Morganson motions to Mrs. Davis, who immediately reaches for a clean bandage. To me he says, "Same time tomorrow."

AND THE NEXT DAY, and the next, and so on, and so forth.

Al needs to stop coming, though a part of me will die if he doesn't visit.

Dr. Morganson needs to start saying something other than "That's fine." Though I'm horrified for him to say anything different.

I exist in the in-between now.

"I should leave soon," Al says.

"Of course."

"But I'll be back tomorrow."

"What if you didn't? I know this driving is a lot on you. Gas is a luxury. I can only imagine the glares you've been throwing at your balance book."

"Sonora." He has my hand again. It's one of the only places on my body he'll touch, save for a soft kiss to my forehead or lips when he says hello and goodbye, too afraid to rattle any other parts of me. He's never seen me this fragile. "I do not want you worrying about expenses. Or the show. Or anything besides healing. Actually, no, I don't want you worrying about that either."

"So what do you want me to do?"

"I don't know, Sonora. This isn't easy for me either."

And it breaks my heart that I'm doing this to him.

"I'm sorry," he amends.

"Don't be. But I think you need the day off. It's not as if I'm going anywhere. Nor are you missing anything here at the clinic. The show needs you."

He fiddles with my wedding ring. "How about one of our compromises? I won't come tomorrow . . . *if* you'll let me bring Arnette the next time."

I grit my teeth.

But boy, do I miss her. Her frankness. Her silliness. She won't treat me like a porcelain doll. I only hope she won't walk away feeling as if I've let her down somehow.

"Bring her," I say. "That's fine."

Chapter 40

A DAY WITHOUT AL TURNED out to be horrifying. Yes, I told him not to come. We made the compromise. But since the troupes combined, and especially since getting hitched, it is the longest we've been apart.

And now that he's been absent one day to focus on other important things—the show—I can imagine one day becoming two, becoming three.

I can't cry.

The doctor says no tears.

And Al and Arnette are supposed to be coming today. Even if my mind is playing evil tricks on me and telling me Al may not show, there's no way Arnette won't.

I ache for the hours to pass until they arrive. I try to sleep. I've found it's the best way to eat up the time. Sleep doesn't come either.

Then, finally, there are footsteps in the hall I recognize. I've been hearing them all her life. Arnette thumps almost everywhere she goes. I'm in the in-between again, filled with elation to be with her, while also dreading that my little sister will turn the corner into my room and find me like this.

Then I realize there's only one set of footfalls, and it's suddenly hard to breathe.

Arnette's thumps quicken, now in my room. A whimpering sound comes, as if she's on the verge of crying.

"Arnette, are you okay?"

She sniffles. "How'd you know it was me?"

"There's no way I wouldn't know. Where are you? Come here."

The mattress dips, Arnette sitting on the edge of my bed. I almost burst out laughing; she unknowingly rocked my body like a boat on water, and I appreciate how Arnette it is. But now she's still as a statue. "I'm right here. Oh, Sonora, I'm so happy to finally see you. I've been so worried."

I twitch a finger, wanting to comfort her. A heartbeat later, her hand covers mine, as if knowing I need it too. "I'm glad you're here. I'm sorry I kept you away. I've been afraid that you—"

"That I'd see you differently? Fat chance of that. You're so brave, Nora." She squeezes my hand. "Look what you've done, what you're doing. How could I ever not want to be like you?"

"Really?"

"Really. In fact, I have to talk to you about something."

"Is it Al? Where is he?"

"Oh, he's fine. Just getting some coffee or something. I asked him for a few minutes alone with you."

I'd palm my chest in relief if I could.

"The thing is," Arnette continues, "Mel ran off. Al found a note this morning. She said something about coming down with pneumonia, but none of us buy that for a second. Lorena said she could try riding, but I don't see how she could stay on with that knee of hers. Things aren't going great with Marty. No one will ride Red. Actually, I should clarify, no one is willing to ride Red, except for me."

"I don't think Mr. Amstead would like the sound of you abandoning his act for ours."

"I don't perform at night. No lights out on the ocean."

I sigh, trying a new tactic. "We've been down this road of you trying before."

"Have we? Your husband fretting over finances? A horse no one wants to touch? The show in jeopardy? How long until that Grover fella catches wind of the fact your riders are being scared off? He's going to wonder why. Al is constantly on tenterhooks about that man, like he's a viper in the weeds waiting for the perfect time to strike."

"You're laying it on a bit thick, aren't you?"

And it's working.

Big-time.

With one little problem: I can't have my sister laid up in a bed next to me. And I have to be honest. "The thing is, I don't know if you can pull it off."

"I can," she insists.

"How?" This is not a conversation I want to have in the position I'm in. Her hand slips off mine, and I don't need eyesight to imagine the hurt on her face.

"I don't know how, Sonora. I guess I was hoping you could help. Maybe you'd have some advice or something on how I can ride more consistently."

"I believe Lorena said 'unorthodox.'"

"Fine, that."

Actually . . . "She also said 'dangerously awkward.'"

"I get it, Sonora."

"I don't. I've never understood what Lorena meant by that. At the time, I didn't question it because I wanted you safe on the ground."

"It means that sometimes we'd go off the tower a bit sideways. Or Lorena would get on my case because I didn't duck swiftly enough for her liking. Then when I did do it quicker, she said it still looked off. Stuff like that. Fix me, Nora."

She takes my hand again, and it dawns on me. She's using her left hand. I think back on my visits with Al, and I can tell from how we fit together that he uses his right to hold mine. It makes sense; that's his dominant hand. But Arnette's always been unique, in more ways than one. She's ambidextrous, something I rarely think about. Other than when someone writes, who takes notice of what hand is being used?

I smile because, yes, I may know how to fix her. "When I grip the harness, I use my right hand. When I duck, I go toward the right. Lorena too. We taught you how *we* do it. But what if you've got your own unique way of doing things?"

She chuckles. "Wouldn't be the first time."

"Try it, from the *low* dive," I emphasize. "Hold with your left, duck to the left. That could be your answer."

"I'm going to need you to tell that to your husband. No way he'll let me dive unless you say it's okay."

"I'll talk to him."

"I want to hug you so badly right now."

"Me too, sis. Me too."

"In the meantime, can we do something about your hair?"

I laugh, resisting the urge to touch my head. "Is it that bad?"

Silence.

"Arnette?"

"I brought Mamie Lou's brush from your dressing room. Now you just keep doing what you're doing, and I'll see to the rest."

She's gentle, running the brush through the ends of my hair. I can tell she keeps away from my bandages and takes care not to tug at any knots, which has to prove difficult considering my hair hasn't been washed in quite some time.

For the next few blessed minutes, it's only the quiet sound of our breathing. Until I ask, "When did our positions reverse?"

"I wouldn't call it that. But maybe we've reached a point where we can help each other."

"I'd like that."

"Me too."

"And thank you," I say.

"For what?"

"Making me feel useful and like I'm still part of the show."

For the first time in a long time, I have a glimmer of faith that everything might turn out okay.

Chapter 41

THE THING ABOUT FAITH is that it's constantly tested. Arnette can, in fact, dive in an orthodox and safe manner when she's using the techniques best for her. I know it the instant she rushes into my room the next day, a ball of energy. Al trails behind, calling out a hello, a pep in his own step.

It's thrilling.

Yet I'm filled with an emptiness on account of not being able to witness Arnette and Red diving with my own two eyes. Here I am, static, yet life keeps going on around me, and without me.

The thought grows legs.

I'm certain that now that Al's been able to rejuvenate the show, he'd rather be at the pier instead of my bedside. I am nothing more than a second job, and I've long grown tired of feeling like a duty. I've long grown weary of another lurking, lifelong fear . . . that I refuse to give a name to.

Dr. Morganson's daily evaluations of "that's fine" add teeth to my unease. It's all he's been saying for weeks now. Three, to be exact, something he points out this morning as he walks into my room.

"Now let's get those bandages off and see what three weeks looks like."

For me, that's barely anything, my eyesight all but gone. My fingertips sink into the sheets and squeeze. Twenty-one days of lying in the dark, and I can't tell beyond the faintest of glows.

Dr. Morganson sighs. "I'll be candid. Your recovery hasn't been what I'd hoped. If I have your consent, I'd like to try a second operation."

The fact he hasn't given up on me is a sliver of promise. "What does this second one entail?"

"It's much different from the first. We've reached a critical point, Sonora. A last-ditch effort, as they say. I'll inject a needle into your eye and pump air through it into the cavity in front of your retina. The theory is that if I exert enough pressure, the retina will press back against the choroid and reattach."

"It's still possible to reattach?"

"In ideal situations, the operation has a fifty percent success rate."

I can do simple math, and I try to keep my unnamed fear at bay. "Will you be able to tell right away? No more waiting weeks to know my fate?"

"Yes, afterward I should be certain if the operation has taken the way we'd like it to."

"When do we begin?"

"Presently, if you are agreeable. It's why I'm here earlier today. Would you like to telephone your husband before we begin?"

"No." I lick my lips. What if he arrives today and I'm on the glass-half-full side of fifty percent? "He'll learn soon enough."

DR. MORGANSON WARNS ME this operation won't be without pain. I'm already uncomfortable, my eyes held open with some contraption. Now I dig my fingertips into the table, bracing myself, staring at empty space so as not to glimpse any inkling of the needle drawing closer to my eye.

At first zero pain incites, and I question if I'm broken, truly beyond repair.

Then the burning begins. The sensation is so intense, so overwhelming, it's as if lava is being poured directly into my right eye, consuming the entirety of my face, dripping and consuming the rest of my head.

I refuse to picture my eye inflating like a balloon. Instead, I think of brushing my horses. Red, with his cow spots. Slow, methodic, even strokes down his neck. The pain interrupts. I whimper, wishing I could vanish into nonexistence. I fight the urge to smack the doctor's hand away, to end his work, but I read his tone before we began: this is my final chance to ever see again.

I lie as still as possible, tensing and flexing my toes, willing for the lava to stop flowing.

Finally, it does.

Dr. Morganson wheels his chair backward, as if needing distance. I do not see him do this. I *cannot* see him do this. I can only hear the wheels.

"What is it? Did it work?" I ask him, already knowing the answer. How could it have worked if the world is mostly lost to me? There was only a light glow before. There is an even lighter glow now. My breath hitches on my next question, and I have to try again to get it out. "What will happen to me now?"

"Sonora, honey, your vision will continue to deteriorate until there is nothing left at all."

I have no choice but to name the fear that's been nipping at my heels all this time: I'll never see again.

"Can you telephone my husband?" I say. "Tell him not to come."

Chapter 42

I THOUGHT I'D CRY.

Al does, once I eventually agree for him to come. I can't so much as hear him, but I can sense his tears. His hand is also damp. After wiping the wetness from his eyes?

But not me.

What I am is numb.

No, that's not true. I still feel, and what I feel is broken. Fractured. Unsure of where I'm to go from here.

I do not know another soul who is blind. Dr. Morganson said he could put me in touch with other patients who are.

"No, thank you," I responded.

"If you're certain." There was a question in his voice.

I nodded. How can someone else know what it is that I'm going through? They haven't lived in my shoes. They don't have a mother who saw an advert in the newspaper for a daring girl and immediately thought of them. Or a sister who has emulated their love of adventure. Or a husband who fell for their bravery and strength on a horse. He fell in love with a performer. But that's not who I can be anymore.

I turn my body and head in Al's direction. I'm without the bandages and eye mask; no point in them any longer. I'm propped up, resting against a stack of pillows.

I'm more comfortable, but the change in my position makes me abundantly aware of how my body's been altered from the muscle I've lost.

"Do I look much changed?"

"Not at all. You're the same Sonora you've always been."

"No," I say. "I am not." Anger builds that he'd say such a thing. "Where's Arnette?" She'll give it to me straight.

"She's at the pier. She wanted to come."

"Take me there. Please. I want to leave. There's nothing for me here anymore."

"EVERYONE HAS MISSED YOU," Al says once we're in an auto. I'd prefer to quickly forget the walk from my room to the passenger seat. I wore dark glasses, which rendered any lasting trace of eyesight completely useless, and Al guided me every step of the way. Voices flowed around me, but who they belonged to was a mystery. My steps were half their usual length, and I held out a hand the entire time. My breath grew labored from unease and the fact that my body hadn't experienced any type of exertion in over a month, causing me to hold the air in my lungs. "Lorena says Claribel especially misses her aunt Sonora."

Al would usually never do such a thing—refer to me as aunt to his sister's dog. He's always thought the way Lorena babies the dog is absurd.

"I miss everyone too," I say flatly, despite it being the truth. "I'd like to see Arnette dive tonight."

Al makes an indistinguishable noise.

Anger builds once more. "I'd like to be there. Is that better? I'd like to hear the splash, the cheers, the reaction to her."

"Of course." His words are hurried, but no touch from him follows. This produces an unmoored sensation, like we're worlds apart. He adds, "We'll go straight to the pier. We should make it in time."

"What time is it?"

"Nearly five. Are you hungry? We can stop at the apartment first to see what Mrs. Van Myers has cooked up."

"Who on earth is that?"

"Sorry, I must not have mentioned her. Arnette and I have been so harried that neither of us have had time to cook. Mrs. Van Myers has been seeing to that for us."

"Oh."

"You'll enjoy her. She's a mountain of a woman, nearly twice your size. I'm surprised the circus hasn't snatched her up."

An awkward pause.

"Funny," I say finally. "No, I'm not hungry."

I am not yet ready to meet this Mrs. Van Myers.

We drive in silence.

How odd, how disarming, to enter Atlantic City without the abundant fanfare of lights. Yet I know when we've arrived. The candied and salt-filled air is a dead giveaway, along with the trill of excited amusement-park-goers.

I'm not able to walk alone. Al takes the upper part of my arm to guide me. Have I caught trouble and he's ushering me toward my punishment? That's how this feels. But I may be overemphasizing his hold on me in my head. Others could merely see a gentleman leading his lady. A ridiculous lady who wears dark, oversized glasses at dusk. I bite down on my lower lip. I bite harder as my toe catches on an uneven plank in the boardwalk. Then I startle as I kick an object I can't identify. Some type of debris.

Suddenly I catch on Lorena's voice at a distance, beginning the show.

"Oh," Al remarks. "It's starting."

"I know," I snap.

"If you're able, we'll need to pick up the pace. Dr. Morganson recommended a walking cane?"

"I do not want one of those. Walk faster. I can keep up."

As the crowd thickens, something I surmise from our slower pace and the way Al weaves us left and right, my unease thickens too. At any moment, someone will barrel straight into me; I'm sure of it. Al twists me one way and then the other. Someone brushes my shoulder. I stumble and Al's grip tightens.

Lorena's voice is louder. She's nearly at the part where Arnette will raise her hand to greet the spectators.

"Here we are," Al says.

"Are we near the tank?"

"It's straight ahead."

He must have brought us in through the employee entrance, toward the back side of the tank where patrons cannot go.

I exhale.

I whip my head in the direction of the tower, hoofbeats all

but vibrating through me, even from where I stand on the ground.

I picture Red. Or maybe it's John. I didn't ask who Arnette was riding tonight. I envision the horse cantering toward my sister. She'll be perched on the railing. In my mind's eye, every detail is crystal clear. Then there's a *clunk*. A *thump*. Two more. It's Red, stomping before they dive.

My throat thickens with emotion.

The crowd releases a collective gasp.

Arnette and Red must be in the air.

I clasp my hands together, waiting for the splash. It comes, immediately swallowed by the roar of spectators.

I startle as Al says into my ear, "A flawless dive, Sonora."

A smile forms on my lips. It may be genuine at first, but my show of emotion quickly becomes a complete sham. Bogus. Fictitious to the nth degree. I experienced the last thirty seconds as if it were me up on the tower. But it was not. Nor can it ever be me again. That is not who I am anymore. I am no longer wanted, no longer the attractive young woman who can swim and dive that the advert spoke of.

Nor do I know where that leaves me.

Chapter 43

"I DON'T WANT ANYONE TO know."

The shows are over.

I've retreated to the apartment—with Al's help.

Mrs. Van Myers was fortunately gone. I'll meet her another time.

I've asked for time alone. Then promptly asked for my sister.

Arnette is with me now.

"Nora, most everyone already knows what's happened."

"Georgie?"

"He was one of the first, you know that."

"Roxie and Irene?"

"They know you've been at a clinic after a hard dive."

"Marty and Jacob?"

"Sonora, Marty's been diving in your place with John. And Jacob, well, I've been spending a lot of time with him. We've grown close."

"As in you're seeing each other?"

"I'm smiling, you should know. I don't know how much you can see."

"With these glasses?" I say. "Absolutely nothing." I toss them onto my bed. "Without them, much the same."

"Oh, Sonora—"

"No, let's not do that right now. Right now I want to know how I'm gone a month and you've already found a beau."

She laughs. "It happened quickly. I made the mistake of mentioning him to Ma, and she's made me promise not to marry him without her present."

I snort. "Like I did. I reckon I'll be all sorts of disappointment to her."

"Stop that."

I absently finger a loose thread on the bedspread, a thread that wasn't loose until I got my hands on it. "What about Mr. and Mrs. Pallenberg?"

"They're so busy with the bears, I don't think they've taken particular notice of your absence. I'm convinced they don't realize you and I are different people."

"We do resemble each other. And Mr. Endicott . . ." I can feel that now I've really messed up the stitching of the bedspread. "What has Al told him?"

"Last I heard, Al hasn't told him a thing one way or the other."

Because he'd been hoping I'd leave the clinic fully restored.

"I don't want anyone else to know," I say. "I don't want to be seen differently or treated differently. Look at me."

"I am, Nora."

I blow out a breath.

"Okay, tell me, how does my face look?"

"Sad."

I close my eyes, the response instinctive. "See that," I say, latching onto my reaction. "Would a blind person do that? I don't know. Will I lose expressions? Remember Margaret Canning's ma?"

"I don't think so."

"She was in geometry with me. It doesn't matter. Her mama, God rest her soul, was blind. And she always had this vapid look to her. I can't be vapid, Arnette."

Her arms around me come as a surprise, not because her hug is unfamiliar, but because I couldn't see it coming. How odd not to anticipate such a thing. "How about," Arnette says, "I tell you if you start giving blank expressions."

"Thank you. I was thinking about buttons too. I'll be mortified if they're mismatched."

She pulls back from our hug. "You've always been meticulous."

"What if I can't be meticulous anymore?"

"I don't see why that needs to stop."

"Am I handling this right, worrying about such stupid stuff like buttons and my face?"

"Nora, I don't know if there is a right way to handle this. What else are you feeling?"

"Anger, that's the biggest. But it's like my anger has different heads."

"Aw, Nora, that makes me think of Medusa, with a sad head, confused, scared . . ."

"Frustrated."

"Yeah." She draws out the word. "But we'll figure it all out as we go. No one says you have to feel a certain way at first, or even as time goes on. How's Al doing?"

"As dutiful as a Boy Scout."

She chuckles. "He'll settle in too." She clucks. "And what about Mama? How do you think she'll handle it?"

"If you're asking if I'm ready to tell her, then no, I'm not."

"You're going to have to at some point."

"I know."

SOME POINT WILL NOT be tonight. Or tomorrow. Or the next day. Telling Mama I'm blind will distress her, and as a result, she'll overcompensate. She'll pity me. She may up and move to wherever I am. I love my ma, but our relationship works best with space between us. So before I break the news to her, I need to be as agile as I can in as many things as I can. I need to have control of myself.

And that's hard when the sensation to cry, to pound my fists and fall face-first into bed and wallow, is the strongest inclination I possess.

Today I wake, palming the other side of the bed. It's cold. Al's up with the birds again, has been since I've been back, and maybe even long before that.

The aroma of coffee is strong, so it can't be too late in the morning. I swing my legs out of bed, fumbling around to find my slippers.

I take one, two, three steps along the bed, then turn, banging my shin into the corner of the bedframe. "You foil me again," I growl at the post. No doubt I'll have the workings of another raised bruise. Tomorrow I'll need to take three larger steps or four normal-sized steps. The problem is, I haven't found consistency with the length of my steps as of yet. When I'm hesitant, they are smaller. When I try for confidence, I lengthen them. Arnette has assured me I'll find a happy medium.

The only other obstacle in the room is an armoire, which I can detect with my outstretched hands. I don't bother doing more than throwing a robe around me. I won't be leaving the apartment, and the only poor soul who'll be seeing me until Arnette and Al get home tonight is Mrs. Van Myers.

She truly is a mountain of a woman. When I first met her, she insisted I all but frisk her. "Go ahead and pat me down," she said. "Get a feel for me, create a picture in your head."

I oddly appreciated the gesture.

And now I envision a hearty woman, big in hips, bust, hair, and mouth. She'll talk as the day is long. I don't mind the distraction.

I leave my bedroom, arms out, footfalls still unpredictable. But I know there's a hall eight to ten steps long, followed by the living room, with an end table only a few steps in.

I'm walking and stepping and tapping with my foot and waving my arm but not coming to the side table.

"Al moved it," Mrs. Van Myers informs me, her voice coming from the direction of the kitchen. "Didn't want you running into it again."

"Mrs. Van Myers," I begin, "is there steam coming out of

my ears? How does Al expect me to learn my way around if he's constantly adjusting the furniture for my so-called benefit?"

"That's exactly what I told him. Let you catch a sharp corner a time or two and you'll learn. Now, come sit. I've your breakfast ready."

She lets me navigate on my own, my shins be damned.

"What are you reading?" I ask, hearing the turn of a page while trying to ignore the laughter outside on the boardwalk, shenanigans that do nothing but dangerous things to my constitution.

"Something that'd make my mother roll over in her grave."

I laugh, aiming my eyes in the direction of her voice so as not to stare at the cupboards. "Mrs. Van Myers, how scandalous." I spoon oatmeal into my mouth, something I'm pleased to say hasn't been a challenge, mostly because it's thick and goopy. Still, it's nice that Al doesn't make a fuss when I use this particular utensil. A knife is a different story; he insists on cutting up my meat for me during suppers. He tried to fork my vegetables too, but I reminded him I could stab efficiently on my own, something I could demonstrate on things other than my vegetables if he didn't believe me.

If he could just tell me where food is on my plate so I didn't resemble a toddler palming around clumsily, that'd be wonderful. But nothing more than that is needed. In many unfortunate ways, autonomy is a thing of the past. "I miss reading."

"I could read to you."

I twist my lips. "That is kind, and while it'd help not to see your face, depending on the nature of what you're reading"—I smile—“reading has always been an escape for me. Something I prefer to do alone.”

“Suit yourself.”

I chuckle. “Speaking of suiting myself, I think I’ll have a bath. And don’t you raise a brow at me for indulging so early in the day. It’s not as if my datebook is full.”

Gone is my old routine.

“I made no such expression.”

And I have no way of verifying. But it’s how I pictured her in my head. I realize it’s a blessing I can still pull up an image in my mind. If someone says the word *red*, an apple appears in my mind’s eye. *Brown*, and I conjure the spots on Red’s coat. When Al’s tone is a certain way, I haven’t lost being able to “see” the slope of his jawline. Not yet, at least.

I stand, needing that soak, and make my way toward the bathroom, doing my best to try to match my old gait. I undress. Turn on the water, double-check that—yes—to the left is hotter. I pull down a towel, having no notion that a box of something or another is stacked on top. It comes tumbling down, the item scattering and pinging all over the floor.

The bath salts.

I curse.

Taking handfuls, I toss them in the direction of the tub. They clang off the tub, the walls, the floor. I throw more fistfuls, not giving a lick about my aim.

So immersed in my frustration, I don’t hear the bathroom door open until: “What in tarnation are you doing?”

I freeze. On my hands and knees. Naked as the day I was

born. “The better question,” I say to my sister, “is what are *you* doing here?”

“You can’t be serious. One of my shows was canceled because of rough water. I thought we could take a walk. Actually get you out of the apartment. But now that I see you, my question is worth repeating. What in tarnation are you doing? The doctor said you shouldn’t be bathing by yourself for the first week or so. Where’s your robe? And, oh my gosh, the water. It’s going to overflow.”

“My robe’s around here somewhere.” Where, I can’t remember. “When I need it again, I’ll find it.”

“Sonora . . . ,” Arnette says through gritted teeth.

The water faucet squeaks and the sound of the water stops. Fabric is thrown at me. “I don’t need this yet. This babying is nonsense. I’m not crippled.”

“No, Sonora, you are not. What you are is learning.”

“I liked it better when you were the little sister,” I mumble.

“You like me just fine.” She hooks her hands under my arms. “Now let’s get you in the tub.”

Once I’m in the hot water, there’s a rustling sound. Arnette’s cleaning up my mess. “Don’t tell Al about this,” I say. “He already thinks I’m helpless. That is, when he’s around.”

“You know,” she says, “you’re not going to like hearing this.”

“So don’t say it.”

“Nope, you’re going to hear it. I think sometimes you take your anger out on Al, like you’re trying to push him away.”

I can feel myself moving my eyes around in their sockets, searching for a response. I’m not sure what to say.

Arnette saves me. “You say he’s not around. If he’s too busy to come to you, you should go to him.”

I purse my lips. “I don’t think so. How many shows are even left?”

“This weekend is our last. You should come. You haven’t since . . .”

I let the buoyancy of the water bob my leg up. I force it down. Let it lift. “I’m aware of the last time I was there.” And that feeling of being replaced, old news, unable to be the old me anymore.

Arnette sighs. “I know you don’t want people to know, but it’d be good to show that pretty face of yours. Everyone misses you. Red, John, and Snow miss you.”

I sink deeper, blowing a bubble against the bathwater.

In every single day of my future, I once saw my horses. I saw myself riding until I was old and gray and my aged body was content to let go of the diving harness.

I am not content to let go.

“No,” I say finally. “It’d be too hard to see them.”

Chapter 44

I realize after my bath, after supper, when I'm methodically brushing my hair before bed, that I used the word *see.*

I said it'd be too hard to *see* the horses.

I'm not entirely sure what to make of that slipup, beyond it leaving an uncomfortable pit in my stomach. Distracted, I fumble the brush. I lose my grip on it. It slips. Then it thunks against the floor.

"No!" I yelp, instantly throwing my hand over my mouth, praying Al hasn't heard me. That he won't come. That he won't try to console me over dropping my most prized possession.

I sink to my knees, patting the ground, finding Mamie Lou's brush. I run a finger down the back of it, scraping my skin on a large crack as I do. Dinged but not broken. Still usable. I hug it to my chest, annoyed, angry, frustrated. All with myself.

Like in the clinic, I'm eager for sleep. But now it's akin to a reset for my mood. Tomorrow will be better. I'll do better. I'll be better for the people around me.

WHEN I WAKE, AL'S there. His warmth radiates. Sleepily, I roll over, snuggling into him, feeling a flutter throughout my body. It's been too long since we've lost ourselves in each other. He stirs, making the deep, rough sounds of a waking man. I inch even closer, opening an eye—forgetting myself for a moment.

Then I clench my jaw, remembering that my world only exists in blackness.

I pull away, as if doused in a bucket of cold water, and ask, "What time is it? I'm surprised you're still here."

Immediately my words leave a sour taste in my mouth as I remember Arnette's.

"I think sometimes you take your anger out on Al, like you're trying to push him away."

He'd have every right to bite back at my snark. Instead, the mattress shifts as he moves. There's a scraping sound of metal against wood on the nightstand. His timepiece. "It's nearly seven. Hungry? I'll whip up something for us to eat."

He's up, out of our bed.

And I'm left ashamed. I have my tail between my legs as I make my way to the kitchen a few minutes later. Wordlessly, I slink into my chair. I put one hand over the other on the table. I'd like to be helpful—to get down plates and glasses from the cupboard—but I'm gun-shy. What if I drop them? What if Al whooshes in and doesn't let me do it myself?

It's easier to sit here and wait. It's easier to be waited on.

"Smells good," I say in a small voice.

The pan's sizzling. "What was that?"

"I said it smells good."

"Oh. I'm glad."

Even though I only just told myself it's easier not to try to jump in, I suggest, "Why don't I put on the coffee."

"Nah, I can do it."

So can I.

Al continues to rustle around in the kitchen. A plate clunks in front of me, then a glass. A liquid is poured. It can't be orange juice, not in these trying times. Milk is my guess. Mrs. Van Myers was going on yesterday about how the prices have been sliced and now many farmers are striking.

Al's next to me, his arm brushing against me as he fills my plate. "Bacon is at six o'clock. Potatoes at three. Bread at eleven."

"Thank you. Been some time since you've cooked for me. Remember the first time you did? Then that birthday cake?"

He snorts. "That feels like a lifetime ago." A moment later his chair scrapes and utensils clink against his plate. "Arnette was saying she wants to get you out into the sunshine today."

I take a large bite of my bread, talking around it. "Is that so?"

"I think it'd be good for you."

"Maybe."

Silence stretches between us.

Al breaks it, saying, "Mr. Endicott wants to lock down next season. We're meeting about it this morning."

"You're going to say yes, aren't you?"

"I am. We have a good thing here. Marty's doing fine with John. Arnette's like a whole new rider. Besides, I think consistency is what's best for you."

I set down my fork but don't let go. Last thing I want to do is try to locate it again and grope around like a fool. "And what is it that I'm consistently doing, Al?"

"Right now? Adjusting. We all are. Myself included."

I stab my fork at three o'clock.

Across from me, Al is doing more than simply eating. I listen, then ask, "Got somewhere to be?"

"What do you mean?"

"You're checking your watch."

"How did you know that?"

"I heard your hand brush against your pocket. Then a ticking sound. It got louder as you held it up to look at it."

"You amaze me, Sonora."

My mouth falls ajar. His words strike me as genuine. And while I wouldn't call my husband disingenuous, I'd call our relationship lately off-kilter, strained, with Al tap-dancing around my emotions. But this comment . . . I like knowing that I can still amaze him.

"Is it your meeting with Mr. Endicott? You shouldn't be late."

I picture him dabbing his mouth on a napkin, standing, pushing in his chair, bringing his plate to the sink. Each sound corresponds.

His footsteps stop beside me. His fingertip goes beneath my chin, turning my face upward. Then his lips are on mine, a peck. But like his comment, it feels genuine.

I'm smiling.

"Got some more potatoes down by four o'clock."

This tone is light, playful. The top of my head gets a kiss.

"Mrs. Van Myers should be here any moment. But I think you can manage for a few minutes, don't you?"

I nod, then send my husband off with a "have a nice day."

"HOW DOES SPAGHETTI WITH carrots and white sauce sound?"

I'm in my bedroom when Mrs. Van Myers enters, along with the question.

She goes on, "It's one of Eleanor Roosevelt's seven-and-a-half-cent meals."

"Al loves carrots. He's similar to a horse in that way."

She laughs. "I got you something, too, that I think you may love. Give what you're doing a rest and join me in the living room."

What I'm doing is still in the messy stage. I've taken every piece of clothing I own and tossed it onto my bed. Now, one by one, I'm feeling and remembering each garment, folding a blouse together with a skirt, and so on. Figure it'll save me half the time getting dressed in the morning if I'm not fumbling around trying to piece together an outfit.

"Wait," I say, "before you go. Which one is blue and which one is light green?"

"Blue is in your right hand."

Got it.

I quickly finish arranging those two outfits, then swiftly yet carefully proceed to the living room.

"I'm on the sofa." Mrs. Van Myers pats the cushion.

I bang my shin; guards like a soccer player wears may be useful. Though, practical or not, I wouldn't dare to put on such a thing. I sit next to Mrs. Van Myers, who adjusts the hem of my skirt. Her help is never bothersome.

"Scooch your hands. I'm going to place something in your lap."

I free the space for her, which she fills with . . . an oversized book? When I put a hand on either side, it's similar in width to a newspaper.

"A photo album?" I ask her.

"Better," she says. "You can't do a thing with a photo album, now, can you?"

She's got me there. "Then what is it?"

"It's a braille book."

"Sorry to burst your bubble, but I can't do a thing with this either."

"Not yet you can't."

I run my fingertips over the small dots. "What's it about?"

"Beats me. I can't read it either. But I borrowed this from the library, and the woman there gave me the name of someone here in Atlantic City who could teach you. That is, if you're interested."

"I am."

Mrs. Van Myers chuckles at the quickness of my response.

"Very well, then. I'll contact this Miss Sadie Cohen and see if she can fit you in. Mr. Carver told me the show is ending soon, but I'll be with you for another three weeks as he wraps up business, which makes me believe that's how much longer you'll be here too. You can learn a lot in that time."

"Learn what?"

It's Arnette's voice, my sister sneaking in like a cat robber apparently.

"Making a habit of stopping in during the day, aren't ya?" I say to her, noticing an uptick in the beat of my voice.

"I'm only glad this time you're clothed."

"Sonora here is going to learn braille," Mrs. Van Myers says, and if I'm not wrong, I detect some pride in her voice.

"Is that so. Glad to see our Sonora getting back on her own two feet. In fact"—the book is lifted from my lap, then both my hands are being yanked until I'm standing—"I have more plans for her two feet. We're going out."

"Are we?" I ask, for the first time more curious than resistant.

"Yep. Just a stroll, some fresh air, some vitamin D—the free kind. It's a beautiful day."

As she speaks, she leads me toward the windows. I realize once we arrive, once I feel the heat of the sun shining through onto my skin. And I think, *This is progress*. I think, *This could be what I need.*

Chapter 45

BEFORE WE GO, I got you these." Arnette clicks the front door closed behind us. "A little more fashion forward than what the clinic gave you."

I cock my head in question.

"Sunglasses. Here."

My sister slides them onto my face, and I feel them with my fingertips. "Round lenses," I comment.

"That's right. Like I said, fashion forward."

My sister positions my hand on her forearm. "This way. We'll go down to the Steel Pier."

I fight to maintain the confidence I began to feel inside my apartment. The sunglasses help, reassuring me that my eyes are concealed. "Tell Al how much these cost you so we can repay—"

"Not a chance. They're a gift."

"For what?"

We begin walking.

"For this new and improved Sonora."

"Hardly."

"No, it's true. You know what I've noticed? I'll spare you the suspense and tell you. I've noticed that your other senses have come to life."

"Hmm." I don't think she's wrong. My other senses do feel like they've been awakened in a way. I wonder if that's normal for others with a condition similar to mine.

"I like how you walk with me," I say to my sister. "I know Al means well, but he holds my upper arm and steers me like I'm a steamboat. It's better how you lead me."

"Have you told him this?"

"No, but maybe I will."

"Like I said, new and improved. Now, we're bound to pass someone we know. I can let you know if I see anyone coming. What if I treat my arm like reins? I'll dip left or right and you'll know to smile in that direction. Show me how you'd smile if you saw Roxie, for example."

She laughs. "Too big."

I adjust.

"Little more teeth."

I adjust again.

"Perfection."

I laugh too.

"Oh. I forget her name, but one of the acrobats is coming our way."

"Marie?"

"I don't know."

"Rosalie?"

"You could say names all day and I still won't recall. She's almost here. Feel for it."

I do, concentrating on my fingertips on my sister's arm. She dips left. I smile left.

"Hello, ladies," the other woman coos. "Beautiful day, isn't it?"

"That it is," I call back.

That it is.

WE MAKE IT TO the Steel Pier successfully, notwithstanding a few mishaps of a stubbed toe and Arnette nearly causing me to collide with a seagull. Truly I don't know if there'd be anything more horrifying than accidentally touching one of those flying rats.

But we've made it. Arnette must have avoided the greenroom backstage and the other performers because she doesn't let on about anyone else who'd recognize me. Then, off in the distance, in the midst of the laughter, joyful voices, and the call of hungry seagulls, I make out a whinny.

I once heard that when a baby cries, a mother's milk will let down. It's the body's natural response, the release of a hormone. When I hear the whinny, something happens deep inside me. An aching sensation. A horse's bray can mean various things. A greeting between horses, for example. A sign of inquisitiveness. Or displeasure when a horse is separated from a companion.

"It's Red," I say.

"You can tell?"

I nod. "It's Red."

"Stalls are straight ahead. Why don't we say hello."

I'm nervous. I can't say intelligently why that is. Perhaps because it's an emotion compounded by various fears, thoughts, holdups, letdowns . . . I could go on. But I'm also excited to see him.

"Hey, Georgie," Arnette calls.

"Sonora!"

"And Arnette!" my sister playfully adds.

"Always a pleasure to see you, Arnette," he says, a hint of something I can't make out in his voice. This is when an expression could do wonders, and I'm curious if my sister's courtship with Jacob has crushed Georgie's, well, crush. "But, Sonora," he goes on, "aren't you a sight for sore . . ." He trails off. "Sorry, I . . ."

"Don't you fret for even a second over that," I say, letting him off the hook. "It's good to be here."

And I mean it.

I hold up my hand. "Take me to Red, will ya?"

Georgie must move quickly to oblige me, so swift, in fact, that he stumbles over a bucket, the metal clanging, and lets a profanity slip.

"And you can see just fine," I point out, earning myself a laugh from him.

Georgie says, "I've got the stall open. Was just in there giving him fresh hay."

I outstretch my arm, Georgie takes my hand, and he guides me until my palm hits a warm, solid surface.

I close my eyes, not needing to, but instinctually wanting to picture Red more clearly. I see him. His cow spots. His big brown eyes. His long mane. "There you are, boy. It's me."

I didn't cry in the clinic. I didn't cry coming home. Now, though, my eyes fill with tears. I lean forward until both hands are on him and my forehead rests between my hands.

He breathes, lifting me, lowering me. I sync my lungs to his. "I've missed you."

A tear falls.

Then there's a tug on the cap sleeve of my dress.

"Oh no you don't," I say, straightening, quickly wiping away the tear. "I'm onto your tricks, mister."

Red nuzzles me, as if laughing at his own shenanigans, and I find his nose with my hand. "How've you been, boy?"

He nickers as I pet him. Then John chimes in. "Don't you worry, I'll come say hello to you, and Snow too."

"Let me help you navigate," Arnette says. "Those buckets will jump out at a person."

John's like a dog that'll keep nudging for pets if you stop. Snow is constantly sniffing me in search of food. Honestly, I could stand here with them all day. But Arnette says, "I've got a show coming up. Would you like to come backstage, or would you rather I help you home?"

Baby steps, I think. "This has been enough."

Arnette's arm winds around my waist, pulling me to her. "Proud of you, sis."

I'm proud of me too.

With my hand resting on her arm once more, we begin our way back. We've gone a handful of steps out of the horse stalls when Arnette tenses.

"What is it?"

"Not what, but who."

"Fine, who is it?"

"Al hasn't told Mr. Endicott a thing yet, right?"

"No."

"Then it's our story to tell however we'd like. He's beelining right toward us," she says from between her teeth. "Get your smile on."

I'll do more than that. "Mr. Endicott," I call out. "Nice to see me back on my feet, isn't it?"

I pray he's not too far away. That I didn't just make a fool of myself by calling into the abyss. I try for confidence, lifting my hand from my sister's arm. Immediately my self-consciousness gets the better of me and I use that hand to touch my sunglasses.

"Sonora in the flesh!" I hear, and I let out a small puff of air. "Al didn't tell me you were out and about yet."

"Only just today."

"Naturally," Arnette says, "her first stop was the horses."

He laughs. He's a large man, Mrs. Van Myers giving him a run for his money. "And you're recovering as expected?" he asks.

I touch the side of my head. "Knocked my noggin pretty good. I'm sure you heard the details." I rush out my next words so he can't question me on that, saying, "But I'm healing up just fine."

"Wonderful. Truly splendid. Guess that means you'll be back in the saddle, as they say, next season? Matter of fact, Al, Lorena, and I began to draft up the paperwork this morning."

"I . . ." I'm at a loss for words. Not about the construction of next year's contract, but Mr. Endicott believing there's riding in my future. If only that was my reality.

The fact that Arnette is going to step in and speak up is something I sense even before she does it. “Marty and I have merely been keeping Sonora’s spot warm for her,” she says. “But my sister is eager to be back on the marquee next season, aren’t you, Sonora?”

I chuckle, buying myself time. From the stalls, Red whinnies some more. He flashes into my brain. Wouldn’t I love to ride him again. My smile widens at the thought. “I’d be eager, indeed.”

Chapter 46

Miss Sadie Cohen is a Southern belle through and through. Kind, sweet, charming. Firm when she needs to be. Though it's a sneaky firmness, by which she makes it seem like something is my idea. "Yes, I believe if you try again, you'll get it this time."

I'm not so sure about that, but I'm wild about the idea of learning braille. It's simply not coming to me as easily as I would've liked.

Whenever Sadie moves, the scent of lavender wafts into my kitchen, enveloping us at the table. Her chair creaks as she readjusts, as if urging me to put my fingertips back onto the page.

The paper is a different texture than a book for sighted people. The texture is pulpy, soft. And while the size of the book is larger, there are fewer words on each page.

One would think with fewer words to absorb, I'd be less overwhelmed. But that is not the case. Sadie has me reading not a full book but a learning page with unrelated sentences. Now that I've mostly learned my letters, she'd like me to put them together into actual words and phrases. The only oversight she's made as an instructor thus far is failing to wish me luck.

Braille is comprised of grids, each with six dots arranged in two columns and three rows. Beginning in the top left corner of the grid is dot 1. Moving down the column to the middle row is dot 2, and in the bottom left corner is dot 3. I can perceive that just fine. And I easily grasp the next portion as well, how each combination of dots forms a letter, number, or punctation mark. A period is dots 2, 5, and 6, for example.

But as I run my index finger over the dots, my brain initially trips up, as a *d* is the exact same shape as a period, only in a different location within the grid.

The preciseness, the similarities, a slip of my finger, making me miss a dot, is enough to fill my mind with sludge and have it ooze out through my ears.

"This can't be a punctuation mark in the middle of a word," I say, exasperated.

"True, so then it must not be," Sadie says sweetly. "Why don't you add your middle finger. Think of it as your peripheral vision."

Very well. "It's remembering all the configurations I'm struggling with the most."

"You'll learn them in time. It takes practice, like anything else in life. You didn't learn to ride a horse overnight, did you?"

My fingers still. I didn't know Sadie was aware of my background or particular situation. Not that I mind, exactly. But the mention of horses is a kick to my confidence.

There I was, only days ago, proclaiming how I'd be eager to ride again. Here I am now, unable to grasp how to read a few simple dots.

I shouldn't minimize. I know reading braille is more than that. But I feel foolish, like I got ahead of myself while talking with Mr. Endicott. So far ahead I can no longer fathom how I'd do such a thing as diving blind.

I sigh.

Sadie rubs a circle on my back. "Why don't we call it a day and come back tomorrow with a fresh brain?"

At the table, I drop my forehead to the page, my fingers still on the raised dots. Two dots as opposed to three, I realize. Not the word *fado*, but *fade*, which makes buckets more sense. "'But let it be. I cannot fade,'" I say into the page, my face mashed against the paper, putting together what I've read so far.

"Well done, Sonora. We could stop there or . . ."

Funny as it is to have my nose on the page, I don't move my head an inch. I like it right where it is. Perhaps osmosis is real and I need my brain touching the book.

Sadie is a dear for not remarking on my position as I begin to move my fingers again. Slowly, quite slowly in fact, I read the remainder of the sentence. "'But let it be. I cannot fade your wish.' Shakespeare, if I'm not mistaken."

"*The Winter's Tale*, act five, scene three. That is correct, Sonora. A job well done by you on all accounts."

Finally, I raise my head, training my practiced smile in Sadie's direction. Though this smile needs no training with how wonderful I feel inside.

And over the final weeks in Atlantic City, my confidence grows. My time with Sadie and my time with the horses become the two highlights of my days. Two parts of who I was before that I'm overjoyed to be breathing new life into once again.

IT TAKES TWELVE LESSONS with Sadie to become proficient in understanding braille. My use of the word *understanding* should be noted. I'm told it'll take quite some time longer—years for many—to truly become proficient in reading. But it's liberating and invigorating to see how far I've come, no longer needing to glue my forehead to the page to engage my brain.

Upon arriving at the Bucks County farm for winter quartering, I contact a distribution center that furnishes blind people in the area with braille books. They've promised to send some along, my first novel arriving just this morning.

That night in bed, the tome atop my lap, I say to Al, "Never before did I imagine this form of reading to include contractions, short-formed words, or a single letter to represent an entire word. For example, *v* can mean *very*. Then there are different dot combinations to convey entire words. An entire raised grid is equivalent to the word *for*."

Al chuckles. "This is all nice to hear. Your enthusiasm runneth over."

I suddenly feel shy, as if I'm being too much for him. But then his hand covers mine where it rests on the book's cover. I can only imagine the intensity of how he looks at me, his voice so earnest when he says, "You're so brave, Sonora. So strong in every way. I'll never not be enamored with your enthusiasm for whatever it is you're doing."

"Even if I'm no longer who you married?"

"And who's that?"

I shrug. "A woman who dives on horseback."

"Is that all you think you are? It's never been about the horses or you as a performer. It's about who you are in here"—he presses his hand over my heart—"and here." His fingertips grace my forehead. "The woman I married is courageous and strong-willed. She's quick-witted and sometimes feisty. She cares deeply. Stubborn too. But more importantly, the woman I married is directly beside me. I hate myself for making you doubt that. I confess I haven't known how to act. I've done a lousy job at being who you need me to be. But I'll keep trying, no matter that you sometimes elbow me away."

I cringe. "Picked up on that, did you?"

"It's not the first time you tried that old trick, but I'm here. If I can stop running, you can stop pushing."

He squeezes my hand, but I wish he'd do more than that. I want his arms around me, all over me. His lips. His body. I lick my lips, searching for the right words, when he asks, "Could you read to me?"

Honesty slips out. "I'm not very good yet."

"I'm still perfecting my creamed chipped beef, and you seemed to like it well enough at supper this evening."

"I'll have you know, I'm a tremendous actress."

His hands are on my stomach then, tickling me. I squeal, pulling up my knees, the book sliding from my lap. It's both unnerving and exhilarating not to know where his next touch will come from. I gasp when his lips are on my neck. I lean my head the other way, presenting him with more skin to do with as he pleases. He takes more and more and more. I may've missed reading and the horses, but I soon learn I've missed this even more.

Chapter 47

THE COUNT OF MONTE CRISTO takes many nights for Al and me to read. In part because my pace is slow. Also in part because *his* hands are often busier than my own.

Both are an excellent distraction from what's coming.

Ma.

I can no longer put her off. I've said it before; it's not that I don't love my mama, nor that I don't wish to spend time with her. The thing is, a large factor of Ma getting back on her feet after Ula left was her reliance on me. With so many siblings, we divided and conquered. It never allowed for the two of us to become close or, with me being the oldest, confidantes.

Clearly, in the gaggle of siblings I was responsible for keeping alive and well, I'd taken to Arnette, a not-so-secret favorite of mine. I picked well, my sister becoming a rock for me the past few weeks. Longer than that, if I'm being honest with myself.

The day Ma is set to arrive, Arnette is by my side on the small divan in the farmhouse's parlor. Al is at the train station to round up Ma when she disembarks. Georgie is visiting his family back in Texas. Lorena says she'll take Claribel for a long ride on Snow at Ralph Stover State Park so neither of them are underfoot.

"You're certain?" I ask her. "You don't need to run off."

"Doctor says I've been too sedentary. Either I use it or I lose it. So I'm going to use it the best I can, even if it's a bit uncomfortable at times."

"Okay, then," I tell her, sympathizing. I've been so caught up in myself as of late that I've failed to realize Lorena's been struggling in her own way, her knee causing her to lose sleep, stay off it more, and generally retreat from doing the things she loves, like those long horse rides of hers.

I know a thing or two about retreating. But I don't want to do that anymore either. I stand and wave her toward me so I can give her a quick hug before she sets off with her small, adorable hairball to saddle up Snow.

After sitting again, I ask Arnette, "Why am I so on edge?"

"Because she'll fuss over you. Mama knows you're strong, but I think she's always failed to see her own strength, and thus she doubts it in others."

"Arnette."

"What?"

"*Thus*?" I shake my head, smiling. "When did you get so wise?"

"I've always been wise, dear sister."

Ain't that the truth.

I square my shoulders to her. "Smears, smudges, or whatnot?"

I imagine Arnette surveying my face. She does something, I'm not sure what, until her thumb traces along my brow. "Tell me you didn't lick your finger."

"Then I won't. You're all set now. And not a moment too soon. You hear that?"

Tires on the gravel drive.

I sit up straighter.

Within moments, there are voices entering the house, two I'd recognize anywhere, even after not seeing Ma for years.

"She'll be in the parlor," Al says.

Then: "My girls!"

Her footsteps are hurried.

"Don't get up. Don't get up," Ma insists, emotion heavy in her voice.

But judging by the slight shift in the divan a second before I stand, Arnette's on her feet too.

Ma's certainly not gentle with her hug. Nor her kiss, which presses against my cheek, leaving behind wetness, not from her lips, but from her tears. "Forgive me. I should be gentler."

I chuckle away her discomfort. "How was your trip?"

"Well enough."

Her perfume is overwhelming, and I have to stifle more than a chuckle when I envision her reapplying it in the car with Al. He can be sensitive to smells. As she moves, the flowery scent leaves behind a trail I can visualize, and I can tell she's hugging my sister, most likely within an inch of her life.

"Both my girls," Ma coos. "Together. I always knew the two of you would end up thick as thieves. Jacqueline isn't cut from the same cloth as either of you. She's made her own way, pleased as punch to be working at Adler's and going out with the girls after her shifts. Then the boys . . . Those boys, each responsible for a handful of my grays. I prayed nightly they wouldn't end up in jail. Let's see, a barber, a mechanic, and maybe the hardest to believe is that Humphrey is set to become a man of the cloth."

"He knows that'll require him to sit still?"

Ma laughs. "As long as he's hearing sins as opposed to committing them."

I smile.

"But listen to me going on and on. Can I get you another pillow, Sonora?"

"I'm fine, and I know there's another on the chair across the way. In fact, why don't you sit. Tell me more about what I've been missing back home."

She answers my question with her own. "Could I get you some tea?"

Al's familiar footsteps enter the room. "Did I hear the mention of tea? At your service."

His timing is impeccable.

"I'll pour," he goes on.

Liquid sloshes into the three cups. There's one, then two clinks of porcelain scraping as Al lifts them, serving my ma and sister. I'm ready with my hand out before he returns for the third.

Ma's voice hiccups. "Careful, sweetheart, it'll be hot."

I force a smile. "Don't you worry about Arnette, Ma. She knows how to drink tea."

"That I do," Arnette says. "No need to fuss."

"It's a mother's nature to flap her wings when a child—"

"Loses their eyesight?" I say plainly. "We don't need to talk around it. I apologize I didn't tell you straightaway." Al perches on the edge of the divan, his arm snaking around my shoulders. "I needed time," I admit to her. "But I'm ready now."

"We don't need to do that, Sonora."

"I'd like to."

So I tell her about the accident, the aftermath, the recovery, how Mamie Lou's brush is now cracked. That may've gotten the biggest reaction from her of all my goings-on. For everything else, I barely heard her breathe.

She takes a large intake of breath now. "And presently, how are you? How do you manage day to day? Who dresses you, dear?"

I laugh. "Why, I do it myself. Why don't I show you. Come, follow me."

Al takes my hand to help me stand. In the past, I'd have yanked away, believing he thought I needed him to do so. But no, I see now he simply loves me. He wants to be there for me. Partners, in a way, like how I've taken to joining him in the kitchen, taste testing our meals as he prepares each one.

I lead Ma—and the others—to the bedroom Al and I share. "See," I say as I open the drawers of my dressing table and chest, "everything has its place. It's merely a matter of remembering where I've put everything."

Ma's been quiet, but now I recognize the humor in her voice as she says, "I lose my glasses atop my own head. How can you find anything specific?"

"It's not difficult, truly." I lift the sleeve of a dress. "This is my blue crepe. It feels different from cotton. It also has a boat-shaped neckline and is ornamented with French knots." I slide a hanger to the next article of clothing. "It's the same with each one. My fingers identify them. I've sorted outfits together. I even put on my own makeup. Believe it or not, dressing myself and caring for my clothes has become one of my easiest tasks."

"Well, I'll be," Ma says, and those three words mean the world to me, so few words that say so much.

By the time she leaves a week later, I'm certain I've convinced her that her blind daughter is going to be more than fine. I think I just may believe it too, which really gets my brain spinning. It gets to thinking about horses.

Chapter 48

IT'S IRONIC; MY MA'S the one, then and now, who's been the spark for my need to be on a horse.

Then, with the advert. Now, with making me believe I could ride again.

There's also a line in *Lolly Willowes* that's always stuck with me, that talks about how a girl threw away twenty years of her life like a handful of old rags, only for the wind to blow them back again and dress her in her old uniform.

Before, I likened it to taking a leap sooner rather than later.

Now it takes on a whole new meaning, and I'd rather not waste twenty years of my life.

"I want to ride again," I reveal to Arnette as we wash and put away the dishes after breakfast.

"Well, let's go outside and saddle up Red right here and now."

"I mean, ride *and* dive, just like you said to Mr. Endicott last season."

"Okay," she says.

"That's all you've got to say?"

"Well, sure. You've got to be the one to do it, not me. And if you think you can, then I think you can too. But the biggest pickle will be getting Al to agree to it."

"Maybe I should talk to Lorena first. She's likely in the office." I twist my body away from the sink, the office on the other side of the kitchen.

"Want my opinion?"

I stop twisting. "Perhaps not anymore."

"That's only delaying the inevitable. And speak of the devil, I can see Al out the window. He's just come out of the barn, talking to some man. Maybe we should get in line."

"What man?"

"Can't say I've seen him before."

"What's he look like?"

Water drips in the sink. I picture her hands hovering over the basin. "It doesn't appear to be a friendly chat. Come on." She leads us to the right, in the direction of the screened-in porch. "Quiet now."

The hinge is broken and the door could slam.

"Should I crouch?" I whisper to her.

"They aren't looking this way. But let's have a seat in case they do."

She backs me up to a wicker set we have out here, and I sit down, immediately rubbing my arms against the winter chill. "What's going on?"

"Al took off his hat."

"Oh no."

"The other fellow is tall, willowy. Has this weasel-like look to him, if that makes any sense."

I growl, then continue to keep our conversation at a whisper as I say, "More than you know. You never met Harold Grover, did you?"

"The man from that animal group? The one who keeps wanting to shut us down?"

"The very one."

"I dislike him already. Clearly not as much as Al does. Flames could be coming out of his nostrils soon."

"What's he saying?"

"If you can't hear, no way I can."

"Can we get closer without being seen?"

It takes Arnette a moment, but she finally says, "This way."

The sun hits my face as we leave the porch. It helps we spent a winter here before I lost my sight. I can still picture the yard in my mind's eye, and I know there to be a long row of rhododendrons. Arnette tucks me behind her as we sneak. I step on her heels no short of five times, mumbling "sorry" each time.

"Shhh. Can you hear now?"

It'd help if my heart would stop pounding in my ears. I take a deep breath, holding the air there, listening with all my might.

My head jerks up. I've heard my name. Well, not "Sonora," but "that wife of yours." Close enough for the sake of finding out what they're talking about. Or rather, who.

"Like I said, Mr. Grover, Sonora plans to take the season off."

"Yet you won't divulge why. And here's the thing, Al. Your wife is the only sufficiently trained rider remaining in your father's troupe. If she's not riding come opening day in May, believe me when I say I'll shut you down and take all 'em horses from you. All of 'em, you hear?"

"On what grounds?"

"These are hard economic times. It's surprising what people will do to put food on the table and support their family."

"Corruption? Lies, bribes. That's your answer? And that's who you are as a man? This has gone on long enough, Harold—"

"You have no idea, sonny. This began long before you. And it won't be over until there ain't a Carver behind the mic."

If only I could see Al's face, but I can imagine it, the confusion there. I hear it in his voice too. "You're right. I ain't sure what you're getting at, and frankly, I don't care. You know we take care of our animals. You know they dive on their own. This isn't about the horses or who you work for. This is about you and . . . what? Some vendetta you've been harboring against my old man? Whatever happened then, he won. And believe *me* when I say you'll never win. Now, if you'll excuse me—"

I duck lower and whisper to Arnette, "Which way are they going? Toward us?"

"Shhh."

An unbearable amount of time passes, enough that I almost prod her again for information. But she beats me to it, whispering, "Coast is clear."

I frown. "Appears to me we're dealing with the exact opposite. That man just won't let things lie, will he?"

I DEBATE GOING STRAIGHT to Al. Though once my fury settles at Grover poking his nose—again—where it doesn't belong, it's not lost on me that both Harold and I want the same thing: for me to dive.

Yet that feels too easy, like I'm missing something, only I can't put my finger on it.

I need to speak to Al.

Already snooping on him has left me feeling bashful, so as soon as I enter his office, I say, "I overheard your conversation with Harold Grover, and I'd like to dive."

He doesn't respond.

He doesn't respond so long that I'm convinced I've entered an empty room. It'd be my luck that he stepped out to use the restroom. But then there's a rustle of fabric. "I know you're in here."

He chuckles. "I'm not hiding from you, Sonora. I'm thinking of how to respond. Cat got my tongue, as the young folk say."

"I can do it, Al. I *want* to do it. The hardest part will be mounting. I've thought this through. The rest is muscle memory and then Red or John doing their part. Remember, ninety-five percent is the horse, five percent is me."

"Sit down. You make me nervous when you hover like that."

"Gladly." I work my way into the room and find the chair.

"Sonora, it scares the living bejesus out of me to have you on a horse again."

"But . . ."

"I'm not sure there's a *but* here, darling."

I cross my leg at my knee and begin bouncing my raised

foot. "There is, Al. You heard Harold's threat; he's got folks willing to be on the take. Let's not let it get to that."

"It may be too late. What I don't understand is how this feels like a personal vendetta. 'Until there ain't a Carver behind the mic.' I have no clue what that means."

"I think I do. Your daddy told me that he and Harold go way back to the first day he met your mama. Apparently Harold wanted her, but your daddy got her."

"And he's been holding a grudge ever since?"

"Trying to tear down what your daddy and your mama built together is my guess. But we *won't* let that happen. I can get stronger. I can train. Don't you think I can do it?"

"That's not a fair question to ask. I think you can do anything."

"So what's the problem?"

"The problem is Harold. Something doesn't sit right with me. You just said it was about my parents, yet he's fixated on you. Then there's the fact Arnette ended the season just fine. Marty came a long way too. The safety of the horses isn't in jeopardy." His pen taps. I jerk my foot harder. "It makes me wonder if something else is in play here. Maybe he knows you're blind."

"How would he know that? Even Mr. Endicott doesn't know."

He clucks. "The hell I should know. You're the one who's described him as being a weasel. Wouldn't it be a grand scheme if he says the only way he'll pull up on the reins is if you dive, knowing full well you can't see?"

I'm waggling my foot so hard that my oxford shoe flies off. I'll find it later. "The joke will be on him then, won't it?"

Al doesn't respond.

"Won't it, Al? You trust that I can do this, right? I can save the Great Carver Show and High-Diving Horses. I can do what I love again. Diving is a part of who I am. Al?"

"You know I'd choose you over the show any day of the week."

"Yes, I know." Anger begins to build in me. "You've expressed that sentiment to me before."

"It hasn't changed, Sonora. To put you forty-five feet in the air? Not being able to see? An animal that weighs over a thousand pounds barreling at you? Please see this from my point of view."

"That's the thing, Al. I can't see."

At that, I stand to leave the room. As luck has it, I kick my shoe that flew off. I snag it and slip it back on, saving me the embarrassment of storming off while missing one.

I'VE NEVER GIVEN MY husband the silent treatment before. It's childish. But so is sneaking along the rhododendrons. I won't make a habit of either, yet I'm sullen about him not agreeing that me diving again is the best thing for all of us, including his daddy's legacy.

So at supper I sit at the kitchen table not uttering a peep.

It's only the two of us. Georgie won't be returning from Texas until next week. Arnette left an hour ago.

"I can stay," she told me.

"Not for even a second longer," I insisted. "Have a marvelous time visiting Jacob. I'll see you in a few short weeks in Atlantic City."

She kissed my cheek goodbye, and I immediately felt the loss of her. Lorena's missing from supper too, someone else who may have had my back about riding again. She knows what it feels like to hold on to something she loves. In fact, she's late for supper because she's out on Snow this very moment.

I intertwine my fingers on the tabletop and lean back in my chair, waiting for Al to serve me.

A plate goes down in front of me. "Meat loaf is at nine o'clock. Peas are at three."

I say nothing.

"I know you're upset with me, Sonora."

I raise my brows, then pick up my fork.

"Why don't you start with the peas." He removes the fork from my hand.

"Al," I snap. "I need that."

"Use your fingers."

"Like a child?"

Is he poking fun at my antics? This is certainly not the way to get back in my good graces.

"Humor me." Al leads my hand to the peas. "Careful so you don't move them out of shape."

"What in the devil are you going on about?" I sigh, but I do as he says, touching the pea he puts my index finger on.

"Dot 1," he says.

He shifts my finger.

"Dot 3," I say, my anger ebbing.

I move to dot 4, then 5.

"Last one is . . . here."

My index finger ends on the bottom right.

I smile. "Yes."

He spelled *yes*.

"Does this mean what I think it means?"

"That I'm willing to *try* to let you ride. We'll start with strength training. Then add in the horses."

I smile bigger. "That, but also, did you learn braille for me?"

"Enough to say I'm sorry and that I believe in you."

I reach up, my right hand unfortunately whacking him in the face. But once I know where he is, I pull him toward me. I kiss him. That is more than enough.

Chapter 49

Yes, I'll be diving again, but Al doesn't want me anywhere near the tower. Which is inconsequential considering we don't have a tower at the Bucks County farm. Too cold.

And honestly, that's fine by me.

I may possess courage for days, but my desire for self-preservation is stronger. I'd be a fool to climb forty feet in my current state, a handful of pounds lighter from lost muscle, and then try to fling myself blindly onto the back of a moving horse.

I could mistime and be trampled.

I could stumble and free-fall into cement-like water.

I could fumble my grip on the harness.

I could lose my strength, my thighs giving out while I squeeze.

I could fail to duck in time, doing greater damage to my face.

That last one is Al's concern, but at first I can't fathom how;

it sounds to me like locking the barn door after the horse has already been stolen. But after Al takes me to Dr. Morganson to get his opinion on the matter, the doctor tells me that advancements in medicine are happening in record numbers. "What if, let's say in ten years, there's a third operation that can be done, but you've done more abuse to your eyes? Protect what you have, even if currently it feels like little."

"So what can we do, Doc?" Al asks.

"Spalding has a manufacturing facility only a handful of miles away. I've sent patients there previously. I'll jot down some specifications for a specialized helmet, one with an unbreakable lens to protect Sonora's eyes."

"But how will that look?" I ask.

"It'll look like a woman who is keen to preserve and persevere."

I twist my lips. How can I fight him on that?

The helmet will take weeks to get ready.

So will I.

Both with a deadline of early May.

I begin my training with bells on, eager to get back in shape. Al hangs a bar for pull-ups in the barn. Every day, with risk of my hands freezing to the metal, I put myself through rep after rep. On my feet, I lunge, I squat. On my hands and feet, I hold a plank and do push-ups until my arms are jelly. At night I roll my muscles over a liniment bottle, preparing for another grueling day of training.

I feel myself growing stronger. When I run my hands down my legs and along my arms, I smile at the progress being made.

Now to get back on the horse.

"I think we should start with John," Al suggests as we walk side by side toward the barn.

I shake my head. "I want Red. He's the more impressive performer. The crowd prefers him."

"He's also more fickle."

"He's who spectators expect. Red's on the postcards and in the adverts. The star of our nighttime shows, when we draw the largest crowds."

Al can't argue reason, and I get my way. He leads Red from his stall.

"I was thinking," I say, "I could sit on the fence rung or something to mirror how I sit up on the tower. You'll run Red to me, and I'll do my thing."

"Yep, where you sit has to be the exact same distance from the ground." Having been a part of the tower's design, he stacks a number of hay barrels to the exact height needed, then says, "These first few tries, I'd like to have Red run straight by you so you can get a feel for his height and where his back is. And please don't fight me on this, Sonora. We'll get to you being on his back."

"I'd never fight against common sense," I say with a side of cheeky grin.

I picture him shaking his head in that playfully exasperated way of his.

"Ready?" Al asks me once we're both set in our positions.

"More than you know."

I hold on to the edge of the top hay bale with one hand and stretch out the other. I listen. I wiggle my fingers. The first time Al leads Red past, I catch nothing but air. I lower my arm. The second time I flick the tip of his ear. Lower still. The third time my hand runs along his neck—and the harness. Winner, winner, chicken dinner.

The fourth time I try to do everything the same.

My hand's too low this time.

How frustrating to get it wrong when I did it perfectly just moments ago.

I try again, slightly higher from where I thought I had it. With my other hand, I feel along the underside of my arm, down my side, beneath my armpit, trying to commit the angles of my body to memory.

"Go," I say to Al.

A moving sound is hard to pinpoint, but I bob my head to the rhythm of Red's hooves against the dirt, doing my best to ignore Al's footfalls beside him. Red will sound different on the tower, more of a *clack* than a *thud*, but the musicality of it will remain. Or at least I hope it will.

He's almost to me.

My fingertips brush against him, trailing, trailing, until the leather of the harness is grabbable. I quickly do so, then release it so I don't get tugged off the hay bales.

I smile, joy infusing me. "I want to mount him this time," I call out.

"All right," Al says. "But I'm stopping him these first few times."

I press my lips together but say nothing. I'll give Al this. I know my actions will need to be precise. A split second off and I'll miss Red. Or I could lose my balance and fall. Or I won't get a good enough grip on the diving harness. A favorite saying of the Carver men: "Crawl before you walk."

Then I have every intention of galloping.

It's the positive thinking I need in this very moment.

We go again, my arm at the height and angles I've tried to memorize through touch.

Al stops Red; I launch myself off the bales, jumping too low, not bringing my leg around high enough, and smack into Red's side. I grit my teeth. "Again."

And again.

And again.

Too much momentum and I go up and over Red, Al catching me.

Not enough momentum and I can't get on or I miss Red completely.

I'm Goldilocks, but for the life of me, I can't get all the arm height, power, grabbing, mounting, stabilizing just right. The kind of right I need to dive safely. I mount Red a time or two, but not with the proper balance. Or confidence.

I sense Al wanting to stop for the day. I don't so much hear it in his breathing or in the way his feet drag. But I have an overall feeling of familiarity with this man, and I know he'll keep going as long as I want to. For me, that's long after the sun's gone down. Wouldn't make a lick of difference for me. But that's not fair to either of my boys.

"Okay," I concede, "that's it for now."

Chapter 50

"THAT YOU, LORENA?" I ask the next morning, my hands wrapped around a warm mug at the kitchen table.

"Not yet. I need coffee before I'm fully myself and human."

I laugh.

"Caught some of your training yesterday."

My laughter abruptly ends. "And?"

"And what?"

"You've got nothing to say? That you're questioning if I can do this or not. That you think Al wants to call it all off."

"I have nothing to say of the sort, but it does sound like you're in need of one of my infamous pep talks. Actually, maybe one of your own. Remember what you said to Arnette to fix her?"

"About using her left hand?"

"Yup. Arnette's way of doing things wouldn't suit either of us, but it fits her. You need to find what works for you. I'm not sure you'll be able to count Red's steps or rely on grabbing a harness that's bouncing six ways to Sunday."

"So what are you saying I do?"

"I'm not sure. Not exactly. I have to imagine your situation is uniquely yours, nor can I begin to understand what it's like to do what you're doing blind. But there's always been something about you that I've admired. It's your gut, Sonora. Your instincts. Your proclivity to be brave and daring. If I had to guess, there'll be a moment when you *know* it's time to go. And when you do, you may find yourself halfway between his head and withers, but it's about getting yourself up there before you go reaching for more."

"Get settled on Red's back, then find the harness, you're saying?"

"You know Red will stand at the end of the platform and stomp his feet for attention before he dives."

I snort. That he will.

"So," she continues, "that'll give you another heartbeat or two to get yourself in the proper position. Maybe don't try to do everything at once. That includes not worrying about things you can't control. Like that horrid Harold Grover."

Practical advice, in more ways than one. I take a steadying breath, then a sip of coffee, already feeling the caffeine go to work. In a few minutes, I do too.

I won't say I get it right straightaway. Or that once I am able to mount Red, I do it correctly every time. But before the week's out, I'm swiftly swinging my leg over a moving Red, and without a moment to lose. Atlantic City awaits.

THE BOARDWALK IN MAY is the quiet before the storm. For us, it's convenient that our tower stands year-round. For the others, this time is spent getting riggings up or assembling the sixteen-foot globe that Eleanor Seufert will defy both gravity and death in as she motorcycles around inside it.

Al and I are getting the horses settled in their stalls. "Now remember, no fuss about my eyesight. I don't want Mr. Endicott or anyone else, worst of all Harold, finding out."

Al closes John's stall door. "You'd inspire so many, you know, if they knew what you're going to do."

His words stop me. I've never before thought about my diving inspiring others. Being courageous is something I've only ever done for myself. Sure, I fancy the applause after a dive. But it's the thrill and the horses I live for. It's the thrill and the horses I haven't been willing to give up. Red gets it, nipping naughtily at my ponytail, the only one of our horses who shows his love in such ways. "Get all your impishness out now," I chastise him, unable to stop my smile.

He nickers, and Al laughs along.

"Sonora?"

I turn toward a familiar high-pitched voice. "Roxie!"

My favorite aerialist hugs me, and I don't miss a beat before throwing my arms around her too. "So you've recovered? I wasn't sure if I'd be seeing you this summer, but boy, am I glad you're here. So much change already this year."

I cock my head. "However so?"

"Didn't Al tell you? Mr. Endicott got the boot. We now answer to a man named Mr. Gravitt."

"No," I say loudly enough for my dear husband to hear from wherever he is in the stables. "Al hasn't mentioned the switch-up. What's he like?"

"Can't say much beyond the fact he's a dish. Orville has been dealing with him for our troupe. But fingers crossed things stay the same. On second thought, he's the only change, but it feels big. As far as I know, all of the same acts have signed on again this year. Your sister back too?"

"She'll be arriving with Jacob and the Hawaiians."

"Oh, that getting serious?"

A second familiar voice rings out, "It sure is!"

My heart swells, not having been with my sister in weeks.

Roxie gasps, then shrieks, "Would you look at that rock? How'd Jacob afford such a thing? I dunno, I may have to talk to this new Mr. Gravitt about the Hawaiians getting paid more than me."

I try to grasp what's causing all the fuss. A rock, as in on a certain finger on my sister's hand? "Arnette!" That must be it. "Congratulations! When did this happen? How dare you not cable me the instant he proposed."

She laughs. "It was only last night. I wanted to tell you in person."

"Well, get over here." I hold out my hand for hers and fake appraise her beautiful ring, or at least I assume as much. "It's perfect," I say, and pull her in for a hug.

Then Roxie's arms are around us both. "This is going to be the best season yet. You just wait."

Only a second ago the woman was fretting. Funny how things can change at the drop of a dime in show business.

WITH LESS THAN A week to go until opening day, all the acts are topsy-turvy. My special eye-protecting helmet is delayed. Then on time. Then delayed again. From my dressing room, I often hear Al grumbling into the telephone as he checks in daily with Spalding. The latest is that we've been told it'll arrive in the nick of time—on opening day.

Dr. Morganson, Al, and I agreed I wouldn't go off the tower—low or high—without wearing it. We all know what this delay means, though none of us want to verbalize it: I may only get a go or two on the tower before I'm performing before eight thousand spectators . . . and Harold Grover.

What can I do but continue to work on my strength? Each day I do pull-ups on rings that dangle from a cross brace beneath our tower. I climb the Hawaiians' 105-foot-high ladder. Then I climb my own tower, counting the cleats as I go. Sometimes I run up the ramp, as if I'm one of the horses, getting a feel for it. Arnette laughs every time, yelling out that I should be whinnying.

I practice on Red on the ground, my intuition improving, even while things are going on all around me that continue to shake my resolve. Perez, a slack wire performer, loses his balance, falls from the suspended wire, and injures his foot. One of the girls from the water sports gang, thankfully not Arnette, slips off her aquaplane, the board flipping all about until cracking against her head. Then, only yesterday, the Pallenberg bear got off his leash, giving a boy named Tommy Kao the fight of his life.

Every occurrence is a pendulum for my confidence, swinging it back and forth. If so many of these trained, talented performers can stumble, then is there truly any hope for me?

It's what I'm thinking right now as I make my way from the exit outside my dressing room and Al's office to the tower. Al has strung together ropes between here and there. If any other performers question what it's for, they haven't let on. I don't use my hand, but I walk alongside it, my clothing brushing the rope as my guide. It's been crucial to keep up the charade that I'm still sighted, everyone who doesn't know the truth assuming last summer's injury has fully healed.

I continue on, nearly at the tower, my focus trained ahead. "Springtime in the Rockies" is playing, and I picture Roxie and Irene in the midst of their routine. Orville, their Al, calls out a direction I can't quite make out as someone nearby coughs, alerting me to their presence. I don't worry about missing them with a hello or a friendly smile; tension is high, and many performers grow serious and preoccupied in the hours leading up to opening day.

I take another step, only to stop in my tracks when there's a scream. A bloodcurdling scream chased by a chorus of alarmed voices.

I stagger, a hand over my heart. What has happened now?

Chapter 51

SOMEWHERE ABOVE ME, METAL creaks and grinds, barely heard over widespread shrieks. Instinctively, I stoop, then retreat a step, stumbling backward over something, landing hard on my tailbone. Suddenly there's a large crash, a cacophony of metal banging and wood splintering, so close to me that the ground vibrates. I cower beneath my arms before scrambling away, not even sure which way to escape.

There's more shouting. The thuds of running feet. "Springtime in the Rockies" still plays. I fight to stand up, but my foot slips. An arm hooks underneath mine to help me get to my feet. As quickly as my savior comes, the arm is removed and whatever they hastily say to me is missed. I stretch my arms wide, trying to gain purchase of where I am or if anyone else is around me. My heart beats with such intensity it feels as if chunks of me will come loose. Someone brushes past and I reach for them, getting nothing but air. In the commotion, I've gotten turned around.

Two giant hands suddenly frame my face. I freeze, out of breath, waiting for a voice. Finally, I hear, "Are you all right?"

I collapse into my husband, tears stinging my eyes. "Yes. Yes, I'm fine. What's happened?"

"It's Roxie." Al's lips touch mine for the briefest of moments, so quickly I'm too slow to respond. "Are you certain you're not hurt?"

"Yes. But Roxie, what's happened to her? Is Irene all right? Orville?"

"This way." Al puts my hand on his arm, keeping his hand on top, and leads me. I believe I'm going back the way I came. Whatever direction I'm going, the hullabaloo becomes more subdued. My tailbone smarts from when I landed on it. I rub there.

"Did you fall?"

"Yes, but it's not me I'm concerned about."

Al yanks me toward him. A gush of something passes. A man, I realize, once I hear his voice, yelling for an ambulance on the telephone outside Al's office.

We continue inside. Al blows out a heavy breath. "Sit. I didn't see it happen, only the aftermath." I'm in his rocking chair. I fold my hands together in my lap, kneading one into the other, awaiting his next words. "From what I can gather, something on the aerial riggings broke. The whole thing came down, including Roxie. As you likely heard, the ambulance is on its way. Everything will be all right."

"Where is she now?"

There is no need for him to answer. The first-aid room is adjacent to our rooms. Roxie's voice calls out, screaming about her back.

I cover my mouth with my hand, terror rippling through me for Roxie, and I say a silent prayer that no permanent damage has been done.

I nearly jump out of my skin at another abrupt sound. "There you are!"

It's Arnette. I feel for her, finding her on her knees in front of me, her head going into my lap. "You're okay," she says. "You're okay."

"Of course I am. What are you doing? Look at me."

I feel the weight of her forehead lift.

"You don't get it, Sonora. I was out in the water, waiting for my turn to go. I saw you walking toward the tower. Then I saw the riggings come down, crashing right where you were standing last time I saw you."

My head jerks to where I know Al is pacing. Then back to my sister. "I moved," I say, at a loss for how to better articulate what happened. "I fell over something."

"A bench," Arnette says. "I saw it as I was running to find you. Half the bench is crushed beneath the riggings." Emotion is thick in her voice. "You could've . . ."

"I'm fine. It's Roxie I'm worried about."

The whirl of ambulance sirens fills the air, and I'm sure every single person stops what they're doing and faces in the direction of the noise.

My chin is cupped, turned. A kiss is pressed to my lips. "Go home with your sister. I'm going to go with Orville to the hospital. Listen to a grand story from Mrs. Van Myers and try to put all of this out of mind."

Fat chance of that, but for his benefit, I nod, force a smile. I tuck my arm into Arnette's, and together we distance ourselves from the horror that's happened here today.

ROXIE ENDS UP WITH a badly fractured ankle and a broken foot. But worst of all is her vertebrae, several of which have been crushed in her lower back. The doctors don't know whether she'll ever walk again.

Al brings me the news, along with my helmet from Spalding, and not a minute too soon; opening night is this very evening.

"I almost don't want to give you this," he says flatly.

"How can I not accept it? Roxie may never do what she loves again. I have that chance."

I take the helmet to test the fit. I've always worn a standard football helmet while diving. This one is heavier and clunkier because of a metal frame on the front that cradles a lens. I put it on, the plastic piece fitting across my nose and covering my eyes. Inside, foam rubber holds it firmly to my head, even more firmly after Al laces up the back and buckles the strap beneath my chin.

He asks me, "How's that feel?"

"I can't hear as well as before," I comment, and the pendulum of my emotions promptly swings to doubt.

Will I be able to hear Red's approach?

Will I be able to mount him?

Will I be able to stay on his back once we hit the water?

They are questions that amass into a pain in between my

eyes, but I know the answer is that I must try. First, from the lower tower. Then tonight, from the top. Without a minute to lose, I'm soon on the tower's lower platform. Georgie has Red at the bottom of the ramp. Al's beside me to stop Red.

"I'm not being foolish, am I?" I ask Al. "Or maybe it's presumptuous of me to think that I can do my act without injury when sighted performers are being injured daily."

"You can do anything, darling. Anything. But if this doesn't go well, then we'll stop there. We'll figure out something else. The show does not rest on your shoulders."

But it sure feels like it does. Either I ride or Harold Grover will call in favors to men more than ready to cash in. He'll finally get what he's wanted all these years since Josephine rejected him and shut down something Doc loved. I shake my head, chasing away the noise, and then I motion for Georgie to release Red.

As always, his hooves thunder through me, now muffled from the pads within my helmet. Still, closer and closer I feel him come, until Al stops him.

My hands find Red first, the familiar shape of him. With him unmoving, it takes little effort to get onto his back and slip my fingertips around the diving harness.

Red proceeds to the end of the platform, where he does his spectator-charming dance.

Then we dive.

My breath hitches.

I duck immediately.

From this lower height and with no perception of the water's closeness, I feel the water hit faster than I ever could have imagined. The impact pulls me free of Red. It's an incredibly dangerous position for a rider to be in. Made even more dangerous by the fact I cannot see where his legs are thrashing. One kick to the head and I won't leave this pool alive. I propel myself to the bottom of the tank—out of reach, I hope—and wait.

Bubbles fizz against my skin.

I wave my arms but feel nothing.

I count to ten, my lungs beginning to burn, then once I'm as certain as I can be that I won't swim up directly beneath Red, I push off the bottom.

I break the surface, gasping for air. I swim a stroke, not sure if it's the right way to the incline, but nevertheless, I reach the side of the tank and hands grab for me.

"Sonora!"

I'm so startled I take a mouthful of water. I cough, smacking away the groping hands. "Al?" I cough again. "Let me go. I'm okay. You'll pull me down."

"I'm trying to get you out." His voice is wracked with fear.

I tread water. The incline's to my right, judging by where I know Al usually stands to watch. "Can we have this conversation on dry land?" I begin swimming, though I keep talking. "I was unseated, so I had to outwait Red. That's all. I'm fine. Next time I'll stay on."

"You want to do that again?"

"Al, I want to do it for the rest of my life. This first time surprised me, that's all."

He's silent.

I swim until there's a touch on my arm, and I assume Al's now standing on the incline. I lower my own feet.

"I'll have you know, Red's standing on the platform looking at us like we're two idiots."

"He may be right about one of us."

Al laughs.

I close my eyes, shake my head, and join him with my own chuckle. "I'm sorry for scaring you."

"I have a feeling you're going to do it a handful of times before the day is through."

"And years after that. But we'll start with today."

Al takes my hand to guide me onto the platform, where I'm promptly nudged by Red for his sugar.

"The high tower—"

I cut him off. "I'd like to save that for tonight. I'm not certain I can work up my courage more than once today for that."

I tilt my head back, as if I can see the high tower. In my mind's eye, I can. And tonight I'll dive blind on horseback from the tippy top for the very first time, all on my own.

Chapter 52

It began with an advert, and it's culminated to what may be the biggest night of my life.

It's fitting that I'm at my dressing table, running Mamie Lou's brush, a bit worse for wear, through my hair. I've sat here so many times before.

As it's done for me for all these years, I try to let the action calm me.

It's proving difficult.

Georgie stopped by only moments ago to let me know that Red is on his best behavior, but also that the crowd may be our largest yet.

"There are a bunch of media folk too," he says. "Cameras everywhere."

With it being our third season in Atlantic City and a more forward-thinking Mr. Gravitt at the helm, the press knows all about "Miss Sonora and Red Lips." Or maybe this media circus is Harold's doing. Did he invite the cameras for his own benefit?

"That worm," I mutter to myself.

"What's that?" Georgie says.

"Did you see Harold Grover out there? I bet he wants to expose me and have all the media here to watch it happen. Big, flashy headlines about a blind woman putting animals in harm's way."

It boils my blood.

I roughly stroke the brush through my hair, then catching myself, I ease up. Me getting riled up is exactly what that man would want.

I hear three quick knocks. Al. Something he always does before stepping inside my dressing room. "There's my girl," he says to me. "Oh, hey, Georgie." Then to me, "What is it? You appear sullen."

I huff. "Just ruminating on the media out there waiting to see me."

"You mean to see you dazzle them?"

Georgie makes his exit, assuring me Red will be ready with bells on. Now, there's a thought.

"Sonora." My table creaks, and I picture Al perched there. I reach out, resting my hand on his leg, wanting the comfort of feeling him. "Are you absolutely certain you're up to this? If you're not, you know we can call it off. Or Arnette can dive in your place. I'm sure Mr. Gravitt would understand."

"He may, but it's Harold and his vendetta that I'm worried about. Doubly so now." There's silence for a moment. Then I add, "I've got to do it."

"Yes, I think you must. Will you let me come up with you? Just this first time from the top to stop the horse? Lorena can announce as well as anybody."

"Yes, she can. But no," I say, squeezing his leg. "I'd rather you didn't. I've got to do it alone."

He's quiet for a few moments more before he says, "Are you afraid?"

"I don't know," I say honestly, thinking, deciding. "I love doing this too much to let fear win."

"You amaze me. Always, Sonora. Just go up there like it's old times. Trust yourself and lean on the hundreds of times you've done it."

"Thank you, Al."

"I'd better get out there. Almost time for us to go on."

"Who is performing for Roxie tonight?"

"Irene is doing a solo show."

I nod, my heart breaking for my friend. "Tonight's for Roxie. For us. For me."

Al swallows roughly. "Tonight's for everyone, my love."

His lips touch mine. As he begins to break our kiss, I hold him there, needing a few more seconds.

"See you out there," he says.

I nod.

"You look great. No smudges."

I can tell he's stalling. I point toward the door, but I'm wearing a smile.

Alone again, I fill my lungs with air, then release it the slowest I've ever done. Then I stand.

I twirl my shawl around my shoulders. I slip on my helmet, leaving it unbuckled for now. I'm wearing my red suit tonight, marked with a button on the right shoulder. I run my hands down my stomach, giving myself one more moment to gather myself.

At that I leave my dressing room, pass through Al's office, and proceed outside. I'm unsure how long until I'm set to go on; different music is playing this evening for the aerialist act. Nevertheless, I find my rope, then begin walking. The fringe of my shawl brushes against the rope until I'm at the base of the tower.

There I hang my shawl and buckle my helmet.

The music ends. Applause takes over. Irene is done. Then Al's voice booms, opening our act. I begin to climb, counting the cleats.

One, two three, four, thinking how familiar it feels to do this very thing.

Five six, seven, eight, reminding myself I'm performing for myself, yes, but for everyone, the future of Doc's show high on the list.

Up and up I go, trembling slightly at the chill in the night air, made cooler with the breeze coming off the ocean. The tank will be frigid this early in the season.

Nineteen, twenty, twenty-one, twenty-two. Fear rears its ugly head, telling me I have more to lose than my eyesight. Earlier Arnette told me she'd be in the grandstand and if I got cold feet to "look" out, knowing she believes in me.

I continue climbing, the numbers ticking by. Al's almost done with his spiel.

Seventy-six, seventy-seven, seventy-eight, seventy-nine . . . I step onto the platform just as Al's voice booms, "And now, ladies and gentlemen, Miss Sonora and Red Lips."

In all my prior dives, I've tried to synchronize my arrival with Al's words. A good omen that I've accomplished it this evening?

I thrust my hand into the sweet-smelling, chilled air, waving to the crowd, reaching for confidence. I grab on; no room for the pendulum to come at me again with fear or doubts. That'd do nobody any good.

I boost myself onto the railing and will away the wobble in my knees. We may not have practiced a moving dive, I may never have ridden without my eyesight from this height before, but I've come all this way to do that very thing. Perform.

The crowd is going wild. I tug at my helmet to create even a sliver more of space for my ears to hear. But it does no good; the excitement of the spectators is nearly deafening.

Intimidating.

Energizing.

Terrifying.

Exhilarating.

I motion for Georgie.

Red is immediately on his way, within steps, shaking the tower. I hold on to the railing with both hands until I know he must be nearing, until I know it's time to reach out my hand.

Not too high.

Not too low.

Goldilocks at her finest.

I can barely hear him, I certainly can't see him, but I can feel him coming. Then my fingertips touch him. I propel myself, throwing my leg in a high arc over him. As luck has it, my hand naturally falls on the neck strap.

I'm seated.

It takes me a breath to realize I've done it. I haven't missed him. I haven't shot myself too far and gone into the railing on the other side.

I'm on Red's back.

A shaft of joy shoots through me and I tighten my legs, preparing for our dive. But of course, he first has to grandstand, stomping one hoof after another. It gives me time to reflect on him, on me, on how what we're doing feels so natural, so perfectly suited to who we are. I'm in the process of finding a part of myself that I thought I had lost forever.

That is, if we can make the dive.

Red ends his dance. He slides over the edge, hanging there for a breath, my body hitching forward, my abdomen engaging to hold me steady. Then he slams his hooves against the panel with a terrific force and launches us out into space.

Nothing but open air.

If I thought it was life-changing to plummet before, with my eyes open, I'm even more transformed as the air pulls at my cheeks in total darkness.

Down, down, down we fall, yet to me it feels as if we're suspended. A ripple goes throughout Red, the tightening of his muscles and the lengthening of his forelegs, and it's my cue to tuck into him.

The water greets us, and I know in my gut we've just performed the perfect dive. I squeeze my legs, my hands. I press my head into his neck. I do everything in my power to stay on, to not ruin it now.

Red jolts, his forefeet touching bottom. He throws his head back and springs toward the surface, surging with such force that when we break the water, he gets so much height that my entire body is exposed to the nighttime air.

The grandstand goes berserk, too loud for me to form any conscious thoughts. Instead, I'm flooded with the overwhelming sensation that we've done it.

Red carries me to the incline, moving so quickly we leave the tank at a brisk canter. I slide off him, two hands catching me. Two hands I knew would be there.

"Sonora!" is all Al says before he speaks into the microphone. "Isn't she wonderful?" he asks the crowd. The volume of their response indicates an overwhelming yes. The moment is made all the more special by the fact the crowd knows nothing about why this dive is truly something memorable.

A sugar cube is pressed into my hand. On a whim, I put it in between my teeth and stretch my neck toward Red. He takes it from me, appearing as if he kisses me while doing so.

Al's so close I can hear the roar of his laughter. Then he speaks into my ear, "The cameras caught that, my love. They're standing for you. A standing ovation."

My heart swells.

At this point, I'd usually leave the stage, the crowd petering out. Not this time. Al whispers again in my ear, "He was here, you know. And he saw it all. You foiled him good, Sonora. In fact, there's a line waiting for you."

"Of fans?"

"Reporters. If you're up for talking to them."

I nod. Let them post headlines and articles, the exact opposite of the ones Harold Grover planned for. That'll make him never want to show his face again.

Al says, “Mr. Gravitt is waving me over. Will you be fine for a few moments?”

“I’ve handled harder.”

The first reporter approaches me before I’m even down from the stage. “Miss Sonora,” he says, “that was remarkable, truly remarkable. What’s it like to do what you do?”

“It’s hard to put into words,” I say. “Maybe you’d like to go through the training and see for yourself one day.”

He guffaws. “I think I’ll leave that to the professionals.”

Someone else chimes in, and I turn toward his voice. “You’re shaking like a leaf,” he comments.

“Not from the act,” I assure him. Not anymore, at least. “The water temperature is less than desirable.”

This garners more laughs. A third voice is added to the mix. “Looking at you even now, I can’t believe it, but a man back there told me you can’t see. Is it true you’re blind?”

I just about swallow my tongue. But Arnette and I have long practiced my expressions, and I maintain one that exudes a calm confidence. Is this question Harold’s doing? Perhaps. Even if it’s not, I don’t want that man chasing us for years to come. So I say, “Yes, it’s true. As if I’d let such a thing stop me.”

A murmur runs through the reporters and those around us. I’m not sure which way this’ll go. I maintain the cool confidence I have on my face, waiting for a reaction.

“Well, then,” one of the reporters says, “I’d like to shake your hand, because I think you’re the most exceptional person I’ve ever met.”

I extend my own. “How can I say no to that?”

The handshaker squeezes mine, covering my hand with both of his.

After that, I'm peppered with one question after another, some about diving, others about my blindness. I try to steer away from the latter, not because I'm ashamed, but because the act is about more than just me. It's about a larger-than-life man who is no longer with us, who made all of this possible. His daughter, who's become a sister to me. My own sister, who's become my best friend. And a devilishly handsome man who once doubted me but has become the one who believes in me the very most.

Speaking of that man, where is he?

I excuse myself, citing how I'd like to warm up, and retreat to my dressing room, an energized pep in my step.

I leave my door open and sit before my dressing table mirror. I stare, knowing I won't be able to see myself but picturing the nineteen-year-old girl in an oversized robe who wanted nothing more than to live life to the fullest on her terms. Never would that young woman have imagined me as I am now. After my accident, I wondered if I'd be the same daring, courageous Sonora, one of the first in the country to dive on the back of a horse.

And yes, it's still me, but only more daring, more courageous. I wonder who I'll be in another handful of years. I'd like to believe I'll surprise myself then too.

I work a sly smile onto my face.

"I know you're there," I say to Al in the open doorway.

"Sonora," he says, an endless amount of love in his voice. "I'll always be here."

Author's Note

THE MOMENT WE JUST experienced together of Sonora's first dive without her eyesight was the beginning of eleven years in which she rode blind. I first learned of Sonora after seeing the 1991 Disney film *Wild Hearts Can't Be Broken*. I've been enamored with her story ever since.

Interesting side note: Sonora attended a screening of the film with Arnette. It's said that Sonora was dissatisfied with its embellishments and felt that it bore little resemblance to her life.

I sought to align my novel more closely with her life and experiences, along with the times, and Sonora's memoir became my primary resource for writing this book. For storytelling purposes, however, some moments, dates, and names I slightly modified. One such example is how I put the media in the final scene and how Sonora's blindness was revealed. In actuality, Sonora hid her blindness for five years. This changed during an appearance in Charlotte. "Say," a reporter said, "somebody just told me that you can't see. I came over to ask you personally because I don't believe it." In response, Sonora revealed that it was true. The next day an article was published, resulting in Sonora being flooded with letters from people all over the country. They shared how much Sonora's story meant to them and how it had inspired them to go on living as normally as possible in spite of various disabilities. Sonora concluded that if knowledge of her blindness coupled with her success as a rider could help others, then it was both rude and selfish of her to keep it a secret any longer.

Sonora dove with horses from 1924 to 1942, the Great Carver Show and High-Diving Horses hanging up its reins shortly after the United States entered the Second World War. As Sonora said in her memoir, "We decided the time to quit had come. We would put Red Lips out to pasture and take to the pasture ourselves. I was ready, but Al was not. Al was and is a real showman, and real showmen love the business as they love nothing else in the world" (Sonora Carver and Elizabeth Land. *A Girl and Five Brave Horses.* Doubleday, 1961. Reprint, Start Publishing LLC, 2012. Kindle).

When I read Sonora's memoir, the love Sonora, Al, Doc, and the others had for their act and for their horses was immediately evident to me.

In an interview, Arnette said that "throughout the show's existence, the Society for the Prevention of Cruelty to Animals was constantly looking for evidence of abuse, but they never found anything because the horses were so well loved and throughout the years not a single one was injured." Veterinarians also visited and checked the horses over the years, all stating that the horses were in excellent health.

I tried to portray such elements in my novel, while including the SPCA's interest in the Carvers' horses. I also felt it was important to include Lightning's death, which is based on a true event. While the SPCA is referred to only twice in Sonora's memoir and no specific employee is mentioned, I chose to create the fictional Harold Grover because I felt this thread deserved greater weight with my novel being published in a different time. The standards for what animals were cleared to do were different when Sonora performed. But Sonora's nephew, Donald French, is quoted as saying, "Regardless of your stance on horse diving, Sonora stands as an inspiration. She represented courage, fearlessness, but also the fun of the times." I have to agree. I didn't tell this story because I wanted to promote horse diving, but rather to showcase Sonora's tenacious spirit.

After the war, Sonora didn't return to horse diving, but acts opened again and remained a fixture at the Steel Pier until high-diving horse shows closed for good in 1978. In the 1990s, some believe on account of the film, attempts were made to once again revive horse diving. It failed to gain traction, and the president of the Humane Society of the United States at the time was quoted to have said, "This is a merciful end to a colossally stupid idea."

In 1942 Sonora and Al moved to New Orleans, where she continued to learn braille and she worked as a typist. Al began work as a hotel desk clerk. Al passed away in 1961. That same year, Sonora wrote her autobiography, *A Girl and Five Brave Horses*, which I wholly enjoyed, and dedicated it to her husband.

Another interesting side note: Sonora mentions Al's full name as Allen within her memoir. Everywhere else on the internet, he's Albert. I kept true to Sonora's version.

Sonora passed away at the great age of ninety-nine in 2003, after seventy-two years of blindness. As far as I know, Sonora never underwent any further operations to try to correct or improve her vision.

Sonora does tell us in her memoir, though, that two years after Roxie's accident, she walked for the first time on crutches. Red Lips lived out the remainder of his days in Houston with friends of the Carvers.

In learning more about what came next for Arnette, I had the pleasure of exchanging email correspondences with her son, Don French. Arnette went on to marry performer Jacob French, whom she met on the Steel Pier in 1929. They married in 1934. Together, they also had a daughter, born in 1938. I love that Don followed in his mother's footsteps, living and working on the Steel Pier as a groom.

Like Sonora—who Don told me was born Nora Evelyn Webster, a fact that tickles me considering I gave Sonora the nickname of Nora prior to learning this—Arnette stopped performing at the beginning of WWII. Along with horse diving, she was a pioneer water-skier, riding the aquaplane with Rex the Wonder Dog, and was the charter secretary of the original American Waterski Association. After Arnette left the Steel Pier, Don says his mother was a "domestic goddess" with quite the green thumb. For many years, Arnette was the president of her local garden club in Pleasantville, New Jersey, and won various awards at garden shows. It makes me smile to know that even separated by a thousand miles, Sonora and Arnette remained very close. Arnette, a remarkable woman in her own right, passed away at the age of eighty-seven in 2000.

Unfortunately, I didn't stumble upon Don's contact information until after completing the writing and editing of the book. I would have loved to have included more about Arnette's inclination for gardening, along with Rex the Wonder Dog. (He sounds so cool!)

The real-life cast of characters in my novel left me feeling truly inspired. I'm so grateful for the opportunity to write this novel, one I've wanted to pen for a very long time, the Steel Pier and Atlantic City a place I've visited on many occasions. A big thank-you to Don for sharing more about his mother with me and, as always, to my agent, Shannon, and to my publishing team: Kimberly, Amanda, Kerri, Margaret, Taylor, Julie, Caitlin, Nekasha, and Natalie. I'd be completely lost without my writerly friends: Lindsay (who reads every single word I write . . . multiple times), Lee, Victoria, Jenn, Carolyn, Rachel, Joy, Kimberly, Sara, Sara, Marie, and all of the fabulous ladies of the Tall Poppy Writers. A special hug to my husband and children, who are the reason I so ferociously chase my dreams. Thanks to God for giving me this passion to write and create.

Lastly, a heartfelt thank-you to the readers and book clubs (especially the Peloton Moms Book Club!) who pick up my novels, share my books, tell a friend about my stories, talk about my characters during book club, and are all-around supportive and amazing. I'm so grateful I get to do what I love and you all help make it possible.

Discussion Questions

1. How did Sonora's family dynamics, along with her mother's experiences and struggles, shape her values, choices, and resilience as an adult?
2. How did her father's abandonment affect the aspirations and mindset of both Sonora and her mother?
3. Sonora described horse diving as "the most fun you could have," not as an act of bravery. How does this perspective reshape your view of courage and risk in her story?
4. After losing her sight, Sonora insisted on maintaining her independence. What does this reveal about her determination, mindset, and sense of identity?
5. Why do you think horse diving became such a popular form of entertainment from the 1880s to WWII, then again into the 1970s?
6. What cultural shifts have made acts like horse diving unacceptable today?
7. Books were important to Sonora. How did reading shape her outlook and choices?

8. What types of books do you think she gravitated toward, and what clues in the novel support this?
9. At the time, books were often either moral (didactic) or purely entertaining. How would you classify this novel, and why?
10. The Disney film *Wild Hearts Can't Be Broken* took great creative license with Sonora's story. In historical fiction, how much accuracy do you think is necessary versus creative storytelling?
11. The novel includes the maxim "Sympathy bolsters weakness and strength is begotten by strength." How do you see this philosophy influencing Sonora's decisions?

Written by Marisa Gothie and Nicholle Thery-Williams from the Bookends and Friends book club.

About the Author

JENNI L. WALSH worked for a decade enticing readers as an award-winning advertising copywriter before becoming an author. Her passion lies in transporting readers to another world, be it in historical or contemporary settings. She is a proud graduate of Villanova University and lives in the Philadelphia suburbs with her husband, daughter, son, and various pets.

Jenni is the *USA TODAY* author of the historical novels *Becoming Bonnie*; *Side by Side*; *A Betting Woman*; *The Call of the Wrens*; *Unsinkable*; and *Ace, Marvel, Spy*. She also writes books for children, including the nonfiction She Dared series and historical novels *Hettie and the London Blitz*, *I Am Defiance*, *By the Light of Fireflies*, *Over and Out*, *Operation: Happy*, and *The Bug Bandits*. To learn more about Jenni and her books, please visit jennilwalsh.com or @jennilwalsh on social media.